D0973435

Dangerous Curves Ahead

SUGAR JAMISON

St. Martin's Paperbacks

This is a work of fiction. All of the characters, organizations, and events portrayed in this novel are either products of the author's imagination or are used fictitiously.

DANGEROUS CURVES AHEAD

Copyright © 2013 by Sugar Jamison.

All rights reserved.

For information address St. Martin's Press, 175 Fifth Avenue, New York, NY 10010.

ISBN: 978-1-250-03297-3

Printed in the United States of America

St. Martin's Paperbacks edition / September 2013

St. Martin's Paperbacks are published by St. Martin's Press, 175 Fifth Avenue, New York, NY 10010.

10 9 8 7 6 5 4 3 2 1

Acknowledgments

It all started with Kristan Higgins who led me to CTRWA. And CTRWA introduced me to Jen Moncuse who founded the 7 Scribes. It was the 7 Scribes who brought me to Casey Wyatt whose unyielding support and encouragement helped make this book possible. And to my Mom and Dad, just because I love them.

Chapter One

Big Fat Fattie and Other Words for "Fat"

Plus-Sized
Zaftig
Big
Overweight
Plump
Chubby
Portly
Fleshy
Curvy
Chunky
Heavy
Rubenesque

"Ellison? Is that you, honey?"

Not today. Please not today. Ellis Garret shut her eyes and prayed hard as she stood in line at Hot Lava Java. Really, really hard. Maybe if she appeased the right god, she would be spared the torture that was Mrs. Agatha Toomey.

Jesus? Buddha? Zeus?

"Ellison? Yoo-hoo!"

Are you there, God? It's me, Ellis. Can't a girl get a miracle here?

"Ellis!"

Apparently not.

All she really wanted was a cookie—and not just any

cookie, but one of those super-big Black and White Cookies with the yummy icing and the oh-so-soft cake-like bottom. She knew she wasn't supposed to be eating delicious giant cookies. It was only Tuesday. Cookies—any and all junk food—were off limits today. She was supposed to be good on Tuesdays and Wednesdays and every day that didn't start with a *Sat* or a *Sun*. *Thou shalt not eat high-calorie snacks on weekdays.*

"Yes, Mrs. Toomey. It *is* me," Ellis said, plastering a smile on her face that she hoped looked genuine. She turned to face the annoyingly slender woman holding a cup of green tea. *Is that you?* Mrs. Toomey asked the question as if she didn't know. *Well, duh.* Ellis wasn't one of those girls who were easy to miss.

"I'm a little surprised to see you. What are you doing *here*?" Mrs. Toomey looked Ellis up and down with her judgmental eyes, seeming to know already why Ellis was there. *Fat girls shouldn't eat cookies.* "Have you patched things up with Jack yet?"

Ellis had known the woman half her life. Agatha was her mother's longtime friend, and the owner of a very successful weight-loss clinic. She also happened to be Jack's aunt.

And she's an undernourished hag.

"I wanted a cookie," Ellis said, ignoring the woman's last question. She would run ten miles naked before she talked about her ex with this woman.

"We sell cookies at my clinic. Very healthy cookies, dear," Mrs. Toomey told her, a disapproving frown on her face. "They are sugar-free, gluten-free, and we don't use any butter or oil. Only natural sweeteners."

They must taste like poop.

"I really wanted a Black and White Cookie and you don't sell those," Ellis explained, trying hard to mind her manners. "Plus your shop is all the way on the other side of town. I figured it would be better for me to stop in and get one instead of robbing a Girl Scout."

"Excuse me?"

Ellis shook her head sadly. "I ate fifteen boxes of cookies the last time I robbed a Girl Scout. And then I gained three pounds. And then I got arrested and then they forced me to do all that community service and let me tell you, my big ass does not look good in neon orange."

Mrs. Toomey stared at her horrified.

A deep male chuckle erupted behind her and Ellis shut her eyes for a moment, choosing to ignore it. Not only had she failed spectacularly at not being rude, but now she had brought attention to herself.

"You have such an original sense of humor, Ellison. I bet that's why Jack fell for you. Why exactly did you two break up?"

"Weren't we talking about cookies?" she asked, trying to shift the conversation away from Jack.

"I guess we were. You really should come down to the clinic. We have tons of other healthy goodies all containing a day's worth of fiber. I'm sure you could use some more fiber in your *diet*." Her eyes traveled to Ellis's midsection. "It helps with the bloating."

"I'm sure it does." Ellis wanted to bite her tongue as she looked down at her relatively flat belly. But she couldn't. "What a nice offer, Mrs. Toomey but I would get kicked out of my fat girls club if I didn't eat at least two teaspoons of butter a day. They are super strict about cholesterol intake."

Another quiet laugh escaped whoever was behind her in line.

"If they kick you out, we'll let you in," Mrs. Toomey said firmly. "Come to my place. My staff can design a diet for you and put you on an exercise plan that will have you shedding the weight in no time. Maybe if you slimmed down, Jack would come back to you."

"I don't want him back. Thanks, but no thanks." Ellis tried not to clench her teeth. "What would all the women think who came to my store and read my blog if I lost weight for a man?"

Mrs. Toomey frowned. "That you would inspire them to stop eating cheese puffs and get off the couch and exercise. Don't you see that by selling them clothes, you are contributing to their obesity? If they don't fit into normal sizes, they'll have to get their behinds in the gym and out of the drive-thru."

Ellis saw red. And like a bull she was ready to charge. She'd opened her shop because she was tired of going into stores that only catered to average women. What about the above average? The tall girls? Or the ones with the big feet? Or long arms? Or the women who couldn't find anything cute in their size? Or the women who just needed a place to shop without being judged? How dare this pompous, wheatgrass-drinking, gluten-free-eating, horse-faced woman talk about her customers like that? Ellis didn't cater to fat women, she catered to all women with unique figures. She opened her mouth to let Agatha Toomey know how it really was.

"Hey, lady," the man behind her said to Mrs. Toomey, preventing Ellis's speech. "Back off. Weren't you the one puffing away outside? Don't you think you should be worried about the state of your lungs instead of what she puts in her mouth?"

"I—" Mrs. Toomey opened and closed her mouth a few times, resembling a suffocating fish. "I have to get back to work. Tell your mother I said hello."

She turned and was out the door before Ellis could mutter a reply.

"That lady is a bitch," her defender said.

"I know, and I was all ready to let her have it but you came to my rescue and took all the fun out of it for me."

"Sorry. You were handling her pretty well." She heard him laugh. "And just for the record I bet your ass looks good in any color you put it in."

Did he just talk about her ass?

Oh no he didn't.

Ellis turned around to face him and BOOM. She felt the earth move and heard bells and saw stars.

OH. NO.

The man was absolutely gorgeous. He was tall with short inky black hair and eyes so dark blue, they were cobalt. And his body! He was brawny, just like the paper towel man, thickly built without being overly muscular, and she had to pull her lower lip between her teeth just to stop from shouting out her appreciation. He was Clark Kent and Superman and super hot. He was beautiful, and grinning at her, and she knew him. His name was Mike Edwards, he used to live in her neighborhood, and this hunk of man had dated her older sister.

OH. SHIT.

She also used to have a serious crush on him.

His eyes narrowed, and the smile faded from his perfectly formed mouth. "Don't I know you from somewhere?"

He doesn't remember me.

Ellis wasn't sure if she should be offended or relieved. She remembered everything about him. He was a cop. His family lived outside of Buffalo. And he tended to get intimate in beds that didn't belong to him. She chose relieved. She didn't want him to remember her or the colossal bitch-fit meltdown she'd had the last time they'd occupied the same space. *Embarrassing* didn't even begin to cover it.

Besides, she was a different person now. There was no use revisiting the past.

"Next," the girl at the counter called, preventing Ellis

from answering his question—which was a good thing because she'd lost her ability to speak.

"Two Black and Whites. A large black coffee." He looked at Ellis for a moment. "And a strawberry lemonade."

"Did you just order for me?" she asked, finally finding her voice. She had to get out of there. First the lady who ran the diet clinic and now the man who'd inadvertently turned her life upside down. The food gods were definitely punishing her. *Thou shalt not eat Black and Whites.*

"Yeah." He nodded as he paid. "I want you to sit with me. I know I know you from somewhere."

Run, run as fast as you can . . .

"But—"

"But sit with me." He cut her off as he grabbed their order and her wrist and led the way to a small table in the corner.

She followed him, not knowing why when she easily could have walked away. *Blame it on the BOOM.*

Normally, Michael Edwards made it a point not to get involved in other people's business, but there was something about the funny girl who sat across from him that had made him open his mouth. It wasn't because she was beautiful, which she was with her dark hair and pouty lips. And it wasn't because her lush body was created for male fantasies, which it was. He wasn't sure why he'd told the skinny Mrs. Toomey to stuff it, but he was sure as soon as Ellis turned around that he knew her from somewhere.

"Why are you staring at me like that?" She frowned at him, looking almost self-conscious.

He was staring at her. The words *You're sexy as hell* almost rolled off his tongue. But he held back. It wasn't her looks that made him unable to pry his eyes from her face but something else. Something almost comfortable that made him want to slide closer and spend all day near her. He shook his head. What the hell was wrong with him? He never reacted this way with any woman.

"I know you from somewhere."

"You do, Mike." She took a bite of the Black and White Cookie he'd purchased. A crumb escaped, falling on her lip, and he watched as her perfect pink tongue came out to lick it up. "We've met before."

"What?" He was so caught up staring at her mouth that he almost missed what she said.

"Oh, Mike." She knew his name. A teasing smile played around her lips. "Have you slept with so many females that you've forgotten me?"

He was right. They had met before, but he knew that he'd never touched her. "I know we didn't sleep together."

"How can you be so sure?"

"Because—" He locked gazes with her. "—I would remember falling into bed with you."

Her eyes widened slightly and she smiled, once again drawing his attention to her lips. "Do you use that line a lot, Mikey?" She rested her hand on her cheek and studied him with interest, like she was cataloging his features and comparing the differences. "Tell me, does that smooth-operator BS really work?"

On most women, yes, he thought. But apparently not on her. She was a ball buster. He felt one corner of his mouth curl. "Usually, but I'm not giving you a line. I know we didn't sleep together."

"Is that because you don't sleep with many fat girls?"

"You're not fat."

"Are you blind?"

"Do you have a mirror?" he countered.

She narrowed her eyes. "Are you flirting with me?"

"No." He shook his head. "I don't know. Maybe. Who are you?"

She looked amazed. "You really don't remember me?"

"Obviously not." But he wanted to. She made him laugh and she didn't seem like a woman who would be easy to forget, and yet he had no idea how their pasts connected.

Her eyes passed over his face as if she was recalling something. "I thought you would have remembered me by now, but I guess you haven't changed much at all in four years," she said, sounding a little wistful.

"What's that supposed to mean?" he asked, sensing her disappointment and not liking that it made him feel guilty. Four years ago? It wasn't like they'd met last week.

"It means it's all for the best." She stood, grabbing her barely eaten cookie with one hand and her lemonade with the other. "Thanks for the snack, Detective."

"Wait." He grasped her wrist. She was walking out on *him*? "Who are you?"

"Apparently, I'm just a girl you don't remember."

She freed herself from his light hold and walked out of the coffee shop. He watched her until she disappeared down the sidewalk. Okay, so maybe he had dated, slept with, discarded numerous women in his thirty-two years, but he wasn't a total jackass. All of his relationships had ended fairly amicably. He never left broken hearts behind. He never entered a relationship he couldn't easily extract himself from. And that meant he had never been with Ellis. She looked like a nester. One of those women made to pop out four kids, bake cookies, and drive the car pool. Four years ago she would have been like toxic waste to him. To this day he shivered at the thought of being trapped with one person forever. So why was he so put out by her? And what the hell had he done to her to cause her to not like him? *Ellis*. The interaction left him feeling a little dazed, a lot annoyed, and more than slightly interested in learning more about the the girl with the cookie.

Chapter Two

Fat Girl Icons

1. *Marilyn Monroe. Curvy. Blond. Sex Goddess. And rumored to be a size sixteen at her biggest.*
2. *Christina Hendricks. The* Mad Men *beauty gives me a girl boner.*
3. *Mo'Nique. You earned that Oscar with your big bad self.*
4. *Adele. Big. Sexy. Unapologetic.*
5. *Fictional Tracy Turnblad. Sigh . . . Hairspray. How I love thee.*

Ellis thought about her run-in with Mike all the way back to her shop. Boom. She'd felt Boom. *Damn it.* It shook her. Why out of all the single men in the world did she have to feel it with Mike Edwards? He was the man who had once ignored her, who had forgotten her, who had slept with her sister. And yet when she saw him, her hormones went crazier than a teenage boy's watching a dirty movie. It must be the lack of sex making her crazy. It had been six months since she broke up with Jack. Six months since she'd had any type of physical interaction with a man. Six very long dry months.

Or it could be that the crush she'd once had on him had never completely melted away, because when Mike's big hand came out to grab her wrist her mouth went dry. It took her back four years. To the first time he'd set his hand on her skin. To that time in life when she still believed in love and loyalty and thought butterflies farted rainbows.

She shook her head.

It probably wasn't Boom. Maybe it was just a severe case of horniness. Or indigestion. Either way she was screwed.

She returned to her shop, Size Me Up, and stopped to speak to Cherri, her college-aged salesgirl, in an effort to avoid the pile of work that was waiting for her.

"How's business, kid?"

"Same as when you left, boss lady."

"No customers?" she said with a sigh.

"No customers."

She wasn't expecting customers to swarm the doors in the hour she was away, but she'd hoped for at least one. Size Me Up had been open five months and Ellis still knew very little about running a clothing store. Except of course what she learned from the Internet when she Googled "how to run a clothing store." Realistically she knew her store would take a little while to get off the ground. With no money for advertising, she had only word of mouth to rely on. On the bright side business was building. She was getting new customers every day, but she was barely breaking even. She had spent so much money on the decor, the stock, and the rent that she estimated it would take at least two years to regain her original investment. She couldn't even afford to take home a paycheck for herself, relying instead on her now meager savings to keep her afloat.

She worked damn hard for no paycheck. The thing that made Size Me Up unique was that in addition to selling cute clothes in a large variety of sizes, Ellis—having amazing skills with a needle—altered clothing. She mostly provided the service for her shorter customers, but she had one seven-foot client who practically kissed her feet when Ellis made her a pair of jeans that covered her heels. Ellis's personal services weren't cheap, but when those women walked out with a garment that fit them perfectly, they were more than happy to pay the price. They were grateful and loyal, and they were the reason Ellis would continue to live on canned soup and boxed cereal.

If things stayed just the way they were, she would be fine. But if anything happened, anything at all—if the air conditioner broke, or her computer died, or the wind blew the wrong way—she would be done for. She couldn't let that happen. She couldn't give Jack the satisfaction of watching her fail. She couldn't go back to the career that made her miserable.

"I can see you thinking," Cherri said. "You are having that daily internal battle where you're wondering if quitting your job, dumping your asshole boyfriend, and opening this store was a mistake."

"You know me so well," she grinned at Cherri.

"I do," Cherri said softly. "I want to be you when I grow up."

Ellis could barely afford to keep Cherri on as a worker, but she would forever. Cherri was a good girl. She was mature. She worked hard, went to school full-time, had another job in her college's library, and took care of her grandmother, but those weren't the only reasons Ellis admired her. Cherri was probably the most beautiful woman Ellis had ever seen, with thick golden hair and a face so classic it should have been painted. But Cherri wasn't like most twenty-one-year-old girls. She was over six feet tall, and while her body was ample and lush it was far from model-like. Far from the notice of boys her age. Ellis knew how she felt. Ignored. Like an outsider. Ellis had opened Size Me Up for the outsiders, and she would gladly forgo a paycheck to ensure Cherri had this place, too.

"I want to be you when I grow up." She gently squeezed the girl's arm. "Now be a good little worker and go to my office and balance the books."

"Sorry. I can't. I'm no good with numbers. That's why I majored in art."

Ellis threw back her head and whimpered. "Please. I suck at the business part of owning a small business. I just want to make pretty clothes."

"You don't have to worry about the books, Ellis. Just let them sit there. Of course if you do, the only clothes you'll be making will be out of old newspapers you find on park benches. We can make it a trend. Call it homeless chic."

"Wow." Ellis blinked at her young friend. "That's some effective guilt."

"I live with a seventy-four-year-old lady. I learned from the best."

Ellis flashed Cherri a grin before taking a huge bite of her cookie. The sugary rush gave her the strength she needed to stop whining and face the mess in her office. "I'm heading back to the grind."

When she got back to her office, papers were still scattered all over her desk and her bookkeeping software was still up. All the numbers were the same as when she'd left half an hour ago. Apparently the office-managing elves had yet to pay her a visit.

"This is fucking depressing," she whispered, taking yet another bite of her Black and White. The cookie was really good. Just like she'd imagined, and she didn't even have to touch a penny from her meager savings to enjoy it. Too bad that whenever she ate one from now on she would think of the man who'd bought it for her.

Mike Edwards played a bigger part in her life than anybody had known. At first he was the hot guy in her neighborhood she fantasized about from afar. Her secret crush. Which became not so secret anymore when she pointed him out to her older sister. To this day she didn't understand what had possessed her sister to go after him. But Dina did go after him. She brought him to Ellis's apartment. Forced Ellis to spend time with them and then had the nerve to try to have sex with him in her bed the night of her law school graduation party.

That was the night things irrevocably changed between Ellis and her sister. After their huge argument they didn't speak for months. Even four years later they could barely stand to be in the same room. Dina had broken her trust as a sister, but Mike . . . Even though he had been inside her home, even though they spent three hours alone talking about everything that came to their minds, as soon as Dina came around he had forgotten about her. He proved to her that hot guys don't go after brainy fat girls.

She wanted to blame him for Jack. For making her feel like she was not good enough. But that wasn't fair because that's just what guys like him did. Maybe she should blog about the experience and call her post "The Man Who Ruined Love for Me." But she disregarded that thought as soon as it entered her mind. It was too dramatic even for her.

"Ellis?"

She looked up to see Belinda in the doorway. Belinda became her best friend in high school. She was curvy and exotic and the most fashionable person Ellis had ever met. But besides just her best friend, she was Size Me Up's store manager. Ellis thanked God daily for her experienced, efficient retail manager. She would have been sunk long ago without her.

"I love you, Belinda," she blurted out. "I mean it. I'm really glad that you quit your job and took a pay cut to work for me. You know I couldn't do this without you and I promise that as soon as we start bringing in more cash I will give you a huge raise."

"I rather have a shrine built to my awesomeness," the redhead grinned. "But honestly, honey, you know I'd rather work for you than that old bitch who was draining the life out of me. That combined with the much shorter commute is worth the shitty pay. "

"I really wish I could pay you more," she said seriously.

"I know." Belinda sighed after hearing that promise for the hundredth time. "I won't leave here until we go down in flames, and we won't. So stop stressing so much. The customers love this place. We're going to be fine."

"From your lips to God's ears," Ellis mumbled, feeling slightly better.

"Well, boss lady." Belinda glanced at the clock. "I came in here to remind you that if you don't leave right now, you're going to be late for dinner at your parents' house."

"Shit." Ellis looked at the clock and then at her calendar. "Shit. Was that tonight?"

She wasn't sure if she could tolerate a dinner with her parents (her mother) after the day she'd had.

"Yes, and hurry before Phillipa calls here."

"I'm going." She stood, shoving the last bit of cookie in her mouth before running out the door.

Instead of driving to her parents' cottage she decided to walk. It gave her a chance to burn off the cookie she'd inhaled and get reacquainted with the town she had left ten years ago. Rhode Island. Boston. Manhattan. The whole time she was away pursuing a career she didn't want she knew that something was missing in her life. It took a brutal breakup with Jack to make her realize that this place was what was missing in her life. Durant was a college town. A cool place with dozens of funky shops and cafés, an expansive green where new bands played every Saturday night, and young idealistic kids filling the streets. But it was more than that. At its heart Durant was a small town, with locals who cared about one another and a sense of community that she had a hard time finding elsewhere.

She opened her shop on St. Lucy Street because it was the lifeline of the small city, and even though she had been away for so long not much had changed. Mrs. Underwood still ran the yarn shop. Postal worker Mr. Conner still stopped into every shop on his daily route, and the guy in the purple bandanna still played his guitar on the patio of the Don Luca Café for lunchgoers every day.

It was good to be home. And good to be near her parents again. Even though they sometimes drove her crazy, she'd rather be near them than anywhere else.

"Ellis? Is that you?" she heard as she entered her parents' home.

"Yes," she answered, hearing that question for the second time that day.

Her father looked up from his spot on the couch, not making eye contact, just giving her a once-over to confirm it really was her.

"Hi, Daddy." She sat next to him, studying her dashing father's ensemble for the day. Blue collared shirt, matching blue tie, and pajama pants. "Snoopy pants?"

"I've always liked Snoopy," he said not looking at her. "*Peanuts* premiered in eight newspapers the day I was born. Snoopy did not appear until the third strip. He wasn't identified by name until November fourth of that year."

Ellis nodded slowly at the wealth of information her father had gifted her. He knew all kinds of useless facts; if he ever went on a game show, he could rack up some serious cash. But Dr. Walter Garret wasn't the type of man who would play or even watch a game show. He was a scientist by trade, a physiologist who studied the physical and biochemical functions in humans and animals. Truthfully, Ellis had no flipping clue what her father did for a living.

"I bought you some chocolates." Walter looked at her nose. "I put them in the cabinet above the sink in between the brown and white sugars."

"Thank you, Daddy," she said.

"I asked your mother to order Chinese food tonight. Chicken with garlic sauce, dumplings, and fried rice. That's what you like."

"Yes, Daddy, I do."

That was how he showed her he loved her. Food. Not once had he ever said the words, nor could she remember him ever embracing her, but he always spent time with her. He always asked her to come in his office and sit with him while he researched, feeding her gummy bears and marshmallows, only quiet foods so her chewing would not disturb his thinking. He was the reason she had eight cavities the year she turned ten. Every filling had been worth it.

She gently placed her hand on his knee, earning her a look at her forehead. "How's work, Daddy?"

"Good, good." He nodded. "Very good. My colleagues and I are studying the heart functions in bears while in hibernation and how the organ adapts to stressful situations. We hope to compare it with the functions of the human heart during rest."

Ellis drifted off while her father spoke in scientific terms she would never understand. "I'm glad to hear that, Daddy," she said when he paused. "Where's Mom?"

"In the garden. The deliveryman should be here in fourteen minutes. Please ask your mother to wash her hands."

"Of course." She smiled at her father and left him to go find her mother, wondering what it was about him that had caused her mother to fall in love.

* * *

She found Dr. Phillipa Gregory sitting in the middle of her tomato plants frowning. Ellis took the chance to study her mother as she rolled a small tomato in her hand. Phillipa was a tiny speck of a woman with a huge brain and big mouth. She was head of Women's Studies at Durant University, author of four feminist-themed books, and a former wild-child hippie. Phillipa drove her bonkers, but Ellis could honestly say she missed the pain in the ass while she was in the big city. And every time she saw her in the garden she thought, *It's good to be home.*

"Ellis, come here," she ordered in her still-thick Queens accent. "Doesn't this tomato look sickly to you?"

"Um." Ellis studied the small perfectly red fruit, not at all bothered by her mother's lack of greeting. "Yes?"

"It's too yellow on the bottom."

"Okay, if you say so."

"I do." Phillipa took off her enormous straw hat, revealing her very long mass of silver hair, and wiped her brow with her forearm.

"Daddy would like you to come in for dinner and wash your hands. The deliveryman should be here in twelve minutes."

Phillipa waved her hand, brushing off her husband's request. "The food will still be hot if I'm three minutes late. Sit and chat with Mommy for a little while." She patted the dirt beside her.

Uh-oh. Phillipa wanted to "chat" with her. Chats weren't good. They usually involved Ellis biting her tongue while Phillipa offered up life lessons.

"How about we sit together on the glider?" Ellis suggested instead of saying no like she wanted. Ellis couldn't control her mother's mouth but she could control where she sat, and she wasn't about to walk around for the rest of the day with brown smudges on her behind. That would give somebody else an excuse to study it.

"Oh, I forgot Miss Fancy Schmancy boutique owner can no longer sit in the dirt." Phillipa rose more gracefully than Ellis ever could, more gracefully than any woman in her mid-sixties should be able to, and joined Ellis on the back porch.

"I never liked to sit in the dirt. Just because you're a crunchy granola hippie doesn't mean I am."

"How did I raise such a smartmouth?" Phillipa looked skyward in mock horror. "My own daughter!"

"I learned it from the best." Ellis shook her head at her mother's bad acting as she sat next to her on the glider. "What did you want to talk about?"

"Oh, nothing." Phillipa gave Ellis a sideways glance. "I'm just waiting for you to tattle on yourself for being rude to Agatha Toomey in the coffee shop."

"She told you?"

What a bitch!

Ellis couldn't believe the woman had contacted her mother so quickly. She thought she had until tonight before the hag tattled.

"Of course she told me." Phillipa shrugged. "She said that maybe if you had a nicer mouth you and Jack would still be together."

"Oh no she didn't." Ellis's head snapped toward her mother. "I hope you set her straight about who dumped who because—"

"Relax," Phillipa cut in. "I told her that you had no interest in Jack-ass and that you were moving on and dating again."

That wasn't true by a long shot but it was better than having Agatha throw Jack in her face at every opportunity. "Why are you still friends with her. She's a bitch. Did she tell you I was there to buy a cookie?" Ellis huffed. "Or that she told me I should eat more fiber to help with my massive bloating or that she was willing to put me on a diet?"

"Yes." Phillipa nodded. "She did, but don't pay her any attention. If Aggie doesn't recruit two new clients a week, a piece of her soul dies. And we're not friends. She's just somebody I exercise with, since my youngest daughter won't." Phillipa gave her another sideways glance. "It wouldn't kill you to go to yoga with me three times a week. It's just good for your heart, your balance. Everything."

"Mom," Ellis warned. Her mother was extremely fit and exercised religiously. She also had the metabolism of a ten-year-old boy. All of that made Ellis slightly bitter.

"Fine." Phillipa put her hands up in surrender. "If you don't want to talk about your health and potentially extending your life span, then we won't. Let's talk about your love life. When's the last time you had sex?"

"Mom!"

"What?" Phillipa frowned as if she were confused, like it was okay for mothers to ask their daughters such extremely personal questions. "Sex is healthy. Didn't you read my book *Your Body, Your Canvas*? It releases all kinds of endorphins."

"We don't have to have this conversation right now. The food should be here." Ellis stood and tried to walk away but her mother grabbed her by the back of her pants, preventing her flight.

"There is nothing wrong with talking about sex, honey. It's a natural expression of our bodies. I thought I raised you to believe that, but I guess our puritanical society has stomped all of that out of you."

Ellis struggled to get away from her mother, but Phillipa proved to be freakishly strong. "I have to go to the bathroom. Please let me go."

"You know your father and I have sex quite frequently, and we both are extremely happy."

"Mother!" Ellis whipped her head around to stare at her mother. "This is not normal! You are not normal. No daughter wants to hear any detail about her parents' sex life, and I can't believe you think that I'd want to share any part of mine with you."

Phillipa rolled her eyes, unperturbed by Ellis's outburst. "I just thought that if you were getting some you wouldn't be so stressed out all the time. I worry about you, Ellie. What kind of mother would I be if I didn't?"

"I'm fine. I promise. Now let me go. Daddy is waiting."

"How is the store doing?" Phillipa ignored her daughter. "It looked beautiful last time I was in but, honestly Ellis, I don't understand why you had to quit law altogether." Phillipa let her go and raised her hands to ward off the inevitable verbal attack. "I know. I know you hated doing corporate law and personally I don't blame you for not wanting to represent those scum-sucking bastards, but couldn't you at least take a few clients here and there? Do some environmental law or some civil liberties stuff? Do you know how much money it cost to send you to Harvard Law?"

Here we go again. Phillipa and she had had this conversation every other week since Ellis announced that she was quitting her high-paying job in Manhattan. At first Ellis valiantly argued why it was better that she stopped practicing, but even all her arbitration skills couldn't win her an argument with Dr. Phillipa Gregory.

Her mother just didn't understand that her old life made her unhappy. Being a lawyer was Phillipa's dream for her, and she went with it because she wanted to make her mother proud. But when she broke up with Jack, she realized that she couldn't live her life for others. She should only do what made her happy.

"Thousands and thousands of dollars."

"There's a guy," she blurted out before her mother could

continue. "We just met and he's gorgeous and I'm crazy about him."

Liar, liar, pants on fire.

"What?" Phillipa stopped her familiar rant. "Who is he? What's his name?"

"Um." Ellis pulled her lower lip between her teeth. "I don't want to tell you because I'm afraid I might jinx it. We really just met."

"Oh, come on! I'm your mother."

You're also a giant pain in the ass. "You want to ruin this for me? I'm superstitious. We're probably going to break up tomorrow because I told you and now I'm never going to get to have sex again."

"Okay, okay." Phillipa relented and Ellis let out a huge internal sigh. "But promise that you'll tell me about him soon."

"Sure thing," Ellis lied again, hoping her nose wasn't growing substantially.

"Ellis, Phillipa." Walter appeared in the doorway of the porch. "Dinner has been here for six minutes now."

"We're coming, Dad," Ellis said, quickly heading inside. She had the awful feeling that she had made a terrible mistake. Her mother would probably never get off her back now. Maybe if Ellis prayed hard enough her mother's memory would be wiped clean.

Yeah right, and maybe pigs will fly and there will be peace in the Middle East by Christmas.

Chapter Three

Every time Mike glanced out the window of Durant's tiny police station he was greeted with a quiet tree-lined street. There were no hot dog vendors. No random homeless people relieving themselves in the alley. No occasional asshole calling him a pig. There was hardly any noise at all. When he'd first landed in New York City ten years ago that stuff excited him. He loved the noise, the energy. He loved the life the city had to offer him, but a few months ago something switched inside and he stopped being able to picture himself spending the rest of his life there. The problem was, he couldn't picture himself anywhere. He didn't know what he wanted out of life and that bothered him. Since he was thirteen years old he'd had his life planned out. Get the hell out of Buffalo. Go to college. Join the NYPD. For ten years he went after those goals with single-minded determination, and he accomplished them all.

Now what?

His thirteen-year-old mind hadn't thought much past that. It wasn't like him to not have a plan. Maybe that's why he came back to Durant, the place he went to college, the city where he had some of the best times of his life.

Everything here was so . . . relaxed. It was the kind of place corporate America had yet to touch, made up of small trendy businesses and mom-and-pop shops. It was a place where people said good morning and smiled when they passed him on the street. And after being a detective in one of the city's most active crime areas, coming back to his college town was like culture shock. In Manhattan he lived. He was always on the move. There was always something there to keep him busy but here . . . he could reflect on his life, decide his next move.

It turned out he sucked at being reflective. He was so used to doing, to being on edge all the time, it was as if he didn't know how to relax.

The only police work he did that came anywhere close to exciting was acting as security for the senior citizen dance-a-thon. And that was exciting only because some ass had spiked the punch, causing a bunch of octogenarians to get a little freakier than they should on the dance floor.

It was entertaining but nothing to stop the surge of restless energy that continuously bugged him. Yet he didn't regret leaving his old life behind. Ten years of working in the city's poorest areas, ten years of violent robberies, ten years of throwing scared kids in jail had done something to him. It changed him. And when some animal brutally beat an eighty-nine-year-old woman for a purse that only contained nine dollars and Mike barely batted a lash, he knew it was time to move on. He didn't want to become that hardened. He never wanted to be a man who couldn't be moved.

And that caused him to wonder if police work was still his passion. But when he thought about it, he realized that there was nothing else he could do. So he left the NYPD and applied to Durant. He made this major move and took a substantial pay cut all so he could think about his life.

He could have gone back to Buffalo. His mother was still there running her flower shop. His sisters and their large families all lived within two miles of where he grew up, but going back to Buffalo was never really an option. There was too much history there. Too many things he didn't want to remember.

"Mike, you hungry?"

Mike looked up at his new partner, Lester, who sat at the desk across from his. Lester was a veteran detective, a little gruff but a nice guy. He sort of reminded Mike of Danny Glover's character in *Lethal Weapon*, which made him secretly wish his partner would utter, "I'm too old for this shit."

"Yeah, I could eat," Mike answered. "What are you in the mood for?"

"Extra-hot Buffalo wings." Lester grimaced. "But those things give me the shits."

Mike grinned at this overly honest answer. "Can't have you on the crapper all day, old man. Maybe we should get you some cream of wheat instead."

"Getting old fucking sucks." The man grinned back, shaking his head. "Don't listen to anyone who tells you it doesn't 'cuz they're full of shit." Lester sat back in his chair and studied Mike for a moment. "How are you adjusting to the new job, city boy? Everybody treating you right?"

"Yeah. I've got no complaints."

Lester nodded. "Durant's pretty safe. I know that this job is going to take some getting used to. We heard about you. You did some crazy shit your rookie year to make detective."

Mike shrugged off the comment. "It wasn't anything you wouldn't have done."

"You're wrong there, partner. I've never single-handedly stopped a robbery in progress, chased the perp twelve blocks through the projects, or gotten my nose bashed in by a dealer. Shit like that will get you killed."

Mike nodded. *Injured* was his middle name back in his early days. He had been twenty-three, newly hired, and itching to prove himself. The last thing his mother wanted him to be was a cop, but as a kid he used to watch *Hill Street Blues* and *NYPD Blue* and salivate over the badass goodness of it all. He did his four years in college, came out with a degree in criminal justice, and instead of going to law school like his mother wanted, he became a cop. He couldn't see himself as a lawyer. His family's roots were entrenched in blue-collar soil. Mike's father, when he was around, worked construction. His mother worked her fingers to the bone with her business and as much as she wanted for him to have a high-powered job and lead a lifestyle she could only dream of, he didn't have the heart for it.

"That's why I'm here. My mom calls me from Buffalo twenty-five times a day just to see if I'm still alive. I figured if I moved to a smaller city, she would call half as much."

He was joking but his mother, Margie, called him often. He knew it bothered her that he was the only one of her children who'd moved away, so he picked up the phone every time with hardly any trace of annoyance.

Lester nodded. "My boy was thinking about going on the job for a little while until my wife laid the guilt trip on him. My son is a mama's boy and Shirley can pretty much get him to do anything she wants. He's now a biology major at the university."

"Detectives," their captain, Maria Montoya called, causing both men to turn and look at her. "There was a robbery down on St. Lucy Street. The shop owner got slapped around a bit when she refused to give up the cash. I've got uniforms on the scene already but I need you to go down there and do what you do."

Mike was out of his chair before the woman could finish her thought. Finally, there was something for him to do.

The sight of police cars on St. Lucy Street attracted a crowd. Apparently the people of Durant weren't used to robberies in broad daylight, which was a good thing. When Mike got out of the car he found about two dozen people milling around the scene, most of them shop owners and customers doing lunchtime shopping.

"Get these people back, please," Mike ordered the uniforms, making his way toward the shaken owner of the yarn shop.

Lester shook his head. "This guy must have some kind of balls. What kind of idiot robs a store in broad daylight in the middle of a busy street?"

"Meth head?" Mike offered, knowing how the addicts were infamous for their lowered inhibitions. He had seen his share of drug addicts while he was on the job in the city and knew many would steal anything they thought was worth a few dollars.

"We don't have too many meth heads around here, but it's possible." Lester pulled out his notebook as they approached. "You talk to the lady. Let me see how a city boy works."

"You want me to school you, old-timer?" Mike grinned at Lester. "No problem."

He dropped his smile as they faced the victim. One of the things Mike was good at was talking to people. Whether it was interrogating criminals or interviewing witnesses, Mike could get almost anybody to talk. He could see Mrs. Underwood was shaken. The first thing he would have to do was get her to trust him. She looked to be in her mid-fifties, petite with ashy blond hair. She owned a yarn shop so she was probably a knitter, maternal, artsy. The big diamond ring on her left hand told him that she was married, and the fact that it wasn't taken by the perp told him the man who'd robbed her wasn't a career criminal.

"Hello, Mrs. Underwood. This is Detective Richards and I am Detective Edwards. We wanted to ask you a few questions."

"But"—the woman's eyes grew round—"I just gave my statement to that other officer."

"I know." Mike placed his hand on Mrs. Underwood's shoulder and gave her a comforting squeeze. "I know this day has been rough for you, but my partner and I can't tolerate some idiot running around our city hurting our people. So we need to talk to you a little bit more to make sure we get this guy and lock him up. Do you think you are up for answering a few more questions?"

"Yes." She nodded slowly. "I think I can do that."

Ten minutes later with some gentle prodding Mike had something to go on. Mrs. Underwood's attacker was short, bald, and hairy with a thick New York accent. According to the shop owner he did not seem to be under the influence or agitated, and he'd only asked for two hundred dollars. Apparently he was fairly polite before the woman refused; that was when he grabbed her by the collar and violently shook her until she relented. It was an odd case for Mike but fairly easy to solve. The man wore no disguise and left fingerprints all over the place. With any luck he would already be in the system.

"That was smooth, city boy." Lester laughed, shaking his head. "You use that pretty-boy shit at your other job?"

Mike shrugged, the corner of his mouth curling slightly. "I use whatever works." Luckily most women liked him.

He scanned the bystanders milling around. In Manhattan they would have been long gone but these people actually seemed concerned. It wasn't every day one of their own was robbed.

"We should probably start questioning some of these people," Lester said, looking at the crowd. "Hopefully one of them saw something."

Mike was about to reply when he spotted a familiar woman standing twenty feet away. *Ellis.* It was as if he'd called out to her or something zapped her because suddenly she looked up at him with her big brown eyes. She looked jolted. The day at the coffee shop came back to him instantly, and he remembered what she had told that chain-smoking diet lady. Ellis owned some kind of store. It must be on this block.

"I'm going to go this way," Mike mumbled, leaving Lester alone.

Mike walked toward Ellis and immediately saw her guard go up as she crossed her arms under her well-formed breasts.

"What are *you* doing here?" she asked as he approached. She looked at him with distrust, as if he were there to steal her virtue. He knew he hadn't been an angel, but he was never disrespectful. He had four sisters and a mother who didn't take crap from anybody.

"I ran out of yellow yarn for the sweater I'm knitting." He shook his head. "Why the hell do you think I'm here?"

She studied him for a long moment, taking him in from head to toe. He did the same to her. She looked good, even better than she had in the coffee shop. A chocolate knit dress with little white polka dots hugged her curvy body. Her long legs were bare and for a moment he wondered how her thick creamy-looking thighs would feel wrapped around his waist. Or had he felt them already and simply forgotten? No. He knew he hadn't. He wouldn't have forgotten that.

"You work for Durant PD now, don't you?" Ellis shut her eyes as if she were in pain. "You're supposed to be in the city. Why are you here?"

Why the hell was she so annoyed with him? "Maybe"—he lowered his voice as he bent his head closer to her—"I wanted to be closer to you."

"Ha!" Her eyes widened as amusement filled them. "And maybe you're just full of shit." She put her hand on her hips. "You don't even know who I am."

"Ellis . . ."

"Oh, you remembered this time!" She clapped her hands. "We're making progress."

"Why do you have to be such a ball buster?" He stepped closer to her, getting a faint whiff of the scented lotion she wore. "You could just tell me who you are and stop playing games."

"It's so much more fun to bust your balls." She crossed her arms under her breasts again and gave him a smile he could only describe as naughty. "Detective Romeo has forgotten a face. You spent the better part of an hour in my bedroom and still don't know who I am. And here I thought I was memorable." Her eyes locked with his for a moment. "Tell me, Mikey, do you still wear Calvin Klein underwear?"

His jaw went slack. She had him there. The designer underwear had been a present from one of his former female friends. But he hadn't had sex with Ellis. He knew he hadn't. She wasn't one of those women who were easily handled. He could see the keen intelligence in her eyes and knew she wouldn't fall for any of his bullshit. Mike knew he would have had to work hard to get anywhere with a woman like Ellis. That's why he only slept with women he could barely hold a conversation with. He wanted no entanglements, and four years ago the work Ellis presented wouldn't have been worth it for him.

She was a tricky one. He took a minute to study her face as he regained control. "If you want to know the answer to that, you're going to have to do some personal research."

Her eyes traveled down to his pants as she pulled her plump lower lip between her teeth. He hardened.

"Thinking about it?" he asked, which caused her to startle and her face to flood with embarrassment.

"You're such a smarmy jackass," she huffed. Her eyes wandered to where her fellow shop owner had stood a few minutes ago. "How is Mrs. Underwood? That was the first thing I should have asked you."

"She's understandably shaken." Returning to business, Mike took out his notepad and flipped it open to a clean page. "You own a business on this block?"

"Yes, I own a clothing store." She absently pointed behind her. "So, Betty really was robbed? I can't believe it. I always felt so safe here."

Mike took note of the store's name, Size Me Up, and mentally complimented Ellis on her choice. "This is still a safe place," he tried to reassure her. "But sometimes there are assholes that have to screw things up for everybody. We'll get him." He reached out and gave her hand a squeeze. "Did you see anything strange or notice a man running past your store?"

"No." She looked slightly worried. "I was in the back doing alterations." She then turned to the women standing behind her. "You girls were on the floor, did you notice anything?"

The women—Mike hadn't even noticed them before—both shook their heads. The tall blonde spoke. "We didn't even know there was a problem until we heard the sirens."

Mike nodded, then jotted down their statements and their names before turning back to Ellis. "Can I have your full name?"

"Why? Do you think it's going to help you remember who I am?"

"Ellis . . ."

She gave him that naughty smile once again. "Yes?"

Not many people got under his skin, but she was quickly becoming stuck there. "I could charge you with hindering a police investigation."

"You could try." She nodded, looking thoughtful for a moment. "But I'd have it thrown out in a matter of minutes. You have no grounds."

It dawned on him: "You're a lawyer?" He still wasn't sure who she was, but the occupation seemed to fit. "Did we meet in court? Did I testify against your client or something? Is that why you've got your panties in a bunch?"

"Wouldn't you like to know the state of my panties?" She raised a single brow at him. "We've never met in court and as you can see I own a clothing store. I'm not a lawyer, either."

She was and he knew it. "But you are a pain in the ass." He would figure out who she was shortly and the little game she was playing would come to an end.

"To some," she said, shrugging. "Now if you'll excuse me. I have to get back to work." She turned to walk away and just like the last time he saw her, his hand somehow gained a mind of its own and grabbed her wrist. *Just let her go*, his brain warned him. *She's not worth the trouble.* But he couldn't let her have the last word. His male ego wouldn't let Ellis leave on top.

She turned toward him, her eyes wide with curiosity, her pink pouty mouth slightly open. "My card." He slipped it out of his pocket and into the palm of her hand, holding it there just a moment longer than necessary. "Call me if you need anything, Ellis."

She nodded once and then walked away.

When Ellis walked back into her empty shop she was torn between smiling and cursing her fate. The smile won out. Mike lived in Durant now. He wasn't there for a visit. He wasn't just passing through. He was here to stay. She didn't know why she found that funny or why she felt the need to rib him so much. It might be the poetic justice of it all. Mike Edwards, the guy who never had to work hard for a woman's attention, had to work hard for hers. Being a pain in the ass was her good deed for the year. Punishing him was payback for all the women he had once walked over.

Saint Ellis. I'll be applying for that halo now.

"Ellis, boss lady, darling?" Belinda called to her.

"Hmm?" Ellis was so lost in her silly thoughts, the voice barely registered.

"Don't hmm me, missy. What the hell was that all about?"

"What?" Ellis turned around to face her friend. Cherri had gone behind the counter and appeared to be busy folding scarves but was grinning ear-to-ear. Belinda, the bolder of the two, placed her hands on her substantial hips and stared Ellis down.

"You were flirting with the hot cop!" Belinda accused her. "And judging by the way you two were mentally undressing each other I take it you are not strangers."

"We certainly were not mentally undressing each other," Ellis protested as an image of a naked Mike entered her head. "At least I wasn't undressing him."

"You were staring at his crotch!" Belinda screeched.

Busted. Shit.

She had hoped Mike was the only one who had noticed. In fact, she had all but forgotten about her two friends standing beside her. Mike Edwards made her lose all kinds of sense. It was the *Boom*. Okay, so maybe she had been kind of sort of flirting with Mike, but it was only a little. A very teensy amount. It was surreal seeing her former crush walk back in to her life. Especially now that she was so different.

"Well, I guess it's a game we were playing." Ellis

sighed and deposited herself in one of the comfy armchairs she kept in the store for tired shoppers. "Mike isn't interested in me. He never was. He doesn't even remember me. "

"We were there," the soft-spoken Cherri put in. "He looked very interested to me, and if he didn't remember you before he surely won't forget you now."

Ellis waved her hand. "You're exaggerating. Mike's the kind of guy who wears a NO FAT CHICKS ALLOWED T-shirt."

"Wait a minute." Belinda sat on the ottoman in front of Ellis's chair. "Back up. What do you mean he was never interested in you? How exactly do you know this man?"

Belinda was her best friend in the whole world but she had never told her about Mike. She had been in San Francisco at the time, and Ellis's crush on him seemed so insignificant.

"We use to live on the same block four years ago. I would see him every morning at the newsstand buying a paper and cup of coffee, flirting with the girl at the counter. I thought he was so . . . I don't know . . . Hot. Charming. Dreamy." She sighed heavily, thinking back to that time in her life she'd rather forget.

"Of course I also saw him with a bevy of big-breasted women every weekend and thought he was way out of my league. But like an idiot, I told Dina about him. Three weeks later she introduced him to me as her boyfriend. And if that wasn't a big enough knife in the gut, she always had him meet her at my apartment when they went out on dates. She claimed she lived too far away. I'd rather think she was still punishing me for being born."

"Why did you put up with that shit, Ellis?" Belinda frowned. "I would have kicked Dina's ass from here to Connecticut."

She shrugged. "I should have. If it was anybody else I

would have, but my sister and I . . . I can't explain our relationship. Sometimes she was my best friend but sometimes I wondered where I could dispose of her body without getting caught."

"That's a little dark and twisted," Cherri said.

"That's Dina and me."

"Yeah," Belinda said. "You're both crazier than a Walmart on Black Friday. Now get back to you and Detective Hottie."

"Him." She nodded. "Right. At first Mike would just pick her up at my place. But after a few times Dina started inviting him over for dinner or to watch a movie. Part of me wanted to kick them out but part of me was a little fascinated with their relationship. Both Mike and Dina are gorgeous, but other than that they didn't seem to have much in common. They barely even spoke, and that caused me to think that Mike was suffering from SHG syndrome."

"What's that?" Cherri's expression could only be described as horrified.

"Oh, you don't know about SHG syndrome?" Belinda said. "SHG. Stupid Hot Guy. A guy who could grace the cover of magazines but couldn't beat a first-grader in a spelling bee."

"Yeah, Mike exhibited all the signs but he ended up surprising me. One time Dina bailed on him and instead of leaving, he came over to talk to me and I realized that he wasn't lacking brain cells at all. The guy is smart. We talked all night, about his family and politics and food and everything that came to our minds, and when we finally ran out of things to say he cupped my face in his hands and gave me the softest, sweetest kiss that I had ever had. And my little crush bloomed into full-blown infatuation."

"How sweet," Cherri moaned.

Belinda, being less sentimental, rolled her eyes.

"Yeah, it was sweet then, but a couple of nights later he showed up at my Passed the Bar Exam Party with Dina and walked right by me like I didn't exist. And then there was Dina. She was all over him that night, cramming her tongue down his throat at every opportunity. I tried to ignore it and worry about my guests, but when they disappeared I knew something was up."

Belinda's eyes narrowed. "I've never been a big fan of your sister, but don't tell me she did what I think she did."

"That's right." Ellis nodded. "I found them in my bedroom on *my* bed." When Cherri groaned, Ellis shook her head. "Mike was just in his Calvins and getting very personal with my sister's unmentionables. And to top it all off, Dina, my only sister, had the nerve to tell me to get out."

"Whoa," Cherri said.

"Whoa, is right." Ellis shook her head. "I literally went bananas. It was my party and *my bedroom* and Dina had been pulling crap like that our whole freaking lives. And then there was Mike. For some reason I thought he was different so when he acted like every other guy in the world I felt betrayed. Of course I started yelling. Actually, *yelling* is an understatement; I think they heard me in Chinatown." Ellis covered her face with her hands, remembering that night. "It was ugly. All of my guests left, and when Mike tried to mediate I threw his clothes at him and told him to get the hell out." She looked up at her friends. "That was four years ago and so when I met Mike in Hot Lava Java last week I was sure he would remember me as the crazy fat chick who lost her shit at her own party. But he doesn't know who I am. He has no clue!"

"Wow." Belinda said. "Self-centered son of a bitch."

"Right?" Ellis laughed glad her friends understood her. "And now that he's in Durant I feel it's my duty to make him pay for being an asshole four years ago."

"Totally understandable," Cherri agreed.

"What happened between you and Dina after that?" Belinda asked.

Ellis sighed. "We stopped talking for a very long time. Things still aren't right between us. But that's not the entire reason we don't talk. It was just the final straw in a long line of things Dina did that made me want to move to a convent. There was the time she showed my underwear to her friends and told them that they didn't make little girl panties in my size so they had to get them from the grandma store. There was also the time she walked out in a bikini in front of my first real date. *On purpose.* And then proceeded to show him the routine her dance class was working on. After seeing Dina's tight, perfect, size-six body stretching in all types of naughty positions he only wanted to come over to drool over my hot sister."

"Oh, Ellis." Cherri shook her head. "That's so sad."

Ellis shrugged. "That's life with Dina."

The little bell rang over the door and three new customers walked in. Ellis stood up and greeted them with a smile while Cherri and Belinda returned to their posts. The time to think about Mike and the past was over. She had work to do. "Welcome to Size Me Up. How can I help you?"

Chapter Four

Why Men Secretly Love Fat Girls

1. Better cooks.
2. Not picky eaters on dates.
*3. More cushin' for the pushin'. (My fav and bow
chicka wow wow!)*
4. Always warm on a cold night.

*Biologically men are wired to like a girl with big hips,
a soft behind, and a small waist. Go to a museum and
check out the paintings from a few hundred years ago.
Does the girl in the picture look more like Adele or
Jennifer Aniston?*

The next morning Ellis arrived at her shop a little before
nine o'clock, wondering what adventures the day would
bring. Besides the robbery and the reappearance of Detective Hot Pants the day before, Phillipa had called. She
had somehow found out about the crime on St. Lucy
Street in record time and wasn't happy about it. "Nobody
ever got robbed when you were a lawyer," Phillipa pointed
out, which wasn't exactly true. One of Ellis's former clients was the mastermind of an elaborate Ponzi scheme,
but Ellis wisely kept her mouth shut.

After Ellis spent an hour on the phone with her mother
and reassured her that she had personally spoken to the
detective in charge, Phillipa let the subject drop. By the

end of the day Ellis was exhausted—but the good news was she had gained three new customers, one of whom decided she needed a brand-new wardrobe. If business kept going like that Ellis might be able to take home a small paycheck this month.

Maybe I'll be able to buy real food this month. KFC, here I come!

Ellis opened the shop every morning and most days stayed well after closing. But she preferred the quiet of the morning. It was then she was most productive. Today was no different. She updated her blog, tidied the storeroom, and wiped all the fingerprints off the huge glass display case where she kept the jewelry. Today in addition to her normal routine she placed the twenty-six-inch expandable metal baton Phillipa had bought her when she moved to Manhattan in the drawer under the cash register. She hadn't told her mother, but the robbery of Mrs. Underwood's shop made Ellis nervous. Durant was her safe childhood hometown. People didn't even lock their doors at night. Ellis had come back here to get away from all the hustle and bustle of Manhattan, to feel safe again.

"I read your blog today."

Holy shit. She also left Manhattan to get away from him.

Ellis looked up to see her ex-boyfriend Jack Toomey standing just inside the doorway. Her stomach dropped. Jack was a beautiful man. And she was the dumb-ass who had taken one look at his dazzling blue eyes and lean body in an expensive suit and fallen hard. He was a lawyer like her. Smart, ambitious, and in the beginning more charming than a bag full of snake oil salesmen. She'd had a hard time believing that he wanted somebody like her. Somebody who was overweight and wore glasses and had been able to recite the Emancipation Proclamation since she was ten years old. But he made her feel beautiful, and after a long line of losers he seemed like the perfect guy. So perfect that she ignored all the signs that he was the wrong man for her.

She never thought he would step foot in her store. It had been six months since she'd walked away. Six months since she'd decided she was worth more than what he thought.

"It's funny. I had no idea you could write."

He looked around her store, taking it all in with that assessing eye that sometimes made her feel self-conscious. For a moment she wondered what he thought about the place she poured her soul into. But she hated herself for thinking that. His opinion no longer mattered to her.

"I have nothing to say to you, Jack." She made herself busy by rearranging the earrings in her display case, hoping the ground would swallow him. It didn't. He moved closer, stopping directly in front of her.

"I think there is a lot left to say, Ellis." Jack placed his hand on her newly cleaned display case, leaving his grimy fingerprints all over it. "Please look at me."

Bastard.

She did look up, not because he asked her to but because she wanted him to know that she was no longer cowed by him. "I think you made everything perfectly clear the night I left."

"Please, Ellis." He placed his warm hand over hers, and when that contact wasn't enough he walked around the counter and set both hands on her shoulders. "I know I made mistakes in our relationship. But I want to make up for them. Please hear me out." He folded his arms around her and buried his face in the crook of her neck.

She shut her eyes, holding her body as rigid as possible, but part of her brain couldn't help but notice that his touch didn't feel as repulsive as she had hoped. He was warm and familiar and he smelled expensive. He was her first love and he used to hold her like this when they began dating. She used to think his arms around her was the best feeling in the world.

Their lives together hadn't been all bad. In fact a small part of her couldn't truly hate him because he had shown her some of the best times in her life. But she wouldn't get sucked in again. Because he was also the man who treated her like shit. "Let. Go. Of. Me."

He took a step back, seeming surprised at her words. He should be. She wasn't the same woman he had met. The one who tried her hardest to put his happiness before hers. She had given up a piece of herself for this man. She wouldn't do that ever again.

"Okay." He held his hands up in defense. "I'm sorry. I just want to talk to you."

"Only employees are allowed on this side of the counter."

He nodded and returned to the other side. It was then she took a breath. His nearness was suffocating. His nearness made it hard to breathe.

"You drove all the way up here. Talk."

"I want you back," he said in a rush. "I never wanted you to leave. You know that."

"You never wanted me to leave?" She laughed humorlessly. "Could have fooled me. You spent the last six months of our relationship going out of your way to make me feel like I was unworthy of you."

He shook his head, running both of his hands through his hair. It was something he only did when he was nervous. "I was going through something, Ellis and I need you to understand that. I needed you to see me through it."

She inhaled harshly. "Are you blaming me for the breakup?"

"No but—" He shook his head. "No, of course not, but can you honestly tell me that you were the same person I met when we broke up?"

"No," she answered easily. "Maybe I do have some fault in this. I thought you wanted me to grow as a person. I thought the man I loved would have wanted me to succeed. I never thought you expected me to spend my entire life catering to you."

"I didn't! But your career was moving so quickly, and there I was at the same firm for ten years and constantly being passed over for partner. I didn't know how to handle being with a woman who was litigating billion-dollar cases."

"You didn't try to handle it. You didn't try to talk to me. Instead you kept putting me down and degrading me and I was stupid enough to let it happen because I thought it was my fault you weren't happy."

"It wasn't your fault. Listen, Ellis, I don't know how to explain what happened. I just know that I want you back. The past six months have been miserable without you."

"Good. Now you know how I felt when I was with you."

"I know you're upset. I know you need more time, but I still love you. I think we can work this out."

"You still love me? You said horrible things to me. You cheated on me—"

"I never cheated on you!"

"I saw you with her. In my house. Don't feed me some bullshit about you two were working. What kind of lawyer works with his paralegal over a candlelight dinner? What kind of work were you doing with her lips on your neck?"

"I didn't sleep with her."

"Well, just because you didn't fuck her doesn't mean you weren't cheating."

He flinched, stunned by her profanity. "It was wrong but I did it to send you a message. To show you that if you didn't appreciate me, I could find another woman who would."

"Oh, you sent a message all right. It was loud and clear and it was telling me to get the hell away from you."

Jack shut his eyes for a moment. "I've screwed this up. I know you need more time but I'm not going to stop, Ellis. I went through some stuff but it's over now. You know we belong together. You know you were meant to be a lawyer. This little store. This move back to Durant is just a phase, and I'm not going to stop until I make you see that."

"Get out!"

Little store? Just a phase? He still had no clue when it came to her and she wasn't about to waste her breath explaining it to him. Maybe she should thank him, because without his betrayal she would have never been brave enough to go after her dreams.

"Fine. I'll go, but it won't be forever."

Her chest was still heaving twenty minutes later. She couldn't believe he wanted her back. Just when she was finally over him, just when her self-esteem returned, he came back to turn her world upside down. She tried to push him out of her mind as she went back to work. But the words *asshole*, and *shithead*, and *butt face* wanted to pour from her mouth like she had some kind of man-hating Tourette's syndrome.

"Honey, what's wrong?" Belinda called to her. She quickly made her way around the counter and grasped Ellis's shoulder. "Ellis what happened? Did we get robbed? Are you hurt?" She looked around the shop, seeing that everything was in its place.

"Jack" was all she said.

"What?" Belinda frowned. "If you tell me Jack was here I'm going to scream."

"He was." Ellis nodded.

"Where's my knife?" Belinda let go of her to rummage

through the drawer. "Oh these will work nicely!" She held up a pair of heavy-duty box-cutting scissors. "I bet you I could cut his balls off with these. Slimy bastard." Belinda continued to mumble. "I can't believe he had the nerve to show up here after what he did to you."

Belinda knew every sordid detail of her life with Jack. It was Belinda she went to after she broke up with him. Belinda knew every harsh word he had said to her, things she couldn't even bring herself to tell her mother, because she was embarrassed that she had let it go on for so long. It was Belinda who'd given her the strength to open this store.

"Give me those." She removed the potential weapon from her friend's hand. Ellis didn't really have time to be a witness in a murder trial, but she was glad she had a friend willing to maim for her. "He's gone now. He won't be back."

"He better not be." She turned to face Ellis, her expression saying a thousand words. "What did he want?"

"To get back together." Ellis never thought that Jack would come crawling back. She never thought she would hear him apologize, either. Throughout their two-year relationship she'd often wished she could hear him say he was wrong. He finally did. It was just a little too late.

"How do you feel about that?" Belinda asked warily.

"There's no freaking way." Ellis shook off her lingering anger. "He's the same asshole he always was. He thinks I'm playing a game. That I opened this store just to get at him."

"But this is your dream. You worked too damn hard to get it."

"I would die before I gave this place up."

"Hey." Cherri walked in for her shift nearly an hour early. "What's going on?" she asked after seeing the look on Ellis's face. "Have we been robbed?" She, too, looked around the store to see if anything was out of order.

"No. It's worse. Jack showed up," Belinda informed her.

"No way."

"Yeah," Ellis said. "I'm feeling somewhere in between murderous and bummed."

"Well then, I have the perfect solution for that." Cherri smiled. "Tonight is trivia night down at Bagpipes. We can get tipsy, show off how smart we are, and bad-mouth Jack-ass all at the same time."

"That sounds like fun. I think we all deserve a little downtime." Belinda looked at Ellis. "What do you say?"

Ellis hadn't been out anywhere with the girls since she'd opened the store. It was time she went out and let her hair down. It was time she forget all about her little encounter with Jack.

"I say Bay Breeze me."

Chapter Five

"When the hell did you start going to trivia nights?" Mike asked his best friend Colin O'Connell over the loud music and dozens of conversations at Bagpipes Pub.

It was the first time they'd hung out since he'd moved back to Durant. He hadn't seen Colin for almost a year, which was not the norm for them. The two of them had been inseparable in college and before that . . . Mike didn't have a lot of friends. He had his mother, his sisters, a few girls here and there, and the flower shop.

His father had walked out on the family the day before Mike turned thirteen. The day Mike ceased being a kid. He became the man of the family, waking up at four in the morning to help his mother and two sisters out at the shop while his older sister took a job in a nursing home to help make ends meet. When Mike's father left he didn't just take himself. He took most of the money in the bank account, leaving his wife with only five thousand dollars to raise four kids.

It was flower shop, school, and home for Mike until he turned eighteen and his mother made him go away to college. It was there he met Colin, who had moved from

Ireland on a student visa. They were both slightly home-
sick, had similar childhoods filled with work and single
parents. Of course, they immediately took to each other
and spent every day of the next four years doing things
they shouldn't have. Colin had come home with Mike on
breaks when he couldn't get back to Ireland, which was
most of the time. He had worked in Mike's family's flower
shop over the summers, broke bread with them on Thanksgiving, and till this day still sent Mike's mother, Margie,
birthday presents. The two had been more like brothers
than friends, which was why Mike felt guilty about not
seeing Colin as often as he should. Yes, they were both
busy. Mike was up to his neck in crime while Colin worked
as a restoration expert specializing in antique furniture.
Mike always thought it was funny that his big, profanity-
spewing friend had such a love for dainty old furniture, but
his love showed in his work and he had the extensive cli-
entele to prove it. Still, going nine months without seeing
his best friend was far too long, and so when Colin suggested trivia night Mike agreed.

"When I hit thirty," Colin responded to Mike's question
in his slight brogue. "One day I turned around and all the
girls at the bar were babies. And instead of wanting to take
them home I wanted to tell them to put on a goddamn
sweater." He took a long swig of Guinness. "My sister is
twenty, for fuck's sake. I feel like a pervert."

"You're getting old." Mike grinned at his friend. He
was beginning to understand what Colin was talking about.
They were about to be thirty-three. Staggering home after
last call didn't seem so appealing. Waking up next to a
girl who was barely out of her teens, even less so. "But
why trivia night?"

"You see, my friend"—Colin playfully slapped him on
the back—"on trivia night you've got more of a variety
for people-watching." He pointed at a gaggle of middle-

aged women sitting at the bar. "Soccer moms. They're a fun group, come every week, usually spend their days up to their elbows in shit and driving the carpool. So when they get a chance to come out they get raunchy. They're loud. They flirt like slags and they know more useless shit than anybody else here. I try to get on their team at least once a month."

Mike shook his head at his friend's perceptive evaluation of those women. Colin had mellowed out a lot in the past few years. The man who was never afraid of a bar fight was now hanging out with soccer moms and limiting his alcohol intake. When had his friend grown up?

"So whose team are we going to be on tonight?"

"Well." Colin scanned the room. "Those frat boys over there are out. They don't know shit and are usually drunk off their asses before the fourth round starts. See if you can find some elementary school teachers or something. They know almost as much as the soccer moms, and they hate losing."

"What the hell do elementary school teachers look like?" Mike searched the room, passing his eyes over multiple groups of women. All he could picture was his fifth-grade teacher Mrs. Larson, who wore cat-shaped earrings and had a mole on her chin with a hair growing out it. He shuddered. He didn't think he could spend the whole night on a team with women like that. But he would if he had to. Colin, it seemed, played to win, and Mike owed him this.

"Look for girls in their twenties that look kind of sweet but serious. They usually aren't the ones with their tits hanging out."

"You should have been a cop." Mike glanced at his friend before he continued to scope out possible elementary school teachers and potential teammates. He saw lots of women, but a flash of red caught his eye. Something, a pull, he couldn't describe it, forced him to focus on the woman who was wearing it. *Ellis*. She was sitting on the other side of the bar with a pink-colored drink in her hand. "I should have known."

She looked up at him as if he'd called her. Her eyes widened with surprise as they connected with his. He wanted to turn away, pretend like he hadn't seen her. The woman irked him but he just couldn't look away. She kept popping into his mind, every day, and he was sure that attraction had nothing to do with it. He found her sexy—but he found a lot of women sexy. It was the fact that he couldn't recall where he knew her from. If he knew, he could then put her out of his mind and focus on something else. Somebody else.

Not wanting to be rude to the woman who had been nothing but rude to him, he nodded his head in acknowledgment, expecting her to do the same.

She stuck her tongue out at him.

"Brat." He found himself smiling, knowing that his earlier thoughts were wrong. She wouldn't be so easy to put out of his mind. He had made that mistake already.

"Huh?" Colin asked, looking in Ellis's direction.

"Ellis." Mike shook his head at her immature gesture. She was next to the same redhead and blonde she'd been with the day of the robbery. Both her friends were staring at him with interest. It made him wonder what exactly Ellis had told them about him. He quickly thought back four years ago to the women he had dated. Michelle, Dina, Rachel, Kara. He remembered them all. Not one of them lasted more than two months. There was no woman in between. He had never been with Ellis.

"Who?"

Mike didn't return his attention to Colin. He was too distracted by Ellis, who was giving him that impish grin of hers.

"The brunette in the red." The only woman in the world who could irritate the hell out of him and yet make him want to get closer. He turned to Colin, thinking that his friend might be able to help. "Do you know her? She says we met four years ago but I don't remember her and now every time I see her she busts my balls about it."

"Her?" Colin took a long look at Ellis. "I've seen her around town a couple of times but I don't have a clue who she is."

"Neither do I. But I know her from somewhere." He grimaced before taking a sip of his beer. "She knows what kind of underwear I wear."

Colin shrugged. "You probably slept with her."

"I didn't." Ten years ago that might have been true, but now he knew it wasn't.

Colin studied Ellis the same way he appraised a piece of furniture, with his head tilted to the side. "I guess she's a little on the chubby side for you but it's possible. Those soft girls are good for a tumble once in a while and she looks like she'd be a good one to tumble with for a couple of hours. Very fuckable."

"Watch your mouth," Mike warned his friend, immediately wishing he hadn't. What did he care if Colin made a comment about her? Mike barely knew her, and the little he did know was a big pain in his ass. But she still deserved some respect.

"You got a thing for this girl, Edwards?" Colin raised a brow at him and then looked over at Ellis once more.

Mike's eyes unwillingly followed. She was laughing at something one of her friends said, enjoying the company of the two women he'd barely noticed last week. Even across the darkened bar he could see how brightly her face was lit up. Her head tilted backward, her mouth slightly opened. It made him want to be in on the joke.

"I don't have a thing for her," he denied, although the

image of her in nothing but red panties appeared in his mind more often than he would like to admit. "I barely know her."

Colin placed his hand over his heart. "I, Colin O'Connell, never thought I'd live to see the day that Mike 'Lady Lover' Edwards would be sweet on a girl. I'm bloody well touched."

"What man talks like that?" Mike shook his head. "You sound like your grandmother."

"I love my granny." Colin finished his dark beer. "And don't change the subject. You always talk about your conquests with me, and now your mouth is shut tighter than a nun's legs."

"There is nothing to talk about." Mike was getting slightly irritated with Colin's sudden inquisitiveness. It made him wish he'd never said anything about Ellis in the first place. She was just a woman. A woman who didn't even like him.

"Fine. We won't talk about your girlfriend anymore. But the blonde sitting next to her is fair game. Come on." He stood up. "Let's go be on their team."

Mike knew that spending the next undetermined amount of hours with Ellis was a bad idea, but his brain couldn't stop his body from getting up and following his friend across the pub.

Ellis watched Mike get up from his seat across the bar. He was probably here to pick up women. *Do men still do that? Do women still let that happen?*

With Mike they probably did. He had that way about him, that smile that made him seem like a badass and good guy at the same time. She tried to keep her attention on her friends but like a magnet he drew her eyes wherever he went in the room. This was supposed to be girls' night out. She was supposed to be relaxing, forgetting about men altogether. Forgetting about Jack. She hated that after six months the sight of her ex still bothered her. It wasn't because she still loved him. It was the fact that she'd spent so long with a man who built himself up by putting her down.

Mike passed the bar. He passed the gang of hot skinny girls. He passed the bathroom. *Frick.* It was like she was watching him in slow motion, like this was a scene from a movie and she was the fat nerdy girl in love with the quarterback who would never notice her. Except this was no movie. She definitely wasn't in love and the hot guy was heading directly toward her, his blue eyes never leaving her face. *Frick!*

"Don't let me do anything stupid," Ellis said grabbing hold of Belinda's hand.

"What? Seriously, Ellis it's just trivia. We aren't going to stone you if you answer wrong."

"Belinda!"

"What?" Belinda asked, following Ellis's gaze. "Oh, the hot cop you were making goo-goo eyes with is on his way over and he's bringing that sexy Irishman with him."

"You know his friend, Belinda?" Cherri asked, clearly interested. Ellis hadn't even noticed the man leading the detective but there he was, just as tall dark and handsome, with that same bad-boy gleam in his eye.

Hunks for sales. Two for the price of one.

"Yeah. He restored my mother's old antique chest and believe me when I tell you that man is good with his hands."

Cherri looked toward the two approaching men. "I bet he is," she said softly.

"That's riveting," Ellis interrupted, "now back to me. Don't let me do anything stupid. Mike's looks seem to affect my brain cells. I need you to remind me that I don't like him."

"But you do like him," Cherri pointed out.

"I can't like him. I'm off men, remember? And he's like junk food on a Tuesday. Strictly off limits." She let out a frustrated sigh as Mike drew closer. There was no mistaking where he was heading. His eyes were still on her. She wished she'd never stuck her tongue out at him. "He slept with my sister," she reminded them at the same time she reminded herself. "Don't leave me alone with him."

"Why not, Ellis?" Belinda asked grinning. "I think you're pretty capable of handling yourself."

"You're wrong there. I'm a stressed-out basket case with an unstable future and Mike's the type of guy who could—who could . . . Holy crap, you guys, I haven't had sex in a really long time." Ellis spoke faster, trying to get it all out before Mike reached her. "Just be good friends and save me from myself. You know I would do it for you."

"Do what?" Mike asked.

Whoa Nellie.

Ellis took a breath and composed herself. She never got so worked up over anybody before but he looked good tonight, really freaking good in a black T-shirt and a pair of low-slung jeans. He looked equally good in a suit and in only a pair of Calvins.

"Nothing." She forced herself to make eye contact and not stare at his chest. She wondered if she could bounce a quarter off it. "What are you doing here, Mikey? Looking for new conquests?"

"Nope." He sat next to her on the booth, his big body pressing into hers and invading her space. He smelled good. Not like cologne but like shampoo and clean skin. It was much different from Jack's expensive scent. It was damn near refreshing. "This is my friend Colin." He pointed to the tall man still standing. "We're joining your team."

"What if we don't want company?" Ellis said feeling the need to rib him. "What if we want a girls' night out?"

"We don't really care." Mike's eyes locked with hers. "Now mind your manners and say hello to my friend."

"Hello, Colin." She didn't want to say hello to his friend. She wanted to say *Go away, go away, go away* but her mischievous side reared its ugly head. "I must not be memorable." She looked at the Irishman with mournful eyes. "I guess you don't recall who I am, either." She glanced at Mike and then back at his friend. They exchanged a glance.

"No, love, can't say I do." He slid his long body into the seat next to Cherri. "Can you tell me what kind of underwear I wear?" He grinned at her.

So Mike had told his friend about her. Ellis wasn't sure if that was a good or bad thing. Probably bad. It was never good when men spoke to each other but she looked on the bright side. Mike didn't remember her, so he couldn't have said much to his equally charming friend.

"Oh, Colin, we both know you don't wear any," Ellis shot back.

Colin's grin melted away and both men stared at each other for a long moment and then looked back at her. Mike did not look happy. Aha! She'd gotten them.

"That was a lucky guess, I swear!" She laughed.

"Brat," Mike said under his breath, shaking his head at her naughty behavior.

What was wrong with her? She was a Harvard Law grad, a business owner. A grown-up, for God's sake. Why was it that every time she got around Mike she acted like a hormonal thirteen-year-old? There was just something about him that made her want to act up. And it was fun.

"I'm sorry, Colin." She did some head shaking of her own. "We've never met before and I didn't know that you enjoyed going commando but now that I do, I know what not to get you for Christmas."

"I like her," Colin said to Mike with a grin before he turned back to her. "It's nice to meet you, Ellis. Introduce me to your lovely friends."

Ellis made the introductions and didn't fail to notice the extra attention Colin gave to the too-young-for-him, very mild-mannered Cherri. Oh Lord, Ellis thought. Cherri would be no match for the sexy grinning Irishman.

"Did you guys order any food yet?" Mike asked as his eyes passed over the menus sitting before him on the table.

Ellis pulled her attention away from her friend and back to Mike. She was about to answer when Belinda beat her to it.

"We can't." Belinda pouted. "Ellis has a no-junk-food-on-weekdays rule and she sort of resembles a starving puppy when we eat it in front of her. We're not sure if we should feed her or send her to the pound."

"What?" Mike slowly perused Ellis's figure, which immediately caused her to shrink back in her seat and get goose bumps all at once.

She inwardly sighed. Her food rule was no secret but for some reason she didn't want Mike and his very cute friend to know about it. She didn't want any excuse for him to study her less-than-skinny body or her eating habits. She knew his type. He went for girls like her sister. Girls with less than 5 percent body fat. It made her wonder why he was sitting with them tonight.

"Ask her about it," Belinda continued, causing Ellis to wonder if she could kick her friend under the table without anyone else noticing. "If it's not Saturday or Sunday she won't eat anything with any fat or sugar."

Mike narrowed his eyes as he studied Ellis once again. She hated it when he looked at her like she was a specimen in a petri dish. "When I met you it was a Tuesday and you were getting a Black and White."

Damn it. He remembered. He witnessed that entire

mortifying scene between her and Agatha Toomey. "I was having a shitty day." She shrugged. "I made an exception."

"Why don't you just eat what you want, Ellis?"

"Because Mikey, us fat girls can't eat what we want when we want it. It's so much easier for you men. You can eat whatever you want and the most half of you get is beer bellies. It's really very sickening. I eat a bag of chips and I can't button my pants. You never have to worry about your ass jiggling or squeezing yourself into a pair of Spanx. Do you know how hard it is to put on a pair of Spanx? Have you ever had to wear a girdle? Or worry about cellulite on the back of your legs? And back fat! Oh, don't get me started on back fat. Nobody ever tells you that you need to lose weight. People don't come up to you in coffee shops and offer to put you on a diet. You don't cringe every time you have to put on a bathing suit." Ellis took a breath. "And why the hell are you letting me rant about this?" She turned to her two silent but grinning friends. "Remember when I said don't let me ramble on like a crazy person? That was your cue to stop me."

"We like it when you rant," Cherri told her. She turned to Mike. "Have you read Ellis's blog? She is hysterical. She says all the stuff all the girls like us think but don't have the guts to say out loud. Her blog is the reason why I went to work for her. Her store is a dream come true for girls like me. It's finally a place we can be ourselves."

Ellis felt a rush of affection for Cherri in that moment. *Guess who's getting Employee of the Month?*

"Blog?" Mike looked at Ellis. "Girls like you?" He blinked. He looked at her confused. She wasn't surprised. Men never got it. "Ellis, what kind of store do you run?"

"It's a store for what I like to call the hard-to-fit yet extremely fashionable population," she explained. "You know, the long and lanky girls. Our large-footed sisters. The petite yet full-figured and your run-of-the-mill plus-sized divas. It's hard for us to find clothes that are cute so I decided to open the store and fill that gap in the market. And if it doesn't fit I tailor clothes upon request."

"What kind of girl are you?" Colin asked with a slight smile. Both men actually seemed to be interested in what she was saying—either that or they were really good fakers.

"Me?" Ellis pointed to herself, surprised he had to ask. "I'm what the politically correct call plus-sized but what most people call fat. But I also have big feet and tend to be on the taller side."

"You're not fat." Mike shook his head. "I think your rule is dumb." He picked up the menus and handed them out, neglecting to give Ellis one. He seemed serious, like he really believed himself when he said she wasn't fat. It made her not trust him. "Everybody order what you want." Mike looked at her and shook his head again.

"I never said they couldn't," she said hotly. He had no right to pass judgment on her eating habits. He was just like Jack, except in the opposite direction. "Just because I want to maintain some kind of control of my weight doesn't mean my rule is stupid. People do what I do all the time. I'm trying to watch my figure."

"I like your figure." He looked at the menu and briefly at her, his eyes lingering on her lips. "I'll watch it for you."

Is he hitting on me?

"What?" She felt a warm flush creep up her neck.

He ignored her outburst. "What do you want? I'm buying."

"You're not buying anything for me." She firmly shook her head. "I had soup before I came. I'm not hungry."

"You don't have to be hungry to eat dessert."

He turned the menu over to the back side, wrapped his long arm around her middle, and grabbed ahold of the menu with his other hand, encasing her in his arms. Her immediate reaction was to snuggle close, but her brain was screaming to get away. Her body betrayed her and instead of fleeing, tingles ran over all the parts of her that had come in contact with him. For a moment she wondered how all this would feel if neither of them wore clothes.

Bad girl. Dirty thoughts. He slept with your sister!

The menu was in front of her face and she had no choice but to look at it. The other options were to look at her traitorous friends, who were doing nothing to stop this man from wrapping himself around her, or at Mike. And he was just as bad for her as junk food.

"What looks good, Ellis?"

She glanced at his profile for a moment. *You*, she thought. He had just a hint of five-o'clock shadow making his already rugged face even better. "Mike, I don't want—"

"I saw your eyes linger on the chocolate nachos." His gaze remained on her face for a moment. "You'll share them with me." He waved his hand, and immediately a cute waitress appeared to take their orders.

Mike had busted her yet again. Her eyes had lingered on the chocolate nachos. Cinnamon tortillas, topped with powdered sugar and drizzled with a decadent hot chocolate sauce. The creator of this masterpiece, the wicked man, placed fresh strawberries, homemade whipped cream, and a scoop of vanilla ice cream on top. That combination shouldn't be good together but it was one of the best things Ellis had tasted. When she was feeling really naughty, she would indulge.

Tonight she was feeling quite naughty.

"You shouldn't have ordered those," she told him as the waitress took the rest of their party's order. Chocolate was her downfall, the only thing that could cause her to break down and binge. "Chocolate is like good sex with a hot man. It's great for a while but eventually it will make you sick."

"What?" Mike's eyes fell on her lips. "Say that again?"

Had she spoken out loud? And why the hell did his eyes always focus on her lips? This day couldn't possibly get any worse—first Jack and now Mike. She had reached her quota of men for the year. The thought of entering a convent entered her head. Her Jewish mother wouldn't appreciate that, but Ellis couldn't please everybody all the time.

She made the mistake of looking into his eyes. *Shit*. He was looking at her with male interest. Well, of course he was. She'd said *sex*. "I didn't say anything. Now get the hell off of me."

Ellis wised up and finally shook herself out of his hold but his skin left its impression on hers, and she felt the warmth from his touch linger long after he let her go. She took a short deep breath, composing herself, and looked toward her friends who were happily ensconced in conversation with Colin. *Traitors*. They were no help at all. She was going to do something stupid shortly.

Mike turned his body toward hers. "What did I do to you that caused you not to like me?"

"Do you remember who I am yet?"

His eyes searched her face once again. "No." He shook his head. "But I know we were never together. I stopped doing the one-night-stand thing a long time ago, and I know that four years ago I would have never gone for you."

"I know," she said, slightly miffed. "Guys like you never look at girls like me."

"I'm looking now, Ellis. Hell, I probably looked then, too, but you look like a breeder."

"Excuse me?" Her defenses went up. If he was referring to her as livestock she'd pop him in the mouth. "What the hell is that supposed to mean?"

"Relax." One corner of his mouth curled. "We call women like you breeders because you look like baby makers. The type of women who want to get married last week and start popping out a bunch of kids. You appear serious when a guy like me is just looking for a little fun."

"Ha! See how much you know. I don't want kids, Detective Know-It-All. I don't want to get married, either. That's so typically male of you to assume that all fat girls are dying to get married and have babies. Some of us are capable of more than domestication."

"This has nothing to do with weight. What is with you?" Annoyance passed over his face. "Why are you so obsessed with fat? Ellis, you're soft and beautiful. You're the kind of woman a man can picture holding his children. You're the kind of woman who seems like she can manage it all."

She rolled her eyes. "Your perception of me is all wrong. I'm a mess. I quit my high-paying job, I cashed in my 401(k) to open my shop, and I'm holding on by a string. Kids and a husband are the last thing I could possibly want." She laughed bitterly. "Even if you don't remember how we met four years ago, I do. You ignored me and went on with your hot girlfriend. I've spent my whole life being overlooked by men like you. And you think I want to get married? Ha. I never wanted to be chained to one man for the rest of my life. Maybe I'm just looking for a little fun myself."

He looked at her with interest. "You don't believe in marriage, either?"

"I do, but for other people. I've worked too hard to get my life the way I want it for some man to come around and screw things up for me."

"I don't believe in marriage for anybody. Go out with me."

"What?" She laughed. A date was the last thing she expected from him. "No!"

"Why not?" He frowned.

"Oh!" She laughed harder. "You're not used to being turned down. Are you?"

"No, so don't turn me down."

"Why are you asking me out?" Ellis stopped seeing the humor in the situation.

She couldn't date him or anybody. It was too soon after her last failure, and there was something about Mike. There was something between them. She didn't like him now, but she could, and if somebody like Jack could knock her on her ass then a man like Mike could destroy her altogether.

"I don't know why." He looked as perplexed as she felt. "We don't even like each other." His eyes returned to her face. "Go out with me anyway."

"No."

They looked at each other for a long time, their eyes locked in some kind of unspoken battle. Four years ago he had kissed her and forgotten her. Would he be any different now? She wasn't stupid enough to find out.

"Sorry for the wait. The kitchen's backed up," the waitress said, breaking the spell between them.

Ellis blinked, trying to clear her head, and focused on the huge platter of cheese fries in front of Colin and Cherri. Belinda had ordered a basket of chicken fingers—but when the waitress placed the nachos in front of Ellis and Mike, Ellis forgot about everything else. They looked better than she remembered. The red of the strawberries beautifully contrasted with all the white of the cream and the darkness of the chocolate. She pulled her lower lip between her teeth. She wouldn't indulge. She had two more whole days until she could.

Thou mustn't eat chocolate nachos on Thursdays.

"Eat one," Mike whispered in her ear, playing the role of naughty devil.

She shook her head. "I can't." But God, she wanted to.

"A few won't hurt." They would. They would hurt her very much, making her feel guilty and punish herself tomorrow by eating nothing but wilted celery. He didn't seem to care about her inner turmoil. She watched as he picked up a chocolate-drenched chip, dipped it in cream, and dropped it in his mouth. "Damn, Ellis," he moaned, and her stomach clenched. "These are amazing."

"I know," she said mournfully. "I hate you, Mike Edwards, and everything you stand for."

He grinned at her, placed another nacho in his mouth, and moaned again. "You've got to eat one."

"No." She folded her arms over her chest and shook her head.

"How about just a strawberry then?" He lifted a whole strawberry, dipped it in chocolate and cream, and held it up to her mouth. "Strawberries are good for you."

"Not the way you dress them." She grabbed hold of his wrist as his hand hovered in front of her mouth. "Mike, no."

He rubbed the strawberry against her lower lip, back and forth, leaving creamy chocolate behind. "Come on Ellis. Just try it."

Her tongue darted out to lick off the mess he made. And as if a choir of angels took up residence in her head, she heard *AH!*

No willpower. She had absolutely no willpower.

"Fine." She relented and took a bite of the ripe strawberry. It was plump and good and sweet, all the things a good piece of fruit should be . . . plus it was covered in chocolate. *AH!*

"Is this a fetish of yours, Mikey?" she asked as she finished chewing. "Does hand-feeding fat girls satisfy some kind of yearning you have? Or does it bring you some kind of wholesome joy like feeding animals at the zoo? Am I like feeding a broodmare?"

"Stop it." He grabbed her chin between his thick fingers and forced her to look him in the eye. She saw anger there. He was angry with her. "I don't ever want to hear you talk about yourself like that again. Do you understand me? It's not funny," he said in a low voice. "It's not some kind of goddamn joke. You're beautiful. You're sexy and any man in his right mind can see that. Why can't you?"

Ellis froze. For a second she felt like crying. After hearing nothing but put-downs from Jack for the last six months of their relationship, Mike's words were like balm to her bruised soul. She had a hard time seeing herself that way, a hard time believing his words because somewhere along the line a tiny part of her had started believing what Jack had said.

His cobalt eyes bored into hers. "I don't want you calling yourself that word around me anymore. Okay?"

She nodded. It was all she could do. He lifted the strawberry to her mouth and this time without protest she opened her lips and let him feed her.

Suddenly the emcee's voice sounded across the bar. Sheet of papers and pens were handed out. Trivia night was beginning.

Mike noticed that Ellis had gone quiet during the first few rounds of trivia. She gave answers when she knew them, showing off her intelligence. He had no idea who wrote *The Glass Menagerie* or the year the first *Peanuts* comic premiered. Colin seemed very pleased with her performance. He nodded at Mike three times, their private signal that he approved of a woman. How could he not approve of her? By the end of round three they were tied for first place and Colin was enjoying himself with Ellis's friends. Or at least he was pretending to.

Colin had always been a good wingman and tonight was no different. He managed to keep Ellis's friends well occupied while Mike was doing things to her he shouldn't have. Rubbing the strawberry across her lips, for example, but Ellis had such pretty pink lips and watching her lick them was like watching one of his fantasies come to life. He was attracted to her and damn it, he didn't want to be.

Sitting next to her, with her soft body pressed into his side, talking for those few minutes, Mike got the chance to learn about her in a way he never got to learn about most women he came in contact with. Some man, somewhere along the way, had convinced her that she wasn't beautiful, which was a shame, because her brown eyes contained little flecks of gold and her skin looked as smooth as the cream they were eating. That man also had probably broken her heart. Mike didn't do needy, insecure women. They were too messy. But Ellis didn't strike him that way. She had steel running through her, and he liked that. She also wasn't looking for the package. The husband-and-family thing. He could be around her without worrying that she had ulterior motives. Tonight he realized he did want to be around her: Even though they bickered and things weren't as easy as he liked, there was something about her that kept him wanting to get closer.

"I like you much better when you're quiet," Mike said into Ellis's ear between the third and fourth rounds.

"Bite me," she griped.

He grinned at her. "Only if I get to pick where." He deliberately took his time studying her body. She wore tight black jeans tonight, with black leather boots and a red wrap top. It was sexy without being slutty and had him wishing she would stand up just so he could see how well her jeans fit her backside.

"God, you're such a smarmy pervert."

He shrugged, unrepentant.

"And why are you sitting so close to me?" She wiggled slightly to get away from him but all she managed to do was rub against him in the process. "You've been with so many women I'll probably get a STD just sitting next to you."

He took slight offense to that. It hadn't been that many. "How do you know how many women I've been with? You don't know me that well." He frowned. "I think."

"I've seen you out in the city at Machado's a few times. Each time with a different girl."

He looked at her. The Cuban restaurant was one of his favorite haunts while he lived in Manhattan and a place he often took women on first dates. "We lived in the same neighborhood?" he asked. She nodded once. "And I never noticed you?"

"You did notice me, but I guess I'm just forgettable."

He racked his brain, searching for her face in his memory, but came up blank. "Don't you think it's time you let me in on this little secret? Tell me how I know you."

"Nope." She shook her head. "Can I have the last strawberry?"

"Yeah." He picked up the last chocolate-and-cream-covered strawberry with his fingers and presented it to her mouth. "I don't see why you just can't tell me. We live in the same town again. We're bound to see more of each other. This game is stupid."

She shrugged, taking a bite of the berry. "I think it's fun."

He watched her chew for a moment, her lips once again driving him to distraction. She was right. He liked feeding her, and not for the reasons she thought. He just liked to see her mouth work. He mentally shook himself out of her spell. This woman was going to cause him to do something he regretted. "Why don't you like me?"

"Can't stand it, can you?" She gave him a slight grin and pulled his hand to her mouth to deposit the last bit of strawberry. "There's more chocolate on your fingers than was on the damn strawberry." She lifted his thumb to her mouth, placed it inside, and removed all traces of food with her tongue.

Holy shit.

His entire body went rigid. All his blood, every ounce went rushing from his head, flooding into other places.

"What?" She looked up at him, his thumb still in her warm, moist mouth.

The silly girl hadn't meant to make him harder than cement, but she had. Mike heard a choking sound and looked up to see Colin wide-eyed. Nothing shocked his friend, but today Ellis had managed to do it. Ellis slowly removed his thumb from her mouth and turned to look at Colin and her friends. Cherri's mouth hung open; Belinda stared at Ellis as if she had never seen her before.

"It's not what it . . . He had chocolate on his . . ." Ellis groaned. "I need a drink." She climbed over Mike, her breasts brushing against his cheek, and quickly headed for the bar. "So freaking stupid," she muttered. "Stupid. Stupid. Stupid."

Ellis made her way up to the bar, her chest heaving, her mind racing. How could she be so stupid? How could she let such an infuriating man make her lose all common sense? She let him feed her! Multiple times! And then she got so caught up in their back-and-forth that she forgot to be rational and sucked on his thumb. The worst thing about it was that she didn't realize how intimate it was, how wrong it was, until Mike froze and looked at her like she was a total slut. And she was a total slut. Who else would suck on a man's thumb in a bar?

"Hey, Red," Ellis heard behind her. She ignored it, thinking the man behind her was talking to someone else. The line at the bar was long and Ellis really needed a drink. She wasn't going to have one, though. A bottle of water was all she was going to be drinking.

Who knew what another dose of alcohol would cause her to do? "Hey, Red." This time she felt a tap on her shoulder.

She turned to face the tapper. "Yes?" It was one of the frat boys she had seen earlier.

"What are you drinking?" He slurred and then looked at her breasts. "I'll buy."

"No thanks. I'm just going to have water." She turned around to wait patiently for her turn. She didn't need this bullshit.

"Oh come on, Red. I've got a bet going with my friends that I could get you back to my dorm before the final round."

She turned around again. *Oh no, he didn't.* "Well, honey, I think you might want to tuck your tail between your legs and head back to your friends because that is a bet you are going to lose."

"Oh, don't be such a stuck-up bitch. How many guys want to take you home tonight? You're like a six. Tops." He wavered on his feet. "You just better be glad I like 'em a little fat." He drunkenly grabbed Ellis's arm. "Give me a kiss."

"Hey, buddy." Ellis looked up and Mike was there. He grabbed the kid's wrist and twisted it into the most unnatural position Ellis had ever seen. The frat boy dropped to his knees. "Watch how you speak to her and the next time the word *bitch* comes out of your mouth you better be referring to a dog. Got it?"

"Yes," the boy panted.

"Yes, what?"

"Yes, sir."

"Good. Now take your drunk ass home."

Mike let the guy go but before he could turn his attention back to Ellis, she left.

* * *

Ellis escaped through a side door to the alley. Her lungs squeezed, gasping for air. Mike had nearly dismembered that kid and all because he called her a bitch. What was up with him? And why did have to look so damn good doing it? Thirty seconds later Mike came barreling through the door, his eyes searching for her in the dark. Why couldn't he be the same asshole who'd tried to get it on in her bed? Why did he have to do little things that made her not hate him?

"Are you okay?" he asked when he found her.

No, she wasn't okay. She was a nut. "Why the hell did you do that?" she yelled at him. "You had to act all macho and nearly break the kid's wrist. I didn't need to be rescued. I could have handled him. It was nothing."

His blue eyes flashed with confusion, then anger. He came at her, pressing her against the brick wall of the bar, one arm on either side of her head. "He called you a name no man should ever call a woman, he put his hands on you, and you have the nerve to be pissed at me?"

He was really angry. That was new for her and she didn't know what to say. Nobody had ever championed her before.

"So what? I have been called a lot worse than fat."

"He called you a bitch!" He smacked the wall behind her in frustration. "Damn it, Ellis, it shouldn't be okay when somebody speaks to you like that. You deserve respect. How the hell could you be mad at me? You need help, Ellis, serious mental help."

Good Lord, she thought. He was absolutely right. Her skirmish with Jack that day must have liquefied her common sense. Mike continued ranting but Ellis stopped listening. All she could think about was how warm his big body was, how good he smelled, how sexy he was when he was all worked up. He was so different from Jack—the way he looked, the way he made her feel, everything about him.

Look out, stupid, here I come.

She grabbed him by the ears and pulled him close, forcing his lips to come into contact with hers. She kissed him hard to shut him up but soon that hard kiss turned hot and her tongue was in his mouth tasting all the chocolate and cream that still resided there. He kissed her back and she felt it deep in her bones. It could be because she hadn't been kissed in such a long time, or because she had never been kissed with such single focus, but she heard that same *Ah!* The choir of food angels seemed to sing for kisses, too.

He broke their kiss with a *pop* and looked at her, his expression bewildered. "Holy shit." He shook his head. "What the hell is wrong with you?" he asked, his large chest heaving. "You don't pull somebody by the ears when you want to kiss them." He looked at her lips, which she was sure were swollen. "You're driving me fucking crazy, Ellis." He ran his fingers through his short dark hair, turned away from her, then turned back. "Half the time I want to strangle you, the other half I want kiss you."

"Go with the second one." She grabbed his shirt and pulled him closer. The BOOM was there. "Kiss me."

The electricity wasn't imagined. Mike leaned into kiss her once again. Ellis's soft body and irrational behavior left him, for the first time in his life, totally unsure of himself. His hands wandered her body as he tasted her mouth. They smoothed down her back, found her neat little waist, and then managed to find their way under her shirt. He pulled her closer, feeling skin that was softer than he imagined. Her breasts squished against him and he groaned into her mouth. All of her soft weight, those pouty lips were his for the taking. His erection returned with force. Ellis was one of those women who knew how to kiss, take pleasure from a man and give pleasure in equal measure. He wanted to crawl out of his body and into hers. It was like his soul was sighing because for the first time in a long time he felt satisfied.

A blunt object connected with his head and he broke the kiss to look at Ellis. Her eyes were closed, her pink lips were puffy and kiss-swollen, and her arms were wrapped tightly around him.

"More," she ordered.

Like magnets his lips sought hers again and this time he felt the smack much harder than before. He turned around to see a pissed-off redhead, an openmouthed Cherri, and Colin grinning like a giant jackass.

"Go away," he told them and turned his attention back to the girl who drugged him with her mouth.

"No," Belinda said firmly. "We're going to take Ellis home."

"I don't want to go home with you," Ellis mumbled as she leaned in to kiss Mike again. This time Belinda whacked Mike so hard with her handbag that he saw stars.

"Damn it, Belinda."

"Ellis." She ignored Mike's outburst. "You told us to save you from being stupid."

"Where the hell were you an hour ago?"

"We didn't think you would be dry-humping him against a wall!" Belinda placed her bag under her arm and gave Ellis a good tug. "He's bad news. He slept with your sister and tried to get it on in your bed without you."

"Oh crap!" Ellis smacked her head. "That's right. You slept with Dina, you dirty man. Get away from me."

She pushed herself away from him and followed her friends.

All of a sudden it came back to Mike. Dina, he remembered Dina from four years ago, but he'd never actually gotten to sleep with her because her sister . . . Her sister! Shit. Ellis was her sister.

"You having a lightbulb moment?" Colin asked, still grinning like a jackass.

"Yeah, I remember who Ellis is. And now I know why she doesn't like me."

Chapter Six

Skinny People Need Spanx, Too!

As a fashionista it's my job to school you about a common misconception. Spanx, girdles, body shapers—whatever you want to call them—aren't just for fatties. Skinny people need them, too! They have jelly bellies and jiggly asses and stretch marks just like us. So next time you're at a bar and see a girl wearing a knit dress, just think: There's a pair of Spanx holding up and sucking in all that stuff under there.

"Do I look okay in this color?" Maryanne, one of Ellis's regular customers, asked.

Ellis looked at the women who had just emerged from the dressing room. She wore an army-green shirt-dress with brass buttons down the front. It was statement-making dress. Military chic. Ellis loved the piece when she ordered it but it took a certain type of woman to pull off the look. Maryanne was in her thirties, blond, sweet looking, round with apple cheeks. She was too cute for the dress.

"No, you don't, honey," Ellis said honestly. "In fact that dress is all wrong for you."

"I thought it was. It looked so cute on the hanger." Maryanne sighed. "I always run into this problem."

Ellis had had that problem, too, and nodded sympathetically. "It's a cute dress and you do have fabulous taste. It's just not the right dress for your body. But don't worry. If there isn't a dress in this store that works for you I'll make one myself." She turned around to search through a few racks when a sapphire-blue dress caught her eye. "See, Maryanne. You're what I like to call diamond-shaped. Girls like you aren't meant to wear such structured clothing, you're meant to be easy breezy and a little bit sleazy with a low neckline." She handed over the dress. "Here, try this. Blue always looks good on blondes." Ellis paused. "Wait." She put her finger on her chin and studied her customer. "I think you need a smaller bra."

"Smaller!" Maryanne laughed. "I haven't gotten a smaller anything ever!"

"You are now. The girls should be squished in and pushed up." Ellis grasped her own bra strap beneath her top and tugged it. "I know," she agreed when Maryanne frowned. "It doesn't sound comfortable, and it's not. But the truth is that a well-fitting bra should fit you snugly. Some man probably invented it. He's probably the same bastard who invented high heels."

"Where can I send my thank-you letter?" Maryanne asked sarcastically.

"Hell," Ellis answered. She turned around in search of her manager. "Belinda, would you mind doing a bra fitting with Maryanne?

"Of course not." Belinda went off in search of her tape measure.

Ellis looked at the dress her customer had slung over her shoulder, satisfied she was going in the right direction. "I think this color blue is going to make your eyes look amazing, although once we get you in the right bra nobody is ever going to look into your eyes again."

Maryanne giggled. "One can only wish. Thank you, Ellis. I'm so glad you opened this place."

"You're welcome." Ellis smiled back, feeling confident that she made the right decision to leave her old life behind. "Now go try it on so I can see if the hemline is right for you. If it isn't I'll fix it for free, because you're such a good customer." She gave a conspiratorial wink. "Just don't tell anybody."

"I won't"—Maryanne's face bloomed into a naughty smile—"if you tell me everything about that hot guy standing behind you."

"What?" Ellis followed Maryanne's eyes to see Mike standing twenty feet behind her in the store.

OH LORD.

A white T-shirt was molded to his hard chest. His hair was damp, his skin glistening. He wore shorts and sneakers. It was obvious that this man had just come from exercising. *Damn him.* He was emitting some kind of pheromones. He must have been because Ellis's feet gained a mind of their own and moved toward him before she could stop them.

For the past two days the kiss they'd shared had played in her head like it was stuck on repeat. She could still feel the ghost of his lips on hers. It was one of the stupidest things she had ever done.

He slept with Dina. He slept with Dina. She had to keep reminding herself. *He's slept with everybody. He's slept with everybody.* She shouldn't be attracted to him. She shouldn't want anything to do with him and yet she found herself stopping mere inches in front of him.

"What are you doing here?"

"I was in the neighborhood jogging and I thought I would stop by."

"Jogging, were you?" Ellis placed her hand on her hip and studied him. "I only run if I'm being chased." He gave her that one-sided smile that she was starting to become familiar with and she didn't like that it did funny things to her stomach. "Nobody jogs down St. Lucy Street. What are you really doing here, Mike?"

"I really was jogging." He looked down at himself. "Can't you tell?"

"Uh-huh." She nodded, pulling her lower lip between her teeth as she once again studied his athletic frame. His shirt was so wet that she could see his skin through it, his pecs, every muscle that he worked so hard to maintain. "Why are you here?" She turned away from him and headed to her office/sewing room. He followed. She could feel his heat on her back.

"You kissed me the other night."

She wondered how long it would take for him to bring that up. She wanted to say that it was a mistake. It was, but she couldn't say she regretted it. Every woman should be kissed like that once. Too bad Mike probably kissed every woman the way he kissed her.

"I did." They came to a stop just inside her office door and she turned to face him. "You've probably kissed thousands of women. You can't tell me that mine was anything special."

His gaze searched her face, resting on her lips before coming back to her eyes. "I watched you help that woman out there. You were good with her—honest, without putting her down." He was quiet for a moment. "This is what you should be doing."

She nodded. "Thank you. This place is my baby."

"What did your parents say when you told them that you wanted to stop being a lawyer and open up a boutique?"

"Same thing yours probably said when you told them you wanted to work for the NYPD."

Mike shrugged and took two steps closer to her. "My parents didn't send me to Harvard Law."

He caught her by surprise. "How did you know I went to Harvard?"

"I remember you now, Ellis." He closed the short distance between them and cupped her face in his hands. "I remember this." He kissed her very softly on the lips. "I remember that you used to wear glasses, and that you always kept your hair tied up, and that you have a thing for ugly Harvard T-shirts. I remember that you're afraid of pigeons and that you idolize Jackie O. I remember that your feet were bare that night and your toenails were painted hot pink." Ellis looked up at him amazed; even she hadn't remembered what color her toes were. "I kissed you that night because I was attracted to that brain of yours. I went off to your bedroom with Dina because at the time I didn't want to be, because being with a woman like you scared the hell out me." His eyes searched her face. "I didn't know that was your bedroom, though. If I had known I would have never done that to you. I'm not as big of an asshole as you think. I never have sex in beds that don't belong to me or the woman I'm with."

"Mike . . ." She didn't know what to say. She wasn't expecting this, for him to remember her at all, much less so incredibly clearly.

He rested his lips against her ear and pulled her close. "I'm sorry, Ellis."

He couldn't be this sweet. She didn't trust it but despite herself she melted a little. "Why are you apologizing?" She said trying to muster up some bravado. "You think if you're sweet to me you'll get me in bed so you can compare me with my sister?"

"Don't be a brat." His hold on her waist tightened. "Not right now. I never slept with Dina. The last time I saw her was that night."

Something inside Ellis whispered, *Believe him*, but the cynical part of her knew that men lied; that he was probably just saying that to get in her pants. For a brief moment she entertained the thought.

Why couldn't she sleep with him?

He and Dina had been through for years, and it wasn't as if she'd had any serious feelings for him. Ellis certainly wouldn't gain an attachment to him. She knew what she was getting into. She knew Detective Edwards was a world-class player. The thought caused her to sigh as he held her close to him. If he had been with Dina, Ellis couldn't be with him. She wouldn't survive the comparison.

"Get off me," she halfheartedly complained. "You're all sweaty." But he also smelled good and she made no move to stray from his embrace.

"No wonder I didn't remember you, Elle. I would have never guessed that the nerdy girl from four years ago would be the one who would stick her tongue down my throat against a bar wall."

"Oh, shut up, stupid face." She slapped his hard chest.

He grinned down at her. "Are we back to childish name calling? I thought we were past that."

"I'm afraid we aren't," she said with faux sadness.

He grinned down at her for a moment. His smile was nice, his lips nicely formed, and she thought about pressing closer and kissing him again. His mouth fit so nicely against hers.

"Ellis? Oh! Excuse me?"

A sign from God. Thou must not kiss sexy bad-boy detectives.

Ellis couldn't see her small mother behind Mike's large frame but there was no mistaking the sound of her voice. *Frick. Crap. Shit!*

"Dr. Gregory?" Mike whipped around and let Ellis go before she had the chance to squirm away.

"Michael Edwards?" Ellis watched Phillipa's mouth drop open; then a huge smile spread across her face. "What the hell are you doing here?"

"I moved back!" Mike stepped toward her mother, picked her up, and spun her around. "How are you, Dr. Greg?" He put her down and smiled at her. "I think about my favorite professor all the time."

"Not enough to come and see me, you big lug?"

"Mom, you know Mike?" Ellis couldn't believe the scene unfolding in front of her. Mike knew her mother? Her mother knew Mike? And they liked each other? *No freaking way.*

"Know him? He was the only boy in my eco-feminism and ethics class. I thought he was dumb as a rock, but what did I know? He turned out to be one of my best students."

He looked at Ellis and then back to Phillipa. "I only signed up for the class because I thought it would get me laid but I actually learned a lot from Dr. Greg. She's amazing." Suddenly it dawned on him. "Did I hear you call her *Mom?*"

"Yes." Phillipa came to stand next to Ellis. "This gorgeous female is my daughter." She raised her graying eyebrow. "How exactly do you know each other?"

Oh crap, Ellis thought. She recognized that look in her mother's eye. Her meddling-pain-in-the-ass wheels were turning. Phillipa wouldn't let this go.

"I had no idea." Mike studied them both, and Ellis knew he was trying to see if there was some similarity between them. He wouldn't find any. "Ellis and I are friends."

"Did you have any idea that he dated Dina?" Ellis said, hoping that it would cause her mother to back off.

"You dated Dina!" Phillipa shrieked. "Oh no." She shook her head. "The lovely Ms. Wild Child is all wrong for you. It couldn't have lasted long."

"It didn't." Mike glanced at Ellis then gave his attention back to her mother. "So how have you been, Doc? You still writing those man-hating books?"

"Yes." Phillipa proudly raised her nose. "I'm two-thirds through my latest man-hating manifesto, and now that you're back in town I expect you to come to my next book signing." She turned to Ellis and in a stage whisper said, "The man is gorgeous. He'll spike my book sales just by showing up."

Mike grinned. "I'll do anything for you, Dr. Greg. How about I take you and Ellis out to lunch today? That is, if you don't mind being seen with me looking like this."

"No."

"We'd love to." Ellis's and Phillipa's words clashed.

No way in hell. No freaking way in hell.

"What?" Phillipa looked at her daughter. "We're going down the street for a sandwich, not to the Ritz. He looks fine."

"Mike's looks are not the reason I can't go to lunch." Ellis's eyes connected with Mike's briefly. She wasn't going to go out with him. Ever. Especially not with her mother in tow.

"Then what?"

"I'm busy, Mom." Ellis motioned around her. "I've got a store to run and three dresses to alter. I really can't go out right now." She narrowed her eyes at Phillipa. "Why are you here anyway? Aren't you supposed to be shaping young minds or something?"

"I had two shaping sessions this morning." She placed her hands on her nonexistent hips. "And do I need a reason to come see my youngest child? I haven't seen you in a week. You can't spare a little time to spend with me. Isn't this one of the reasons you left Manhattan? Oh, and your father! He asked me about you three times this week. He thinks you're starving to death!"

Ellis sighed "Okay, Guilty Mcguilterson. I'll come over for dinner."

Mike caught Ellis's eye and gave her a sympathetic

look. If he'd spent a semester in Dr. Phillipa Gregory's class, he knew how compelling she could be. "I'll leave you ladies to talk."

He was out the door before she could say anything, which left her alone with her smiling mother.

"Is Mike the guy you were telling me about?" Phillipa's eyes lit. She was smiling so broadly her face looked as if it would crack. She grasped Ellis's arms and shook her. "Oh my God, Ellis! I'm so excited for you. Have you slept with him yet?"

"Mom!"

We aren't having this conversation. We just can't be.

"Oh, don't be a prude." She waved off Ellis's objection. "That boy was legendary on campus. The girls said he could give multiple orgasms. Has he done that for you yet?"

"Mother!"

"Honey." Phillipa gave her a considerate look. "You probably never had one of those before. Jack-ass wasn't a very good lover, was he? I never experienced a multiple orgasm until I met your father."

"Phillipa Elizabeth Gregory!" Ellis slapped her hands over her very red ears. "If you say another word on this subject I'll commit matricide."

"Oh, please." Phillipa rolled her eyes. "I'm shaking in my shoes. Listen, my love, it's all right to share these things with me. Mike is a great guy. I totally approve."

"He dated Dina! Doesn't that matter to you at all?"

"Not really." Phillipa shrugged. "They were no good for each other, but he's good for you. He likes you. A mother can tell these things."

"Can you, O Wise One?"

"Yes." Phillipa stood on tiptoes and gave Ellis a loud smacking motherly kiss. "Come for dinner tomorrow night. I'm going to see if I can get your sister to show up, too."

"Really?" Ellis tried to contain her frown. Oil and water. Ellis and Dina.

"Yes, really. When was the last time we all had dinner as a family?"

"I'm not sure," Ellis said softly. It had been too long, probably years.

"I'm not, either, which means tomorrow is family night. Be prepared to do some bonding."

"Of course," Ellis sighed. "Looking forward to it."

Phillipa left the store a few moments later and when Ellis returned to the front the only person she found besides a few customers was Belinda. There was a tiny little ache in her chest. Mike had gone and she was okay with that, but he could have at least said good-bye. She didn't know why she cared; it was probably his MO. She wondered how many women he had left without saying good-bye to.

"Hey, where did your mother go?" Ellis whipped around at the sound of Mike's voice. He was there again, standing just inside the front door with a brown paper sack in his arms. "Why do you look so surprised to see me?" A smile spread across his face. "Did you think I wasn't coming back?"

"I didn't care either way," she lied. The smell of french fries hit her nose and she began to move toward him. "What's in the bag?"

"Lunch." He walked over to the register where Belinda was standing, handing her a sandwich. "Turkey sub for the redhead with the mighty swing."

Belinda grinned at him. "You shouldn't have bought me lunch. It almost makes me feel bad for trying to knock your brains out."

"Then my evil plan worked." He turned to face Ellis. "It's the weekend, Harvard. I've got some good stuff in here for you and I don't want to hear any bullshit about you not wanting it." He walked toward her and she held her ground. Today was her day to be wicked, to eat whatever she wanted. There was no way she was going to turn down free food from a hot man.

"I ate carrots all day Friday to make up for all the damage I did on Thursday."

"That's ridiculous. You had two strawberries!"

"No." She pulled her lower lip between teeth. "After I left Bagpipes I ate half a bag of chocolate chip cookies."

"Really?" Mike bent his head close to hers. "After you left, I smoked a cigarette."

It took Ellis a moment to get his joke but when she did her eyes widened. "Perv." She shook her head. "Let's go eat in the storeroom. I hope you've got french fries in that bag."

She turned to lead the way and he was right behind her. Too close. So close that she could feel his breath on the back of her neck. She stopped short, causing him to softly collide with her.

"You didn't really think I would leave without saying good-bye, did you?" Mike asked. Ellis said nothing because that's exactly what she thought. "I'm not as big an asshole as you make me out to be."

"The jury's still out on that one." She turned to face him. "Why are you really here?"

"I don't know." His answer seemed honest. "Can't a guy buy a girl who kisses like a porn star some lunch?"

"Mike." She didn't want to smile, but she couldn't stop her lips from twitching. "I still want to hate you for forgetting me, so quit being a nice guy."

His blue eyes searched her face in a way that always disarmed her. "Haven't you ever met a nice guy before?"

"I didn't know they made men in nice."

Instead of Mike smiling at her little joke concern spread across his face. His warm fingers came up to touch the underside of her chin.

"What did he do to you, Elle?"

The bell over the front door sounded and Agatha Toomey walked into Ellis's shop.

"Oh God." Ellis slapped her forehead. "Why is she here?"

Mike turned his head to see what Ellis was talking about. "Oh, it's the bitch from the coffee shop," he said so matter-of-factly she smiled.

"Yes, she also happens to be my ex's aunt and the bane of my existence. Go wait for me in the back. I'll be there as soon as I can get rid of her." Ellis attempted to step around Mike but he grasped her hand before she could go.

"I don't like the way that lady talks to you. Let me come with you."

"Why?" She raised her brow at him. "Are you gonna try to break her wrist if she gets too sassy?"

"No, but if she gets really nasty I'll have her car impounded."

"Oh." That funny little ache in her chest appeared again. Slowly all the preconceived notions she had of him were melting away and she was seeing Mike for the man he really was. A caretaker. "That might be nice." She gave his hand a gentle squeeze. "Go eat, Detective. I'll call for backup if I need it."

Ellis took a deep breath before she lifted her chin and made her way to Mrs. Toomey. "Welcome to Size Me Up, Mrs. Toomey. Can I help you find something?"

"Oh God no." Agatha looked around the store, her face pinched as if she smelled something sour. "I came to speak to you about Jack."

"Wow!" Ellis said with faked enthusiasm. "You picked the last topic on earth I want to talk about. Let's talk about the fifty grams of sugar I ingested on Thursday instead."

"This is no time for your little jokes," Agatha snapped.

"I came to talk about my nephew. *You* are making him miserable." She pointed a bony finger at Ellis.

A wall of anger rose inside her but she wouldn't show it. She wouldn't give either Toomey the satisfaction of knowing they could get to her. "I refuse to discuss Jack with you. We are broken up. End. Of. Story."

Agatha's thin cheeks grew red. "What is wrong with you, Ellison? Jack is the best that you can do. He's smart, handsome, and successful and he doesn't want any other woman but you. I think he could do better, but you're all that he wants and I'm here to see that he gets what he wants."

Jack's mother died when he was just a kid. Agatha doted on him, but Ellis didn't understand why Agatha cared so much about their relationship. However, it did give her a tiny glimpse into Jack's brain. If he'd spent his whole life being catered to by this woman, no wonder he expected the same from her. "Not this time. Now if you'll excuse me, I have work to do." Ellis moved to walk away but a bony grip on her wrist held her still. The hold hurt. Agatha's perfectly manicured nails bit into Ellis's skin.

"You had better smarten up, girl, and go back to Jack because if you don't you'll be sorry."

Because there were customers in the store Ellis knew she couldn't make a scene and knock the woman's lights out like she wanted. She was going have to channel Gandhi and go the nonviolent route. Agatha had never been a fan of hers, but the hatred rolled off of her today like a thick fog.

"Ellis, baby, are you okay?" Mike emerged from the back room. His big body was relaxed, but his intense gaze concentrated on Agatha's hand. Ellis could handle herself but she felt comfort in knowing that he was there in case she couldn't.

"I'm fine, Mikey. I was just saying good-bye to

Mrs. Toomey." With a twist of her wrist Ellis broke free
from the woman's hold. She lowered her voice. "Get out
of my store, Agatha. And don't ever show your face in
here again."

Agatha's eyes traveled to Mike and then back to Ellis.
"Whore," she quietly spat.

"Skinny bitch," Ellis returned.

Agatha gave her one last long chilly look and walked
out. Ellis took a deep breath, gave a warm smile to her
curious customers, then headed toward Mike, who was
still standing in the doorway to the back rooms. When
she approached he stepped aside to let her through but
guided her to her office instead of the storeroom where
she assumed they would be eating.

She was surprised to find that her desk was tidy when
she walked in, all the papers stacked into neat piles with
sticky labels attached to them. "Snooping through my
records?" she asked.

"Your organizational skills are lacking," he shot back
as he shut the office door with his foot. "Are you okay?"
He gave her a gentle push toward the love seat that used to
be covered with sewing supplies and sat down next to her.

"I'm fine, Mike," she lied. She didn't feel fine at all.
She felt woozy and lightly leaned against his side.

He lifted her wrist to study it, examining the little
crescent-moon marks. "I'll fucking kill her."

"Mike . . ."

"Where does she live?" He lifted her wrist to his mouth
and gently kissed it.

It was yummy, so yummy that she allowed her eyes to
drift shut while he lingered there. "I'm not telling you."

"I need to know so I can be your alibi for the day you
go over there to kick her ass."

She smiled, thoughts of slapping the smug look off of
Agatha Toomey's face floating in her mind. "Thank you,

but it's no big deal. My ex is her beloved nephew. She just wanted me to reconsider my decision to dump his sorry ass."

"I can make her life a living hell for you. Give me something to go on."

He was too protective. It must be some sort of macho male thing. She kind of liked it. "She drives a green Beetle convertible with a vanity plate. Put a boot on her car for me."

"Done." He pressed another kiss to her wrist, gentler this time, longer. His thumbs massaged away the red marks on her skin, and for a moment Ellis was very content with the world. Mike worked his rubdown up to her palm, kneading her tired stiff hand muscles into submission. It was heavenly. Her eyes once again drifted shut as he worked his magic.

"Tell me what happened between you and your ex," he said softly.

Ellis's eyes came open at that comment and she looked up at him. The way he was looking at her . . .

"Nothing." She couldn't tell him what Jack had done to her. She had a hard time facing it herself. "I realized that two years was too long to be with him. He disagreed."

His eyes locked with hers. "I don't believe you."

"Well, I don't want to talk about this with you." She shook her head. "Why do you care?"

Mike lifted his hand and brushed a stray lock of hair behind her ear. "I don't know. I don't know why I do half the things I do when I'm around you."

He lightly stroked her cheek with his thumb and for a moment Ellis was speechless and senseless. She wanted to kiss him again, to hold on to him, to run her hands along his hard warm body. Mike was one of those guys a woman could lose her heart to if she wasn't careful. *Careful* was Ellis's middle name.

"Okay, enough feeling me up." She inched away from him and reached for the paper bag that was resting on her desk. "What did you bring me for lunch? I hope you remembered the ketchup."

"It's simple, Ellis. You can do it," Mike said.

He hadn't left her store yet, the time getting away from him. He had never spent so long in a woman's clothing store in his life but he kind of liked it there. Her store was cute. Almost homey in a way. It reminded him of his mother's flower shop. Some aspects of running a small business never changed. Ellis, like his mother, had orders to fill and customers to cater to. He remembered his mother staying well past closing to fulfill a big order for a wedding or going out of her way to make a special arrangement for a longtime customer. She always went above and beyond, and he saw some of that in Ellis. The love for her store, the drive she had to make it successful, the need to make her customers leave happy. The only difference was that his mother had him and his sisters to help run the store. Ellis was doing it all on her own.

"Explain this to me one more time, Mikey." Ellis turned to look at him, her scent distracting him from the task at hand.

When he woke up this morning he hadn't planned on coming here. He planned to do his normal two-mile jog, go back home, shower, eat, and go on with his day. But things didn't work out that way. A memory of Ellis's deliciously soft body popped in his head and instead of taking his normal route through the park his feet led him into the center of the city and down the street that led to her store.

"Open the spreadsheet." He reached over her to point to the icon on the screen. "Go to the functions menu and hit calculate. Now you can see what is selling and what isn't."

She did what he said and then spun her chair around to look at him. "Is it really that simple?"

"Yup."

Her face broke into a large grin and she clapped her hands like an adorable toddler. "Thank you! You just saved me hours of work."

Mike rested his hands on the arms of her chair and leaned in close. She smelled good, like lotion, a different scent than before. He fought the urge to bury his nose in the soft skin of her neck. "What's the reward for all my expertise?"

She sighed and leaned back in the chair, resting her arms on the top of her head. He got a chance to give her body a good long look. Today she wore a tight skirt and white blouse that opened in a vee over her breasts. Her legs were crossed, smooth, long, and bare. But what kept his eyes wandering was her feet, which were encased in gray suede heels with a little bow on top. Her toes were bared, showing off her bubblegum-pink-painted nails. He barely took note of a woman's feet but Ellis's, like everything else on her, were sexy.

"Reward?" she asked after a moment. "How about the satisfaction of knowing you did a good deed? Your reward will be in heaven."

"Bullshit." His gaze fell upon her lips. "I'd rather have a kiss."

"Drop dead," Ellis said, but her eyes traveled to his lips and Mike knew she was thinking about their last kiss.

It needed to be repeated or Mike would go insane. "Go out with me, Ellis."

"You went out with my sister." She pushed on his shoulders and rose from her chair. But Mike didn't back up. Ellis was nearly as tall as he was in her heels, and for the first time Mike stood eye-to-eye with a woman. "Isn't one of Phillipa Gregory's offspring enough?"

Apparently not. He couldn't believe that he had it bad
for his favorite professor's daughter. He really couldn't
believe he had also dated Dr. Greg's older daughter. Small
world . . . or fate, but Mike wasn't the type of guy who
believed in that kind of crap. He had met Dina by chance.
She was cute, a little self-centered, a little out there, but
fun to hang out with. He knew that it wasn't going to go
anywhere the day they met. But with Ellis things were
different. Something about her kept pulling him in when
all he wanted to do was run away. It didn't make any sense
because everything he did seemed to bring him closer to
her.

"I didn't sleep with your sister, if that's what this is
about."

Ellis nodded. "You told me already."

He could tell that she didn't believe him and it bugged
him even further. "Ask her. We only went out a few
times."

"It doesn't matter if you did or didn't; I have no desire
to be another notch on your bedpost." She pushed her
face closer to his, and once again he noticed those little
gold flecks in her eyes. "Tell me, Mike, do you and Colin
have a master list? Redhead. Check. Swedish girl. Check.
Is fat chick the only thing left on your list? Is that why
you want me?"

"Don't." Mike grabbed her waist, pulling her close to
him. Only she could manage to piss him off. "I already
told you not to put yourself down in front of me. I don't
like it, damn it. You are more than how much you weigh.
Don't you get it?"

Her eyes grew wide. "I'm not putting myself down!
I'm not your average girl. I opened this store because I've
finally embraced it. I'm a big girl. Don't tell me you can't
see that."

For some reason her little impassioned speech did

something to his insides. She noticed and tried to take a step back, but he wouldn't let her. They were so close. All he had to do was lean in a mere inch or two and take what he wanted. It wasn't going to happen that way. She was going to have to come to him willingly. It might take a little more time than he was used to, but he would wait. The urge to feel her naked and underneath him struck him at the most inconvenient times. Maybe if they got together the constant thoughts of her would fade from his brain. Maybe they wouldn't. It was a chance he was going to have to take.

"Are you still in love with your ex?" he asked. Every time he bought it up she brushed him off. It was none of his business, and he wasn't sure why it was important to him. But if she was still in love with that guy Mike would walk away. He didn't compete with other men no matter how great the woman was.

"No," she said with such conviction that he believed her. "This has nothing to do with him."

"Then what, Ellis?" He couldn't figure out why she kept turning him down. "So what? I slept with a few women. Did you expect me to be a virgin?"

"No but—"

"But what? I don't want to marry you. I just want to take you out to dinner."

Her eyes searched his face for a long moment. He wondered what she was thinking. "My refusal is just killing you?" She gave him that naughty smile of hers that caused him to go hard and infuriated him at the same time. "Karma's a bitch, isn't it?" She stood on tiptoes and placed a kiss on the bridge of his nose. "Thank you for putting all of the paperwork onto my computer."

She backed away from him and this time he let her go. "Things will be easier on you if you're organized," he said gruffly.

"Really?" She tilted her head to the side and studied him. "How do you know so much stuff about running a business? You're a cop."

"My family owns a flower shop in Buffalo. I helped out sometimes."

"Oh." She blinked at him. "I'm having a hard time picturing you among hundreds of flowers."

"Try envisioning me naked. It might make it easier."

Her mouth dropped open and Mike got the huge satisfaction of knowing he'd gotten her. It was too easy sometimes. "See you next time, Ellis."

And on that note, he left. He had already spent too much time with the girl he was going nowhere with.

"Where the fuck have you been?"

Mike walked up to the front door of his rented town house to find Colin sitting on his steps.

"Shit." He had forgotten all about Colin. They were supposed to watch the game together but instead Mike had been busy with Ellis. And not busy in a good way. This was a sign. She was no good for him. All she ever managed to do was make him horny or angry. "Sorry. The time got away from me."

Mike glanced at his watch and saw that it was nearly five PM. He had been at Ellis's store for hours. How could he have not noticed that?

"For fuck's sake," Colin swore. "I've been sitting out here for the better part of an hour freezing my bollocks off."

Mike shot his friend a look. "It's seventy-five degrees, asshole."

Colin shrugged. "Figuratively speaking, then." Colin unfolded his long body and waited for Mike to ascend the stairs. "Don't tell me you've been out jogging all this time? I know you bloody Americans love your exercise, but six hours is pushing it."

"I wasn't jogging the whole time," Mike said as he fished his key out of his pocket and let himself and his irritated Irish friend into his house.

"Then where were you?"

"Are you my mother?" Mike flopped down on his black leather sofa and flicked on the television. The baseball game, already in its second inning, was on. "Don't tell me you were worried about me?"

"You were with the girl from the pub, weren't you?"

"What makes you think that?" Mike asked, not looking at Colin. How the hell could he have guessed that?

"Because if it were any other girl you'd be blabbing like a schoolgirl after prom."

Mike laughed hard at his friend's odd saying. "Where the hell do you come up with those?"

Colin, who didn't see the humor in it, frowned at him. "Were you with her? With Ellen?"

"Ellis," Mike automatically corrected. "And yeah, I was."

"You like her." Colin finally came over and plopped himself next to Mike on the couch.

Mike did and he had no idea why. "She drives me fucking crazy." And she made him want to get closer.

"Any girl who can kiss the way she was kissing you is well worth a little insanity, don't you think?"

"No." Mike shook his head. "I don't know. She's Dr. Greg's daughter."

"What? The hippie man basher?"

"Yup." Mike sighed.

"So that means you've been with both of Dr. Gregory's daughters?"

"No." He hadn't been with either of them, at least not in the way Colin meant. "Listen, I'm done talking about Ellis. Let's just watch the rest of the game."

"All right, but first get off your ass and get me a beer

and some crisps if you got them." When Mike shot him a look Colin added, "You made me wait an hour for, fuck's sake."

"They are called potato chips here." Mike got up and made his way to the kitchen. On his way he noticed the voice mail light blinking on his phone.

He pushed PLAY and walked in to the kitchen.

"Mike, it's your father." Mike froze, literally froze; even his heart stopped beating. He never thought he would hear his father's gravelly voice again. "It's been a while. I think we should talk . . ."

Colin stood before him in the kitchen. He knew the whole story. Knew that Mike had no love for the man who walked out on him. "Holy fucking hell," he said after a while. "What are you going to do, Edwards?"

"Nothing." There was no going back now. Mike walked over the phone and erased the message.

Chapter Seven

Mother Lover . . .

*I'm one of those unfortunate women who has a mother
who is way skinnier than her. As a teenager this used
to bug me. But as an adult I've had a chance to rethink my position.*
There are some definite pro and cons.

*Con: She always asks me and not my skinny sister to
exercise with her.*
*Pro: She calls my sister, and not me, three times a
week just to make sure she's getting enough to eat.*
Con: I can't fit into any of her clothes.
*Pro: I can't fit into any of her clothes! My mom has
terrible taste.*

Dina was late for dinner. *What's new*, Ellis thought while
she sat waiting in her parents' living room. They had
been waiting for her for nearly an hour, so long that their
father nervously paced in front of the telephone.

"Indian Star gets crowded at six o'clock," Walter said
as he held the menu to Dina's favorite restaurant in his
hand. "If Dina doesn't get here in four minutes it will take
twice as long for our meal to get here."

"Just order now, Daddy." Ellis threw a look at her
mother, who was sitting at her desk working. Only Phillipa could stop her father's anxiety-ridden pacing.

"I want to wait," he said firmly. "Dina has not come to dinner four times in the past three months. I do not want to spend eleven dollars and eighty-five on her rogan josh if she is not going to be here to eat it."

"Walter, my heart." Phillipa rose from her chair and offered her hand to him. "Let's go in the kitchen and put Indian Star's number on speed dial so when Dina shows up we don't have to waste our precious time dialing."

"Doing so will only shave four seconds off our ordering time," he grumped but took his wife's hand and headed into the kitchen.

Ellis was left alone to wait for her sister. Somebody in their family was always waiting for Dina Gregory. Ellis tried not to let it bug her. Once upon a time she'd longed to be close to her sister, but as they grew up, instead of growing together they grew apart.

"Hey, Smelly Ellie." Dina breezed in fifty-six minutes late for dinner. Looking like a young Phillipa, she was dressed in a pink leotard and a long paisley printed skirt, her long auburn hair thrown up in a messy bun. She must have come from her second job teaching modern dance.

Ellis rolled her eyes at her childhood nickname. "You're late. Daddy's ready to bust a blood vessel. You know how he hates to order after six." She turned her head toward the kitchen. "Daddy, Dina is here. You can dial now."

"Whatever." Dina sucked her teeth. "I don't know why you play into his Asperger's bullshit. So what if he has to wait? He'll get over it."

Ellis wanted to defend Walter but she kept her mouth shut. Walter wasn't Dina's birth father. He wasn't Ellis's birth father, either, but unlike Dina, Ellis had only known Walter Garret as her dad.

Ellis was adopted but Dina was Phillipa Gregory's flesh and blood and she never seemed to get over the fact that she had to share her mother with a man. "You know, Dina, if you're going to be late all you have to do is call. Last time I checked your fingers weren't broken."

Dina admired her hands for a moment. "No, they aren't broken—"

"But I would be happy to break them for you," Ellis said, finishing her sister's thought.

"Hungry, Ellie? Is that why you are being such a cranky bi-otch." Dina flopped herself on the couch next to Ellis and rested her head on Ellis's shoulder.

"I'm cranky because *you're* such a bitch sometimes," she said softly. "I don't like it when you're mean about Daddy."

"I know." Dina shifted her eyes to look up at Ellis. "Is that why you don't love me anymore?"

"Oh, Dina." Ellis groaned, a little less irritated with her sister. This was the nature of their relationship. Dina would be offensive and then say something sweet, causing the world to love her once more. "I love you but you're still a bitch, and a self-centered one at that. People don't tell you that nearly enough."

"You're right. I am." She sighed. "My therapist says I deliberately do things to sabotage my relationships. He thinks I constantly alienate people to test their love for me."

"What?" Ellis looked down at her sister. "You're in therapy?"

And actually learning something?

"Yeah." She shrugged. "I'm thirty-four, unmarried, and living in a studio apartment above a bar. Something went wrong in my life."

Ellis had to stop her mouth from dropping open. "I can't believe it."

"Believe it. I know why we don't get along," she said softly. "I'm jealous of you."

"What? Dina, you're drop-dead gorgeous. You've got

two percent body fat and you date the hottest men on the planet."

"Men just want to fuck me," she said, shrugging. "But you're smart. Everybody is always talking about how smart you are. I've been mad at you my whole life because of it. Now I can see that I was jealous of you when you passed the bar because you're six years younger than me and had accomplished so much more. I wanted to stick it to you. I knew the one thing that I always had over you was a way with men. That's why I took that guy to your bedroom that night. I wanted to hurt you. But God, Ellie, I didn't think you would stay mad at me for years."

Ellis didn't know what to say to that. She never thought she would have this conversation with her sister. She never thought they would clear the air. Boy, was she glad they did.

"Did you ever manage to have sex with that guy?" Ellis knew she shouldn't have asked. Dina and she had barely spoken for years, and instead of having a moment Ellis was asking about Mike.

"Unfortunately not."

He told the truth. Ah!

Dina rolled her eyes again. "I never saw him again after that night. He went all self-righteous on me and claimed he couldn't be with a woman who would do that to her sister." She sighed wistfully. "It's a pity, too. I liked him. He was really freaking hot."

"He still is," Ellis mumbled. Her mind flashed back to him standing in her store all sweaty, his wet T-shirt clinging to his muscles. She found herself wanting to lick him, wanting to know what his big damp body would feel like on top of hers.

"What?" Dina sat up and Ellis's mind snapped back to the present. "Have you seen him?"

"Yeah . . . Uh, we bumped into each other. He didn't remember me," she said quickly.

It wasn't exactly a lie. Mike hadn't remembered her, but for some reason Ellis didn't want Dina to know that eventually he had. Or that there was a strange but powerful attraction between them. Or that they'd shared a kiss that literally took the breath out of her. But why? Mike and Dina had only dated for a few weeks, but Ellis didn't want her sister to know that the guy who was the catalyst for their rift was the same guy Ellis had a hard time controlling herself around.

"I'm surprised he didn't." Dina said with a frown. "You had a colossal bitch fit."

Ellis raised a brow at Dina. "It was justified."

"It might have been. So"—Dina nudged Ellis—"do you forgive me now?"

Ellis didn't like being estranged from her sister. Of course Dina was forgiven, but Ellis couldn't help herself. An apology from Dina Gregory was a rare thing. "Only if you tell Daddy you're sorry for being late."

"Fine," she huffed. "I'll apologize to the Mad Scientist." She got up and tugged on Ellis's hand. "Come with me. We can tell Mother that we're all made up. Maybe she'll stop inviting me to dinner now."

"Fat chance." Ellis said. "Now she'll insist on doing this once a week."

The next morning Ellis woke up to a ringing phone. She glanced at the clock: six fifty-eight. Two minutes before her alarm was due to go off.

If this is my mother asking me to go jogging I'm going to scream.

Phillipa had asked her last night. Apparently word of Agatha Toomey's visit to Ellis's store had gotten back to

Phillipa and the jogging partners had severed ties. On the one hand Ellis was glad her mother would no longer be associated with the skinny hag, but on the other she was sad that Phillipa would no longer have a friend to run with. Maybe one day she would strap on a pair of sneakers and join her mother.

Yeah right. And maybe one day I'll be a size two.

Mike's face entered her mind. The sexy detective liked to jog—and more important he liked Phillipa. Maybe he could go in Ellis's place and save her from all that embarrassing huffing, puffing, and sweating.

Ellis shut off her about-to-go-off alarm and picked up on the fourth ring. "Hello?" she said, not happy that someone had robbed her of two minutes of precious sleep.

"It's Jack."

Her stomach sank. "I don't want to talk to you, Jack. I thought I made that perfectly clear the last time."

"I told you I wasn't going to give up on us," he said quietly. "We need to talk about our relationship."

Ellis looked at her nails and sighed. "Nope. Don't want to talk to you."

He had controlled so much of her life before. What hours she worked, where they lived, what she wore, how she felt about herself. No more. Her rose-colored glasses were gone.

"Ellis, if this is about my aunt, I apologize. I had no idea she was going to your little store but she's right. I'm unhappy without you. I want you back in my life."

He'd called her store *little* again. That one word diminishing all the hard work she put into it. Acid burned in her gut. "Oh, really? Well, I'm not your girlfriend anymore so it's not my place to care about your happiness. Everything is not about you, Jack. I come first from now on and I don't want to be with you."

"Why won't you let me explain?" His voice grew

sharp. "I did a lot of thing wrong but I did a lot of good things for you. I can't believe you are going to let a bad six months ruin a year and a half of good times."

"You don't get it, Jack. This isn't just about you. I wanted a new life."

"Your old life was fine. Ellis, you need to rethink this breakup. You know how much I love you. If you don't you'll regret it."

"I'm sorry, Jack but I don't think I will."

She hung up on him. It was the first time she had done so and damn, it felt good.

Belinda had a doctor's appointment and Cherri wasn't scheduled to arrive until one. Ellis was left manning the store alone. She didn't mind. Saturdays were their busy days; only a few shoppers came in early in the week, and not usually before lunchtime. This gave her time to sew. On days like this she brought her form to the front of the shop to do her alterations. Today she worked on a dress for a high school reunion. One of her customers had a very large bust, a tiny waist, and a hard time find clothing that worked on her. Ellis helped the woman try on every dress in the store but nothing came close to fitting her. The reunion was in four days, which left Ellis with a challenge: lose a customer, which she couldn't afford to do, or redesign a dress. The customer, Lydia, had fallen in love with a red silk number that looked great against her skin. Silk was a hard fabric to work with but Ellis worked carefully and the dress was nearly ready.

"I deserve a treat for this," Ellis said, studying her work. "A piece of red velvet cake. To honor this dress." She nodded, smoothed her hands over the silk, and made a mental note to call Lydia.

The bell over the door sounded, alerting Ellis to a customer's arrival. She turned away from the dress and smiled, expecting to see a woman. Instead she saw a man, balding, big belly, in his mid-forties with a giant, gaudy ring on his left hand. He was probably looking to buy a gift for his wife.

"Welcome to Size Me Up. Can I help you find something?"

"Yeah." The man approached the register. "Cash."

"Excuse me?" Ellis's smile dropped a fraction. "Like an ATM machine?"

"No, honey." The man put his hands in his pockets. "Empty out your register. You're getting robbed."

"What?" Ellis put her hands on her hips. "Are you freaking kidding?" Robberies didn't happen like this. Short, fat middle-aged men didn't just walk into stores and demand money.

"No. I'm not. Empty out your drawer."

"No!" She rolled her eyes. First Jack-ass's call and now this. "Who robs a store in the middle of broad daylight? And a clothing store at that? Why didn't you try the jewelry store on the next corner? They've got way more money than me." It dawned on her then. "Are you the same guy who robbed the yarn store?"

The man took a small step back and frowned at her. "You think I'm going to admit that to you?"

Ellis shrugged. She should be afraid but she wasn't. This guy was four inches shorter than she was. He didn't look dangerous—plus he was stupid enough to rob her store. He was no criminal mastermind. "I guess not. Listen, I don't have any money. Why don't you just go away and we'll forget about this."

The thief took a step closer. Thankfully her glass display case stood between the two of them. "Open the register."

"No. Go rob somebody else. I just told you that there is no money in there. We opened an hour ago and most of my customers pay by credit card. This is not a convenience store."

"The jewelry then." The man looked down at her case.

"It's all costume. It's not worth that much."

"Listen, bitch." His head snapped up. "I'm tired of talking to you. I'm not leaving here empty-handed, so shut up and open up the case."

"Fuck off. I'm calling the cops." Ellis turned to get the phone, her heart pounding.

A hairy hand grabbed her by the back of her shirt and forced her around. "I'm not playing around. Open the damn case."

"Okay." Now she was scared. "The key is in the drawer. I need to get it."

"I'm watching you."

He let her go and Ellis took the opportunity to rummage through her drawer. She felt the keys but she also felt cool metal against her hand. The retractable metal baton. The most thoughtful present a mother could give. She reached for it, pulled it out ready to strike, but the man with the big stomach and the hairy hands was quicker than he looked. He grabbed the baton with one hand and delivered a viscous backhanded slap to Ellis's face, his gold ring slicing into her cheek.

"I warned you not to fuck with me, bitch." In one quick move he slammed the baton down on her display case, causing it to shatter. Pieces flew into Ellis's face. "Don't try anything else."

She nodded, watching him as he emptied the display case, burning his image into her mind as he did.

"Have a nice day, ma'am." He tipped his nonexistent hat at her and walked out the door as if nothing had happened.

Chapter Eight

"Did you watch the game the other day?" Lester asked Mike. They were at their desks going over paperwork and old case files.

Mike nodded and then shook his head. "It was pathetic. Being a Mets fan is like getting your heart broken, then stomped on repeatedly, then put back together and shot."

Lester nodded. "That's some deep shit, man. Why do we even bother?"

"Hell if I know." Mike looked down at a file. "Hey, did you ever follow up with the lady who thinks her neighbor stole her cat?"

"Yup and she's batshit crazy. Cat showed up the next day. I still can't believe she made you fill out that incident report."

"Believe it. She says that her neighbors are out to get her because she has five rusty Chevys parked in her front yard."

"Five." Lester shook his head. "That's not enough to kidnap a cat over. Eight." He nodded. "That's when it gets to be ridiculous."

Mike laughed at his partner's musings and returned to

his paperwork. A couple of minutes later his cell phone rang and when ELLIS popped up on the caller ID, Mike smiled.

"You changed your mind about going out with me? I knew you would come to your senses eventually."

"Mike," Ellis said, her voice shaky.

His whole body went on alert. "What's wrong, Ellis?"

"I-I. Can you come down here? I've been robbed."

It only took Mike four minutes to get to St. Lucy Street. He didn't remember the drive over or Lester's complaints about their safety.

Ellis. Her face flashed through his mind; her soft shaky voice stayed in his ears.

I've been robbed.

He never expected it to happen to her. Not on St. Lucy Street again. They still had no leads on the last robbery. Not a clue as to who the perp was. No pattern to follow. Mike didn't think they would ever find the guy. But now they would.

He threw the car into park as soon as he saw the sign to Ellis's store, ignoring Lester's shouting that the car was parked diagonally.

"Ellis!" Mike ran up to the entrance of the store. Before he couldn't enter Ellis came rushing out.

"Mike."

She rushed into his arms and hung on to him for a moment before looking up at him. He wished she hadn't. His stomach clenched, his throat tightened, and his eyes burned all at once. The left side of her face was battered. The skin beneath her eye was slashed, blood slowly seeping from it. Little scratches marked the rest of her face. She'd been through hell.

"Don't look at me like that, Mike," she said in a quiet voice. "You're going to give me a complex."

"Oh, honey," he said as he softly cupped her face in his hands. "You look awful. What happened?"

"I got the sass slapped out of me and then I got robbed, but don't worry, I took it like a champ."

"Like a champ?" He gave her a soft smile, not wanting to upset her. He could tell she was in shock. Whoever did this to her really did a number on her face. It was already starting to bruise.

"Yup, like Tyson." Her grip on him suddenly tightened, her fingers biting into his shoulders. "Mike?"

"Yes?"

"I feel a little woozy."

"Okay, honey. Let's find you a place to sit."

Before he could move her she slumped in his arms, completely passing out.

Ellis opened her eyes nearly ten minutes later. Mike had never been more relieved.

"Elle, are you okay?" He brushed the hair off her pale, rapidly bruising face.

"Yeah." She attempted to lift her head but quickly settled back into his arms. "Ouch. No. Why are you holding me? Did you drug me?"

"Not funny." Mike frowned. Ellis was the only person who could be robbed, assaulted, and a pain in the ass. "Would you like me to let you go?"

"No." She frowned and then winced. "I didn't say I didn't like it."

"Okay then." He brought her body closer. In the fifteen minutes since he arrived half of Durant PD had shown up, an ambulance had been called, and Belinda had showed up for her shift. It was absolute insanity outside. Once again a crowd had formed on St. Lucy Street. Another robbery, this one worse. The people of Durant were beginning to get afraid.

That's why Mike took Ellis to her office, her curvy body sprawled against his as he sat on her sofa. When she collapsed his heart stopped beating. He had been scared, really scared, and stopped thinking rationally for a moment.

"What happened?" She blinked up at him. "How did I get here?"

"You were robbed. Don't you remember?"

She shook her head as if trying to clear it, then nodded. "Yes, but how did I get here? Last thing I remember was talking to you."

"You fainted, Ellis," Mike responded softly.

"I did not! I've never fainted in my life."

She had the nerve to be outraged by this. It made him smile. "You did today."

"Really?" She looked into his eyes, searching for the truth.

"Why would I lie about that?"

"Bummer," she sighed. "So much for taking it like a champ."

Mike noticed his boss and Lester hovering just outside the door. It was all going to begin soon. The questions, the visit to the sketch artist, the evaluation by the paramedics, the crime scene investigation. It was a rough process for anyone to go through and since Ellis's robbery had been violent, it was going to be even more involved. He wanted to spare her from it. He wanted to make it all go away before it began.

"Can you tell me what happened?" he whispered so that only Ellis could hear him. "You are going to have to tell your story a dozen times."

"Oh Mikey, do you want to be my first?" She gave him half of her naughty grin, and his heart pounded.

"Yeah, this time I do."

She told him what she remembered, giving him the

most detailed description of a perp he had ever heard. He
recalled the sketches he had found around her office the
day he had tidied up. Some were of elaborate dresses,
others were of people. She had an eye for detail, an ability
to pick up on the smallest facet.

"I can draw him for you." Her eyes filled with tears but
she quickly blinked them back. She was unable to even
allow herself the luxury of shedding a tear. "This is my
fault, Mike. I should have kept my mouth shut and given
him what he wanted. But there was no money in the register and I couldn't believe I was getting robbed. We're
barely making it as it is; I couldn't let him take away what
I worked so hard to get."

"Shh, honey." He ran his fingers through her thick hair.
"This was not your fault. I don't want you blaming yourself."

"I was going to hit him with the baton but he snatched
it from me." She took in a deep breath. "My mother gave
it to me. I wish I could have hit him."

"You were brave," Mike assured her.

"I was stupid."

"That too."

He was glad she realized it. Mike stopped himself
from shaking her for trying to defend her store. Didn't she
know that people died that way? How many store owners
had he seen sprawled lifeless on the floor because they
tried and failed to defend what was theirs? If that criminal had had a gun, if he had shot . . . Mike stopped himself from thinking. She was here, awake, alive, and only
bruised.

"I look like a prizefighter, don't I?"

"Yes, but a beautiful prizefighter. Much better than Ali."

Her lips curled into a smile, causing her to wince once
again. "Don't make me laugh, dummy. My face hurts like
hell."

"I'm sorry." He rested his hand on her uninjured cheek and pulled her face closer to his. He couldn't help himself. He needed to kiss her. Just before his lips met hers two EMTs entered the room, followed by his boss, followed by Lester. That didn't stop him. He knew what the consequences for kissing her would be but he didn't care.

Chapter Nine

Life Is Like . . .

*Life's a bowl of cherries? I hate the saying. Pour some
sugar on it, wrap it in crust, and serve it to me on a
plate. Mmm, cherry pie . . . What was my point?*

Ellis noted the line of people entering her office just before Mike kissed her. She thought it was going to stop
him but instead he pressed his lips to hers and let them
linger, making the kiss sweet and unhurried. When it was
over he looked down at her with his dark blue eyes and
gave her a soft reassuring smile.

"I have to talk to my boss. The paramedics are going
to clean up your face." He gestured toward a tall African
American man in a gray suit. "That's my partner, Lester.
He'll take good care of you. I'll be back in a little while."

"Okay," Ellis said even though she didn't want him to
leave her. It was a foolish thought. He had a job to do.

She watched him nod at Lester then follow his boss.

"Hello, Ellis," Lester said as the paramedics hurried
toward her.

She absently returned the greeting as a funny feeling
settled in her belly.

Lester was quiet for a moment, as if he was unsure how
to behave around her. "Are you related to Walter Garret?"

"Yes," she said wincing as the male paramedic poked
at her face. "He's my father."

"He works with my son Cameron at the university."
Lester paused. "My son says he's brilliant."

"He is." Ellis hissed as some kind of antibacterial solution touched her face.

"Hurts like a bitch, doesn't it?"

"Mike is getting in trouble, isn't he?" She could tell something wasn't right by the uneasy look on Lester's face, by the awkward way he was treating her. If Lester was as seasoned as he looked he should be much more comfortable around robbery victims. It made her realize that she probably shouldn't have called Mike. She didn't know why she called him instead of 911 like she was supposed to. After her thief had left it was the only thing she could think to do. His name was the only one that came to mind.

"Uh." Lester hesitated and Ellis had her answer. "Not too much. We're probably off this case, though. The captain shouldn't be too mad at him for coming to help his girlfriend."

"But I'm not his—"

Lester gave her a pointed look. "It's better for him if you are. Do you get my drift?"

She nodded. "I didn't mean for any of this to happen."

"Nobody is blaming you for this. Don't worry about him. Mike did what he had to do."

Ellis needed stitches to close the cut on her cheek. The paramedics wanted to take her to the hospital but she balked. She balked again when the doctor at the clinic across the street took out a needle to sew up her face. Mike watched her go pale and then asked the doctor if they had any liquid stitches available. She would be really mad if she fainted twice in one day.

"It was only a four-inch curved needle, Elle. I thought you were tougher than that."

"Bite me," she grumped.

"Just tell me where." Mike looked her up and down, feeling the need to tease her when what he really wanted to do was haul her into his arms and kiss her.

She frowned at him and then winced, making him feel bad for bothering her. Ellis had been a trouper through it all. She remained calm, answered all the questions thoroughly, and drew a very good sketch of the perpetrator. She was a model victim and now she had every right to be cranky.

"Don't tease me. My face hurts."

"You should have taken the pain meds." He grabbed her hand as they left the clinic. "Come on, let's get your prescription filled and go get something to eat."

She pulled away. "I don't take pain meds. They make me all fuzzy and I can't go to lunch, I have to get back to my store. I have three dresses to finish and I need to start cleaning up."

She was so damn determined. He admired that about her, but this time she would have to put herself before work. He wanted to flat-out tell her no but he could see she was ready to fight him and this time he wanted as little argument as possible.

"I'm sorry, Ellis. You can't go back to your store yet. It's still a crime scene."

"But you're a cop. You can let me back in there so I can get some of my things."

"I can't." He wasn't supposed to but he could. She needed the night off and if a couple of dresses hung in limbo, so be it.

She looked at him, her eyes searching his face. "Would you get in trouble if you did?"

"Yes."

"Okay."

"Okay?" He was ready for an argument but she didn't give one. "No smart-ass remark?"

"I don't have the energy."

He grabbed her hand and this time she didn't pull away. "You must really be hurting if you don't have the energy to be a pain in my ass."

"I am. You are going to find me an ice pack and buy me a big bag of chocolate." She shut her eyes for a moment, and the urge to tuck her into bed nearly overwhelmed him. "Scratch that. I need something I don't have to chew."

"How about some ice cream?"

She opened her eyes. "With hot fudge?"

"Anything you want."

Just as he was leading her to the nearest scoop shop Ellis's cell phone rang. "Crazy" by Gnarls Barkley played.

"Shit. It's my mother." Ellis pinched the bridge of her nose, looking more pained than he had seen her all day. "I'm never going to hear the end of this."

"She's probably just checking to see if you're okay. Answer the phone."

"I don't wanna," she pouted.

"Do it anyway."

She relented and slowly pulled the phone out of her bag. "Hello, Mother."

"Ellis, are you okay?" Mike clearly heard Phillipa's loud voice pour from the phone. "I just heard about the robbery. And on the radio! Why didn't you call me? The DJ said that the owner had been assaulted. What happened? How badly are you hurt? I'm on my way."

Ellis looked at Mike helplessly. He took the phone. Dr. Greg could be a steamroller. "Dr. Greg? It's Mike. You don't have to worry. I'm here with Ellis."

"You are? Thank God! She never tells me anything. How is she?"

"She's fine," he lied. Once Phillipa saw Ellis's face she was going to have the proverbial cow.

"I'm coming down there."

"Don't!" he said. The store didn't look much better: Besides the smashed display case, there were still cops around. "I'll bring her to your house."

Twenty minutes later Mike had pulled up to the house. It was a cute little bungalow, with flower boxes in front of the windows. It wasn't what he expected from Dr. Gregory. When he took her class ten years ago he didn't think of her as a real person with a family. He only saw this little woman with a bigger-than-life presence. But today, speaking to her on the phone, hearing the worry in her voice, he realized that before she was a professor and a feminist she was a mother.

"How do I look?" Ellis asked him. They had been parked for a few moments now, neither one of them in a hurry to get out of the car.

"I'd date you," he said with a shrug. The truth was she looked battered but he didn't want to tell her that. Before they left, Ellis tried to cover most of her bruising with makeup, but Mike refused to let her put any near her stitches. No amount of makeup would hide the state of her face. The only thing she managed to do was look like she'd tried to cover it up.

"That doesn't make me feel better," she mumbled.

She tried to arrange her hair in front of her face in vain. He already knew that her parents would see through it. They were parents, after all, and just hearing that their youngest child had been robbed was enough to keep them worried about her for a year.

"Come on, Ellis. They're waiting for us."

She looked down at her hands. "I don't want to go in."

"Why not? What's the worst they can do? Fuss over you?"

He knew as soon as he said that that Ellis was a woman

who wasn't used to being fussed over or coddled. She was one of the strangest females he had ever encountered. Most women he knew would have been weepy messes by now but Ellis had remained strong the entire day. She didn't blame the asshole who hurt her—only herself. It worried Mike a bit.

"My mother is going to drag me by my hair to the nearest law firm and make me apply. She didn't like it when I quit. Now she has a good excuse to nag me forever."

"Really?" Mike was surprised by her statement. "I thought your mother was one of those free-spirited go-where-your-heart-leads-you kind of mothers."

"She used to be. She was that way with Dina." She looked out the window. "With me they took a different approach. They had different expectations."

"I take it Dina ran wild as a teenager."

Ellis nodded. "They let her do whatever she wanted, hoping that it would turn out for the best. Even though my mother is a feminist I think she thought that somewhere along the line a nice man would come and take care of my sister. They knew that wasn't the case for me so they stressed academics. Dina got to be the beautiful creative one while I got to be a lawyer."

"But you're creative." Mike said. And beautiful, he didn't say. He didn't understand why she didn't see it. "I saw the sketches in your office. The one of that lady at the vanity was really good."

"Oh." Her cheeks reddened. "That was just something I was fooling around with." She shrugged. "Dina is a hostess at a restaurant and I'm the owner of a fledging clothing store." She smiled wryly. "I guess none of my mother's plans worked out."

He was about to tell her that she was talented. That she was just as lovely as her sister. That her drive would get her far in this world. But he never got the chance. The front door opened and man in a yellow tie appeared.

"That's my father," Ellis said. "We'd better get out." She placed her fingers on the door handle but then looked back at Mike. "My father is not like other fathers but I love him very much."

"Okay." Mike nodded at the warning. If this man had married the outspoken über-feminist that was Phillipa Gregory, he must be extraordinary.

"It took you four minutes and thirty-seven seconds to get out of the car," Ellis's father said as they approached. "It should take you less than thirty seconds to get out of the car. I was concerned."

"I'm sorry, Daddy. Mike and I were talking."

"Mike?" The man's eyes settled on him for a too-brief moment before he looked away, and down at his feet. "Is this your new boyfriend? I did not like your last boyfriend. Your mother said not to say anything but he wasn't good to you."

Again Mike wondered what Jack had done to Ellis. He would make it a point to find out later.

"Mike is my friend," Ellis said patiently as she stepped past him and entered the house. "I would like you to meet him. Mike, this is my father, Dr. Walter Garret. Daddy, this is my friend, Detective Michael Edwards."

Mike extended his hand to Walter. He took it but his eyes never met Mike's. Mike was beginning to understand what Ellis was talking about in the car. "It's very nice to meet you, sir. I was in one of your wife's classes a few years ago."

"I remember her speaking about you. Only five men have ever taken Phillipa's class. I was one of them."

Walter stepped farther into the house and shut the door behind him. He took a large flat box from the table and handed it to Ellis, never once looking at her face.

"I bought you a box of chocolates. You like these. All of them have nuts. No coconut. You hate coconut."

"I do," she said with a soft smile. "Thank you."

Walter finally pulled his eyes up to Ellis's face, and as an outsider Mike could tell it actually was a struggle for the man to look at his daughter. "Your face."

Walter lifted his fingers and lightly touched the skin under Ellis's injury, concern in his eyes. "Ellis." He quickly removed his hand. "We will have banana pancakes tomorrow for breakfast. Tonight you will sleep in your old bedroom and you will watch movies with your mother and I."

Ellis glanced up at Mike, her eyes misty. He nodded. Ellis might not want to stay but her father wanted her to. For Walter's own peace of mind he needed her here tonight. She had a father who actually loved her. Mike had no idea what that felt like. Ellis was blessed.

"Can we watch *Forrest Gump*?" she asked.

Walter nodded. "Mike, would you like to stay for lunch? We are going to have pizza from Michelangelo's."

"Yes, thank you."

Mike spotted Phillipa across the room. He gave her a look hoping that she would read his meaning and remain cool around Ellis. It had been a rough day for her, and the last thing Ellis needed was more excitement from her mother.

"Ellis . . ." Phillipa walked over and wrapped her arms around her much taller daughter. "I'm so glad you're here. I was very worried about you. I almost had to take a Xanax. You know I don't do very well under pressure."

"Liar," Ellis accused softly. "I once saw you bang out a four-hundred-page manuscript in two weeks."

"That's different. Deadlines inspire me. My children give me heart palpitations."

"I'm fine, Mom."

"Your pretty face," Phillipa said when she pulled away. "I'll take out a steak. We'll put it on there."

"No raw meat near her cut," Mike admonished. "A bag of frozen peas will work."

Phillipa rolled her eyes. "Men always think they can tell a woman what to do." She walked over to Mike and hugged him. "Thank you for taking such good care of my baby. I'm glad you were there."

"Don't mention it," he said. "Your girl is a trouper. You should be proud of her."

Mike studied the Garrets, realizing that Ellis just didn't look like Phillipa. She didn't look like Walter, either. No facial features, no traits, no similarities. Both parents had peach complexions while Ellis was olive. Neither possessed her thick chestnut hair. Plus Ellis was just built differently. Without heels she stood as tall as her father.

"Oh, we are. Now tell us what happened."

"Later," Mike said when Ellis paled. "After she eats."

"You aren't seriously suggesting I wait to hear my daughter's story."

He glanced at Ellis. She was exhausted. "I'm not suggesting. I'm telling you that you're going to wait."

Phillipa narrowed her eyes at him, challenging his ruling. He wasn't scared of her. He'd grown up in a house full of strong females. "Fine." She backed down after a moment. "I'll wait but I won't wait forever. I want every detail, Ellison Elizabeth Garret."

"How could I deny you, Mother." Ellis sighed. "I need some air. Mike and I will be outside until lunch arrives."

Ellis led Mike out the kitchen door that opened into her parents' backyard. It smelled like fall. She inhaled deeply, taking a moment to stare at the sunny yard. Physical exhaustion was beginning to set in, but she fought against it.

Her day was far from over. She would be staying here all night watching movies with her parents. She loved them and understood their concern but Ellis needed time to think, time to regroup. Her store would be closed all day tomorrow due to the investigation and probably the next day for cleanup. Two days closed. Two days of lost revenue. Two more days where she had no control of her destiny. There had to be a way to recover from this. All she had to do was discover how.

"You grew up here?" Mike asked from beside her.

"Yes." She looked up at him, still in his work clothes, looking a little disheveled and yet sexy. "This house used to belong to my grandmother. My father's mother," she clarified. "But she left it to him when she moved to Arizona. It was a nice place to grow up."

"It looks like it."

They fell silent for a moment as Ellis went to step off the back porch and into the yard, but Mike gently caught her arm and tugged her over to the glider. He sat next to her, and soon the gentle rocking of the chair began to soothe her.

"No walking, Elle. You're too tired."

"No, I'm not." She only half lied. She was more than tired. She was mentally worn out.

"Fine, then I'm tired. I want to sit."

"Okay." She leaned against him. The glider was so small it was hard not to. His body was warm, his shoulder solid, and her common sense fled for a few moments. "You can go home if you want. I'll be okay now."

"And miss pizza from Michelangelo's? Fat chance."

"Oh, okay." She was glad he was staying. Her parents could be overwhelming sometimes.

"They really love you," Mike said reading her mind. "Your parents."

"Your parents love you, too."

"My mother," he said quietly. "My father walked out on us."

"I'm sorry." She didn't know what else to say, but she could tell by the sound of his voice that the abandonment bothered him.

"Don't be. He's a deadbeat who couldn't handle us. We were better off without him. But you're lucky. You can always come home, and a lot of people don't have that."

"I'm adopted," she blurted out, not sure what possessed her to do so. "That's why I don't look anything like them or Dina. My birth mother was one of Phillipa's students."

Mike turned and looked at her with interest. She didn't know why she told him that. She didn't tell many people where she came from but for some reason she wanted him to know. "Is that why your skin is olive?" He lifted his hand and ran it gently down her uninjured cheek. He stared at her for a long quiet moment. "Damn it, Ellis," he said, sighing. "You scared the shit out of me today."

"Oh." His statement took her by surprise. She looked away. "Why? You've never witnessed dramatic-damsel-in-distress fainting before? I asked you to come all the way down there; I had to make it look good."

"You're one hell of an actress." He shook his head. "You were out for ten minutes. If you wanted to wake up in my arms you could have gone to bed with me last night."

Ellis rolled her eyes. "Why do you have to be such a perv all the time?"

"Why do you have to put up a wall every time I say something serious to you?"

His words disarmed her. He was right. She didn't know how to behave around him. Every time she thought she had him pegged, he did or said something to surprise her. She hated feeling unsure. She hated that she couldn't trust him not to destroy her. Jack kept popping into her mind. She had fallen in love with him, she'd trusted him, and he cheated on her, he degraded her. He had hurt her. She knew Mike and Jack weren't the same man. She knew Mike wasn't cruel but she kept thinking back to four years ago when he had kissed her and then ignored her. If that little slight had stung for months after, she could only imagine what it would feel like if she fell in love with him and he broke her heart.

"Ellis, look at me."

She couldn't, so she changed the subject. "Did you get in trouble because of me today?"

"No," he answered after a moment. "But my partner and I are off the case."

"Is it because you kissed me?"

"Yes, that's one of the reasons."

She finally turned to look at him. "Why did you kiss me in front of all those people?" It was as if he didn't care who saw. "In front of your partner? In front of your boss?"

Mike shrugged. "Because you needed to be kissed and because I needed to kiss you."

Shit. He's trying to make me fall in love with him.

"Mikey." She slid her hands over his cheeks and brought his mouth to hers. This kiss, it was so much better than their nearly perfect first. He was gentle. He let her control it, let her make it as deep as she could stand, let her pull herself closer and closer while she sought his tongue. He gave it to her, allowing her to sweetly suck on it, allowing the kiss to take on a new meaning.

Ellis felt like she was falling. She pulled away. It was all too much for her but Mike wouldn't let her go far. "Shit," he breathed as he peppered tiny kisses along her throat. "Shit."

She knew how he felt. Neither one of them could explain this attraction. Neither one of them could seem to stop it no matter how hard they tried. "That was just a thank-you kiss," she said, trying to put some distance between them, but he was having no part of it. His hands wandered up the back of her shirt, stroking her skin, feeling her flesh. The insecure part of her wanted to run away. The rest of her wanted to stay put. "Don't—" Her voice wavered. She could feel his heat, his hardness. It was more sensation than she knew what to do with. "Don't think I'm going to be so nice to you in the future."

Don't think I'm going to fall in love with you.

He kissed the wounded side of her face softly and then her mouth. "I want you so bad, Ellis." He hugged her close, speaking into her hair. "Come home with me tonight."

Chapter Ten

A Fat Girl's Guide to Guilty Pleasures

Best place to find decadent Black and White
Cookies: Hot Lava Java.
Best place to find decadent hot men: See above.

"No," she breathed and kissed him again. She wanted to go home with him. She wanted to feel his heavy male body on top of hers. She wanted to kiss him from his eyebrows to his ankles. She wanted to feel him inside of her but she knew she couldn't. She couldn't risk it. Contrary to what she had told him at the bar she wasn't one of those women who could take sex lightly. But right now she could kiss him, because he was sweet to her and because she'd had a bad day and because he was so damn good to kiss.

"Ellis." He broke away panting. "Stop kissing me."

"Why?" She softly kissed the corners of his mouth.

"Because I'm not the kind of man who can just kiss you."

"And I'm not the kind of girl that you can just sleep with."

They stared at each other for a long, hot moment. Mike parted his lips to speak but he never got the chance.

"Kids," Phillipa called. "Come inside. It's time to eat."

* * *

The following morning a detective called Ellis to tell her
she could return to her store. Ellis took the long route to
work, not knowing why she chose it. It wasn't planned but
after leaving her parents' house and stopping by her place
to shower and change, she got in her car and took back
roads. She got stuck behind a school bus, and for the first
time she didn't mind. Thoughts that she had put off all
day yesterday came rolling into her brain.

Her store.

Was it a mistake to keep going? Had it been a mistake
to open it in the first place? To take Belinda away from
her higher-paying job? To give those women false hope?
What if she couldn't deliver? What if she was a fraud? She
hated doubting herself. Doubt was for the old Ellis. The
one who lived and breathed on a kind word from Jack.

*Look at you, Ellis. Do you have any idea what people
think when they see us together?*

"Stop," she said aloud. She wouldn't let Jack enter her
brain, poison her self-worth. She loved her store. It was
the right decision. This robbery was just a tiny bump in
the road, not a sign from God. She had to continue. There
was no other choice.

She parked her car in the alley beside the store and got
out slowly. Normally she rushed inside, eager to start her
day, eager to update her blog. But today was different. She
could still remember the feel of the man's hand as it connected with her face. She could still hear the sound of the
glass shattering.

"Hey."

Ellis looked up at the greeting. She was surprised to
see Mike there. Last night was torturous. Sitting beside
him all night, knowing how his lips felt, knowing that he
wanted her and that she could never be with him made
movie night almost unbearable. Her parents thought it
was the ordeal at the store that caused her to be so quiet,

but it wasn't. She could barely think about that when he was near her.

"I didn't think I would see you so soon."

"Is it because you turned me down when I asked you to come home with me?"

There he goes, totally knocking the wind out of me again.

"I wasn't sure your fragile ego could take it."

"It almost couldn't." One side of his mouth curled. "I cried a little."

Ellis laughed even though she didn't want to. "I have that effect on men sometimes."

He came toward her, a tool belt in hand and heavy-duty black garbage bags in the other. It was then she took him all in. He was in ratty cargo shorts and a faded blue T-shirt. His hair was still damp as if he had just gotten out of the shower and come straight to the store.

"Don't you have to work today?"

"I do, and I'm ready to take orders."

"Really?" How was she supposed to stay away from him if he kept coming close to her? "Drop and give me twenty."

"Shirt off or on?" He continued to grin at her then sobered, his eyes passing over her face then resting on her lips. He looked into her eyes, regret filling his voice, "I shouldn't have asked you to come home with me last night."

He shouldn't have but she didn't mind that he did. "We seem to lose all sense around each other."

He shook his head. "I had all my senses, Ellis. I meant what I said—the timing just wasn't right."

Would it ever be? "I'm sure I'll be fine doing the cleanup alone. Belinda and Cherri are coming this afternoon. You're absolved of any guilt."

"I don't feel guilty." He handed her the garbage bags

and placed his hand on the small of her back, guiding her toward the door. "I just don't want you alone in the store today."

"It's not like I'm going to get robbed again. That would be statistically impossible." She walked toward the door, her heart pounding. Why couldn't she be as confident as she pretended? "Has that ever happened?"

"Do you always have to argue?"

"I was a lawyer. I still am technically. It's in my nature to argue."

Through the window Ellis could see glass scattered across her floor. A physical ache entered her. She tried to ignore it and turned to Mike. "I'm thirsty. I think I could go for a frozen lemonade. You want one?"

"Yeah," he said. "I'll buy us both one later." He stood behind her at the door. "Open it," he insisted.

Her hand shook slightly as she turned the key in the lock. Mike increased the pressure of his hand on her body, a little reminder that he was still there. She pulled the door open, walked in, and looked around. It almost looked the same as when she'd entered yesterday. The clothes were still neatly arranged on the racks. The red dress still hung on the form. The display case was the only difference, broken beyond repair, all of the items it held gone, shoved in some criminal's pockets.

"Where do you keep the broom, Ellis?" Mike asked, breaking her trance.

"In the back."

He gently squeezed her shoulder. "It's time to get back to normal."

"You have a nice day, too!"

Mike watched Ellis slam the phone back into its cradle as he finished sweeping up the last remnants of glass on her floor. He could feel her frustration rolled together with the love for her store. To him the place was just a bunch of clothes, but to her it was her life. He never had anything he cared about as much as she cared about this place. Something inside him wanted to make this all better for her.

"Stupid, cheap assholes," she muttered to herself. "If I didn't pay my premium every month I could afford to have five display cases by now!"

"I take it that things didn't go well with the insurance company?"

"No." She grabbed the discarded broom and furiously swept the clean floor. "They'll only cover the jewelry that was stolen, not the display case." She blew a strand of hair from her face as she swept the same spot on the floor over and over. "The display case cost a fortune. I don't have any money to replace it. I can't leave it like this." She stopped her furious cleaning and looked at him. "Maybe my mother is right. Maybe I should go back to being a lawyer."

"Stop." Mike confiscated the broom before Ellis had a chance to use it as a weapon. "You're being dramatic. It's broken glass. You aren't going to let that make you want to give up on this place."

"No, not give up. I would die before I'd do that, but maybe I could start taking on a few clients here and there until things pick up."

"And when would you have time to do that, Ellis?" He grabbed her by her shoulders and gave her a little shake. "You spend fifteen hours a day here as it is. You need to take a breath and prioritize."

"Sleep is entirely overrated," she grumped. "And when did you become so sensible? Detective Hot Pants giving sound advice. Who would have thunk it?" She sighed. "It's your fault I'm in this situation as it is."

Mike frowned at her. "How did you come to that conclusion?"

"Because you're here. Duh! Who else am I going to blame?"

He grinned at her. "I'm glad you're being logical about this."

She gave him a wobbly smile, and it caused him to want to kiss the side of her mouth. Why was he here? He'd told her that he didn't want her to be alone at the store today, and that was true—but it wasn't the whole truth. She got on his nerves. She snapped at him, teased him, drove him crazy, and was more trouble than she was worth. And yet he went out of his way to be near her.

Maybe because he kept thinking about his mother and her little shop that was just as much a home to him as the house he grew up in. He could only imagine how she would feel if somebody had desecrated her store. He would want somebody there for his mother.

Or maybe he was full of shit. He liked Ellis. He liked her little store and being here, helping her clean up, made him feel a hell of a lot better than sitting behind his desk doing police work. When he was with Ellis that restless feeling disappeared. He didn't need to be reflective, he didn't need to think about the direction his life was taking because he could only think about her.

"I'm being a brat," she said softly, meeting his eyes. "I would have left a long time ago if I were you."

Mike shrugged. "I think I've developed a fetish for having pain inflicted upon me."

"Kinky." She gave him that naughty grin that always got to him. But it caused the nasty bruise on her cheek to shift upward and Ellis to wince slightly.

If he ever caught the guy who'd hurt her, the man would suffer. He wasn't surprised he had been pulled off the case. His captain told him he was way too close to it, and she was right. All rationality left his brain when he was around Ellis.

"I think we can have your case fixed for cheap." He dragged his eyes off her pretty but damaged face and back to the object they had been discussing.

"Are you a glass supplier in your free time?"

"Nope, but Colin is a restoration expert. I'm sure if we get him the measurements and take a few pictures he could find us a deal and do the work for cheap."

"You really think he would do that, Mike?"

Mike nodded even though he hadn't asked. Colin wouldn't mind. At least Mike hoped he wouldn't. "Do you have a tape measure?"

Two minutes later Mike was on his knees measuring the busted case when the bell over the door sounded.

"Ellis?" a man called to her.

Ellis, who was standing beside Mike jotting down the measurements, froze for a moment and took a step closer, her bare leg brushing his arm.

"What's wrong?" Mike started to stand up but Ellis's hand on his shoulder kept him where he was.

"It's my ex," she whispered as Mike angled his head around her legs to see the man coming toward them. He wore khakis and a pink polo accompanied by a watch that cost more than Mike made in a year. "Stay right there. Please."

Mike nodded even though he wasn't sure that he wanted to respect her wishes. He immediately disliked the guy. He had *pompous jackass* oozing out his pores.

"Get out, Jack. I have nothing more to say to you. I thought I made that clear yesterday."

She talked to him yesterday? When?

"My aunt told me that you got robbed." Jack stepped closer to Ellis. Mike stopped pretending to measure and looked up at Ellis, who held her body stiff but her head high as if she was expecting to be knocked down. "I needed to see for myself that you were okay."

"I'm fine. You can go now."

"You're not fine." Jack's eyes zeroed in on Ellis's cheek. "Fucking animal," he cursed softly. "Did he do that to you yesterday?"

"No, I've taken to castigating myself for dating you."

Mike had to repress his smile. He cheered Ellis's quick and caustic comeback.

"Enough, Ellis! This robbery should prove my point that leaving me and your old life behind was a mistake. It's time for you to give up this foolish dream and come home. It's time for you to stop being stupid and realize what a huge mistake you made when you left me."

Mike was halfway off the floor, ready to smack this asshole in the mouth, when Ellis dug her fingers into his shoulder. He knew she could handle herself so he stayed where he was. But if this guy said one more nasty thing to her he was going to get a fist in his face.

"You better watch how you talk to me, Jack. I will not be disrespected by you anymore."

Good girl.

"I'm sorry, honey." Jack's expression softened immediately. "I always say the wrong thing to you, but I can't accept the fact you are going to let a bad six months get in the way of the great year and a half we had. I know I hurt you and I'm willing to change but I can't do it alone. You have got to help me through it."

Ellis shook her head. "You hurt me, but my quitting my job and moving away wasn't just about you. Couldn't you see that I wasn't happy being a lawyer? Couldn't you see that I wanted more out of my life?"

Jack reached for Ellis's hand but she pulled away. "I don't accept that. We were fine until you found me with Louise. You never said anything about being unhappy with your job."

"That's because you were too self-centered to see the

signs!" She turned away, trying to compose herself. "Can't you see that I'm not alone? I have company. I don't want to rehash our failed relationship right now."

"Do you think I care if the help hears this?" he hissed. "I want to talk to my girlfriend."

"You're wrong again, buddy." This time Mike stood with no interference from Ellis. "I'm not the help and she's not your girlfriend." Mike wrapped his arms around Ellis and pressed a kiss to her forehead. "She's moved on and it's time you do. Don't call her. Don't come by here. Tell your aunt the same thing. I've been understanding these past few weeks but now you're starting to get on my nerves."

Jack puffed his chest up. "Who do you think you are?"

Mike let go of Ellis and took a step toward Jack. He backed away. Mike had this guy pegged. He was all talk, the type of man who put others down to lift himself up. "I'm Detective Michael Edwards and I'm the only one she's coming home to from now on." He took another step toward Jack. "Get out."

"You traded down, Ellis," Jack said, giving her a disgusted glance as he backed away. "You'll have to learn your lesson the hard way. You better hope I'm around when he moves on to greener pastures. He will eventually. I'm your best shot."

Mike lunged toward Jack but the weasel was quick and darted away before Mike could lay his hands on him. He could kill the man.

"I could have handled him myself," Ellis said from behind him. He turned to face her. His blood still simmering. "But I'm glad I didn't have to." She wrapped herself around him and held tight for a moment. "I'm sorry you had to see that," she said into his ear. "But thank you for being here, Mikey. I'm not sure I could make it through this day without you."

"Don't mention it." He hugged her tightly, ignoring the huge lump that formed in his chest. He was starting to feel something for this girl, something way bigger than lust, and it scared the shit out of him.

Ellis watched Mike all day while he played handyman around her store. He helped her put out the new stock and took out the trash. All of her current and fulfilled orders were now on the computer thanks to him. He even came through with his promise about her display case, calling Colin soon after Jack left. At the moment he was on a ladder changing a bulb that had gone out the day before. She hated to admit it but she liked having him around. He was helpful and efficient and free.

She knew why he was here. The man was a fixer, a caretaker, a protector by nature. If she ever met his mother she would have to thank her for raising such a nice boy. But Ellis felt his presence in her store was more than just being there for her. He seemed to like being there. He seemed to like discussing numbers and merchandise. He seemed like he was in his element. She could have kicked him out long ago. She could have assured him that Cherri and Belinda would help her clean up her store but part of Ellis felt like Mike needed to be here.

It made her wonder if maybe he was more attached to that little flower shop in Buffalo than he let on.

"I can see smoke coming out of your ears." Mike climbed off the ladder and came to stand before her. "Stop thinking so hard. You're making my head hurt."

"I've got a lot on my mind," she answered.

Mike pulled her close and slid his hands down her back. "You want to talk about it?"

"No." She rested her head on his shoulder, unable to describe how surreal it felt to actually have him to lean on. Four years ago she had written him off as a self-centered asshole. Now every moment they were together he was proving to her he was not.

"Want to talk about the proposed tax hike for the upcoming year?"

"What?" She looked up at him. His eyes were twinkling. It made her smile. She looped her arms around his neck and reached up to kiss him.

But before her lips touched his, the bell over the door sounded and a harried brunette came rushing in. "Oh, Ellis. It was awful!"

"Karen, what was awful?" Ellis looked at her very good customer's red blotchy face. "What happened?"

"I can't find a wedding dress." She collapsed against Ellis's chest and wept. "I lost thirty-five pounds and I still don't fit into any of the dresses. I went to six stores. Two of them didn't carry any dresses over a size twelve and the stores that did carry my size . . . Everything looked like something my grandma would wear. My wedding is in less than a month. What am I going to do?"

"Oh Karen, I'm so sorry." Ellis knew how she felt. When she was in high school she couldn't find a prom dress that fit her unconventional body. She, too, had gone to many stores and ended up empty-handed and sobbing into her pillow. That was when Ellis learned to sew. If there wasn't a dress for her to buy, she would make one.

"I couldn't think of anyplace else to go. Do you know of a bridal salon that would help me?"

Ellis gently removed the weeping bride from her chest and squeezed her shoulders. "Take a deep breath, babe. I can't think of any places off the top of my head but we are going to put our heads together and come up with a solution. Because you need to look hot on your wedding day."

"Forget about hot. I just don't want to be naked!"

"We could try the city. There's always the Internet. We

could search the Internet for a dress and then I could alter it for you."

She took out the pad of paper that she kept behind the register and studied Karen. "Tell me how you envisioned yourself looking on your wedding day. Forget about size. Forget about what you think a fat girl should wear and tell me how you dream of looking."

"I don't know what you mean."

"Do you want to be a sexy, pinup bride? Do you want to feel like a goddess, or a princess, or do you want to be simple and chic?"

Karen sniffed. "I've always loved the way Grace Kelly looked on her wedding day. Maybe like that?"

"Ah." Ellis smiled. "Good choice. Now we have something to go on." She started to sketch a basic outline. "So you like lace. The long sleeves looked good on Grace but you don't want to copy her. You want to be original. Cap sleeves, I think. And lace over satin." She sketched furiously, getting lost in the design. "Empire waist, beading here. A-line."

"Ellis . . ." Karen sighed.

The sound of her name pulled Ellis's attention from her sketch and back to her customer. "What do you think of this dress? Do you like it?"

"I don't like. I adore it. Forget about trying to find that on the Internet. You have got to make it for me."

"What? I've never made a wedding dress before. You can't trust me with something so huge."

"But I do. Please, Ellis. You're my last hope."

Ellis stared openmouthed at Karen for a moment. Could she really do it? Did she have the time? The talent? What if she sucked at it? The thought of letting Karen down on her wedding day was almost too much to bear. But then she locked eyes with Mike, who reached out and gave her hand a comforting squeeze. She wasn't sure why that made it better, but it gave her the strength to nod.

"I'll do it."

"You will?" Karen screamed and hugged Ellis so hard she could barely breathe. "My budget is five thousand. Can you do it for that?"

Ellis nearly swooned at the amount. Five thousand dollars would not only keep her afloat but help her out tremendously. It was just that she didn't think she could take that much money from Karen. "I could do it for less than that. Like half that."

"No, Ellis." Karen shook her. "You are designing and hand-making a gown that I was going to spend five thousand dollars on at a store. You deserve every penny. In fact I wish I could pay you more."

"But Karen . . ."

"It's settled. I can't wait to tell my mom. When do you want me for my first fitting?"

"Um . . . Tomorrow? Ten o'clock?"

"Great! I'll see you then."

Karen floated out of the store, leaving Mike and Ellis alone again.

"You were very good with her, Elle." Mike backed Ellis against the register and brushed his nose against her cheek. "This is what you are meant to be doing."

Was it, though? It felt right. She felt more competent making dresses than she ever did practicing the law. "I've never made a wedding dress before, Mike. What if I suck at it?"

"You won't." He buried his nose in her neck and inhaled her scent. "I don't know anything about clothes but I know you do good work."

Suddenly all the emotions of the past two days hit her. Her face throbbed. Her head ached. Jack kept bugging her.

She was worried about everything and Mike was there being sweet to her again. She wasn't sure she could take it. Her vision went blurry. "Why are you being so nice to me? I don't know how to handle it."

"It's okay if you want to cry." He pulled away a little and gazed down at her. "You've had a rough couple of days."

It was as if she needed permission to cry. She let the first few tears fall as he gathered her close, smoothing his big hands down her back.

"Oh, stop crying, you big baby," he said into her hair.

Ellis laughed as she stood on tiptoes to bring her mouth to his. "Thank you. I'm glad you were here today," she told him again.

"You're welcome." He cupped her face in his hands and gave her a long deep kiss. She felt him everywhere this time. Her nipples tightened. Her breath grew shorter. She throbbed in places she thought were long dead.

He broke away slowly, stroking the tendrils of hair off her face. "You're tired. I think you should go home and rest."

She nodded. She was tired and she did want to go home but she didn't want to go home alone.

Chapter Eleven

Things I Would Sell My Mother to Have . . .

1. A lifetime supply of Lindt milk chocolate.
2. The Rock, aka Dwayne Johnson, smeared in said chocolate (yummy).
3. A big plastic sheet for my bed. (I'm a messy eater.)

"I should feed you. Come home with me and I'll find something for us to eat."

Mike looked at Ellis for a very long moment, his eyes settling on her lips. He stared so long she grew afraid of his answer. They both knew what it would mean if he came home with her. They both knew that things between them would irrevocably change.

"I would like that." He stroked her cheek with the backs of his fingers before he pulled away. "I'll follow you home."

Ellis took the direct route home this time, Mike following her in his vintage black Mercedes. She tried not to think about what was to come. She tried not to think about him as the anticipation filled her body. It had been so long for her, so long since she felt desire or desirable. Jack had taken that away from her. He'd robbed her of her joy in sex, of her confidence, of her pride. His words came rushing back.

Do you have any idea what it's like to sleep with somebody like you?

Ellis shook her head as she pulled into her little drive-way. She was going to put Jack out of her head for good. He had no place there anymore.

She stepped out of her car just as Mike shut his off. They said nothing to each other as she let them inside but she could feel the heat of his gaze on her back. She felt his need as much as she felt her own.

They stopped in her living room. She turned to face him, wanting to say something to him, something mean-ingful, something profound, but her mind turned to mush as his eyes raked over her body.

"Are—are you hungry?" she managed to say.

"Yes."

He grabbed her arm and pulled her into his hard body as his mouth slammed down on hers. This kiss was dif-ferent: There was no finesse, no slowness, no time spared. It was hot, needy, and deep. It was all-consuming and before she could process the silky feel of his tongue on hers, cool air brushed across her bottom. He peeled her shorts off, his hands reaching inside her panties to cup her behind, to push her against his very hard erection. She rubbed against him, her mind going blank, her body taking over. He let out a visceral groan.

First his shirt came off, revealing a chest too perfect for words, then her panties slid to the floor and pooled around her ankles. She was almost naked, just a few more pieces of clothing to go before he saw all of her. Insecurity, her old friend, filled her. She had never had sex in broad day-light before and never in her extremely bright living room. With Jack it had been in the dark and under covers. With Mike it was all so different. She would be exposed.

He dragged his lips from hers long enough to remove her tank top. "Undress me," he ordered.

She did what he asked, her hands going to the fly of his shorts. They shook as she unbuttoned, unzipped, and freed him from his pants. It was beautiful, big, smooth, and as dark as the rest of him. She wanted to kiss it, to run her tongue over it and taste him but her knees were too wobbly to bend. Instead she took him lightly in her hand and ran her thumb across the tip, smearing that little drop of liquid over him. His body jerked violently and she backed away, afraid she had done something wrong.

"Oh honey, I'm sorry," he whispered, gathering her close. "Your hands feel too good." He led her to the couch where he sat on the arm and she stood facing him. "Let's slow down a little."

He reached up to unhook her bra, leaving Ellis completely naked in front of a man for the first time in her adult life. As her nipples were exposed to the air they painfully stiffened, begging to be touched. Mike said nothing. He did nothing, only stared for a moment. Then his hands and eyes began to slowly travel her body as her mind calculated all her imperfections. They slid over too-wide hips and around to her slightly rounded belly, then down to her fleshy behind and over her thighs. All he did was rub her skin with his slightly rough hands and stare at her with such intensity that it caused tears to come to her eyes.

"What's wrong, baby?" His gaze was full of concern. "You're shaking."

"The way you look at me . . . You don't think I'm ugly?"

"God no." He cupped her face in his hands and brought her mouth to his, kissing her, slowly sucking her tongue into his mouth as if it belonged there. "You're beautiful, so beautiful."

The way he said it, the way he looked at her and touched her, made her believe it. Mike Edwards wanted her, and the knowledge of it made liquid pool between her thighs.

"We fit." He linked his fingers through hers as he placed his head between her breasts, his lips fluttering against her pounding heart. He cupped her breasts in his hands, squeezed them, tested their weight, lifted them to his mouth to kiss her aching nipples. Her breath shortened as he took one into his mouth. He suckled, she moaned. He pulled deeper with his wet lips and she arched her back, trying to bring herself even closer to him.

"Mike, please." She begged, for what she did not know. She just knew she wanted to be closer to him. "More."

He touched her between her legs, finding her dripping wet. "Ellis. You're ready for me." He trailed his fingers along her cleft, slid them up to her clit, and lightly rubbed. She fell apart, coming so hard her knees buckled. Mike caught her before she fell and lowered her onto the couch. He hovered over her, a slight smile forming on his beautiful lips.

"Oh don't look so pleased with yourself."

His slight smile bloomed into a full one. "Can't help it."

He kissed down her throat, licking, tasting her skin while he lifted his fingers to her hair to remove the band that confined it. His hard body felt heavenly as it settled on top of hers, and for a moment she was content with just holding him. But soon, simple touch alone wasn't enough and she wrapped her legs around his hips, causing their inflamed parts to brush against each other.

"You're going to be the death of me," he told her.

"What a way to go." She lifted her head off the couch, needing to be kissed. He obliged, nipping at her bottom lip, sucking it in, licking inside her mouth. She started to rub against him, feeling his member slide against her swollen lips.

He abruptly broke their kiss. "I'm sorry, Ellie. I can't wait any longer."

"Who was asking you to?"

He gave her a quick, wicked grin before he slowly slid into her. It had been so long and Mike was so big. She stretched to accommodate his girth, feeling him at her womb. An insuppressible moan escaped her lips. He paused for a moment, his blue eyes boring into her. This was new for her, the connection, this tenderness. It felt like a first time.

He thrust slowly, his eyes never leaving her face. He studied her every expression, stroked to accommodate her needs. Sex wasn't supposed to be like this. It wasn't supposed to be this . . . this . . . good. She kissed his Adam's apple, unable to tolerate even one part of her body not touching his. He thrust over and over, each time a little harder. The orgasm came so quick and strong her entire body convulsed, her toes curled.

"Honey." Mike rested on his forearms and gazed down at her. "Wait for me next time."

She tried to nod but he took her nipple into his mouth, sucking hard, and it caused her to lose all control of her body. It had been too long. He felt too good. She couldn't keep that promise.

Mike found a slow hard rhythm that drove Ellis crazy. So crazy she barely noticed the car honking as it pulled into her driveway. But the red color of the car woke her from her sexual haze. "Mike!"

No!

"Ellis," he moaned.

God? Buddha? Zeus? Anybody?

She heard the engine die and knew what was coming.

Why am I being punished?

"Get off me!"

"What?" He stopped moving. "Why?" Concern filled his handsome face and feelings Ellis didn't want to face entered her mind. "Am I hurting you?"

"No, my parents are here."

"What!" He turned to look toward the window and violently swore. Ellis's blinds were up. Her curtains tied back. If her parents got any closer they would be able to see into her house. See Mike inside of her.

"Hurry, they've got a key."

"Will they use it?" he asked as he disconnected his body from hers.

"Of course they will! Especially since I don't plan on answering the door like this."

Mike growled. "What the hell are we going to do?"

Ellis didn't look at him as she was busily grabbing all the loose items of clothing scattered across her living room. "Run."

She tossed his sneakers at him and made a naked mad dash upstairs to her bedroom, Mike right behind her.

"Ellis?" She heard her mother's voice from outside the house accompanied by the ringing doorbell. "We called the store."

"Shit." She dropped the pile of clothes in her arms on the floor and grabbed for her panties.

"Don't bother with them, Ellis. We don't have time."

Mike was already nearly dressed and was buttoning his shorts when they heard the front door creep open. "Help me," she cried as she tossed her bra at him. They worked together to get her in it as the she heard her mother's voice calling her name again.

Mike handed her tank top as she was kicking their discarded underwear beneath the bed. She put on her shirt and faced him. "Do I look like I was just having hot sex?"

"Yes." He grinned at her. "What about me?"

His erection tented his shorts. "I'm afraid so." She couldn't help but laugh. "Can't you do something about that?"

"Ellis, where are you?" Footsteps sounded on the stairs.

"I wish I could," he whispered but stuck his hand in his shorts to adjust himself. "How are we going to explain why we are up here?"

Ellis couldn't think of a single reason besides the obvious, and as soon as she got her mother alone she was going to have a very long talk with her about entering her house uninvited. "A puzzle!" Ellis spotted the five-hundred-piece Big Ben puzzle her grandmother had given her three years ago. She grabbed it off the top shelf in her closet and threw it along with herself on the floor just as the door to her bedroom opened.

"Oh, there you are." Phillipa walked in followed by Walter, both of them looking confused. "Didn't you hear me calling you? And why the hell are you two on the floor?"

"We're just doing a puzzle." Ellis's voice sounded defensive even to her own ears. She could smack her mother for interrupting the best sex she'd ever had but her father was there, too, and the poor man did not need to know what she had been up to.

"Yeah," Mike added. "I read somewhere that puzzles release stress and keep the mind sharp."

"Okay." Phillipa looked doubtful. "We bought you some groceries but we really came by to see how you were doing."

"I'm fine, Mom."

"You don't have to worry, Dr. Greg," Mike said, looking as innocent as a newborn baby. "I'm keeping her occupied."

Occupied is a good word for it.

A hysterical bubble of laughter formed in Ellis's chest and she had to bite her lip to keep it from escaping.

"I'm sure you are." Phillipa looked from Mike back to Ellis. "Come on, Walter. Let's get the groceries out of the car."

They left and as soon as Ellis heard their footsteps on the stairs she began to laugh. She couldn't help it. The mad dash up the stairs, the naked scramble to find their clothes, the stupid puzzle that they were never going to finish. It was all too surreal.

"Are you crying?" Mike asked her.

"No," she gasped. "It's just . . . I can't believe . . ."

"It is pretty funny." The laughter was contagious and soon Mike flopped on his back and joined her. Together they laughed until tears streamed down their cheeks.

"I'm so sorry, Mike." Ellis crawled across the floor and threw her arm over his still-shaking chest.

"You should be." He turned on his side and gathered her close. "I was planning to give you a dozen orgasms today."

"Really?" She smiled up at him. "Somebody thinks highly of himself."

"No." He cupped her cheek in his hand and sweetly kissed the side of her face. "Somebody thinks highly of you."

Ellis looked into his eyes and suddenly it hit her.

BOOM. BOOM. BOOM.

He's making me fall in love with him. Holy Freaking Shit.

Chapter Twelve

Mike glanced at the clock on his nightstand. Ten thirty-seven. He sighed, punched his pillow, and forced his eyes to shut again. Sleep eluded him. He had been in bed for over half an hour trying to fall into a dead dreamless sleep. He wasn't surprised the Sandman hadn't visited yet. He never went to bed this early but tonight, after a long hot shower and reading the entire newspaper, he crawled into bed. He hoped sleep would stop Ellis from invading his every thought. It didn't work. Every time he closed his eyes he saw her face, or remembered the way her luscious body felt against him or the way she moved her hips when he was deep inside of her.

His eyes popped open. He sighed again, got out of bed, went to his living room, and flicked on the television. Maybe the news would help clear his mind. Ten forty-six. Ten forty-eight. Ten fifty-two. It didn't. No one else had ever managed to have this kind of hold on him. It could have been that sex wasn't just sex with Ellis. It was different with her. Too intense, and something inside of him told him that if he ever made love to her again he wouldn't be able to walk away easily.

He should stay far from her, and normally he would. He didn't do attachments or commitments, but Ellis wasn't asking for any of those things.

Her parents. He'd never had the urge to strangle anybody, but when Dr. Greg and her husband showed up he could have. He understood they were still worried about their daughter but did they have to stay all night? Did they have to insist on making them dinner? Did they have to put every last damn piece of that puzzle in place?

Poor Ellis must have mouthed *I'm sorry* a dozen times over the course of the evening, and when Belinda and Cherri showed up slightly before eight PM he thought she was going to scream. Apparently waiting them out wasn't going to work, so at eight thirty Mike decided he had enough for one day and went home. Only now he was regretting it. He'd had the best sex of his life and they didn't even get to finish what they'd started.

He had two options. He could sit around his house all night hard as a rock thinking about her, or he could go get what he wanted. The choice was easy. He sprang off his couch, grabbed his keys, and shoved his feet into his jogging sneakers. Mike opened the door and froze.

"Ellie." His heart raced. He had finally met a woman who wasn't afraid of going after what she wanted.

She was standing at his front door, dressed in a short black trench coat, her hand raised to knock. "Were you going somewhere?" Her eyes went wide. "I—I should have called but—"

She screamed as Mike lifted her off the ground. The trip to his bedroom seemed to take forever but once they arrived he dropped her on the bed, smiling as she bounced softly. "You read my mind, honey. I was coming to see you." He covered her body with his and kissed her.

She caught his face in her hands. "I can't believe you

picked me up." She gave him a hard hot kiss. "You don't know how much that turned me on."

"Good, because I've been hard as steel all night. You aren't going to leave this bed for a very long time."

"Thank God." She let out a dreamy sigh. "Just promise me my parents won't show up again."

"I promise." He kissed the length of her throat, the underside of her chin, her cheeks. "Now you promise me that you confiscated your mother's key."

"I wrestled it out of her skinny little hands two hours ago."

"That's my good girl."

Her shiny black coat was tied in a bow at her waist. With a yank the bow was gone and the coat fell open, revealing her nearly nude body beneath it. All she wore was red satin panties. His mouth watered.

Could she see into his mind? Did she know that he often thought about her in that particular garment?

"You like?" She gave him her naughty little grin. His chest tightened.

"How did you know?"

The need to feel her skin was overwhelming. She was lying before him like some kind of morsel to be feasted on. He wanted to devour her, to pump into her hard and fast until they were nothing but sweaty bodies and panting breaths. But he couldn't. Not yet.

He lowered himself till his lips touched her soft belly. He kissed it, trailed his tongue around her perfectly round navel until she shivered.

"Naked," she whimpered. "I want to feel your skin."

He let her sit up and pull his shirt over his head. Her hands trailed over his chest. Her fingertips brushed over his nipples and he did some shivering of his own.

"I've never seen a body so beautiful," she said more to herself than to him. "I shouldn't have said that." She glanced up at him. "I don't want you going around thinking that I'm attracted to you."

He grinned. "You even give me a hard time during sex."

She wrapped her arms around him, gently kissing the side of his face. "There's something about you that makes me want to be happy."

His heart stopped beating for a moment. He pulled away from her so that he could see into her gold-flecked eyes. She was serious. It wouldn't be easy to walk away from this one, and for once he didn't want to.

Shit.

He pushed her down on the bed, ready to please her body, but she wouldn't stay down.

"You're not naked yet." She reached for the waistband of his shorts and slid her warm hands inside, stroking his too-hard manhood as she worked them down his legs.

"Stop it, baby," he breathed. "I'm not going to last thirty seconds if you keep that up."

He pushed her hands aside and her body down on the bed. His head went between her legs, kissing the insides of her soft thighs.

"Mike, don't," she moaned.

He licked her through her panties. "I want to taste you."

"Please, no foreplay. I need you now."

"You have me." He slipped her panties to one side, revealing her soft sweet flesh. "You are even pretty down here." He kissed her mound, used his fingers to spread her, and then licked the length of her.

"Please." She curled her fingers in his hair. "Please, Mike. I don't want to wait anymore."

Hearing her plea, he stopped and held his face to hers. "But I want to kiss you all over and when I'm finished I want to start again."

"Later." She pushed her body against his. "Love me now. Kiss me later."

How could he refuse a plea like that? He smashed his mouth to hers, kissing those pink lips that drove him to distraction. Her legs wrapped around his hips. She rubbed her mound against him. He could feel how wet she was and it was hard for him to maintain self-control.

"Now, Mikey. Please."

Pushing those little red panties aside, he entered her in one slow thrust. He gritted his teeth. Tight. Wet. Silky. She felt too good around him. He throbbed. He was close to coming, which was a shame because he wanted to make it last all night. He pulled out slowly and thrust again. Harder this time. She came immediately. *Thank God.* He could slow things down.

He disconnected them and she moaned in protest. He peeled off her underwear as he covered her erect nipples with his mouth. She tasted as sweet as she smelled, and he suckled her until she was writhing against him.

Slowing things down wasn't working. She made him too hot. She made him want to throw his self-control out the window. He pushed inside of her again, forgetting about taking his time. Ellis didn't seem to want him to. She met his every stroke, urging him to go faster with her moaned pleas.

He felt her tighten around him and he knew she was ready to come again. He fastened his mouth to hers, pulling her tongue deep inside. She went rigid and then started to tremble with orgasm. This time he joined her, spilling himself deep inside her.

"I'm stretching out your T-shirt," Ellis said to Mike as she stood beside him in his tiny kitchen. He was making a ham-and-cheese omelet because after three bouts of rigorous, toe-curling sex a little protein was needed.

He looked up from the eggs and gave her body that slow perusal that usually made her tingle. "You look better in it than I do."

Ellis sighed as he stared at her very voluptuous chest. "I was never the type of girl who looked good in her boyfriend's clothes. You know how those girls in movies always look so sexy in a man's white buttondown shirt and nothing else? Not me. I can't even button them over the twins."

Mike stopped what he was doing and pulled her into his arms for a slow kiss. She melted. The sex was ahmazing and when he was inside of her she could think about nothing but how wonderful he felt. Now that it was over all her insecurities returned. She was unsure of how to act around him. She didn't do this. She didn't have casual sex. And now she didn't know how to behave, which was why she was chattering like an idiot.

"Do you like cranberry juice?" he asked as his lips grazed her ear.

Ellis moaned her answer. She couldn't believe she was actually here. She gave her body to Detective Hot Pants, something she swore she would never do. Now she understood why women couldn't get enough of him, why he never stayed with one long enough to see the seasons change. He was easy to fall in love with, and if she wasn't careful she would be in the ranks of women that Mike Edwards had loved and left.

Their time together was wonderful and she had no regrets but for the sake of her heart they could not repeat tonight.

"Grab it out of the fridge for me. Cups are in the cabinet over the sink." He pecked her mouth. "Our snack is ready."

She turned away to do as he asked, her lips still warm from his kiss. He was seated at the table when she turned around, a steaming omelet in front of him. When she went to pull the chair across from him out it wouldn't budge.

She looked at him in question.

"Sit here." He patted his lap.

Is he on drugs?

"I'll break you."

He frowned at her. "That's what you said when I asked you to be on top. I think we both know how well that turned out."

Ellis's cheeks burned at the recent memory. It had worked out. Very, very well in fact. "That was different. We were—you were—" She sighed in frustration. "—on a bed."

"Come here, Ellie." He lifted his arms, urging her closer.

"Fine," she grumbled. "I hope your chair is sturdy enough to handle this."

She gingerly sat on his lap, holding most of her weight off him. He wasn't happy with that and squeezed her against him until she relaxed. She expected to hear the chair groan in protest but it remained blissfully quiet.

"I love the way you feel, Elle."

She wrapped her arms around him and rested her head on his shoulder.

You like making poor defenseless women fall in love with you, too.

"I think you have a secret fetish for fat girls. Did you know some men have a thing for being squashed? They pay money for big women to sit or lie on them. It's a good business. Maybe I should charge you."

Mike sighed heavily, "Why do you always have to say things like that?"

"Why do you pretend that I'm not fat? We both know I am."

"I don't see you as fat."

"Really? Aww." She grinned at him "We need to get your vision checked."

He cupped her face in his hand. "You're curvy and sexy and have an ass I would photograph and frame if you let me. Why can't you just accept the fact that I'm seriously attracted to you?"

"I accept it," she said after a moment. "And I don't say those things because I don't like myself or because I'm looking for reassurance from you." She smiled softly at him. "But every girl likes to hear she's super sexy once in a while." She kissed the tip of his nose. "I'll never be a size that has single digits and my thighs will always touch when I walk but I'm okay with that. And I want you to know that and try to ignore my insanity."

Thoughts of Jack entered her mind. He was so different from Mike. Jack had claimed to love her. He had told her every day but as soon as she did something to displease him the comments about her appearance would begin—or about the way she ate or spoke or smiled. She didn't realize he was slowly tearing her apart, that he was trying to break her until their very last conversation when the words *fat pig* were spat at her. It took a long time to build herself back up from that point.

She knew Mike wasn't looking for forever but she was also beginning to learn that he wouldn't tolerate anybody tearing her down. It was nice to know that.

"I get it, but it still bugs the shit out of me."

"I'm sorry, Mikey."

"Don't be." He picked up the fork and dug into the rapidly cooling omelet. "Eat up. It's getting cold."

They fed each other, shared kisses, and for the next twenty minutes talked about their childhoods. Ellis inwardly sighed. Tonight had been the most romantic night of her life. It reminded of her of the night they'd shared four years ago and the conversation that had made her fall for him in the first place. She was sad it was all over.

"I should get going." She attempted to get off his lap but once again found herself stuck.

"It's two thirty."

She glanced at the microwave, discovering he was correct. "I guess time flies when you're having fun."

"It does." He paused for a moment. "Stay."

"Stay? You can't possibly want to have more sex? Aren't you . . . exhausted?"

"I am exhausted and I always want to have sex with you but that's not why I am asking you to stay."

"You don't do sleepovers." She searched his face to see if he was serious. He was. "Why do you want me to stay?"

"I don't know. I want to wake up with you tomorrow."

"Oh." She blinked at him. Her stupid heart was pounding. BOOM. BOOM. BOOM. Tomorrow her life would go back to normal. She would reopen her store, finish her dresses, return to her happily single status. It was too soon after her breakup to be falling in love. She had too much on the line this time. Her store. Her future. Her heart. The risk was too much. But tonight was a different story. Tonight she would enjoy her time with the man she'd never dreamed of being with.

She stood, extending her hand to him. "Okay. Let's go to bed."

Chapter Thirteen

Mike stared at himself the next morning as he shaved. He looked tired. He *was* tired after managing only a few hours of sleep the night before. Ellis asked him to make love to her again before they fell asleep, and when they woke up he spent an hour doing the same. Yes, he looked tired, but he also looked dumb. He couldn't stop his lips from curling in a stupid self-satisfied grin. It was foolish for him to think that once he had her he wouldn't want her as much.

He tapped his razor on the sink before rinsing the blade. If he didn't hurry he was going to be late for work. But for some reason he couldn't make himself move faster. He opened his medicine cabinet to pull out his aftershave when he spotted them. The condoms. An entire box that he should have used last night. His stomach clenched.

All women were on birth control nowadays. Weren't they? It wasn't like him to be so careless. He never forgot to use protection. He had never had sex without it before. That must be the reason it felt so different with Ellis. So damn good.

"Shit."

Sex at her house. At his house. All those times that

neither one of them paused to think about the possible consequences. He was going to have to speak to her, to find out if there was any possible chance that she could be pregnant.

"Shit."

Work that day went by in a blur for Mike. He couldn't stop thinking about Ellis. In between panicked thoughts of fatherhood came ones about them in bed. He wanted to regret their night together but he couldn't. He would do it all over again if he had the chance.

He walked into her shop right before closing time. A few customers were scattered about. Cherri was manning the register.

"She's in her office," she told him with a little smile.

Mike thanked her, wondering if Ellis had shared any details of their night together. Probably not. She didn't strike him as that type of women. The truth was he barely knew what kind of woman she was. He did know that she'd told him she didn't want kids. He believed her. He also believed that if she did have his baby she would be good to it. Motherhood may have not been her chosen path but his gut told him that she would be a natural.

"Hey," he said to her when he walked into her office.

Her eyes went wide. "I didn't think I would see you today."

"Here I am." He gave her a halfhearted smile. Shutting the door behind him, he leaned against it. "I need to talk to you."

Immediately her expression grew wary. "Okay." She put down the dress she was working on and spun her chair to face him. "Shoot."

"We didn't use any protection last night . . ." Mike wasn't sure how to continue. "I wanted to—I was just wondering if—Are you okay?"

She rose from her chair with a smile on her face. Her arms came around him. "Of course I'll marry you, Mikey. I always wanted a spring wedding but I'll be too big by then. You think I'll be showing by Christmas? A Christmas wedding could be a lot of fun. We could dress as Santa and Mrs. Claus." She giggled. "Our wedding pictures would be so cute. Don't you think?"

"Um . . . yeah." He shut his eyes and buried his face in her hair, trying to slow his rapidly beating heart. Marriage. He felt queasy, but not panicked. He wouldn't be like his father. He wouldn't let her raise a kid alone.

"Mike?" Her hands touched his face. "You do realize that I'm joking, don't you?"

His eyes snapped open. She was frowning at him. "Uh, yeah."

"No, you didn't!" She backed away from him, crossing her arms under her breasts. "Oh, how typical! You *would* think I would want to marry you. Well, I don't, even if I were pregnant."

"Wait a minute. If you were pregnant we would be getting married. I'm not going to let you raise my baby without me."

Shut up, you idiot, he told himself. *You don't want to get married.*

"Thank God I'm not pregnant," she huffed. "I'm on the pill. You don't have to worry about me trapping you into a loveless marriage."

He opened his mouth to tell her it wouldn't be loveless but then shut it. Where the hell did that thought come from? "I wasn't worried. I wanted to make sure I did the right thing by you. This is the first time I forgot to use something."

"I forgot, too, and I know better." She locked gazes with him. "Maybe this is a sign that last night was a mistake."

Her words were a punch to the gut. "A mistake?"

"Yes." She looked away from him. "You've been with a lot of women and I didn't think about that before I slept with you. You could have man-whore cooties or something."

Mike wanted to defend himself, to tell her that she was wrong but he couldn't. "I haven't slept with as many women as you give me credit for. I haven't been with anybody but you for a year."

Ellis's mouth formed a perfect O. She was speechless for the first time since they had met. She was right about one thing: Even though he was careful to protect himself and his partner, he could never be sure. But she was wrong about them. Last night was not a mistake, and he would make sure he proved it to her.

When Ellis returned home that evening her stomach was in knots. That morning after Mike had given her a long kiss good-bye she'd floated home on a cloud of sexual satisfaction—but all of that died when she noticed the light blinking on her phone.

"Hey, it's Dina. Where the hell are you? I sent you three texts."

She had forgotten all about her sister. They had been trying to make an effort to stay connected since that dinner with their parents but Ellis hadn't spoken to her in days. She was too wrapped up with Mike. Maybe she should come clean about them.

She disregarded that idea almost immediately.

Dina didn't need to know that Ellis had slept with Mike because it was over between them, just one night of very good sex. It didn't matter that she thought about him one hundred times that day or if her heart leapt when she saw him walk into her office. Michael Edwards was officially off limits. Being with him was too risky. She was just finding herself. There was no way she could lose herself in another man.

Ellis sat down on her couch and dialed her sister's number.

Dina answered on the first ring. "Why the hell didn't you pick up your phone last night? I was worried sick."

"What?"

"Where were you last night? Mom told me your store got robbed. She told me you got hurt. She said your face was all busted up. Damn it, Ellis. I kept trying to call you to see if you were okay. "

"I was . . . uh . . . in bed," she said, telling a half-truth. This was not what she expected to hear from her sister when she picked up the phone. She never thought in a million years that her sister would actually care. "You spoke to Mom. She told you I was fine. Didn't she?"

"Yes, but I needed to hear from you myself." She was quiet for a moment. "Listen, Elle, I know that I have spent the majority of your life treating you like the stuff that grows under rocks. But I happen to love the stuff that grows under rocks very much and would hate it if something happened to it."

"Dina . . ." Tears clogged Ellis's throat as guilt tore up her insides. While her sister was worrying about her, Ellis was having hot sex with her ex-boyfriend. *Classy.* "I'm okay, I swear. You don't have to worry."

"Oh, I'm not going to worry anymore because I'm picking you up and we are going to the shooting range."

"What? Guns. I'm pretty sure New York State doesn't just give out gun permits willy-nilly. And you know our nonviolent pacifist mother will not approve of this adventure."

"So what? We won't tell her. I know you're all brave

and shit but I need to do this. I need to know that if the time ever came you'll be able to protect yourself."

"Where the hell was this sister when we were kids? I could have used you in junior high."

"Nah, it would have never worked then. I had too much fun torturing you."

"Bitch."

"Brat."

"Thanks for calling, sister."

"I'll call again. We will get this sister thing right eventually. I promise."

They disconnected and for the first time in a long time Ellis was really hopeful that things would work out with her sister.

"I'm hungry," Colin complained as he studied the contents of Mike's refrigerator.

Mike stared at his friend's back, wondering if he could burn a hole through his shirt with his gaze alone. He had been in Colin's company for over half an hour and for the first time in the fifteen years Mike had known the man he wanted to punch him. How could one man have so many jokes?

"Forget about your goddamn stomach for two seconds and get me an ice pack."

Colin glanced over his shoulder and grinned at him. "Your head hurts, does it?"

"You know it does," he snapped. Mike had been through few experiences in his life in which he was truly embarrassed; today was one of them. Today took all those other experiences combined and made them seem like small potatoes.

"Don't get your knickers in a knot." Colin opened the freezer and tossed Mike an ice pack. "You know you're scared of needles. I don't know why you had to go rushing off to the doctor today."

"I'm not scared of needles." Mike winced as held the pack to his forehead. "I don't like them. Big difference."

"I'd say passing out, knocking your head on the exam table, and needing me to pick you up is more than not liking them."

Maybe Colin had a point. "It wasn't the needle," Mike admitted. "It was all the blood." They stuck the needle in my arm and kept filling vial after fucking vial. When she put the fifth in I'd had it. It's not right to take so much fluid from one person."

"Why'd you look at it? Always look away, man. Especially since you tend to faint like a little girl." He pulled a couple of beers out of the fridge, tossing one to Mike. "Did they have to get the smelling salts to revive you?"

"Fuck off." Mike gingerly felt the throbbing lump on his head.

"Shouldn't you be saying thank you instead? I had to stop working to come get you."

"I'm sorry if I took you away from reupholstering a settee. It wasn't my idea anyway. I wanted to drive myself home."

"I was restoring a vintage slot machine and that's beside the point." He took a long swig of beer. "Why did you go to the doctor in the first place?"

"Physical," he grunted, before taking a swig of his own.

"Next time have a girl come get you from the doctor. She can play nurse a hell of a lot better than I can." Colin studied him for a moment. "What's going on with you and Ellis?"

Ellis. He hadn't seen her for a few days and he would be lying if he said he hadn't thought about her a thousand times. Every time he stepped foot in his kitchen he remembered her curvy body in his T-shirt and her red panties. Every time he lay in bed he could faintly smell her scent on his pillowcase. He could almost feel her nestled against his chest. "She reopened her store a few days ago," he said, deliberately misunderstanding. "I think she's doing pretty well."

"Don't play dumb. You know what I'm talking about. Did you make any progress with her yet? Did you seal the deal?"

Mike took his time answering. He had no secrets from Colin but this time he wasn't so eager to share. Ellis was somebody he wasn't comfortable talking about, even with Colin. Mike wasn't exactly sure what was going on with them. She had claimed that their time together was a mistake. It wasn't. They weren't done yet.

"We're hanging out." He shrugged. "I like her."

A slow smile spread across Colin's face. "Come on, lad. Don't be shy now. Will I be Uncle Colin soon?"

"You sound like the Lucky Charms guy when you say shit like that." Mike sat back, crossing his arms over his chest. "Let's talk about you instead. You haven't been with anybody in a long time."

Colin had been dating a woman for about a year and Mike was sure his friend was heading toward walking down the aisle. But something had happened between him and his love. Something that Colin hadn't shared. Colin had been single ever since. It seemed Mike wasn't the only one with a closed mouth when it came to women.

"I'm keeping my options open." He stood up and opened the drawer where Mike kept his menus. "Let's order pizza. I'm starving."

Apparently the conversation was done.

Ellis was busy stitching the hem on a dress when Belinda poked her head into her office. "Hey, Ellie, Mike's on the phone for you."

"Mike?" She honestly didn't think she would hear from him so soon after their little fight. She'd seen the look on his face when she told him that what they'd done was a mistake. It was subtle but she could tell by the slight tightening in his jaw that it had hurt him.

She didn't lie to him that day. She knew she shouldn't have slept with him and it had nothing to do with the women in his past. If she let herself fall in love with him she would end up giving her heart away, and this time she was afraid she was never going to get it back.

"Yes, Mike. Detective Hot Stuff. The guy who has been paying you an awful a lot of attention lately." Belinda studied Ellis for a moment. "What's going on with you two?"

"I slept with him," she blurted out.

"You hussy!" Belinda accused. "Was it good?"

Ellis nodded. "Best sex I've ever had."

"Why don't you seem happy about it?"

"Because I'm one of those unfortunate people who goes all girlie and gets stupid feelings for the guy I'm sleeping with."

"And you're afraid that sex is all he wants?"

She shrugged. "Partly. I just don't want to fall in love again, Belinda. It's too hard."

"Oh, girl. I know. Why the hell do you think I'm avoiding it?" She gave Ellis a soft smile. "Pick up the phone and talk to the man. We can have some girl time after work. I'll pick up some booze and we can meet at my place."

"Sounds good." Maybe a talk with her best friend would do her good. Maybe she was blowing this whole thing with Mike out of proportion. "Thanks, Belinda."

She winked at her and left the room.

Ellis picked up the phone on her desk and took a deep breath before she answered. "Hi, Mike." She tried to sound cool, like she hadn't thought about him at all the past few days.

"Hey." His voice sounded different. Heavy. She sat up in her chair. "I called your cell phone, but you didn't answer so I figured I'd try you on this line."

"I'm sorry. It must be on silent. What's up? You missing me already?"

"Maybe. I haven't talked to you in a couple of days. I was just wondering how you were."

"I'm fine, but how are you? You don't sound like yourself."

"I'm okay, just a little tired."

It was more than that. In her gut she knew all wasn't right in his world. "Where are you?"

"At work. I know you're working, too, and I don't want to take up your time but . . ."

"But what, Mike?"

"I just wanted to say hi."

"Oh." She was speechless for a moment. "Hi."

"I've got to go, Elle. Maybe I'll see you around."

He disconnected before she could say another word.

Mike hung up feeling like a total jackass. He didn't know why he'd called her. Twice. He should have taken the first missed call as a hint and not bothered her, but something drove him to dial the number to her store. He wanted to hear her voice, not because he missed her but because he wanted to take his mind away from his thoughts. From the heaviness that was making it hard for him to breathe these past few hours.

His old partner had called him that morning to tell him that the fifteen-year-old kid they had busted for armed robbery last year had been killed in prison. After ten years on the job it shouldn't have surprised him. But it did. And more than that, it bothered him.

Darryl Peters was from the worst neighborhood in the city. He was poor. His high school was dangerous. He wasn't exceptionally smart. He wasn't athletic. Crime seemed like his only choice. Normally Mike wouldn't have batted a lash when he threw a perp in jail, but this kid had stayed with him. He looked younger than his fifteen years. He cried when they arrested him. He asked for his mother when they hauled him in for interrogation. And now he was dead.

How many poor kids had they sent to prison? How many kids could have made something of themselves if they had been born in a different zip code?

Knowing that the boy was dead made him hate his job a little. Prison didn't rehabilitate kids. Throwing fifteen-year-olds in with the adult monsters wouldn't cure them. It would only turn them into monsters. Or it would kill them.

"Mike?" The officer at the front desk called to him. "Somebody's here to see you."

He looked up to see Ellis with a cup of coffee in one hand and a pink bakery box in the other.

"Elle?" He stood up. "What are you doing here?"

"I got a thing for cops," she said absently as she crossed the room to meet him. "I came to see if I could pick one up. What happened to your head?" She put the coffee and the box on the nearest desk and reached for his face. "Mikey . . ."

As soon as he felt her warm hands on his skin he leaned into her touch. He couldn't help himself.

It was one of the few times he'd seen Ellis unguarded. She was worried about him. She couldn't hide it.

"Who did this to you?" She brushed her lips over his bruised forehead.

"I did it to me," he said, not wanting to tell the truth. "I was getting blood drawn and I passed out and knocked my head on the exam table."

"Oh." She covered her mouth with her hands in a vain attempt to smother a giggle.

"You're not supposed to laugh at me." He frowned at her. "You're supposed to coo and fuss over me and kiss it better."

"I'm sorry," she said, still giggling. "I'm having a hard time picturing you passing out. It seems like nothing ever gets to you."

He studied her face, still marred from her run-in with the asshole who'd robbed her. "Things get to me, Ellis. Things get to me all the time."

They were quiet for a moment as they stared at each other, something indescribable passing between them. "Judging by the look you're giving me, I'm guessing I still look like I went twelve rounds with Tyson."

"I didn't think it was possible, but your face actually looks worse than before."

"You mean, you're not a fan of the greenish yellow tinge my cheek has taken on? Or is it the intermittent spots of purple that turn your stomach?"

"Hmm." Mike gently ran his thumb across her cheek. "I think it's that scabby gash that does it for me."

Ellis nodded as she leaned into him, her warm soft body doing wonders for his shitty mood. "It's a sight to behold. Well, at least we match. We could bring home the title for most battered couple."

"We could," he said softly. "Why are you really here, Ellie?"

"I told you. To pick up men. See." She motioned to the coffee and bakery box she'd discarded on Maloney's desk. "I even bought cop bait, but pickings seem to be slim around here." She looked into his eyes and gave him that slightly naughty grin he was growing inordinately fond of. "I guess you'll have to do. Want to come out with me tonight?"

"Yes," he said without thinking. "I do."

It was just after six PM when they left the station. The

streets of Durant usually grew quiet around this time on a
weeknight. The college kids were in their dorms. Families were sitting down to dinner. Ellis and Mike were
strolling through town. They were quiet for a while and
instead of it being awkward, instead of one of them
searching for something to say, the silence was comfortable. He'd never really had that with a woman before.

He never just took walks with a woman, either. Every
girl he had dated in the past he'd had a plan for, a purpose
for being with her. But with Ellis . . . They just were. No
plans. No thoughts. He didn't even know where he stood
with her half the time. He just knew that he liked her.

Ellis stopped in front of the window of McKeel's
Hobby Shop and peered into the window.

"This is Durant, you know." She lightly pressed her
hands to the glass as she studied the intricate set of min-
iature buildings on display. "This was how the town
looked in the 1950s before all the hippies moved in and
funked up the place. See? There's the university and that's
St. Lucy Street. The third store in is my shop."

She looked up at him and grinned. "My father used to
bring me here when I was a kid. But only around Christ-
mastime. Every shop on the street does a window display.
The bakery always does theirs out of gingerbread. The
accountant makes a Christmas tree out of shredded tax
forms, but McKeel's . . . They do the best one. This town
turns into a winter wonderland." She pointed to the pond.
"That becomes an ice-skating rink, and those people beside it get dressed up in winter clothes, and the whole
thing is dusted in this glittery white snow. It's beautiful."

So was she, he couldn't help but to think. Her face lit
up with excitement when she described the town. He
didn't think anything had ever made him so happy.
"You'll have to show me when they do it this year."

She nodded and slid her arm around his as they head

farther down the street. "You have to do all the Christ-massy things there are to do in Durant. There's the tree lighting on the green and parade of houses and the fruit-cake bake-off."

"Fruitcake bake-off? I'll pass on that one."

"You can't! It's a good time. Usually whoever can cram the most alcohol into their cake wins."

He smiled at her enthusiasm. "I've never been here for Christmas. Classes ended before that. I had no idea there was so much to do."

"Durant's a great town. I missed it when I was gone."

They came to end of the street but instead of turning down the next one, Ellis surprised him by walking onto the empty playground. She wore a little brown fluttery skirt, ridiculously high heels, and a khaki-colored jacket. She wasn't dressed to go play in the park.

She turned back to him, extending her hand. "Let's swing."

"That's not the first time a woman has ever said that to me, but nobody else has meant it the way you do."

"Perv." She gave him that sassy grin of hers. "I bet I can swing higher than you."

Ellis kicked off her shoes and took the swing on the end, her legs pumping back and forth, taking her higher and higher, causing that cute little skirt she had on to fly up. She wore yellow panties with black polka dots. He couldn't pull his eyes away.

"I haven't done this since I was eight," she said sounding slightly breathless. "I'm going to jump."

"Ellis," he warned, "you'll break—"

Before he could finish her sentence she was screaming and hurtling toward the grass. She landed flat on her behind and without thinking he rushed to her.

"Are you okay?"

She blinked at him for a moment, then grabbed his

arm and yanked him down on the grass with her. He landed half on top of her curvy warm body, and when he looked into her face he found her laughing uncontrollably.

"That was almost as fun as sex."

He smiled down at her and then when he couldn't help himself anymore, he pressed a soft kiss to her mouth, hoping that some of her happiness would seep into him.

"Mmm," she moaned, closing her eyes for just a moment. "Now tell me what's wrong."

"What?" He stiffened, her question taking him by surprise. "Nothing."

"Something." She ran her fingers through his hair. "Tell me."

He looked at her for a moment, prepared to tell her he was fine, but he couldn't. She caught him off guard. She saw right through him. "A boy I arrested was killed in prison yesterday. He was only fifteen."

She was quiet for a moment, her eyes taking in every inch of his face. "You feel guilty," she said, reading his mind. "You feel like if you hadn't busted him he would still be alive."

He nodded. "There are kids that are just bad but then there are kids who just need a leg up. Darryl's father had died the month before the robbery. Hit by a car, crossing the street. The kid was reeling and poor and running with the wrong crowd. If somebody would've taken the time out to help him I know he wouldn't have robbed that store."

"But he did, Mikey. And you were doing your job. There's nothing you could have done differently. No reason you should feel like shit."

"I know that." He shook his head. "But it bothers me. I've thrown so many kids in jail only to find out later that prison has made them more violent, that they have really hurt someone when they got back on the streets. It makes me hate being a cop sometimes."

She ran the back of her fingers across his jaw. "Is that why you moved here, because you weren't happy anymore?"

"I moved here because some asshole nearly beat an eighty-nine-year-old to death and I barely batted a lash. I didn't like that about myself. I didn't like what I was becoming so I moved here. I figured the risk of being disgusted with myself was lower." He'd never admitted that aloud to anybody and now that he had it off his chest he couldn't stop himself from telling her more. "The only thing I've ever wanted to be in life was a New York City cop. I don't know what happened. I don't know when that stopped being enough."

"What do you want out of your life?"

"I don't know. I came here to figure that out."

She cupped his face, kissing the tip of his nose. "You're damaged and confused. I like that about you."

"So you're admitting you like me now?"

"I've always liked you. I had a crush on you four years ago, even before we met." Her cheeks went red.

"Did you?" He was surprised by her statement and surprised how damn good it made him feel.

"Yeah. I shouldn't have told you that," she grumbled. "It'll probably make your big stupid head swell to epic proportions."

"Ellis . . ."

"Oh yeah, I was being nice to you, wasn't I? There's something good about you, Mike. Even before I knew you I sensed it. You're a good man, and a good cop. You should be happy, and if being a cop doesn't make you happy anymore I want you to find the thing that does."

He looked down at her for a moment, unable to describe what was going on inside him. This woman . . . She was making it hard for him to be miserable.

"You've got grass in your hair." He slid his lips along

her cheek. "We should probably get you off the ground. It's getting cold out here."

"Really?" She wrapped her arms around him. "I'm not feeling it."

He wasn't, either. With his body pressed to hers he was feeling warm all over, but as comfortable as he was, he knew he couldn't lie in the grass with her all night. He reluctantly pulled his body off hers. "I want to buy you dinner."

"Okay. Anything but sushi." She got up, dusting off her behind. "I hate sushi."

"I do, too." He retrieved her shoes. "If you're going to give me fish, cook it."

"I know. And don't just cook it. Deep-fry it. I don't want to feel too healthy eating it."

He took her arm and led her out of the park. "Yeah, and whole fish gives me the creeps. Who the hell wants to have the eyes of the thing they're eating staring at them?"

"Exactly! Every time I see someone eating one I keep thinking that there are worms in its belly. And I keep imagining them squirming around in there."

Mike frowned at the visual. "I think we should stick to beef for dinner."

"Cheeseburgers." She nodded. "And milk shakes. Do you know they have beer-flavored milk shakes now?"

"I'm not sure how I feel about that."

"My mother loves them. Can't get her to eat a piece of chicken but she can slurp down two beer milk shakes in less than twenty minutes."

He listened to Ellis go on about her mother as they walked down the street, and for the first time in a long time he was perfectly content.

Ellis discovered that she really loved making Karen's wedding dress. All the delicate white fabric, the intricate needlework, the skill she used to make the sketch come to life made her feel accomplished. Of course the dress was nowhere near done even though she had less than two and a half weeks to Karen's wedding. Her finances were still dismal and she had more work than ever before, but she felt good. Happy even. She knew that changing the course of her life was the best thing she could have done.

"It's going to be gorgeous," Cherri said to her from the doorway of Ellis's office. "Karen is going to cry when she comes in for her next fitting."

"You mean like she cried at the last one?"

"Yeah." Cherri smiled at her. "But way harder this time."

"Remind me to stock up on tissues."

"Will do." Cherri fell silent for a moment, a tight look on her face.

"What is it, honey?" Ellis worried a little about her young employee. The girl never seemed to slow down.

"My grandmother." She sighed. "She fell in the shower this morning. She's fine but I keep thinking about what would have happened if I wasn't there."

"Go home, Cherri. Be with your grandmother."

Her eyes widened. "But I'm supposed to work another two hours. You have so much sewing to do."

"I'll be fine," she said truthfully. No job was more important than family. "Go home and don't feel guilty. You deserve a little time off."

"Yes, Cherri," a deep voice said. "You do. I'll help out around here."

Mike appeared behind Cherri wearing a gray hooded sweatshirt with his alma mater plastered across the front. Ellis's heart beat faster.

"You will?"

She was surprised to see him so soon after last night. They had spent three hours together, doing nothing but talking. It was one of the best dates of her life because it didn't feel like a date. She felt like she was with an old friend that she was wildly attracted to. And that scared her. She knew she was falling hard and fast for this guy. She didn't want to. It was too soon after Jack. This time in her life was supposed to be all about her. Plus she wasn't sure how Mike felt about her. There were hundreds of reasons for her to stay away but there was only one reason she wouldn't. He made her feel good. He made her feel like it was okay to be herself.

He nodded. "You could use some dumb muscle, couldn't you?"

She nodded, feeling a little shy around him for the first time. "You don't have to. I can manage here by myself."

She barely noticed that Cherri had disappeared as Mike crossed the room. He stopped in front of her, pulling the lace out of her hands and pulling her body into his. "I'm here, Ellis. In a dress shop. There's only one reason for this."

She leaned in to kiss his cheek, hoping that her face didn't betray how much his words affected her. "Admit it. You can't live without me."

"You wish." He hugged her tighter, his face falling to the curve of her neck. "What do you need me to do tonight?"

"This." She slid her hands under his sweatshirt and rubbed his lower back. They had both gone home alone last night. Not because she wanted to. She had forgotten all about keeping some distance from him. But he didn't ask her to be with him. He didn't make a single move. He just softly kissed her good night and escorted her back to her store.

"How are you feeling today, Mikey? I was thinking about you."

He froze, pulling slightly away so that he could look at her face.

"What?" she said self-consciously. She hadn't meant to let the last sentence slip. She didn't want to give away how close she was to falling for him.

"Nothing. I'm fine. I'm good." He shook his head and stepped completely away from her. "Put me to work, Ellie."

She did put him to work, confused by their interaction. For two hours she watched him as he cleaned out the storeroom, updated her software, and made himself useful around the shop. He barely said two words to her or spared her more than a passing glance. At one point she was tempted to send him home. She wasn't sure why he was there. Her shop was no longer the big mess it had been after the robbery. She didn't need rescuing but she had the sneaking suspicion that his presence in her store had more to do with him than with her. It was as if he needed to be there. He needed to feel useful.

She knew part of him was a little lost. He was, like her in a way, at a crossroads in his life. But Ellis was sure she'd found the thing that would make her happy. She knew Durant was the place she wanted to spend the rest of her life, but he wasn't there yet. He had no idea what to do with himself. It was another reason she should stay away. He could decide that Durant wasn't the place he wanted to be. He could pick up and move tomorrow and she could be left a little in love with him.

"Who's the guy, Ellis?"

She turned to look at Macy, one of her good customers, surprised she was so caught up staring at Mike that she didn't hear her come in.

"Oh him? He's . . . Just a friend. What can I help you with?"

"Well, I came in to see what kind of dresses you had on sale but I'd rather spend my time gawking at the man merchandise you've got on display."

"I saw him first," she said as she gave Macy a little push toward the dressing rooms. "I'll bring you some dresses."

"Would you like to have dessert with me?"

Mike came up behind her and wrapped his arms around her waist as she waited for Macy to finish dressing.

She kept herself rigid, a little stung by his behavior tonight.

Say no. You don't need this bullshit right now.

But his lips grazed the back of her neck and she unwillingly relaxed a little.

"Say yes," he urged. "And none of the bullshit about you not eating junk food on a weeknight."

"We had cheeseburgers and milk shakes last night," she said, feeling a little petulant.

"Say yes anyway." He rested her chin on her shoulder.

"No."

"But I worked hard tonight. I even got a paper cut cleaning up the disaster area you call a desk. See?" There was a tiny cut on his index finger. "You owe me."

"Okay," she said, hating that it took so little prodding to get her to cave. "You were helpful tonight. So helpful that I think you should quit your job and work as my shop boy."

"Only if you agree to pay me in sex."

She closed her eyes as not-so-clean thoughts flooded her mind. Thoughts of him running his hands all over her naked body, of his lips brushing against her nipples, of him stroking between her legs. Her face grew hot. If she was ever going to have a shot at escaping with her heart intact she needed to stop thinking that way.

Like that's ever going to happen.

"Oh, honey, say yes."

Ellis opened her eyes to see Macy staring at them with a huge grin on her face.

"Ellis didn't tell me we weren't alone," he said. "But I'm Mike." He extended his hand without removing his arm from around Ellis. "It's nice to meet you."

"You too. Listen, Ellis, I'm going to take the green dress and the black pants but I need both of them altered. I'll come back tomorrow to get measured. You go enjoy dessert with your *friend*."

A little while later they were in a booth at Hot Lava Java, sharing a warm decadent blueberry crumble topped with vanilla ice cream. It was the first time she had been back there since they had bumped into each other the first time. She was beginning to wonder if she could ever walk into this place and not think of him.

"I'm going to make love to whoever made this," Ellis said, sighing with happiness as she licked her spoon.

"I made it," Mike lied. "It took me all day."

She raised a brow at him. "Prove it?"

"Can't," he shrugged. "I'm a cop. I got rid of all the evidence."

"That's too bad then." She placed a big spoonful of ice cream in her mouth and let it melt on her tongue, watching Mike as he stared at her. He made her feel self-conscious and comfortable all at the same time.

Her phone rang. "You Drive Me Crazy," by Britney Spears. It was Dina. She didn't pick up. A little guilt seeped into her. She'd seen her sister two days ago and still hadn't told her about Mike.

"What's wrong, Ellie?"

"That was Dina. I haven't told her about us yet."

"Why not? We're not a secret."

His words surprised her. That was the last thing

expected him to say. "She won't like it. She says she really liked you."

"I doubt it." Mike dismissed her concern. "It was just a fling."

She looked away. His words didn't comfort her. Mike had no idea how Dina thought. He didn't grow up the insecure wild child who needed to have everything for herself. Her father stopped coming around regularly when she was six. Only seeing her once or twice a year when he felt like it. And then when she was twelve he stopped coming around altogether. She had daddy issues and man issues and she never saw things from anybody else's perspective. Ellis knew Dina well enough to know that this would upset her. Not because she wanted Mike so much but because Mike was the one who broke things off and now he was with the chubby little sister whom she thought wasn't good enough for him in the first place.

He left his side of the table and slid in next to her. "Why do you seem so bothered by this? It was four years ago and if I remember correctly she tried to bang some guy in your bed while you were having a party."

"What exactly would I tell her? That we slept together?"

"No." He cupped her face in his hands. "You're going to tell her that we are seeing each other and we're going to keep seeing each other until we're sick of each other."

"That could happen very soon," she said as she leaned in to kiss him. "I'm nearly sick of you already." Her lips brushed his and as soon as they made contact she let all the reasons why they shouldn't be together fly out of her head. She needed to stop overthinking things. She needed to let herself live in the moment. She needed to do what made her happy.

He moved to deepen the kiss but as soon as his mouth opened over hers they heard, "Hello, son."

Mike's body went rigid. Ellis turned to see the owner of the gravelly voice that had that kind of power over Mike.

Oh shit.

The man had black hair liberally streaked with strands of sliver and eyes a shade of blue that Ellis had only seen in one other place. He looked exactly like Mike.

His father!

Ellis turned back to Mike to see his face expressionless, but she could feel the angry heat rolling off him.

"Mike . . ." The man sat down across from them. "I came here to see you. We need to talk."

"Well, Harry, that's too bad. I stopped wanting to speak to you twenty years ago." Mike gave a gentle push to the small of Ellis's back. "Come on, Elle. I'd rather be someplace else."

Ellis rose, looking from father to son. They shared the same mulish expression but Harry couldn't hide his feelings as well as his son. Ellis didn't know what had happened, didn't know if the man was even worth Mike's time, but she recognized the look in his eyes. Regret. Shame. Sadness. Mike didn't seem to notice or care. He didn't bother to spare his father another glance as he grabbed her hand and led her toward the door.

"Son, wait."

"Don't!" Mike stopped but didn't turn around to face the man who gave him life. "You lost the right to call me son the day you walked out on us. Stay the hell away from me."

Chapter Fourteen

He clearly remembered the day his father walked out. It was a Thursday. His mother and older sisters were at the flower shop preparing an order for a big wedding that was to take place that weekend. He was home alone with his baby sister, Janice, waiting for Harry to return from work. He was supposed to be there by four, home in time to feed them dinner and take Mike to baseball practice. Four o'clock came and went, and there was no sign of him. So he waited, put on his uniform, and made Janice a grilled cheese sandwich when she got hungry. Five o'clock rolled around. No Dad. Mike started to worry. Car accident, work mishap, something gone wrong? Not wanting to worry his sister, he went into his parents' bedroom to use their phone to call the shop. But as he reached for the phone he spotted a yellow piece of legal pad paper on his mother's pillow.

I'm sorry Margie. I can't live like this anymore.
I'm leaving. Please forgive me.

The bastard couldn't bother to tell them in person. The coward couldn't face them to tell them good-bye. It was the next day they learned he had nearly cleared out the checking accounts, only leaving them enough money to make it through the end of the year. At thirteen, Mike knew what it felt like to have love die. His father, his hero, walked out on them the day before his birthday. The day before they were supposed to cut work and school and spend the whole day away from the women who ruled the house. Instead he spent it watching his mother worry and his sisters cry. It was that day he vowed never to let anybody get that close, close enough to make him feel more than indifference when they left.

Ellis's rapidly clicking heels on the pavement alerted him to the fact that he wasn't alone with his thoughts. Looking down at her he could see that her cheeks were slightly red and her breathing heavy.

"Ellis." He slowed his pace. "I'm sorry. I was going too fast."

"I'm okay," she puffed. "All this speed-walking is a good way to burn off dessert. I only wish I wasn't wearing four-inch heels."

"I'm sorry, Elle. I—I wasn't expecting to see him."

She nodded and squeezed his hand. "So that was your dad, huh? At least he didn't walk in on us having sex like my parents did."

Despite himself he laughed. "No, he's much better at walking out."

She was quiet for a moment then tilted her head to study him. "Was that the first time you've seen him since he left?"

Mike nodded. "I didn't recognize him at first. I wasn't sure if he was dead or alive until a couple of weeks ago."

"Oh," Ellis pursed her lips. "How does that make you feel?"

Her question stunned him for a moment. Nobody ever asked him how he felt about his father leaving. "I don't

know. I'm done talking about him. He doesn't deserve
our wasted breath."

"I'm sorry." She pulled her lower lip between her teeth.
"I wish I knew what to say in situations like this. I wonder
if Hallmark makes a card?" She thought for a moment.
"Something like: Sorry your deadbeat dad returned. Hope
his tires get slashed."

Something tugged at his heart again. It was the same
feeling he got in the park yesterday. It was the same
feeling he had this evening he was with her in her store.
Somehow Ellis had firmly planted herself under his
skin.

It was the last possible thing he wanted.

It scared the shit out of him.

Twenty years ago he'd promised himself that nobody
else would ever have that kind of power over him, the
power to change his world as he knew it. Ellis might be
able to do it, might be able to affect him. He couldn't let
that happen.

"You should apply for a job with them. You seem to
have a knack for writing greeting cards."

She shrugged. "I'm multitalented."

He nodded and continued to walk her back to her store,
his chest feeling heavy, his brain racing. He'd moved to
Durant to get away from his hectic former life. He never
guessed that he would run into a whole different, more
troubling set of problems.

A few minutes later they were standing beside her car.
She stared up at him and he could see in her eyes she
wanted to say something. Whatever it was he didn't think
he could bear to hear it.

"Good night, Ellie." He leaned down to kiss her cheek,
but she turned her face so that her lips connected with
his. She wrapped her arms around him, giving him a
comforting kiss. In that moment he knew he didn't want

to go home alone. He wanted to stay in her soft hold all night, forgetting about every unpleasant thought that clawed at his brain. But he couldn't. He wouldn't let her have the same kind of hold over him that his father had over his mother.

Breaking the kiss, he stepped away. "Text me when you get home."

He opened the car door for her, helping her in, and when the car started he walked away from her, forcing himself not to look back.

Nine days had gone by since Ellis had seen or heard from Mike. She hated herself for knowing that it was nine days, for counting their time apart. She hated herself for finally letting go of the little piece of doubt that plagued her. She should have trusted her gut. She should have kept him at a distance. She shouldn't have let herself care about him so much. One night, she told herself. One night of earth-shattering, heavenly sex, but her statement was quickly forgotten after spending a few hours in his company. He was like potato chips: One night was not quite enough.

At first she was understanding. She thought he needed a day or two to sort out his father's reappearance. It was a big deal but after five days of ignored texts and unanswered phone calls she realized that maybe it was more than that. That maybe she had read more into his feelings than she should.

She made a pact with herself to forget him. Her life had moved on without him. She had lunch with Dina twice. The shop was getting busier. She had taken in more altering. The wedding dress she was working so hard to complete was coming to life. Her display case had been fixed. Her finances were less dismal. Her life was good. She just hated that she felt so damn crummy.

She was going to fix that. She had two whole days off.

Two whole days to herself where she would see nobody and do absolutely nothing. Maybe she would take a bubble bath and read the book she had been putting off for a year. Maybe she would sleep all day and not bother to get out of pajamas. It was rare she got to do anything for herself. It used to be all about Jack-ass, seeing that his wants and needs were met. Before that it was making her way through law school and studying for the bar exam. Now her life was consumed with making the store work. Ellis had never taken personal time. She never relaxed.

Which was probably why she was wide awake on a Sunday morning, filled with restless energy. She glanced at the clock: seven oh two. She shouldn't be up this early. She turned over, trying to find a new spot that would make her instantly comfortable and drag her back into dreamland. That spot didn't exist.

She sighed. Maybe she would visit her parents or check out the local vintage store for inspiration. Ellis was no good at doing nothing.

The doorbell rang as she sat up. It had to be her mother. Nobody else would dare to visit her this early on a Sunday. If Phillipa had on her jogging gear Ellis would scream. No amount of restless energy would ever make her want to go jogging.

It rang again and this time she forced herself out of bed and rushed down the stairs. She didn't want her mother calling her name, waking up the entire neighborhood in the process.

When she opened the door, the hairs on her arms rose. It was the last person she expected to see. The one she had just put out of her mind. "What are you doing here?"

Not you. Not now. Not today.

Just when she starting to forget about him he showed up and knocked her on her ass. Mike stood before her, looking a little tired, unshaven. Not himself. Her heart squeezed painfully. She wanted to pull him in and hug him. She wanted to slap him.

"I want to spend the day with you."

Nine days. Nine whole days without a word. She cared about him. She worried for him and he ignored her. It was like the night of her party all over again.

No. She wouldn't let that happen. This was her life. She wouldn't play on his terms.

"I'm busy." She tried to push the door closed but Mike caught it and pushed it opened again.

"You aren't. I called Belinda yesterday and she told me you have two days off."

She paused at his words. He called? She shook her head, her resolve strengthening. "I do and I plan to spend them in bed. Alone."

He grabbed her wrist when she began to step away. "You're mad at me."

"I'm not. I don't care enough to be mad."

"Bullshit," he spat. "You're mad at me for walking away. I get that I—"

She wrenched herself away from him. "I'm not mad at you for walking away. I'm mad at you for ignoring me and thinking you could just come back whenever you please. I don't know what kind of woman you think I am, but I'm not here for you to pass the time with when you get bored. I'm not just a good time. I'm not just sex when you want it. You don't get to stroll in and out of my life when you want to. This thing goes both ways."

He shook his head, his expression softening. "It's not that, Ellie. I—I just—"

"What? Found somebody who looks better naked?"

His jaw tightened. "Don't go there, Ellis."

"I knew I shouldn't have gotten involved with you. I

should have run the other way." She pinched the bridge of her nose to lessen the throbbing in her head. "Screw you, Mike. Getting involved with you is always a mistake."

She turned and left him where he was, not bothering to slam the door in his face. She didn't expect to be so angry. With him for thinking he could walk in and out of her life whenever he wanted—and with herself for falling for the last man she should.

Mike watched Ellis stomp up the stairs toward her bedroom. He should leave. He should shut the door and walk away for good.

Mistake.

She'd used that word and it hit him in the chest. There were many words he would used to describe what they were. *Mistake* wasn't one of them.

He knew he'd been wrong to ignore her. He wanted so badly to pick up the phone and hear her voice. But he didn't. He knew he was getting too attached to her. His body craved her in bed but his mind and every other part of him craved her conversation, her naughty smile, her presence in his world. He wasn't in Durant for a serious relationship. This place was just a rest stop—a place where he could gather his thoughts before he moved on. He didn't want to fall in love. But staying away was too damn hard. He had to proceed with caution.

He shut her door behind him and ran up the stairs to her bedroom. He could tell by her anger that the last nine days had been just as rough on her as they had on him. He'd counted their time apart, hating himself for doing so. The thing he hadn't counted on was missing her.

She was huddled under the covers when he arrived in her bedroom. Unsure of what to do next, he stared for a moment. He'd never had trouble with women before, but when it came to Ellis he never seemed to do the right thing. It was as if he never found his balance when he was around her, and that was one of the things that bothered him the most. Stripping off his boots, jeans, and sweatshirt he slid in bed beside her, his body sighing as her soft figure came into contact with it.

"Go home, Mike." Her muffled voice came from beneath a pillow.

He yanked it away. "I'm not leaving."

"I won't let you do this to me." She turned to face him. "I'm not a doormat. You can't just walk in, out, and all over me."

"I'm not going to. I was dealing with—"

She cut him off. "I would have been there for you."

"I know." And that's what scared him. He stroked a lock of hair from her face. He pulled her closer and was glad to feel her body slightly relax against his. "I'm sorry." He kissed her forehead. "I missed you being mean to me. I didn't know what to do with myself."

"You should have jumped off a cliff." She frowned up at him, but he could tell she was softening. "Your beard is scratching my skin. Oh, and I hate you."

"That's my girl." He pulled her into his body, wrapping both arms around her. His lids grew heavy. He'd spent nine days restless, jumpy, unable to relax, but now all that left him.

"Mike?" Ellis called as he was shutting his eyes.

"Hmm?"

"I was serious, you know. If you walk out again, don't expect to ever come back."

Chapter Fifteen

Back Fat Bitch Fest

I generally like the way I look. Most days.
I stare in my full-length mirror and think I'm looking
all foxy.
But then I turn to the side.
Back fat. Bra bulge. Chub flub.
The bane of my existence.

Ellis stared at the big sleeping man in bed beside her. He
needed a haircut. His formerly short hair had transformed
into small black, silky curls. He looked yummy with them.
Unable to stop herself, she lifted her hand to run her fingers through it and sighed. He was gorgeous even in his
sleep. He didn't snore. He didn't drool. He didn't sleep
with his mouth open. And there she was in her rumpled
monkey-printed nightgown, her hair probably looking
like a rat's nest.

Where's your willpower, woman?

She was going to end up hurt. She could feel it coming.
It wouldn't be like it was with Jack. It would be worse.
Mike wouldn't mean to break her heart. She should end
things once and for all. Before it all came crashing down.

"I like your monkey pajamas," he said, startling her
from her thoughts.

"Thank you."

He pulled her closer, brushing his fingers across her

cheek. She didn't want to bask in his nearness but as soon as his skin came in contact with hers she tingled. "Your bruise is finally gone," he said sleepily. "You're back to being gorgeous again."

"Hey, didn't you think I was gorgeous with it?"

He placed a soft kiss on her cheek. "Every time I looked at you I wanted to kill the guy who hurt you." He dragged his lips across her skin, kissing the place where her ear met her neck. "It almost made it hard for me to make love to you those six times but somehow I managed to solider through."

His words brought a smile to her face and she shut her eyes, enjoying the smoothness of his lips on her skin, the tingles of pleasure that shot through her body. She'd missed him. Despite everything she'd missed him. But she didn't want him to break her heart. "You should have stayed away, Mikey." She opened her eyes to see his face. "It was for the best."

His eyes shuttered a bit before they moved to the clock on his side of the bed. "I can't believe you let me sleep for almost three hours. What do you want to do today?"

"Mike." He wasn't going to make things easy for her.

"It's been a long time since I've laid around all day. We can do that. Maybe go to the movies later? Or go for a walk in the park?"

"Mikey . . ."

"You want to take a bath? I can run you one and put all that smelly girlie shit you women like in there. By the time you get out I can have brunch on the table."

He slid out of bed and headed into her bathroom, where she heard the faucet turn on. "Do you have any food in here or should I order out?" He stuck his head out the door waiting for her response.

She should send him home, remind him what a mistake they were, protect herself from heartbreak. This was

her time. She needed to be focused on her store—on growing her business. She needed to make a clean break. But
not just yet.

"Food? You know I don't keep any in the house. We'll
have to order out."

The day passed quickly. Too quickly, Ellis thought. She
took a long hot bath, and when she got out the food he
promised was waiting. Warm bagels, cream cheese, fresh
fruit, and orange juice. They ate in bed, and afterward
dozed a little. Ellis finally got the chance to begin the
book she had been meaning to read while Mike read the
newspaper. They didn't talk much, didn't kiss, and barely
touched. Ellis kept waiting for him to make his move, to
attempt to make love to her. But he didn't try a thing. She
would welcome it if he did. Too many times she'd thought
about him, his mouth, his body, his hands over the past
week. Too many times she caused herself to grow damp
because she couldn't stop herself from thinking of him.

Tomorrow she would officially cut the ties between
them. She knew she wasn't the type of girl who could just
have sex. And she knew they weren't the type of people
who could just be friends.

Mike set down his paper, placed his warm hand on the
back of her neck, and settled his gaze upon her mouth.
She knew he liked her lips. She remembered how much
time he spent kissing them on that night they spent in his
bed. "Put the book down, Elle."

She did as he asked, anticipation filling her. Finally. It
had been hours. Actually it had been weeks. She deserved
this. His lovemaking. When she was with him she stopped
feeling like the insecure little fat girl and more like the
desirable women she always wanted to be.

"Want to play Rummy?"

"What?"

"Rummy? I saw a deck of cards on your shelf. Or we can play Hearts. Actually, I could go for a game of Spit. I haven't played that since I lived at home with my sisters."

Ellis shook her head, not sure if she was hearing him correctly. "You want to play cards with me?"

"Yeah." He looked at her as if it were obvious.

"You've got me in bed and the activity you want to engage in is card playing?"

"Yes." He frowned. "Unless you want to take a nap."

"No," she sighed. "I don't want to take a nap. Go get the cards."

Mike stood in front of Ellis's door preparing to leave for the night. It was nearing eight PM. He had been there all day and still he was finding it hard to step over the threshold and leave.

"You've had enough of me today?" she asked him.

No, he wanted to say. He wanted more. "You cheat at cards. You think it's funny to put your cold feet on me and you kept stealing my fries at dinner. I think I've had all I can take."

"I didn't cheat." She tried to keep a straight face but was failing miserably. "I lost, remember?"

He shook his head, smiling at her outrageous lie. "I didn't say you were a good cheater, but you switched hands while I was in the bathroom and that constitutes cheating. I should have known better than to play cards with a lawyer. They always cheat to win."

She pulled her lower lip between her teeth. "If it makes you feel better, I felt slightly guilty about it."

"Only slightly?"

She nodded. "If I'd won I would have felt really guilty."

He smiled at her, wanting to pick her up and carry her upstairs to the bed they spent all day in and bury himself inside of her. "I have to go."

"Oh." He watched her shoulders slump a little. He felt the same way. "I had fun today."

"So did I."

He grabbed her hand and tugged her into his arms, an erection forming as soon as her body touched his. It was almost enough to set her away from him. Almost. Instead he brought her closer, tipping her chin up so that he could taste her. He purposely kept his kiss light, only allowing his lips to brush over hers, keeping the flame from growing into a fire. But Ellis wasn't content with that and deepened the kiss, slipping her sweet tongue in his mouth, inviting him to consume her. She set his damn heart racing. He gently broke the kiss before it could go any farther, before he found himself stripping off her clothes where they stood.

"Mikey . . ." She hugged him tightly. The silence stretched between them for long moments as his mind raced with uncomfortable thoughts. "I don't think we should see each other anymore."

Her words hit him like a punch but he knew she didn't mean it. Her words said one thing but her body, her actions told him another. They weren't done yet.

"No." He kissed her forehead. "I'll see you tomorrow."

As he drove home the restless feeling returned. He tried to ignore it, tried not to think about spending another night alone. During their nine days apart he had thought about going to a bar, picking up a girl, satisfying his baser needs, but night after night he couldn't bring himself to do it. Finally last night he grew tired of fighting with himself and resigned himself to the fact that he was about to enter a real adult relationship.

He wasn't sure what had changed his mind. Maybe it was the fact that Lester's wife had surprised him at the station yesterday. She brought him lunch. She asked him how his day was going. She kissed him good-bye.

Mike saw that and it didn't make him feel lonely. He had spent most of his adult life alone. It made him miss Ellis. It made him wonder why he was so hell-bent on staying away from her when she was the only one who could make him feel good.

Opening his front door he found his phone ringing. He was tempted to ignore it, but glancing at the clock he noted that it was his mother's usual calling time; if he didn't pick up she would keep calling.

"Hello, Ma."

"How did you know it was me?" He could hear the smile in her voice.

"Who else calls me at eight o'clock every single Sunday without fail?"

"You're my only son," she reminded him. Mike could picture her face in his head. Her eyebrows raised as they always were when she was making a point. Her mouth softened with a smile. "And you live hundreds of miles away. If I didn't call you I would never hear from you."

Hearing her voice flavored with that thick western New York accent made him miss home. He should go see her. "That's not true. I would call you on Mother's Day and your birthday if I remembered what day it was."

"Ha ha, son," she said dryly. "How are you? You sounded a little down last week."

"I'm fine, Ma. I like it here."

"Are you sure?" She paused momentarily. "Colin mentioned that there might be a girl. Is there anything you want to tell me?"

"What? Colin told you?" He shook his head, wondering what kind of punishment he should deliver to his best friend.

"Of course Colin told me. Who do you think I call every Sunday at eighty thirty?"

Mike wasn't surprised that his mother stayed in contact

with Colin. She was the type of woman who fiercely protected those who were important to her. "There is nothing to tell."

"What's her name?"

"Ma!"

"I would like to see you happily settled before I die, Michael. You are going to be thirty-three in a couple of weeks and it's time I start getting some grandbabies from you."

He was about to remind his mother of his feelings about marriage and children but he saved his breath. "Okay, Mom."

"Did you hear from your father again?" At the mention of his father, Mike's stomach clenched.

"No." There had been a message waiting for him the night he bumped into his father at the coffee shop, asking for the chance to talk. Mike hadn't returned the call and his father hadn't tried to contact him again. "Has he tried to talk to you?"

She was silent for a long time.

"Mom?"

"He did. He wanted to make amends." She took a breath. "I've forgiven him, Mike."

"You've forgiven him?" Mike raked his fingers through his hair. "He walked out on you, left you with four kids, and you've forgiven him? Have you forgotten all of that?"

"No, I haven't forgotten, and it was my choice to do so. You don't have to forgive him if you don't want to but I will not have you judging my decision to do so."

Thoroughly chastised, he apologized. "I shouldn't have raised my voice. I'm sorry."

"I forgive you, too, son. There are some things about your father that you don't know. You might want to think about speaking to him. It could change the way you see him."

"I doubt it."

Mike knew he could never forget the look in his mother's eyes the day Harry left her, or the stress of not knowing whether they were going to have enough money at the end of the week to keep food on the table. His mother never moved on, never dated again, stopped smiling like she used to, and all because of her worthless husband. She may be able to forgive, but Mike wasn't so kind.

"He's not a bad man but it's up to you, son. I will support you either way. Your sisters are all torn about it."

"How are my sisters?"

"Good. I think Lara is pregnant again, but she hasn't said a word. I honestly don't know how they are making it. She and Bobby are working fifty hours a week. I don't know how they are going to manage a fourth baby."

"Things will work out. They always do."

They chatted a few minutes longer, Mike barely focusing on what his mother was saying. All he could think about was her ability to so easily forgive the man who had destroyed their family.

"I bet if I could see you, your eyes would be glazed over."

"Huh?" Her words snapped him back to attention.

"I'm going to go now. My adopted Irish son is expecting my call. I love you."

"I love you too, Ma."

Mike walked up to Ellis' house the next morning a little before eight AM. It had barely been twelve hours since he'd kissed her good-bye. Twelve hours since he'd spoken to his mother. The conversation with her tilted his world a little. She forgave. Out of all the things Margie should have done, out of all the things Harry deserved, forgiveness wasn't one of them. It caused Mike to think about Ellis's family, how unconventional, how slightly overbearing they were, how loving. He wondered how she would handle it if her father walked out—if Phillipa would be able to forgive. He wondered if he were wrong for not wanting his mother to do so. He knew forgiveness wasn't something he was capable of.

He reached her door, rang the bell, and waited, wondering what cute little nightgown she would wander down the stairs in this time.

"Hey." She opened the door and he was surprised to see her dressed but barefoot in a pair of super-tight jeans and a brown turtleneck.

"Damn, I was hoping to catch you half naked again."

She blushed. "Want me to change?"

"Yes." He sighed. "But don't. I'm taking you out today."

She smiled, motioning for him to come in. He liked her cozy house. How it felt like a home.

"Do you want coffee? I would offer to feed you but you know the state of my refrigerator."

It was empty. The only food she had in her house was ramen noodles, a block of cheese, and some Ritz Crackers. "I'll take some coffee. You go put on some comfortable shoes, maybe something without a heel."

She frowned at him and went to her hallway closet. "I don't own any weather-appropriate shoes without a heel."

When she opened the door Mike saw rows and rows of shoes, sandals, and boots, some neatly lined up on the floor, some hung in an organizer on the back of the door.

"Holy shit. Do you need all those?"

"Yes." She pulled out a pair of brown boots, the kind that reminded him of the ones horse riders wore, but with a bigger heel. "The first thing I did after I broke up with Jack-ass was buy twenty-five pairs of heels. One for each month I spent with him. He wouldn't let me wear heels. Said it made him feel short. So for two years I relegated myself to only wearing ugly sensible shoes. That's all over now."

"Wouldn't let you?" He frowned. "Ellie, I can't imagine anybody stopping you from doing anything."

"You would think," she said softly.

Mike looked at her for a long moment. The more he learned about Jack the more he regretted his decision not to knock the guy on his ass. "Why were you with him so long?"

"I don't know." She sighed. "He was good to me at first and successful and all the things a woman thinks she wants in a partner. I was a rule follower back then. I thought the only path to happiness was the route I was taking. Become a lawyer. Get married. Start a family. And even though I wasn't sure I wanted those things I threw myself into getting them. I threw myself into trying to make sure Jack was happy and in the process I lost a little bit of myself. It took me six months before I realized the man I had fallen in love with was treating me no better than dogshit on a sidewalk. And that's when I left." She looked up, locking her eyes with his. "I deserve more. I deserve to be treated well."

He nodded, heeding her subtle warning. "Put your shoes on, Garret. We've got places to be."

Chapter Sixteen

"Apple picking?" Ellis grinned at Mike as he pulled up to Wilde Orchard after a picturesque forty-minute drive. "I never thought Detective Hot Pants would ever bring a woman apple picking. I assumed it was all candlelight and black satin sheets."

Mike shrugged. "Actually, I'm more of the chicken joint, cheap wine type of guy, but I thought I might change it up a bit."

"Mmm." She sighed dreamily. "Chicken and cheap wine, my two best friends. Do you think they make apple wine here? Or hard apple cider?" She looked at him. "I sound like a lush, don't I?"

"A little, but I like a girl who likes her liquor."

They grinned at each other before stepping out of the car.

She was pleased with his choice. Mike released a breath that he didn't realize he was holding. He had never taken a woman apple picking. He had never taken a woman anyplace other than a restaurant, but with Ellis things were different. He had to prove to her that taking a chance on them wasn't a mistake. He had to prove to himself that he could be with her without losing himself.

* * *

"Inhale," Ellis ordered Mike. "Doesn't it smell like fall?"

"What does fall smell like, Ellie?"

They had been strolling the orchard for over two hours without picking a single apple. It was empty, being a Monday. There were a few parents there with their small children, a couple of classes on field trips. It was quiet, breezy; the sun shone brightly. The perfect fall day.

Ellis sniffed the air. "Like sunshine, rotting leaves, and apples. It's heavenly."

Mike smiled at her as she turned her face to the sun and breathed in once more. "I think the rotting leaves are my favorite part. We used to make giant piles as kids and hide from my—" A powerful memory jabbed him and for a moment he lost the ability to speak.

"What?" Ellis looked up at him in concern. "Tell me."

"My father," he said, hating that a good memory of the man infiltrated his bad thoughts of him. But things weren't bad when his father was around. In fact they were pretty damn good. "We used to make giant piles of leaves and hide in them and when my father came home from work we would jump out and surprise him." He shook his head. "You think we would have realized that he wasn't really surprised after the first few times, but he always pretended. Always clutching his chest like we gave him a heart attack."

Ellis took his hand in hers and led him toward the small pond in the middle of the farm. "Do you want to talk to me about it?"

He hesitated for a moment. He had never discussed his father's abandonment with anybody. Not Colin, not even with his sisters. Growing up, they lived with the knowledge that their father had walked out. They shouldered on, pretending like it didn't affect them.

"My mother said she forgave him." He looked down

into her big brown eyes, watching for her reaction. She gave none.

"You don't agree with her decision?"

"No." He shook his head. "It was bad when he left, Ellie. Really bad. He didn't even tell us why he was leaving, just left a note on my mother's pillow and her with four kids to raise alone." He looked away from Ellis. "She used to cry at night," he said softly. "She didn't think we heard her, but I did. I saw her once and then I used to listen outside her door. She cried every night for three months."

"Oh." She softly squeezed his hand. "He deserves to be drawn and quartered."

"He deserves worse than that." Mike lifted his eyes off the spot on the ground he was so intently studying and looked back at her. "I'm not sure how she could forgive him."

"It serves no purpose to be angry," she started. "Bitterness makes a person feel ugly. I don't think she forgave your father for his sake but for her own."

He was surprised by her words. "You agree with her decision?"

She shrugged. "I don't have an opinion either way. I wasn't inside their marriage. Maybe there are things about your father only your mother knows. Maybe she forgave him because in her eyes he truly deserves it."

Mike shook his head, having a hard time absorbing what Ellis was saying. "Do you think I should forgive him? He disappeared for twenty years and now he wants back in. I don't know if I can. Could you?"

"I don't know." She paused. "Do you want to? My birth parents are still together. I met them when I was sixteen. My entire life my mother had told me that they were scared college kids, and that they gave me up so they could give me a better life. But when I met them I was surprised. They live in a huge row house in DC. My birth father is an investment banker. My birth mother works on Capitol Hill. They drive Beemers. They're rich." She shook her head. "I thought they gave me away not to give me a better life but to give themselves one."

"They sound selfish."

She nodded. "That's how I felt—like they couldn't be bothered to love me. I came home from meeting them sobbing. Nothing my mother said could make me feel better about them giving me away. " Ellis smiled in memory. "It was my father who changed my view of things. 'I'm pleased that they didn't want you. I'm much more satisfied with you than they would be.' In his own tactless way he made me realize that things happen for a reason. That my birth parents gave me away so my real parents could love me."

They stared at the pond in silence for a few moments. "I forgave them, not because they asked for it but because their decision gave me some really weird, but very loving parents. I forgave them because it was the best for me. It might have been the same for your mother."

"All right," he relented. "I guess you're saying that I shouldn't stop questioning my mother's sanity."

She nodded. "You might not want to forgive him, but you might want to think about letting some of your anger go. What type of man would you have been if your father had stuck around? Do you think you would have been any better?"

"I don't know." He shrugged. "Maybe."

She reached up on her tiptoes and pressed a kiss to his cheek. "I kind of like you the way you are."

"Such high praise." A smile formed on his lips.

She smiled back at him for a moment then sobered. "All I'm saying is that instead of focusing on how bad life was when he left, think about how good it's been since he's been gone." She wrinkled her nose adorably. "Did that make any sense? Or do I sound like a less charming version of Dr. Phil?"

"Yes and no to both." He gathered her into his arms, kissing the bridge of her nose. "You gave me something to think about."

"You don't have to listen to anything I said, you know. My family is just as dysfunctional as yours. My father's kind of autistic. My mother's a raging feminist and my sister is stuck in her teen years."

"What about you?"

"Me?" She looked up at him. "We both know I'm perfect."

"Of course. How could I forget?"

She burrowed into him as the breeze picked up. He felt better after talking to her and he wasn't sure why. Nothing had changed. He was no closer to forgiving his father than before but having someone to talk to eased the tightness in his chest.

"You should buy us apple cider doughnuts," she said after they'd spent long minutes huddled against each other.

"And a pie." He rubbed his hands over her back. "And some apple butter and maybe some juice."

"What about a pumpkin? We can't leave here without one of those."

"Of course not." He smiled at her child-like exuberance. "I think I saw pumpkin doughnuts in there, too. Should we get a few? And how about some ice cream?"

"And maybe after we eat all of that we can hire a contractor to widen my door because I won't be able to get out of it."

"I'll call around for some quotes." He winked at her as he pulled away. "Come on, Ellie. I think it's time we wandered back to the shop."

* * *

It was a long walk back to the orchard's storefront, but Ellis didn't mind. Being with a man like this was a new experience for her. Talking, joking, not feeling like everything she said or did was going to be judged was totally foreign to her. She was afraid to like it, to trust it, because it seemed too good to be true.

They walked through rows and rows of Granny Smiths, watching for mushy fallen apples. Mike had already stepped on one, smashing it against the sole of his shoe. He carried the smell of sweet overly ripened apples with him as they walked. Combined with his natural scent, it made Ellis want to eat him up. She thought that he would have taken her to bed yesterday, but he only gave her a kiss that ended too soon before he walked out. It left her feeling frustrated, confused, and a little unsure of herself. Why else would he come back if not for the sex? Friendship? Ellis disregarded that notion quickly. Mike wasn't the type of man who collected women friends. He wasn't the type of man who entered relationships, either. He was out to have fun with whomever he was with. Today they were having a good time but Ellis wasn't sure if she was the type of girl who was cut out for just having a good time.

Thoughts of sending him away entered her head. She'd made a few halfhearted tries the day before but she had little willpower when it came to him. She was going to have to resign herself to being with him until whatever heat they had fizzled out. Hopefully if she prepared herself their inevitable break would only be bittersweet.

The sounds of a child crying shook Ellis's thoughts. Ahead of them she spotted a little boy in a red hooded sweatshirt and denim jacket sobbing. Something in her heart twisted. He couldn't have been more than four, his sweet face fearful and innocent.

Letting go of Mike's hand, she carefully approached the child. "Hello, my name is Ellis. Are you okay?"

"No." The little boy's lower lip quivered. "I-I-I can't find her."

"Who?" Before Ellis realized what she was doing she picked up the boy and cuddled him close. "Who can't you find, sweetheart?"

"My mommy. I went to look at the red bird but when I turned around my mommy was gone." A fresh wave of tears streamed down his face.

"Oh, honey," she breathed, feeling sorry for the little blond child. "I'm sure we'll find her. Try not to worry." She looked toward Mike, who was studying her with a slight frown. "This is my friend Mike. He's a policeman. He'll help me make sure you get back to your mommy."

The boy stopped crying for a moment. "Do you have a gun?"

"Yikes, kid! Not at the moment." Mike shook his head. "What does your mother look like?"

The child's eyes watered again. "I don't know."

"Really, Mike," Ellis said smoothing a kiss over the child's wet cheek. "You expected him to give you a full description?" She patted his back. "What's your name, honey?"

"Jared." He rested his head on Ellis's shoulder. "You smell like animal crackers. I like animal crackers."

"So do I, Jared," Mike said, giving Ellis a wink. "Come on, let's head back to the store. I'm sure your mother will show up there soon."

Twenty minutes and two cider doughnuts later, Jared was reunited with his harried but relieved mother. She wasn't what Ellis expected when she walked up. The woman was a bombshell wrapped in a pink sweater and tight jeans. Long legs, thin body, breasts too well formed to be all natural, and once her child was safely back in her arms she eyed Mike like he was devil's food cake and she was on a diet.

"Thank you again for finding him," she said, placing her hand on Mike's bicep. "I turned around and he was gone. I'm so glad he found a police officer to take care of him."

"I didn't find the police officer, Mommy," Jared said, sounding annoyed. "Ellis found me and she bought me doughnuts."

Katie, Jared's mother, barely tossed Ellis a look. Ellis was used to being dismissed by women who thought they were more attractive. "Of course she did, sweetheart. I hope those doughnuts don't ruin your lunch."

Bitch.

"Sometimes a kid needs a little comfort food." Mike said, ruffling the boy's hair. "Speaking of lunch, I think it's time we got out of here." He glanced at Ellis and then back to the mother and child. "Don't lose your mom again, kid. You have to watch her. It's your job to keep an eye on her."

"Okay, Mike. Good-bye, Ellis."

"Good-bye, Jared."

Mike put his hand on the small of Ellis's back and led her from the store.

"I thought you didn't want kids."

"I don't." She looked at him, surprised by his accusatorial tone. "I would never lose the baby weight and God knows I don't need any more weight issues."

"Really? The way you were looking at that kid, I wasn't sure you were going to give him back."

There were moments when she felt a slight ticking of her biological clock, but she ignored it. All women felt that way around very cute small children.

"And the way his mother was looking at you I wasn't sure she was going to give you back."

"What?" He shook his head. "She wasn't giving me *the look.*"

"Oh, Mikey." She sighed. "Have you gotten so many looks from women that you don't notice them anymore? It must be a downfall of being super gorgeous."

"Super gorgeous, Ellis?" He gave her a smile that melted her insides. "Why, I had no idea you felt that way. What exactly about me do you find super?"

"Oh stuff it, Copper." She blushed, wishing she hadn't said that. She didn't want him to know that her feelings for him were growing. She didn't want to give him any clue as to how she felt. And though the day was wonderful she knew there wouldn't be many more days like it.

They walked back to the car, hands empty, both quietly lost in their own thoughts.

"We didn't buy anything." Ellis stopped. "How could we leave an apple orchard with no apples?"

Mike tsked and shook his head. "It's an abomination. We need a pie or at the very least some cider."

"On the way home we can stop for vanilla ice cream."

"And maybe some chicken potpies from Roma's?"

Ellis nodded. "And wine?"

"Absolutely." He smiled at her as he fished his wallet out of his pocket. "I'll call in an order. Get whatever you want from the store."

"Ah." Ellis grinned back him. "That is probably my most favorite phrase ever."

Mike watched Ellis skip away, the smile still on her face. She was happy today, and seeing that made him feel confident in his decision to pursue things with her. His brain warned him to take things slow but his body was screaming to take her to bed. He would take her to bed again. He just needed to wait a little while longer. He wanted her to trust him, which was odd for him. He never cared if a woman trusted him, but then again he'd never cared about a woman so much before.

"Detective?"

At the sound of his title he looked up to see Jared's mother coming toward him, minus her child.

"Don't tell me she lost him again."

He had to admit the kid was pretty cute, even though he spent the better part of half an hour crying. Mike had limited experience with children. He had a couple of nieces and nephews back in Buffalo but didn't see them often. When he did, he was always bearing Christmas presents, which made him a very popular uncle.

He didn't expect to see the look in Ellis's eyes when she picked up the boy. It was a little bit of longing. It made him wonder if all women had that look in their eyes when they held a small child or if, despite what Ellis had said, motherhood was in her future. She would be a good mother.

His chest suddenly grew heavy. He could picture her pregnant, and this time the thought of fatherhood didn't freak him out as much as it used to.

"Hi, Mike," Katie said, approaching. She flipped her hair over her shoulder and smiled at him. Her teeth were too white. He didn't trust her smile.

"Did you need something?"

"No." She rested her hand on his arm. "I just wanted to thank you again for finding my son."

"You should thank Ellis. I didn't find Jared. She did. I happened to be with her."

"Oh! Don't diminish your role. What you did was wonderful. You comforted my son."

"I really didn't—"

"I want to thank you properly." Her smile took on a predatory quality. "My mother is willing to watch Jared tonight." Katie slid her hand up Mike's arm, squeezing his bicep. "We can have drinks, maybe go back to your place for a nightcap."

Shit. Ellis was right. He smiled, wondering how much she would gloat when he told her. "I'm sorry, Katie, but I can't see you."

"Is tonight not a good time?" She pouted and ran her fingertips up his chest. "We can make it later in the week. Jared goes to his father's house Friday night. I'll have a whole week to prepare for us."

Mike removed her hand from his body. "I can't have drinks with you ever. Didn't you see I was with Ellis?"

"Her? You're with her? Like on a date?"

Mike frowned, not liking her tone. "It's more than a date. We're together."

"Really?" Katie shook her head. "But she's—she's . . ."

"What?"

"Fat."

"Don't," Mike warned. "Don't be a bitch just because you got turned down."

"I'm not being a bitch," she snapped. "I just couldn't fathom a man like you going out with somebody who looks like her. But now that I see what your taste level is like I'm glad I won't be wasting my time on you."

"Yeah? Even if I weren't with her, I wouldn't consider going out with a woman who's too self-involved to keep track of her kid. Do the world a favor. Don't have any more."

Katie stomped off. Mike watched her go, sad that she felt the need to put down somebody else to lift herself up. Shaking his head, he pulled out his phone to place the order he promised Ellis he would make.

Chapter Seventeen

Stupid Things I've Done to Look Skinnier

Plastic wrap around my belly, arms, thighs and ass.
(I felt like lunch meat.)
A corset over a girdle over two pairs of Spanx. (I felt like sausage.)
The lesson in all that: Learn to love the way you look.

"Why are you so quiet?" Mike asked Ellis. "Is something wrong?"

She was seated next to him on her couch, piping-hot chicken potpies in front of them. They had been back from the orchard for twenty minutes. As soon as they stepped inside her house Ellis excused herself to her room. She washed her face. Changed her clothes. Stalled so she could get herself together. She didn't want her mood to affect their day. She tried to keep the smile on her face. Tried not to wear her heart on her sleeve, but she knew she was failing miserably.

"I'm fine," she lied.

She had seen what transpired between Mike and Jared's mom. She heard the disbelief in the woman's voice when Mike told her that they were together. Saw Katie's thoughts even before she had said the words.

You're with her?

She should have been used to it by now. Every time they went out together, every time they passed a woman on a street they would get looks. Women who wondered how the hell she managed to get a guy like Mike or women who silently cheered her on.

Way to go, fat girl. You've got a cute boyfriend.

The confident Ellis wanted to shout them down. Of course Mike was with her. Why wouldn't he be? She was beautiful, too. But the insecure girl thought they were right, thought that Mike should be with somebody who looked the part. Somebody thin like her sister, like every other girl Mike had dated.

"You tired?" Mike put down his lunch and placed his hand on the back of her neck, slowly rubbing away the tension with his thumb. "Did not picking apples at the orchard take it out of you?"

She nodded, unable to speak for a moment.

"So, no five-mile hike in Wilbur Park tomorrow?"

"No." She wrapped her arms around him and buried her face in his neck. Her eyes were burning.

Knock it off. Be happy. Don't be a whiny fat girl.

"What's wrong, Ellie? I'm not used to you being so quiet." The concern in his voice was deep. "I don't like it."

"I'm fine. I promise."

He didn't believe her.

"If I asked any other woman that question she would blab for hours. Talk to me."

Stop it, damn it. Don't cry. Don't let some bimbo with a boob job and a tight sweater ruin your day.

He cupped her face in his hands and pulled it away from his body. His gentle concern made it worse. She couldn't look at him. She shut her eyes tightly to keep them from filling with water. She was sick of not feeling good enough.

He likes you. You like yourself. What's wrong with you?

She had blamed Jack for making her feel that way but

maybe she should shoulder some of the blame. Maybe her confidence wasn't what it ought to be.

"You haven't said a mean thing to me in hours." He pressed kisses to both of her cheeks. "I'm starting to think you don't like me anymore."

"You have ugly man feet," she managed.

"Thanks." He gave her a half smile, pushed her down on the couch, and pressed his lips to hers.

Her body sighed, with pleasure, with relief, as his came into contact with it.

Thank God.

Something was up with Ellis. Mike couldn't put his finger on it but he could tell by her expression that it was more than just sleepiness affecting her. It made his gut clench, made him want to make whatever it was that ailed her better.

Fix it for her.

He pushed her down on the couch, the overwhelming need to kiss her driving him. Her soft thighs came around his waist, welcoming him. He felt at home.

Shit.

He wasn't used to this. Caring so much. Wanting happiness for another more than he wanted it for himself. He hated the feeling, but more than that he hated not knowing how to fix something.

He wanted her to tell him what was wrong but Ellis wasn't in the mood for talking. Kissing. Yes. Lovemaking. Absolutely. Her body relaxed beneath his. He ran his hands up the back of her bare thighs, as a little part of his brain whispered that what he was doing wasn't right. But damn, it felt good.

He broke his kiss to study her face.

"Don't stop."

Lord knows he didn't want to. "We should talk."

"About what?" She lifted her head off the cushion to kiss him.

"Mmm," he moaned. "Stop that! We should talk about what's bothering you."

"The only thing that's bothering me is you not kissing me." She let out a frustrated sigh. "What's wrong with you anyway? What kind of man would rather talk than have sex?"

"What kind of woman would rather have sex than talk? Oh, and for the record I'd rather have sex." He rubbed his lower half against hers to prove his point. She smiled that naughty smile, and part of the tight ball in his stomach dissolved. "I want to know what's wrong with you."

She blinked at him. "Why do you care?"

"Why don't you understand how much I like you?"

She still didn't trust him, and as much as it bugged him he almost understood why. His track record, his past with her sister—none of that inspired much confidence, and for the first time in his life he realized that what he had was too good to give up. He was going to have to take things slow with her.

"Kiss me," she ordered.

He wanted to force her to answer him but instead he did as she asked, feeling her melt as he slid his tongue into her sweet mouth. Her hands slid up the back of his shirt, causing his skin to burn, causing him to want to peel off every inch of their clothing. Skin to skin. Body to body. The memory of their last time still hung in his mind. Just thinking about her made him hard. Knowing what she felt like around him made it impossible not to want to slide inside her and pump away until they both melted into oblivion. But it wasn't the right time. Not yet. He had to prove to her that she was different from the others. That he could be different with her.

"Mike," she panted when he broke the kiss.

He placed his hand between her thighs, inside her panties. She was wet. Wet and he hadn't touched her breasts, or stroked her nipples. He hadn't done much more than press his lips to hers.

He rubbed his thumb across her nub, causing her to shiver and smile and moan all in the same moment.

The way she looked when they made love made him want to memorize her face to capture the moment forever.

"You're so pretty, Ellie." His kissed her jawline, the smooth skin of her cheek, the tip of her nose. All while his hand worked to bring her pleasure. Her orgasm came mere moments later. The intensity of it left them both panting and him so turned on that he had to leave her. If he didn't he wouldn't be able to control himself.

She had that kind of effect on him.

"I have to go, honey." He watched the confusion, the hurt sweep across her face before he leaned in to kiss her. She would understand soon. He wasn't about to end things.

Chapter Eighteen

The Cracks That Kill

*As a girl who spends her days trying to help other
women look their best, there is something I simply
must say. Nobody, and I mean nobody, wants to see
the crack of your no-no space.
You have to realize it's out. Seriously? Don't you feel
all the air rushing down the great divide?*

"An unsolicited visit?" Phillipa said as Ellis stood at the
door of her parents' home. "What good deed did I per-
form to deserve this? Wait a minute." Her hand shot out to
check Ellis's temperature. "Are you sick? What's the matter? It's the time of year where you tend to get sick. Are
you congested? Constipated? I have cod liver oil in the
bathroom. That will work out whatever you got stuck up
there."

"Mother," Ellis groaned. "How do you manage to speak
so many words in such a short amount of time?"

"I'm talented." She ushered Ellis inside, kissing her
cheek as she did. "Tell Mommy why you came."

They sat together on the couch, Ellis muting the television as she did. "Daddy called me at work today and told
me to come for dinner."

"He did?" Phillipa frowned. "He didn't tell me that.
He tells me everything."

"I wanted to surprise you." Walter walked in wearing

a pumpkin-printed tie with a starched salmon-colored shirt. "I called Tomatillos and ordered you a cheese quesadilla, rice, and beans with no cilantro." He nodded. "You don't like cilantro. You said it tastes like soap."

"Thank you, darling, but I already started making my low-fat vegan macaroni and cheese. We've been eating out a lot lately, and I thought you would enjoy a home-cooked meal."

Ellis watched her father nod and walk away. She smiled. Her father only did that when he was about to say something that might hurt Phillipa's feelings.

"Mom," Ellis started gently. "Nobody likes your vegan macaroni and cheese. It's possibly one of the most awful things in creation. In fact, whoever invented it should be arrested for trying to pass off that goopy yellow sauce as *cheese*."

"Well damn, Ellis. Tell me how you really feel." Phillipa looked skyward as if praying for divine intervention.

"I was just saying what Daddy was thinking, but loves you too much to say."

"Yes." Phillipa smiled, looking at the door her husband had just left through. "He's a very sweet man."

Ellis watched the slightly dreamy expression that crossed her mother's face and swallowed the enormous lump in her throat. Phillipa loved her husband. Her genius, non-eye-contact-making, social disaster of a husband. And he loved her, too.

Mike's face flashed in Ellis's mind and left her wondering what love truly was. He'd walked out on her yesterday after kissing and comforting and bringing her exquisite pleasure. Watching him go made her feel like lightning had struck her chest. It was the first time in her life she was ever sorry to see a man go. She kept fighting with herself, warning herself not to let him get too close, that things with him were bound to end.

Enjoy him.

But don't give away your heart.

Only God knew how badly she wanted to do that.

"I'm glad you're here, sweetheart. It saves me from calling you tonight." Phillipa turned her body, placing her hands on Ellis's shoulder. "I have something to tell you."

Immediately a knot formed in Ellis's stomach. It was never good when her mother looked her in the eyes and took on her famous all-business expression.

"What is it, Mom?" Ellis began bracing herself for the worst.

"Your sister has met somebody," she said gravely.

"Jesus, Phillipa," Ellis swore, placing her hand over her still-beating heart. "You nearly caused me to wet myself."

"Well, I wanted to relay the news to you as dramatically as she related it to me." Phillipa waved her hand dismissively. "Dina says that she's not letting this one get away from her, that this guy is the one. Do you know how many times I have heard that phrase from your sister? I love her but she wouldn't know the right man for her if he snuck up behind her and goosed her."

Ellis tried not to frown at her mother's negative outlook on her sister's man-picking abilities. Ellis wanted to be hopeful for her big sis. If Dina found the right guy, then maybe Ellis wouldn't feel so enormously guilty about not telling Dina she was seeing Mike. "Don't be so quick to judge, Mom. What do we know about this man?"

"He's an actor. He does off-off-off-Broadway plays and has been an extra on some of New York's finest shows. I think he played dead body number two on *Law and Order* last year. They met in her modern dance class. He has a five-year-old son and still lives in his mother's basement. And she thinks he's the one? I think he is a disaster waiting to happen."

"Damn." Ellis sighed. "Okay, so he doesn't sound like a dreamboat, but maybe he's a decent guy." But even as Ellis said those words she knew he wouldn't be. Dina never picked decent. She picked charming and sexy. She picked poor and temporary. But this time it might be different.

"Mom?" Ellis bit her lip for a moment, not sure she wanted to open a can of worms. "Why haven't you told Dina that I was dating Mike?"

"Because you're in love with him, Ellie. That's something you need to tell your sister, not me."

Ellis nodded. There was no use fighting it anymore. She loved Mike Edwards. She wasn't falling anymore. She wasn't infatuated. She was very much in love and it took him walking away yesterday for her to realize that.

"Dina will hate that."

"Yeah, but things didn't work out between her and Mike and even under different circumstances they never would. She should be happy for you—and if she isn't, I'll have to take the blame, because I didn't raise her the way I should have."

"Mom . . ." Ellis leaned over to kiss her cheek. She was ridiculously close to tears again. "I might not have to say anything. I have no idea what's going on between me and Mike. You know him. He's not the relationship kind of guy and I probably shouldn't even entertain the idea of entering a relationship when I'm just getting my life in order. And then there's Jack. Doesn't it seem a little crazy to you that I could fall in love so quickly after such a bad breakup?"

"I don't think you ever really loved him, honey. Not the forever kind of love anyway. Once you really love somebody you can't let go of them so easily. You can't just move on with your life. Your father and I broke up for three months before we got married. I couldn't move on,

Ellis. I could date other men. I could even like them, but nobody ever came close to making me feel like your father did. Mike might be that man for you." She reached up to pinch Ellis's cheeks. "Mommy likes him. Plus he's so hot I get burned just looking at him. Tell me, daughter, is the sex as good as you thought it would be?"

"Mom!" Ellis blushed to the soles of her feet.

"Oh don't play coy with me, missy. Puzzle my ass! I would've called you out that day but your poor father was there and I didn't want him to know what you were up to." She looked skyward. "He actually thinks you and Mike are puzzle enthusiasts. He's talking about getting you one for Christmas."

"Yikes. Try to talk him out of it."

"Out of what?" Walter appeared through the kitchen door.

"Nothing, darling."

He nodded, deeming whatever they were talking about unimportant. "The food should be here in twenty-two minutes. When I called this afternoon I asked for it to be delivered at seven PM." He nodded again. "I would also like to discuss a new project the university wants me to lead over dinner."

"We'll talk about whatever you want, Walter," Phillipa said to him.

He disappeared through the door again.

"He's so weird," Phillipa muttered.

Ellis burst out laughing. "I always wondered if you thought that about him or if you were immune to it."

"Immune? How on earth could I be? We knew each other for a year before I could get him to look in my eyes."

"Then what about him made you fall?"

Phillipa shook her head. "I have no idea. He's an odd-ball, a nerd, and a Republican but I took one look at him and knew I had to spend my life with him. As un-feminist as that sounds, I just don't feel right when we aren't together."

Shit.

Ellis knew the feeling.

The doorbell sounded, causing both women to glance at the clock.

"We still have eighteen minutes," Ellis muttered, but she got up to answer the door.

"Hey, Elle." Mike leaned in, giving her a lingering kiss, and walked in. "You look pretty today."

Ellis stared at him, her mouth agape. What the hell was he doing here?

"I told you I was going to see you today," he said.

She realized she must have spoken aloud. "Yeah, but—but—"

He bent to kiss Phillipa's cheek before he turned around and grinned at her. "I called your father and asked him if we could all have dinner together."

"You did?"

"Yes." He shifted the bag he was holding from one arm to the other. "And since we are having Mexican I bought all the fixings for peach sangria."

"You voluntarily agreed to have dinner with my parents?"

"Yeah. Why is that so hard to believe?"

"Yes, Ellis," Phillipa added. "Why are you so surprised? You know I was Mike's all-time favorite professor. If I wasn't married to your father I'm positive Mike would have tried to date me. It's no wonder he's so fond of my offspring."

"Eww." Ellis crossed her eyes. "Say it ain't so, Mikey."

He shook his head. "It broke my heart when she told me she was happily married, but my spirits lifted when she said two single daughters."

"Perv," Ellis muttered. She had to bite her lip to keep from smiling.

Mike shrugged. "You can't blame a guy for going after what he wants." He winked at her. "Come help me make the sangria, Ellie."

She followed him through the kitchen door, watched him put the bag on the table, and then was swept into his arms. Her heart rate shot up as his lips came down on hers. It was a hard, heated kiss that made her tingle all over and confused her at the same time. Why the hell did he walk out on her yesterday and kiss her like that today?

"Mike," she whimpered.

"Hmm?" He kissed her hair, hugging her close. "I thought about you all day." He dropped his voice to a whisper. "Have I ever told you how much I like you in red? It does something to me." He slid his hand down her back, stopping on her behind.

"Stop it!"

Ellis and Mike jumped away from each other after hearing that voice. Her father was standing by the refrigerator, his face red, his mouth pressed into a thin line.

"Daddy . . ." Ellis wanted to die. Her face burned so hot she was sure it was going to melt off.

"I'm sorry, Walter. It's my fault. I didn't see you there."

"Are you committed to my daughter?"

"Dad!" Ellis looked from her father to Mike, panic filling her. He was never like this. Never so protective. "You don't have to answer that."

"Yes, you do." Walter narrowed his eyes. "Are you committed to my daughter?"

"Yes." Mike nodded, his neck growing red. She wished the floor would open up and swallow them. That a mythical creature would swoop down and pick up her father. She was used to her mother making a scene but not her father.

Are you there, God? It's me, Ellis. Again.

"Are you going to treat her kindly?" Ellis watched in amazement as her father lifted his eyes to Mike's and held his gaze. "I did not like Jack. He was very bad to her. He hurt her. I will not let you hurt my daughter. I will not tolerate it."

Mike nodded. "I'll be good to her, Mr. Garret. Hurting Ellis is the last thing I want to do."

She noticed that Mike didn't promise. He couldn't. Inevitably things between them were going to end. They both knew that.

"See, Daddy? Mike's a nice guy. You don't have to be so protective." She left Mike's side and hugged her father's stiff body. "But I'm glad you are."

"I love you," he said so quietly she almost missed it.

She blinked at him for a moment. "I love you, too."

He gently extracted himself from her. "Dinner will be in nine minutes. Please wash your hands." He nodded once more and walked out of the kitchen.

"Are you crying?" Mike grasped her arms.

She hadn't noticed the tears running down her cheeks until he pointed them out. "I guess I am."

"What's wrong?" He looked so bewildered, it caused her to smile.

"Nothing. My dad loves me."

Dinner started without incident. It arrived exactly at seven, which caused Walter to be very pleased. And after washing their hands as he asked, they congregated at the dining room table. Ellis couldn't help but get nervous butterflies in her stomach. Mike had planned this dinner. He wanted to be around her family. He was so unlike Jack, who'd never wanted to be around them. Only his own. And she knew Jack was serious about her. What did this mean for her and Mike?

"Tomatillos is the best Mexican restaurant in town," Walter announced in the middle of piling arroz con pollo on his plate. "Followed by The Aztec followed by Mojitos. I would like to talk about work now, if that's agreeable with everybody."

"Of course, sweetheart," Phillipa encouraged.

"I am having trouble understanding a new project the university wants to me head."

Ellis was prepared to mentally check out for the next ten or fifteen minutes. Her father's scientific talk was always way over her head; she'd learned early on that if she tried to follow it she was soon lost. She glanced at Mike, who looked genuinely interested in what Walter was saying. Or he was a great faker. She was fine with either one. He was also great to look at.

He wore an aqua-colored vee-neck sweater that made his eyes glow. She wondered what female in his life bought it for him. Men never picked out colorful things like that for themselves. Was it from his mother, one of his sisters, a former girlfriend? It wouldn't surprise her if it were. He probably had many gifts lining the insides of his closets.

"—if penis size is relative to body size or if it solely based on genetic makeup, or if it is a combination of things. It could purely be luck, too, but the scientist in me doesn't believe in genetic luck."

Ellis's mind snapped back to attention to when she heard the word *penis* come from her father's mouth. She expected her mother to be the source of outrageous dinner conversation, but apparently it was Walter's turn to act up.

The next moments seemed to go by in slow motion. Looking back, Ellis wished she could have stopped what was happening, but nothing beside an act of God could have changed the direction of the conversation.

"Michael, do you find your penis size proportional to your body size, and if not would you say it was above average or below average?"

Kill me now, Ellis prayed to a God who wasn't listening. *Oh please, kill me now. Kill me now. Kill me now.* She opened her eyes to look at a grinning Mike. "For the love of God don't answer him."

She looked to her mother for help, but all Phillipa did was shrug. "Actually, I'd like to know the answer to that question myself."

Ellis glared at her mother, wanting to smack her head in frustration. "Daddy, you cannot ask people, especially my boyfriend, about the size of his penis. You're not at work. We're eating dinner and you're embarrassing Mike and me."

Walter looked at Mike and frowned. "Mike doesn't look embarrassed."

He didn't. The goofball was laughing at her. At her! *Jackass!*

"I am aware that sometimes I don't understand social situations. Do you think this is an inappropriate topic of conversation?"

"Yes!"

"No," Mike chuckled. When Ellis glared at him he sobered a bit. "I think the conversation itself is fine but some people find scientific talk at the dinner table troubling for their digestion."

"So for future reference should I refrain from asking personal-anatomy-related questions during social and family gatherings?"

"Bingo." Mike smiled. "Who wants more sangria? I'm pouring."

Chapter Nineteen

Mike followed Ellis back to her house. He was a little nervous about what was to come tonight. It was almost like he was a teenager again, anticipating his first time with a girl. It clearly wasn't his first time, or even his first time with her, but it was the first time he was going to take the huge scary step toward having a real relationship with a woman.

Out of all the women he had been with, he knew in his gut that Ellis was the girl to go forward with.

When he wasn't around her he didn't feel right. He felt like he was just going through the motions. Why settle for feeling blasé when he could be happy with a beautiful girl? It made him wonder why he couldn't let himself fall in love with her. She was lovable, he realized that, but if things didn't work out, when things failed, because inevitably they did, he wanted to be able to pick himself up and go on like nothing happened. He knew it was selfish to not give 100 percent of himself to her. But his mother loved his father, gave more of herself than she had to give, and look where it got her.

"I'm sorry about tonight, Mikey," Ellis sighed once they entered her house.

"Don't apologize. I had a lot of fun tonight. And I asked for this. Remember?" He had. After leaving her yesterday he knew he had to do something to show her he wanted to stick around. Dinner with her parents was odd but it was no hardship. It made him miss being a part of a family.

"I have to apologize. First my father twists your arm into saying you're committed to me, which I'm not holding you to. Then he asks you how big your penis is. If he asked how our sex life was I was going to off myself right at the table. And my mother! She all but encouraged it. Why on earth did you ask to have dinner with them?"

"Because I wanted to be your boyfriend," he said seriously.

She gulped. "Wanted to? As in past tense? As in 'The dinner with your parents was so bad I no longer want to be your boyfriend'?"

He grabbed her hips and pulled him into her, smiling at her rambling. "As in you called me your boyfriend tonight in front of your parents. I think it's official now."

"Did I call you my boyfriend?" Her eyes widened. "Do you want to be my boyfriend?"

He nodded. "Did you think I would go through all this trouble for a girl I didn't want to be with?"

"Gee, I don't know." She pulled her lower lip between her teeth. "I'm a wreck. An emotional, financial wreck. You shouldn't want me as a girlfriend. You should get somebody more like you." She broke eye contact and fiddled with the collar of his shirt.

"What's more like me, honey?"

"You know." She bit on her lower lip so hard he was afraid she might break it.

"I don't."

"Someone who likes to jog."

He inhaled deeply, determined to be patient with her. "Do you expect me to base an entire relationship on one common interest? Besides, jogging is my alone time. Do you think I want some mouthy broad ruining that for me?"

She gave him a tiny smile before her worried expression returned.

"What else, Ellie?"

"Somebody who likes sports."

"Again, that's man time. No girls allowed." He patted her bottom. "You're losing this argument, baby."

"You should—" She paused, briefly making eye contact with him before returning her eyes to his neck. "—date somebody who's thin."

"What!" He wasn't the shallow asshole she thought he was. He loved her body and every soft curve she possessed. He was sick of her preconceived notions and was about to tell her so—until he saw the tears in her eyes.

He melted. No other woman had such an effect on him.

"I—I saw what happened between you and Jared's mother yesterday."

"So?" He was confused. "I'm not attracted to her, and even if I was I wouldn't even consider her when I'm with you."

" 'I never thought somebody like you would be with somebody like her.' "

The woman's words—he couldn't even remember her name now—came crashing back to him. She'd called Ellis fat. He didn't think it was much more than a cheap shot at the time but now he knew better. Now he understood how Ellis saw it.

"Somebody beautiful?" He kissed her forehead. "And smart?" His lips traveled down the bridge of her nose.

"And sweet?" He kissed her cheeks. "And sexy?" His mouth found hers. "And funny?"

"And fat. Don't forget fat." She smiled sadly and hugged him tightly. "I know you like my body but you're a total weirdo. When we walk down the street together women look at us. They're wondering how the hell I managed to snag you."

He didn't think that was true but he humored her. "Men look at us, too. Didn't you notice that guy in Roma's yesterday? If he looked at your ass one more time I was going to punch him."

"The one by the cooler?" She raised her brows. "Really? He was cute."

"Not the point." He frowned at her. "I've never dated a girl for more than two months in my adult life. But I want to keep seeing you. I want to be with you, Ellis. Stop trying to push me away."

"Fine. You win." She should feel happier. He was saying all the things that she wanted to hear, that any woman wanted to hear, and more important she believed him. He wanted to make this work, to give them a shot. Why was she so reluctant to take a chance on him? "Just promise me that when you're ready to bail you'll talk to me about it. Don't get all weird and mannish on me."

Don't be like Jack.

Her heart couldn't take it.

Anger flashed in his eyes, and she knew she had said the wrong thing. "Why do you assume it's me who'll bail? Why are you predicting the end of us before we begin?"

Because the end is coming, she didn't say. It was just a matter of time and as much as she wanted to trust him not to hurt her, she couldn't. She was in love with him and unless he loved her, too, they wouldn't work. "Why didn't you have sex with me yesterday?"

She changed the subject to a safer one. She didn't have the energy to argue with him. She wanted to enjoy him while she could.

"Because of this." He pulled a piece of paper out of his pocket. "I wanted you to be sure."

"Test results?" She frowned. "Negative for . . ." She read down the list, her heart rate slowing. "You got tested? For me?"

"For us." He looked bashful for a moment. "It bothered me when you told me that we were a mistake. But you were right. You don't know who I had been with. You're the only one I've never used . . ." He looked her helplessly at her for a moment. "I want you to trust me." He raked his fingers through his hair. "Say something."

BOOM.

"I'm going upstairs to get naked now." She headed toward the stairs, smiling at him over her shoulder. "Are you coming?"

The first time they made love that night was quick, hard, and explosive. It had been weeks since their last time. Weeks of pent-up sexual frustration to fuel them. She came twice before he did and he gave her that little cocky smile that she found both infuriating and adorable. The second time was slower, more leisurely. He took his time exploring her body with his mouth, kissing every exposed inch of her skin, licking her in her most sensitive places, till she was a quivering happy mess. And when he finally entered her, he experimented with rhythms and positions. He asked her what she liked, what she wanted from him, what he could do to make it better. It brought her to tears. She didn't know that sex like that existed. She didn't know that there were men on this earth who were made to please a woman.

"Are you okay, Ellie?"

He was propped on one elbow, looking down at her, his free hand stroking the hair from her face.

She shrugged. "I've been better." She was a bad liar, unable to stop the grin that spread across her face.

"When I saw the tears in your eyes I—I thought I had hurt you."

"No. No! Of course not." She raised his hand to her lips kissing his palm. "You were very good, so good that I'm thinking of renting you out."

"Really?" he grinned. "How much would you charge?"

She shook her head. "Can't tell you. It could affect your ego."

"It could?" He absently touched his fingertips to her nipple, causing it to pebble. "If it's anything less than a grand an hour I will be sorely disappointed."

She smiled at him. "The truth is that I don't like to share, so I guess I can't rent you out."

He gave her a gentle peck on the mouth. "I want you to do something for me."

"Anything."

"Tell your sister about us."

"Oh."

She nodded. They were no longer just sleeping together, just seeing each other on occasion. They were a couple now. Tonight made it official. It was only right that Dina should know. But telling her big sister was the last thing she wanted to do. She knew how Dina would take it. They were just starting to get along. This would undo everything—but Mike wasn't just some guy to her anymore. He was her boyfriend. She loved him. It shouldn't be a secret. But she still didn't want to do it.

"Give her more credit, baby. She'll be cool with this. It's not like you stole me from her."

"Okay, Mike," she said.

"We can do it together if you want. Ask her to come to lunch."

"No." The last thing Ellis wanted was to have Dina see her with Mike. This was something she was going to have to do alone. She would need to think of a gentle way of informing her sister that she was dating that once tore them apart. "I'll tell her, Mike. Please don't worry about it."

Chapter Twenty

Lactose Overload

I apologize for the short blog today, but I ate half a gallon of strawberry cheesecake ice cream and I've got a bad case of the sugar shakes. Please feel free to shame me in the comment section.

Ellis, Cherri and Belinda stood side by side in the storeroom, their heads tilted, staring at Ellis's work.

"Wow."

"It's breathtaking."

"You like it?" Ellis bit her lower lip and studied her work.

Karen's wedding dress was complete and it looked like a . . . wedding dress. A bona fide designer gown that you might pick out of any bridal salon. And it was pretty. Ellis was surprised with the outcome. She'd never thought she was capable of creating something so . . . complicated. Her chest swelled with pride. Making a wedding dress was a better high than selling clothes, for the simple reason that Karen would wear the dress on the day she started her new life with the man she loved. She would look back on it fondly. It would always mean something to her.

"I don't like it. I love it," Cherri gushed. "I want you to make mine."

"Yeah, Ellis," Belinda added. "I thought you were out of your mind when you told me you were going to make one, but it's gorgeous, and not Bitzy's Bridal gorgeous but Vera Wang Couture gorgeous."

Ellis's cheeks burned. "You're only saying that because I sign your paychecks."

"No." Cherri squeezed her hand. "We wouldn't lie to you. The five grand you're getting is what you deserve. I think you stumbled upon your calling."

"My calling?" Ellis blinked at Cherri. She thought owning Size Me Up was her calling—but it wasn't selling clothes that she was passionate about. It was altering them, redesigning them, seeing the looks on her customers' faces when she presented them with garments that were made just for them.

"Have you ever considered designing bridal wear?"

She shook her head. "Whoa. We're just getting on our feet with this place. I can't imagine taking on something else right now."

"But you're so good at this. Besides, you won't do it alone. We'll help you," Belinda said. "I'll take over the books, and my mother is great with a needle. She can come in a few times a week to help. She gets bored being at home all day."

"I could come in earlier," Cherri volunteered. "It's not busy in the mornings, so I could do some of my school-work here."

Ellis's throat tightened, slightly uncomfortable but infinitely touched by their offer. "You're both so sweet but I can't ask you to do that. I barely pay you enough as it is."

"You don't have to pay me any more, dummy," Belinda said. "I don't just want to be an employee; I want to be an investor. I was with you when you dreamed of opening this place. I want to be with you when you expand. I've got some money saved up. I think your work is amazing. I think we could go far with bridal."

"I'll be an investor, too," Cherri added. "I'm broke but

I'll invest my time and whatever else I can, so long as you promise to make my dress for free when my day comes."

Ellis stood absolutely still for a moment. This was too much. Too far beyond the scope of her dreams. "I cannot take your money, Belinda."

"Look at me, Ellis." Belinda motioned to herself. "Does it look like I am a person who would ever settle for being broke?"

"Huh?" Ellis rubbed her throbbing head.

"Listen to me carefully, honey. I'm not just giving you money. I'm investing, and I don't invest unless I know I'm going to get a return. I know I'll earn my money back plus loads more with your fingers on the needle."

"But I don't have anybody else who wants a dress. I don't even know if Karen will like this one."

"You know she will. And if there is a Karen out there, imagine how many women are out there like her. I mean, look at me. I have never been able to just buy clothes off the rack. You've had to alter nearly every item of clothing I own."

Ellis studied her best friend. Belinda was the curviest of the three, reminding her of every pinup girl and sexpot of the past. She was exotic and gorgeous with red hair and bronze skin and a way about her that made the world want to stop and look. But she was an outsider. Just like Ellis. Just like Cherri, who was nearly six feet tall. They had bonded because they had a hard time finding clothes that fit. From her blog followers alone she knew that there were many women out there like them. Who didn't fit in. And out of those women who didn't fit in, some of them had to be getting married.

Holy shit. This could work.

Belinda grabbed hold of Cherri's arm and headed for the door. "Just think about it."

They left her alone with the wedding dress and a head

full of thoughts. Mike's face flashed through her mind
again. She needed to talk about it with him, ask him how
he felt. Maybe when he came home tonight they could
make this big decision. The wheels in her mind stop turning with that thought.

They?

Home?

Ask Mike how he feels?

Why bother? As much as she valued his opinion, this
store was her baby and her dream. This was her life, and
she'd vowed never to let another man have a say in how
she lived it.

The bell over the front door sounded. Ellis paid little
attention to it as she tidied her work space, thinking one
of the girls had forgotten something. She yawned, trying
to stretch the exhaustion from her bones. All she wanted
to do when she got home was eat, take a hot shower, and
fall into bed, preferably with Mike. He'd waited for her to
get home every day this week. Sitting on her doorstep,
smiling when she pulled in. Every night they went to bed
together. Every morning they woke up in each other's
arms. And every day part of her wondered when the time
would come when he wasn't waiting for her to come home.

"Smelly Ellie?" Dina called from the front of the shop.

Ellis startled. *Dina?* Her sister had only been to the
shop once before it opened. She was the last person Ellis
expected to visit, the person she had been hoping to avoid.
Mike had asked her to tell Dina about them. She hadn't
yet. She was afraid. Afraid that Dina would blow up,
would hold a grudge, would sever ties. They were getting
close again. Mike Edwards had come between them once.
She couldn't bear for it to happen again.

"I'm in here, Dee."

Dina sauntered in in a pair of skintight leather pants,
motorcycle boots, and a gray leather jacket. She was abso-

lutely gorgeous with her mane of auburn hair flowing behind her.

"Going to a biker bar, dearest sister?"

"Concert in Albany. I just wanted to swing by the
'rents' house first. I'm a little short on funds this month."

Dina was always a little short on funds but Ellis held
her tongue. It was none of her business if her parents
wanted to give their thirty-four-year-old daughter money
every other week. Ellis had her own issues to deal with.

"So," Ellis said, changing the subject. "I heard you
have a new boyfriend."

Dina shrugged. "Yeah, he's out in the car. We finally
ditched the kid tonight. Hey, I like kids as much as the
next person but this one is so needy. He won't even go to
bed without Vigo tucking him in. He needs to grow up
already."

Now, isn't that the pot calling the kettle black?

Ellis suppressed an eye roll. "Isn't he five?"

"Yeah, but he's messing up my mojo. It's hard to get
intimate with a guy when he's always worried about his
kid."

The guy actually cared about his kid. Maybe he wasn't
so bad. And listening to Dina talk about him he seemed . . .
nice. Maybe it wasn't the guys Dina choose. Maybe it was
Dina.

"You should probably make an effort to get to know
his child, Dina. Mom said you were serious about him."

Dina gave a long sigh. "I was wrong. He's nice but he
lives in a basement apartment. And honestly he doesn't
ring my bell if you know what I mean. Now, Detective
Mike . . ." She sighed. "He had it all—a good job, no
kids, no criminal record. I wonder what he's up to."

Ellis said nothing, afraid she might give herself away.
Mike was right, she should tell Dina and let the consequences be what they were.

Tell her now!

I can't.

Chickenshit.

"I know. I know." Dina put her hands up in defense. "I need to move forward, not look back. I need to make choices for the me I am now, the me I think I should be."

"Your therapist is good, Dee. Worth every dime."

"He is." She leaned forward and pecked Ellis's cheek. "I gotta go. Call me later. We'll have a girls' night in."

"Okay," Ellis agreed, feeling guilty. They hadn't had a girls' night in years. They hadn't acted like sisters in years. "I'll call you tomorrow."

Dina left. Soon Ellis heard the door again. This time Mike appeared, scaring her half to death. Immediately she wondered if he had seen Dina.

"What the hell are you trying to do to me, Edwards? Give me a heart attack?"

"Sorry." He grinned, leaning his tall frame against the door and studying her.

She studied him, too, taking note of how good he looked in his dark suit, how his dark hair curled around his ears.

"You're here late tonight," he said after a moment. And even though there was no censure in his voice, her guard went up.

Toward the end Jack started wanting to know her whereabouts. He wanted times, and names of people she was with. He wanted details. Ellis balked at being controlled. The arguing started. Jack's criticisms grew harsher.

"Did you expect me to call you?"

"No." He shook his head. "I just worry about you after the robbery. I don't like it when you're alone in the store."

"Oh." She was at a loss for words. He wasn't Jack. She needed to stop expecting Mike to act like him. She needed to stop waiting for him to hurt her. "Do you know what's going on with my case?"

He closed the gap between them and stroked her cheek with his thumb. The bruise was long gone but the memory of that day stayed with her. She could still see her attacker's face, smell his overpowering cologne, feel the bite of his ring as it slashed her skin.

"They have nothing. I'm sorry." Mike sighed in frustration. "I thought he would have hit again but he's not as stupid as we hoped. I wish I was on the case. I don't like that the bastard's still out there."

"You shouldn't have kissed me that day. You'd be on the case right now."

"I had to kiss you." He shrugged and then gave her a little grin. "These are for you." He pulled a set of keys out of his jacket.

She stared at the shiny silver objects. "What . . ."

"The first one is to my front door. The second is my mailbox key."

She looked up at him.

UH-OH.

She wasn't prepared for this. Exchanging keys was a big step, one she wasn't sure they were ready for. "These are . . . for me?"

"No, they're for your parents so they can walk in on us again." He looked at her as if she were insane. "Of course they're for you!"

"I—I just wasn't expecting them."

"No shit." He grabbed her waist and pulled her into him, boring his beautiful eyes into hers. "I don't want you doubting us. Okay? This isn't a fling. This is real for me."

She fiddled with his tie, unable to look in his eyes any longer. The playboy was trying his hand at settling down and she wanted to believe it. Wanted to. She swallowed the golf-ball-sized lump in her throat. "I suppose you want a set of my keys, too?"

He nodded. "It's starting to get cold outside and I rather not freeze my ass off waiting for you to get home."

She rubbed against him. "But it's so much fun warming you up."

"Don't tempt me." He kissed her brow and set her away from him. "If you don't want to give me your keys right now it's okay, but when you're ready to . . ."

She nodded, not at all sure if she was making the right decision. "You can have the key I wrestled from my mother's hand."

"Good. Now get your purse and let's get out of here. I'm taking you out for dinner."

Mike watched Ellis from his seat on the couch. She was across the room with Belinda and Cherri, all three of them laughing at something. She was so different around her friends, so unguarded. He could see it in the way she threw her head back and laughed, the way she openly smiled at her friends. Things weren't always like this between them. She seemed surprised every time she came home and found him there. It made him feel like she waiting for him to screw up.

She didn't trust him. It wouldn't have bugged him so much if he didn't care about her. But he did. And there were times when he caught her looking at him, when her expression was soft and her shield down, that he thought she might be in love with him. He wasn't sure how he would handle it if she told him that. Women had told him that they loved him before. He was horrified the first time he heard it, wondering how the hell somebody could love him after such a short time. He wasn't looking to be loved by those women, but if Ellis loved him . . . it wouldn't be so bad if she loved him. He might like to be loved by her.

"Are you afraid she's going to vanish if you take your eyes off her?"

Colin sat beside him on Ellis's couch. It was Sunday, one of those rare days when they all had time off from work. Ellis had invited them over for dinner. They had drinks, played cards, talked for hours. It was comfortable. It wasn't his usual nightclubs and drunken nights but after years of that lifestyle Mike kind of liked this better.

"She looks good in green," he said, acknowledging his friend's comment.

"I'm guessing you'd say the same thing if she wore blue, orange, or yellow."

Mike shrugged. "What's your point?"

"You're more pleasant when you're getting some." He glanced at Mike before returning his gaze to the television. "You're not such a cranky arsehole."

"Fuck you," Mike said without heat. He liked this whole relationship thing.

"You think you can bear to be away from your sweetheart for a few days? Your birthday is coming up."

Mike raised a curious brow. "No Vegas. I left two thousand dollars, the contents of my stomach, and half my brain there last time we went."

Colin flashed him a wide grin. "I know," he sighed. "I stank of tequila for two weeks afterward. But that's not where I was thinking. A client of mine has a skybox in Pittsburgh. He was so pleased with the slot machine I restored that he gave me the box seats as a tip. Wanna go?"

Mike thought for a moment. It had been a long time since he and Colin had taken a trip. It was their tradition, but for the past few years it had been forgotten. "Ellis, can you come here for a second?"

She crossed the room, a slight smile on her face. She looked pretty with her hair around her shoulders and the sweater hugging her curves. He pulled her into his lap.

She let out a squeak but quickly settled, looping her arms around his neck.

"You must want something." She gave him a naughty grin. "Which means I get something in return." She looked at Colin. "What do you think I should ask for, Colin? An all-day trip to the Garment District? Oh! How about to the outlets?"

"Too small, love. Go bigger. I'm thinking diamonds."

"Tennis bracelet? Studs?" She shook her head. "We'll negotiate after you tell me what you want."

"There's a football game in Pittsburgh that I would like to go to."

"Go. Have fun. You don't have to ask my permission."

He was a little disappointed that she acquiesced so quickly. "It's next weekend."

"Okay." She blinked at him.

"That's my birthday weekend."

"I know. I'll just have to give your very special birthday present to somebody else." She got off his lap and lightly deposited herself on Colin's. She hugged his best friend, rubbing her nose against his cheek, teasing Mike with her naughty smile and gold-flecked eyes.

"How would you like Mike's present, Colin?"

Before Colin got the chance to respond, Mike tugged Ellis off him.

"What?" She feigned innocence. "I got you some thick socks. It gets cold here. " She kissed his cheek. "Your birthday is on a Monday. We can celebrate when you get back."

"You sure?"

She nodded and he almost believed her. But there was something off about her lately. There were things she was keeping from him. He would have to talk to her when everybody left. "I'm sure. Now let me go. I've got warm chocolate brownies and ice cream waiting. I'll bring you some."

They watched her walk away. Colin let out a low whistle. "Damn it, Edwards. Now I get why you're nuts about her. " He watched her hips sway. "I'd . . ."

Mike punched his best friend of fifteen years on the leg. Hard. "Watch it, Irish."

"Ouch! That hurt for fuck's sake." Colin rubbed his throbbing thigh. "I was giving you a compliment. I like her." His eye settled on Cherri for the moment. Mike followed his gaze, seeing her through his friend's eyes.

Cherri was a beautiful girl with long golden-blond hair that fell to the middle of her back and big bright green eyes. Her lush body was one that would be pleasing to any man. Plus she was sweet, and wholesome, always smiling, always polite. But she was just a girl, not even out of college, and yet Colin's eyes were feasting on her. It was a look he had never seen from his friend.

"She's only twenty-one."

"What?" Colin tore his gaze from Cherri.

"Cherri's a baby. She's only twenty-one."

"She's my sister's age. Bloody fucking hell," Colin cursed softly. "But I talked to her. She never told me she was twenty-one. She doesn't look twenty-one. She sure as hell doesn't act it!"

"She's not your type anyway," Mike pointed out. Colin liked worldlier women, with grace and elegance. Cherri was none of those things, and while she was sweet she was no match for Colin O'Connell.

"And Ellis is yours?" he said hotly.

Mike didn't respond, not wanting to get into it with his friend. It seemed Colin had a thing for Cherri, and Mike hoped for all their sakes that he stayed away from her.

Ellis stared at the pan of leftover brownies. She was supposed to be tidying the kitchen but she got distracted. Homemade. Fudgy. Chewy. Orgasmically delicious. All words she would use to describe them. She already had one brownie, a big one, with a side of vanilla ice cream. But she wanted another one.

Throw them out.

DON'T! What's wrong with you? There are starving children in Darfur.

Then send them the damn brownies.

A pair of strong male arms wrapped around her, distracting her from her nemesis. Warm lips found the back of her neck. She sighed. They were finally alone. With their friends gone their night could finally begin. Falling in bed with him was the best part of her day. It was right up there with sweets, shoes, and clothes.

"What are you doing?" Mike asked her, his voice low and seductive.

"I'm having an argument with myself."

She stared at the evil brownies. She had no willpower when it came to food or Mike. He was always bringing her sweets. Two days ago it was warm bread pudding. Today he made brownies. But he also took her on long walks. Sometimes he would put on Cuban music and dance with her until they were panting and laughing. Every night he made love to her until she was sweaty, out of breath, and exhausted. She moved more with him than she had her entire life. And there were moments with him when she was happier than she had ever been.

"What were you arguing with yourself about, Ellie?"

She picked up a brownie, breaking it in half before turning in his arms. She pushed a piece through his lips and then kissed him. Her tongue slid across his perfectly formed lower lip. "About whether I should dump you or not."

"What?" He looked alarmed for a moment.

"You make me eat too much junk food." She slid another piece of brownie into his mouth and then followed it up with another kiss, deeper this time, tasting chocolate and a little bit of ice cream. He was as yummy as he looked.

"Mmm." He cupped her face. "Stop that for a minute. I want to talk to you."

Her stomach knotted. "I don't like it when you want to talk instead of kiss."

"I wanted to make sure that it's really okay that I go to Pittsburgh."

"Of course it's okay," she lied. It wasn't really. She had made plans for them to have dinner in the city. But they could have dinner anytime. It seemed selfish of her to ask him to stay because of that. They had barely been together a month. He and Colin had been friends for fifteen years. She didn't want to be demanding. She knew what it was like to have a boyfriend who tried to limit her time with her friends. She wouldn't do that to Mike. "You spend your weekend how you want to. I'm not going to pout and moan every time you go away."

He studied her face for a moment. "What if I want you to?"

"You've got the wrong girlfriend for that, buddy."

He pulled away from her, and she had the feeling that he wasn't happy with her answer. "You're brutal for my ego."

Ellis shook her head. "I'm sorry, Mike, but why are you making such a big deal about this? Did you want me to tell you not to go? I'm not going to do that. We're in a relationship but our worlds don't revolve around each other."

He took another step away from her. "No?"

"No."

"What's it going to take for that to happen, Ellis?" Mike's voice grew quiet. His shoulders stiffened. "Ever since we started dating you've been acting weird. I can't tell if you want me to hang around or leave you the hell alone."

"You know I want to be with you."

"Do I?" His eyes flashed. "Belinda told me about your plans to start making wedding dresses. She told me you got two more orders yesterday. *More.* She thought I knew that you were expanding your business."

"Oh." Her heart stopped beating for a moment. "I—I . . ."

She had no retort for that. She didn't want to tell him that she'd kept that huge news to herself because she was desperately seeking a way to keep some of herself away from him. "I didn't think you would care that much."

"You didn't think I would care," he snapped. "Why not? I want success for you more than you want it for yourself. What kind of asshole do you think I am?"

She'd hurt him. The realization came as a sharp blow. "Mike . . ."

He put his hand up to stop her, his angry eyes burning her skin. "What's it going to take for you to trust me?"

She said nothing. She didn't know if she ever could. She'd learned the hard way that the only person she could always trust was herself. She didn't want to let her guard down only for him to step on her heart.

"Tell me, damn it. And don't you dare lie and tell me you do because I feel it here." He touched his chest.

"I don't know." She tried to push past him. She was in no mood to fight with him. She felt guilty for keeping the secret from him and angry that she had allowed him to become such a big part of her life in such a short time.

"You do know!" He grabbed her arm and swung her around to face him.

"Marriage!" she shouted. "Forever. For you to love me like my father loves my mother. That's when I'll trust you. But we both know that's never going to happen. We aren't ever going down that road."

He gaped at her. "You said you didn't want to get married. You don't want a family. Do you?"

"I don't know anymore," she said, but even as her lips formed the word she knew she was lying to them both. "I don't even know why we're fighting. You wanted to go to the football game and I want you to go."

"That's not why we're fighting and you know it." He grabbed his keys on the counter. "Good-bye, Ellis."

He walked away from her and her heart fell all the way to the soles of her shoes. What just happened? She was so afraid of him breaking her heart that she didn't take into consideration that he had one of his own.

Mike lay in bed that night, his arms pillowed behind his head. He felt like an idiot, like a dumb-ass, like a petty teenage girl. He should be rejoicing. She didn't want a serious commitment from him. Why was he pushing things? He had what he wanted. Her in his bed. In his life. She wasn't demanding. She didn't ask much of him. But he wanted her to. For the first time in his life he wanted to be more to someone.

It bothered him that she didn't trust him, that she thought so little of him that she kept her success away from him. He'd waited his entire adult life to find a woman he wanted more than sex from and she . . . Well, she was being how he always had been. Never allowing anybody to get close enough to leave a mark.

But then she shouted those words at him.

Marriage. Love me.

Was that what she really wanted? Could he do that? Could he love her? He wasn't sure he was capable of it. He thought his father loved his mother but he'd walked out on her. Could he be any better?

Maybe she was right. Maybe they were doomed from the start. Maybe he should let her go.

He heard the distant sounds of keys jangling. His complex was quiet, the walls thin. He often heard his neighbors' comings and goings, but the sound got louder. He heard the creak of the door, heels clicking softly on the hardwood floors. And then she was there, in the same green sweater she had on earlier, the light from the hallway illuminating her in the dark room.

"Ellis." He sat up, the sight of her causing his heart to slam into his rib cage.

She flicked the light switch and shut the door behind her. "Two things," she started, her voice shaky. "I want to be with you."

He nodded. He was wrong to blame her for being reasonable, but he wouldn't admit to that tonight. "And the second thing?"

"I'm not good at apologizing." She stripped off her sweater, revealing her nude-colored bra to him. He hardened. When she slid her jeans down her curvy hips it throbbed. "I should have told you about the dresses but you've got to cut me some slack." She lowered her voice as she unhooked her bra. Her nipples hardened as the air brushed them. "I don't know how to have a normal relationship. You've got to give me some time."

He watched mesmerized as she stripped off her panties. She was baring herself to him. He had seen her naked countless times, but not like this. The back of his throat burned with emotion.

"Come here," he choked.

She slowly walked toward him, her arms moving in an attempt to cover herself. He could feel more than see her self-consciousness. Didn't she know how much he loved her body? How much he craved the sight of her light brown nipples. The sight of her soft rounded belly, of the plump thighs that he loved to slide between.

She pulled the blanket off him and stared at his tented

boxer shorts. Tonight there would be no lighthearted love play, no easy smiles, no silly words. The anticipation of her touch on his body made him want to jump out of his skin.

"Lie back," she softly ordered. She reached for the waistband of his boxers. He lifted his hips as she tugged them off. It was one of those rare nights when he wasn't in the mood for foreplay. He wanted to pull her down and pump inside of her till she screamed. But she wasn't having any of that.

She knelt before him on the bed, her lips brushing his toes, then the tops of his feet.

"Ellie . . ."

"Hush." She kissed his ankles, his knees, his thighs, all while her hands stroked the length of his body. He reached for her, multiple times, but she pushed him away and kept kissing her sweet, nearly worshipping kisses. She cupped his balls and kissed each. She trailed her tongue over them, then up his shaft. He jerked, not sure if he could take any more of her exquisite torture.

"Please, baby. I need you now." He begged her. He never begged.

She shook her head and then took the whole length him into her hot, wet mouth. He groaned, gripping the sheets. This was different for him. He wasn't used to being on the passive side of lovemaking. He was always in charge, always directed lovemaking. Not tonight.

"Stop, Elle. I'm going to come."

Her sweet sucking didn't stop and he exploded. He was still breathless when she rose above him to kiss his chin before she moved to his neck and shoulders. More tender kisses. She climbed on top of him, and he sighed with pleasure.

He loved when she was on top. He loved to feel all of her soft weight pressing into him. Her smooth skin, the rasp of her nipples as they scraped his chest. He was getting hard again. She rubbed her mound against him, taking her pleasure while making him fully erect. It didn't take long. She was panting, her wetness seeping from her onto him. He couldn't take it anymore and grasped her hips, angling her toward his throbbing cock.

"No," she said firmly. "Let me do it." She gently took him in one hand and guided him slowly, inch by inch, until he was buried so deep inside of her he felt like they were one person.

"Ride me," he said in a ragged whisper.

She lifted herself, wiggled her hips, bore down on him once more—and then she hit her peak, her nails scrapping his arms as wave after wave of climax struck her.

He was greedy tonight. He barely let the waves die down before he took over, furiously pumping in and out her body while she lay breathless and moaning on top of him. *Sex isn't supposed to be like this*, he thought as her mouth met his.

It wasn't supposed to consume him.

He pushed inside of her harder, faster, ruthlessly. She bit down on his shoulder, dug her fingers into his skin, and then cried out. He felt her wetness squeeze around him and he lost all control. They came together this time. Hard.

It took a while for them to recover. Ellis had dropped into an exhausted slumber on top of him, her legs still spread across his hips. His cock still buried deep inside of her.

He kissed her forehead, twined his fingers through her hair, and drifted off to sleep. He wasn't ready to let her go. Not yet.

Chapter Twenty-one

"Is this about the water balloons?" the worried kid asked Mike.

The Durant Police Department had received multiple complaints about a roving band of teenagers. Some concerned citizens called them a gang. And he was a ballerina. They had yet to do anything illegal except loiter. However, the mayor's mailbox had been stolen and Mike and Lester had been assigned to the investigation. A stolen mailbox? Two detectives? Durant's tax dollars at work.

Mike sighed as he studied the fifteen-year-old suspect. The kid, Eric, who was reportedly the ringleader, looked more like a dopey Abercrombie model than a juvenile mastermind. Truthfully, nobody in town gave a shit about the stolen mailbox, but ever since the two robberies on St. Lucy Street, the mayor had taken on a zero-tolerance policy.

Ellis's robbery still ate at him. The more he thought about it, the more he wished he was still on the case. Two stores, two doors apart, both owned by women. There had to be a connection. Every day Mike studied the sketch Ellis had done of her attacker. If he ever caught the guy . . .

"Seriously!" Eric threw up his hand in frustration. "We were just going to throw them at some freshmen. Who told?"

"You did, jackass," Mike said, rolling his eyes skyward. "And if you're going to pelt underclassmen with water balloons, make sure there's only water in them and try to avoid their faces."

"We called you in for the mailbox," Lester informed him.

"Mailbox?" The kid blinked and looked from Mike to Lester. "Is that some kind of drug?" He put his hands up in defense. "Hey, I don't do any drugs. I'm on the lacrosse team and they randomly piss-test us."

Mike shook his head. He wasn't in Manhattan anymore. Despite the robberies, Durant was still a nice place to raise kids and he was glad to see that this kid was still innocent enough not to know about every drug on the planet.

"The mayor's mailbox, Eric." Lester grimaced. "Somebody stole it."

"You're shitting me." The kid grinned. "Somebody took that old blowhard's mailbox? Asshole had it coming. It's in the shape of an eagle."

Mike raised a brow at that comment. "An eagle?"

"Yeah," Eric said, laughing. "The dude is Captain Patriotic all of sudden. He's up for reelection next year. You should see the size of the American flag he's got hanging on his house."

"Ah," Mike said, nodding. "You can go now."

"I can go?" Eric blinked at him.

"Yeah." Mike got up from the table in the interviewing room.

"And I can still do the water balloon thing?"

"I'm not encouraging it. But if you do, try to hold off

till spring. It's too damn cold to be hit by a water balloon."

"All right." Eric flashed them a grin. "You guys aren't the stupid pigs people call you."

"Gee thanks. Now get the hell out."

Lester waited till Eric had disappeared before he turned to Mike. "You let him go quickly."

"The kid's a goof, but he's not a thief, and now that I know that it was an eagle-shaped mailbox I'm even less inclined to bust the kid who took it. Hell, I might have taken it if I saw it."

They left the small room and headed toward their desks.

"Nah." Lester shook his head. "I would like to see a turkey-shaped mailbox. Now, turkeys, those are some regal birds. They got all those feathers sticking out of their ass and they taste damn good with some gravy. You can't eat an eagle. Wouldn't want to eat them. They don't have enough meat on their bones. What the hell did they ever do for anybody? Majestic my hairy ass. Can't eat them. Can't shoot them. Whatever."

Mike laughed at his partner's musings. "Do you think about this kind of stuff on your days off?"

Lester shrugged. "My head wanders when my wife starts yammering about her clients at the salon. I can't tell her I don't give a shit if Mary Lou What's-Her-Face is having a hard time going through the change. So I have some Lester time and think about things."

"You're unstable."

"Michael."

He stopped short. His father stood beside his desk. Twenty years and Harry Edwards had barely changed. His hair was a little grayer around his temples, his eyes had a few more lines around them, but he was still the same man. And Mike felt like he was looking in some kind of fun-house mirror.

He pushed the sensation away and hardened his heart. "I told you I have nothing to say to you."

"Well, that's too damn bad. I need to talk to you and I won't leave until you hear me out." Mike stared at his father, taking note of his tone. It was the same tone he'd used when they were kids and he meant business.

"You okay, Mike?" Lester placed a supporting hand on Mike's shoulder. Mike glanced at his partner. Lester was a good man, a good father. He loved his kids. He'd never walk out on them. Bitter-tasting bile rose inside him. Harry Edwards had once been like Lester.

"Yeah. I'll be back in a few minutes."

"Okay, son." Lester squeezed his arm before returning to his desk.

Mike motioned toward the interrogation room they had just left. His father followed him silently. He tried not to think about all the missed baseball games. All the questions the other kids asked. *Where did your father go?* He had no idea. Twenty years gone. Twenty missed birthdays. All their graduations. His sisters' weddings. His grandkids' births.

Mike wasn't in the mood for explanations or a heartfelt talk. He only wanted to know one thing.

"Why now? Why did you come back now?"

"I'm sober," Harry said and the blow from that admission nearly knocked Mike on his ass. "And I'm rich."

"What?" Sober? Mike never saw his father drink more than the occasional beer. They were middle-class, went to church every Sunday. The boy he used to be thought that people like his father were immune to addiction but the man he was now knew that was wrong.

"I went to Mexico to get clean and started my own boating business." Mike wanted to look away from his father, unable to stomach the admission, but his father's gaze was powerful. He locked eyes with Mike's in a hold that was impossible to break. It was hard to look at his father, to hear him speak after such a long silence. "I contracted with the cruise ships to take the tourists on excursions. I made some money. I've earned respect and now I got something to offer you."

Offer him? All Mike had ever wanted from his father was time. "Don't gloss over the sober part. What the hell are you talking about? You weren't a drunk."

"No." Regret flashed in his eyes. "I was addicted to pills."

Mike shook his head. "I don't believe you." Mike had been his father's shadow. He would have noticed if his father was high.

"Remember when I hurt my back when you were eleven and I was laid up for about a month?" He waited for Mike's acknowledgment before he continued. "They gave me oxycodone, and when that didn't help they gave me something stronger. Pretty soon I was addicted and depressed. They wouldn't let me work on sites anymore and I was no good sitting behind a desk then." He took a step toward Mike. "I couldn't take coming home every night to you looking at me like I was some kind of hero when I knew I was nothing but scum. Remember that fifty dollars your grandmother sent you that you thought you lost? I took it. I—"

"Stop." Mike held his hand up. "I don't want to hear any more."

"But I've got so much to say, Mike. I love you. Leaving you was the hardest part."

"No." For some reason those words stung him more than anything else. "You're a fucking coward."

"Maybe I was but I'm back and I want to make amends."

"Make amends." He laughed without humor. "Is that one of your steps? Because you can take it and shove it up your ass."

"Mike. I know you're angry but—"

"Angry! You have no fucking idea who I am or how I feel. I don't want you back in my life. So go back to where you came from and leave me the hell alone."

Go see Mike.

Thoughts of him distracted Ellis as she sat across from her newest client. Ellis had done her research on bridal fashions in the short time since she'd started making them. She bought bridal magazines. She went to wedding trade shows. She watched every single episode of *Say Yes to the Dress*. And it was paying off. Audra, her latest bride, had come in as a referral with a big budget and even bigger wishes. Audra wanted to stuff her short, very rotund body into a fit-and-flare mermaid gown. No way in hell. It wasn't a surprise that she couldn't find a dress that looked good on her. Ellis had to explain to her, not so gently, that her body was completely wrong for that type of gown.

She had done three sketches before the woman picked one. They decided on beaded lace in pure white, with a three-foot train and a matching veil. Audra wanted a ball gown, of course, and she wanted it in two months. It was going to be a tremendous amount of work. Lace wasn't easy to work with and neither was this Manhattan bride, but she was offering to pay ten grand. Ten thousand dollars for one dress. Ellis couldn't believe someone would shell out that kind of cash for something she was only going to wear once. But she was glad for her client. That check alone could pay rent on the store for the next few months. Plus she was glad for the challenge. More than the money, the pride she would feel finishing the garment would be her reward. Every good review, every smiling bride, every tearful groom was money in her spiritual bank.

Check on Mike.

"Ellis," the bride's mother asked. "Do you think you could design my dress, too? It's a black-tie event. I don't know if we told you but we are holding it in the New York Public Library."

"Just like Carrie Bradshaw did in *Sex and the City*." Audra sighed.

They had told her at least half a dozen times. She got it. They were rich. Big deal. "How exciting, but I design for plus-sized and hard-to-fit women." She glanced at the slender Mother of the Bride and suppressed an eye roll. "You, Mrs. Landry, could walk into any store and buy a dress."

"Yes, dear, but I want *you* to design it for me. I saw that dress you did for Lydia Chase at our reunion. I never liked her in high school but even I had to admit she looked exquisite. Work with me, honey. I can help you make a name for yourself. You know we have contacts in the city."

Then why didn't you have one of them make a dress for your—oh who cares? Go see Mike.

The thought was nagging her, had been for the past half hour. She tried to ignore it but it kept at her. At first she thought it was because of the argument they'd had a few days ago. But things were fine between them. Her heart thumped faster as the thoughts of him circulated in her head. She had called him once already but his phone went straight to voice mail.

He's a cop. Cops can . . .

"Thank you for your offer but I'm focusing on my bridal designs at the moment and I want to stay true to my market. I want to design dresses for the women who have a hard time finding them."

"Say no more." Mrs. Landry put her elegant hands up in surrender. "I want my pumpkin's dress to be perfect. But think about expanding your market to include MOB dresses and bridesmaid gowns."

Mike. Mike. Mike.
I'm sure he's fine. Stop bugging me!

Go check.

"That's a great suggestion. I'm so sorry to cut this meeting short, but I have something very important to do."

She stood, unable to focus on the conversation because her breath was coming short. The more she thought about it, the more unsettled she felt. Calling wasn't enough. She couldn't settle for just hearing his voice. She needed to see him.

Ten minutes later she walked into the Durant Police Department to find Mike sitting at his desk. He was alive. She didn't know why she'd had the nagging feeling that he wasn't okay. It was odd. She'd never felt that way before, never felt such panic. She couldn't stop picturing him hurt.

"Ellis?" He turned. He must have sensed her. "What's wrong?" He stood up, unable to hide his concern. "What happened?"

"Nothing." She kissed both his cheeks half a dozen times as relief flooded her. He looked exhausted, and she wondered if the long nights of lovemaking were catching up to him. "Can you leave work early today?"

He raised his brows. "You need help at the store? I can get off a little bit early."

"No." She took his hand, needing to pull him closer. "I don't need help at the store. I meant, can you leave work now?"

"Right now?" He searched her face for a reason.

"Yes." She nodded. "Right now."

"For God's sake, Mike," Lester said. "What do you want her to do? Beg? Go with her. I've got you covered."

"Hi, Lester." Ellis blushed. She hadn't noticed Mike's partner sitting there. "Do you think you could bear to work without him for a few hours?"

Lester glanced at Mike. "If you don't go with her I will."

"Thanks." He nodded at Lester, grabbed his jacket, and took her away.

* * *

Ellis led him out of the police station, her fingers locked with his. He barely felt the chilly air on his skin because he was still so heated from the encounter he'd had.

My father is a drug addict. That thought kept pounding in his brain. A drug addict. How could he not have known? How could his mother not have told them such a huge thing? No wonder she could forgive. She knew. She knew for twenty years the reason behind her husband's departure and never breathed a word of it to any of them. He thought he was angry with his father and but his mother's lie was more like a betrayal.

Ellis lifted his hand to her mouth and pressed a kiss to the backs of his fingers. "What's wrong, Mikey?"

"Nothing. I'm just tired." He looked down at her. She wore dark denim, flat black shoes, and a blazer with a colorful scarf that made her eyes stand out even more than usual. "You're not wearing heels."

"I'm dressed to take a walk with my boyfriend."

She'd come down to the police station in the middle of the day when he knew she was swamped at work.

"I'm not complaining, but why did you pull me away from work today?" He forced his lips to curl into a smile. "You missed me that much?"

She nodded, which surprised him. He was expecting a sassy comment but all she did was look up at him and study his face. "You still mad at me?"

"No." He shook his head then wrapped his arm around her, pulling her close as they walked down the street. "You are hard to stay mad at. Where we walking to today? Want to head back to the pond? Or we could head to the other side of town and go to that tea shop you like? I won't even complain about drinking out of those ridiculous little cups."

"I'll go wherever you want, babe."

They walked along in silence for a few minutes, Mike feeling a bit better with each step they had taken away from the police station, from the place his father had spilled all his demons. He was glad she'd come.

Things had been better between them after their fight. Now she cautiously shared everything with him. She still didn't trust him completely. He could feel her holding a little piece of herself back. Mike wasn't sure if she ever would be able to give her all, but it was something he was going to have to live with if he wanted to be with her.

"Mike," she said, sighing in frustration, "something's wrong with you." She stopped walking and pulled him to one of the many benches that lined the streets of Durant. "I know this is going to sound crazy coming from me but I couldn't stop thinking about you for the last hour. I know something is wrong. I need you to tell me what it is."

He wasn't sure why he didn't want to tell her at first. He just knew he didn't want to keep thinking about his father. He didn't want to give him any more space in his head than he deserved.

"My father came to visit me today."

"Oh." She blinked. "Thank God. I thought you were going to tell me that you wanted a sex change."

"What? You're insane."

She shrugged. "I caught my last boyfriend in my apartment with another woman. You wanting a sex change is not such a big leap."

"Jack cheated on you?" That explained a lot. It gave him a glimpse into why she was the way she was sometimes.

"Jack did a lot of things. Tell me what happened today. I was worried about you."

He kissed her forehead, letting his lips linger on her cool skin. "Sometimes I think you like me even more than you let on."

"Yeah, yeah. Tell me what happened."

"My father says he left because he was a drug addict."

Her eyes widened, a little sadness filling them. "Did your mother know?"

"How could she not have known? They lived together, slept together. If you were on drugs I would know."

"You think so?" She gave him a curious look.

Of course he would. He knew her better than she thought. He knew when she was keeping something from him. "You think I don't know about the bag of Snickers you keep under the sink in the empty tissue box?"

"Son of a bitch," she cursed softly. "And I thought I was being sneaky about it. It's only for emergencies, you know."

"See? If I know about your secret candy stash, my mother had to know my father was abusing pills."

She wrinkled her nose at him. "You sound like you're mad at your mother."

He thought about it for a moment and realized he was. "She lied to us. For years we had no clue why he left."

"And if you'd known, would it have changed the way you felt about his leaving?"

"I—I . . . Yes. It would have. I wouldn't have wondered all those years."

"How do you tell your thirteen-year-old his father left because he was a drug addict? How does a kid process that? I might have thought that my father left because he chose the drugs over me. When the truth could have been that he left because he didn't want his addiction to ruin your life."

He was silent for a moment, once again amazed by the way she interpreted things. She made him think in a totally different way. "I still hate him," he grumbled. "And I'm mad at my mother for not telling me. I would have understood when I was older."

"Mikey," she said softly. "You barely understand now."

"Why can't you be on my side just once?" he pouted.

"I am on your side. I'm always on your side. I just don't like seeing you so hurt."

"I'm not hurt. I'm pissed off."

"Typical macho male response." She pecked his cheek. "You are hurt. You looked up to him. You trusted him, how could you not be? I'm not saying you should forgive him. But being pissed off for the rest of your life isn't going to get you anywhere. Talk to your mother. See what her take is on it and make sure you listen to her. Don't be mad at her, either. You have no idea what it was like for her. I've never met her but I know she did what she thought was best for you."

He leaned down to kiss her, cupping her cold cheeks in his hands so he could keep her closer longer. "I hate it when you expect me to be rational."

He knew he was going to have to have that conversation with his mother. But it would have to come a little later. He was in no mood to speak to her now or even think about his shaky relationship with his parents.

"What do you want to do now, Elle? We've got the rest of the day to ourselves."

She sighed. "I want to get warm cinnamon rolls from the bakery and then I want to go back to my place and have sex."

He grinned at her. "Cinnamon rolls and sex. I think I can suffer through that."

Chapter Twenty-two

A Few of My Favorite Things . . .

*Law and Order in any form. It's like an old
friend or your favorite pair of jeans, always
there for you. Spanx. (Enough said.)
Fun-sized candy. It makes me want to say
WHEEEEE!
And men with hard chests and dreamy smiles . . . le
sigh.*

Ellis had no idea what to get Mike for his birthday. She
even blogged about it, asking her followers what to shop
for. She got dozens of suggestions, but nothing that seemed
right for her boyfriend. As simple-minded as men were,
they were hard as hell to shop for. Mike was no exception.
He definitely wasn't Jack who lived for designer suits and
manscaping products. Mike didn't wear cologne or play
video games. He wasn't into cars. He liked football but
Colin had offered up box seats to a game so Ellis really
couldn't compete with that. She wanted to get him something special. Which was why she dragged Colin to the
mall with her.

She studied the beefy Irish hunk, who was more brother
than friend to Mike. He was scowling at a pair of cuff
links Ellis had asked to see.

"I take it you don't love them?"

"No, Ellis I don't." He ran both his hands through his dark brown locks. "I don't know why you dragged me here in the first place. I don't know nothing about shopping. I hate it."

"Then why did you agree to come with me?" She put her hands on her hips and stared him down. He either hated everything she picked or had no comment at all, which she found infuriating. They had been here two and a half hours without a single thing to show for it. "You didn't have to come. You could have said buy him some towels and hung up, but no, I've got to stand here and put up with your pissing and moaning . . ."

He grinned at her, his smile slightly crooked. "Oh shut it, lass. I came because you're the first girlfriend who has ever asked me to come, and you're the only one I think is going to make it for the long haul."

"Really?" She tilted her head and narrowed her eyes at him. "Exactly how many girlfriends has Detective Hot Pants had?"

"One. Only you."

"Colin!"

"I'm not stupid enough to fall into that trap. For fuck's sake, Ellis. Don't you realize what he did for you?"

She blinked at him. "No."

"He's asked your permission to go off with me. Don't you understand how huge that is? I'd cut of my bollocks before I'd ask a woman for permission to go anywhere. He's serious about you. I might be losing my best mate."

"You think so?" She got happy. It was wrong of her but everybody loved a little validation sometimes. "That sucks for you. So you basically accompanied me to see if I was up to par for your friend?"

"Yup."

"And?" She batted her lashes at him.

"You're a world-class ball buster with a big mouth but that only makes you hotter in my book."

"Oh Colin." She threw her arms around him and loudly kissed his cheek. "You're a big help."

"What?" He shook his head when she released him. "But you still haven't gotten him a present."

"Right. Shit." She sighed. "What should I get him? Custom bowling ball? Flask? Gold-plated handcuffs? Give me a clue."

"I've known Mike for fifteen years and the only thing I can tell you about him is that he likes good food, sex, and sports."

"So a Yankees jersey?"

"Yeah, just make sure you're in it with nothing on underneath it. Or we can go lingerie shopping." He looked her up and down. "I'm sure he would appreciate that."

"You're a perv," she shot back, but secretly thought that wasn't a bad idea. Maybe she would get Cherri to come back with her later. The girl was innocent but Belinda was on vacation and Ellis would need another set of eyes. "Come on, Irish. I'll buy you a giant pretzel for being such a good boy."

On their way to the food court they passed workers putting up Christmas decorations. Halloween had barely passed. Sigh. Thanksgiving was coming up shortly. She and Mike hadn't discussed what their plans would be. Truthfully, she was afraid to bring it up. Even though Colin had told her that Mike was serious, her constant companion, doubt, lingered in the back of her mind. Would he want to spend it with her family? Would he rather go home to his?

"Ellison?"

Shit. Not again.

Agatha Toomey stood in front of the GNC, her skinny

hand clutching a bottle of supplements. Ellis should have known she hadn't seen the last of this woman. Durant was a small city. They were bound to run into each other from time to time.

"Oh, hello. Nice to see you, Mrs. Toomey. Hope you have a good holiday." Ellis thought she could be slick and walk past but Agatha's other bony hand shot out and grasped her arm.

"Wait." The exercise freak was strong and stopped Ellis in her tracks. Colin stopped, too, and gave her a curious look. "I spoke to Jack and he told me I should apologize for coming to your shop. He thinks I'm making things worse."

"Trust me, you aren't," Ellis said but Agatha continued on as if she hadn't heard a thing.

"It's just that my sister died so young. I'm like a mother to him and I want to see my Jacky happy and settled."

"I'm sure he'll find a nice girl." She released herself from the woman's grasp. "I have to go."

Agatha leveled her gray gaze at Ellis. "He only wants you." She gave Ellis's body a thorough once-over. "Even if you keep packing on the pounds."

Still a bitch.

"Well, that's a shame because I've moved on. It's been months. Jack needs to move on, too."

Agatha looked to Colin and her normally sour expression turned into a scowl. "I see you moved on again. What happened to the last guy, Ellison? Did he get tired of going to bed with an overweight big-mouth or are you just being the tramp I always thought you were?"

Colin opened his mouth to defend her but Ellis quickly cut him off. "Tramp?" Ellis used her stature to force the woman to take a couple of steps backward. "If I'm such a tramp why did you fix me up with your precious nephew in the first place?"

"Because," she sneered. "I was friends with your mother and she was always complaining about how she thought you were never going to meet a nice guy. I knew my Jacky was lonely but I never thought he would go for you. I thought you would put out and move on. I had no idea you would sink your claws in him. You ruined him for other women and now you throw your horrible behavior in his face by parading around town with multiple men dressed like a slut."

"Slut?" She took another step forward, knocking Agatha into a wall and causing her eyes to indignantly bug from her head. "Your nephew degraded me. He tried to control me. He brought another woman into my home just to hurt me. And you have the nerve to call me a slut? Well guess what, you rat-faced, unstable bitch. I don't care what you think and next time you call me something that isn't my name, I'm kicking your underfed ass. And my boyfriend is a cop so you won't get help from the DPD. I'm done being nice." She poked Agatha in the shoulder, and the women gulped. "You better avoid me like the plague next time you see me or it won't be pretty. And one more thing, stop obsessing over your nephew. It's getting creepy."

Ellis straightened and Agatha took the opportunity to scamper to her left. "I'm glad the guy slapped you around when you got robbed. It was exactly what you deserved for messing with my family."

Ellis took a step toward the woman. She fled without saying another word.

"Bloody fucking hell," Colin cursed.

She exhaled, her skin feeling hot, but her soul feeling soothed. "I'm sorry you had to see me act like that. It wasn't pretty."

"No, love, it was the sexiest thing I have ever seen."

"Shut up, Colin!"

"No." He linked arms with her and led her off once again. "I've gotten a wee bit excited. Your boyfriend will probably bash my head in when I tell him. I think you're my dream girl. I could take you back to Ireland and not worry about you in a bar fight."

Colin was due to pick him up any minute for their trip to Pittsburgh. He was looking forward to this trip, but part of him wanted to stay home. When they were younger they used to tear up the town. Somehow on every birthday trip he managed to be single; both of them had. If only for a little while. It was their excuse to talk to the women who flocked to nightclubs in skimpy, usually shiny outfits. Women who drank too much and could twist their bodies in pretzel-like positions. It would be different this time. Thirty-three, and now Mike was the one thinking he was too old for that shit. However, Colin was still single, and Mike wondered if he would still want to carouse like they used to. Maybe not. Lately he had been more into trivia nights than techno beats. Hopefully they would have an uneventful trip.

He watched as Ellis rummaged through his refrigerator, her beautifully rounded backside distracting him from his thoughts. He wasn't sure he wanted to leave her this weekend. It wasn't just the sex he would miss, but her. He used to get that itchy, jumpy feeling, and he'd know it was time to move on to another woman. It hadn't happened with Ellis yet and he wondered how long it would take for that time to come. Or if it ever would.

"You want pickles on your sandwiches, Mike?"

"No," he answered absently.

Ellis was going to stay at his place while he was gone. Her landlord was redoing their floors. That thought shook him. Somewhere along the way he'd started to think about her place as home. He swallowed. When had he stopped thinking in terms of *I and me* and started thinking in *us and we*?

"I made you some cookies to take with you," she said, straightening up. "They're still warm. Of course, I ate half of them already but there's still plenty for you and Colin."

She pulled the soft cooler she had purchased out of the plastic bag and began to pack it with the massive quantities of food she'd prepared. A whole roasted chicken, sandwiches, cookies, snack cakes, soda, and beer. He walked up behind and wrapped his arms around her as she poured coffee into a thermos.

"You know they sell food in Pittsburgh, Ellie. You didn't have to go through all this trouble."

"It's your birthday. I want to do this for you." She screwed the top on his thermos and turned in his arms. He held her for a moment, inhaling her soft vanilla scent.

"Come with us," he said without thinking.

She laughed, her whole face lighting up. "Thank you but I'd rather have my mother give me a bikini wax."

"I thought you liked football. You watch it every Sunday with me."

"I hate it. A lot. Really. Freaking. Hate. It."

"What?" he asked, amazed. She always sat pressed against him, asking all the right questions, never bothering him when the game got intense.

She shrugged. "I like you."

A rush of warm, unmanly feelings came over him, and he squeezed her against him. He didn't want to leave her. "Maybe I can stay home. I'm sure Colin can find somebody else to go with him."

"No, Mike." She shook her head firmly. "You are going to this game with Colin. We talked about it."

I'll miss you, he stopped himself from saying. Damn, he felt like a girl. He must have it bad for her. Those thoughts had never entered his mind before. "Why didn't you tell me about your run-in with your ex's aunt?"

She growled, cutely, but it was still a growl. "Colin has such a big freaking mouth." She looked up at him, her eyes wide. "Listen, Mike. I didn't tell you because I didn't want you to get all psycho-cop on me and show up at her house. This isn't like the thing with my business. I'm trusting you. Okay? It's hard for me but I'm doing it."

She was. He had to give her credit for it. He couldn't complain. "You sure? What if some hot girl hits on me in Pittsburgh?"

"I'm sure you'll do the right thing. If not I'll castrate you."

He winced. "I believe you. Colin told me how you got up in that starving lady's face." He scowled. "He also told me how sexy you were and that he had to keep reminding himself that you were my girlfriend."

"Really?" She blushed. "I would date him if you weren't in the way."

"Over my dead body."

"For fuck's sake, Edwards. Get your hands off the girl and get in the car." Colin stood behind them tapping his foot like an old fisherman's wife. They hadn't heard him come in.

"Hold your goddamn water."

"Hi, Colin," Ellis said, beaming. "I packed some snacks for you. I even got some Guinness."

"Ah, love. Thank you." He looked back to Mike. "I'll be in the car. Kiss her and let's go." He was out the door after that.

"Good-bye, Elle. I'll see you Monday." He tilted her head back and gave her a very long, sweet kiss. "We'll celebrate my birthday when I get back." He let her go and hardened his expression. "Oh, and stay out of my night-stand."

He walked out the door wondering how long it would take her to look.

It took her twenty-seven minutes before she peeked in the drawer. She was supposed to trust him, respect his privacy, but her curiosity beat out her conscience. She sat on the side of his bed staring at the closed drawer. At best she expected to find porn. At worst a drawer of women's underwear in *his* size. What she found was entirely unexpected and supremely lovely. Sitting on top of some hardcover books were a dozen yellow roses and a heart-shaped locket.

"Damn him." She teared up. The brat in her wanted to close the drawer and pretend like she'd followed his order, but she couldn't. She put on the locket, found a vase for the flowers, and called her boyfriend to thank him.

"It's barely been half an hour," Mike said into his phone. "I thought you would have made it at least an hour." He ignored Colin's grumblings about his manhood and listened while Ellis thanked him and promised him that she would gladly show her appreciation when he got home. It was almost enough to make him want to tell Colin to turn the car around.

Eventually he hung up and glanced at Colin, whose eyes were focused on the road. "Sorry," he muttered.

Colin shrugged. "I like her so it's okay. I never thought I would live to see the day when you fell in love."

"What?" That comment shook him to his core. "I'm not in love with her."

Colin snorted. "The hell you aren't. You're with her all the time. You look at her like you want to eat her and you get this goofy look on your face whenever she's around. If you're not in love then I'm bloody English."

"Nah." He shook his head. "I really like her. That's

all." He couldn't be in love. He wasn't capable of such deep feelings. It was impossible. He had promised himself years ago that it would never happen to him. Sure, the thought of her with somebody else killed him, but that was normal. Wasn't it? So was wanting to be with her all the time. Right? He couldn't love her, because if he did it meant that if she walked away it would destroy him. He wasn't going to let any woman fuck with his head like that. It wasn't going to be like it had been with his father and his mother.

But now that he knew the truth behind his parents' breakup, behind his father's leaving, that argument didn't seem to hold up anymore.

Marriage. Love me. The nasty fight they had a week ago came back to him. He had asked for her trust and she told him exactly how to earn it.

But love? He couldn't let himself think about her walking away. Somehow she got in there and lodged herself in his chest. She made him feel right. *Shit.* This was his fault. He asked for this. He pushed for them to be together. He forced her to let him in when all she wanted from him was . . . she never wanted anything from him. She tried to push him away.

"Shit." He did love her. He loved her more than he could handle. How the hell did it sneak up on him like that?

He wasn't supposed to fall in love. He was only supposed to be in Durant for a little while, until he figured out what he wanted to do with his life. He still didn't know. In fact he hadn't thought about it very much until the moment he started things up with her.

"It's okay, Edwards. You're in love. It happens to the best of us."

But never to him.

"If I were you I would put a ring on her finger and a baby in her belly as soon as possible."

Forever? No. Children? A life that was no longer his own? No. No! That was not the life that he wanted. Was it?

He didn't know anymore. He still needed to figure himself out. He was in love for the first time in his life. So why the hell did he feel like there was a vise grip on his chest?

"Can you pass me the ice cream, please?" Cherri asked Ellis.

"Only if you pass me the chips." Ellis picked up the pint of Chubby Hubby and passed it over as she received a bag of barbeque Popchips.

"Are you sure your boyfriend is going to be okay with us eating this junk-food feast in his bed?" Belinda said as dumped a handful of chips in her lap and reached for the bag of Peanut M&M's.

Ellis had been a tiny bit lonely without Mike these past two days, so she'd invited the girls over for a pig-out sleepover to help take her mind off missing him.

Your sister wanted to do this with you.

Guilty thoughts bugged her at the most inconvenient times.

She should have invited her sister but she couldn't. Not here. Ellis still hadn't gotten up the nerve to tell Dina about Mike, even though things seemed to be getting serious between them. She was letting herself trust him. She finally decided to stop waiting for him to hurt her. It was time to tell her sister.

Tomorrow I'll stop being a chickenshit.

"We eat in bed all the time," Ellis said between bites.

"Really?" Cherri raised one of her dark golden brows. "What else do you do in bed?"

"Yeah, Ellis." Belinda gave her a teasing smile. "How's Mike in bed? You've been very close mouthed about him."

"You've seen him." Ellis raised her nose, like she was

queen of the world. "I don't think I have to say much about him."

"He is hot," Belinda agreed

"You think he's the one," Cherri asked.

Ellis didn't want to answer that question. She had never been in love like this before. But *The One*? That was a phrase her sister threw around. She didn't see marriage for them. She didn't think about it, didn't want to expect the impossible. They both had been so against it before. She may want it now but she couldn't expect him to get on bended knee just because she had softened. She couldn't expect him to tell her he loved her even though she was starting to believe he did. Mike Edwards wasn't that kind of man.

"We're not getting married," she said, trying to shrug off the heaviness that covered her heart. "Hey, did you guys see *Housewives* this week? That Teresa needs to take a pill."

"You're right, she does." Belinda frowned. "Now let's get back to Mike. Are you in love with him?"

"You've seen him," she sighed. "What do you think?"

"Have you told him?" Cherri poked her in the arm, her face alight with excitement.

"Of course not! He would know then."

"Wait?" Cherri frowned. "You don't want him to know?"

"Oh sweet, innocent Cherri," Belinda started. "You never tell a man like Mike that you love him first."

"Why not?"

"It's simple." Belinda told her. "He'll freak out."

The phone rang just after eight PM Sunday night. Ellis reached for it, hoping it was Mike again. She had spoken to him earlier that day when the game was just ending. She could hear the roar of the exiting crowd in the background, and despite the noise she could hear something in his voice that wasn't right. She hoped it was exhaustion or strain from screaming for his team but something inside her told her it wasn't that. He sounded like he was holding back something. They had joked about women hitting on him. She had laughed then, but the comment jarred her slightly. He was a good guy. She needed to trust him. Maybe her mind was playing tricks on her and it was nothing. Or maybe he really was just tired. She needed to hear from him again to confirm.

"Hello?" she said cheerfully.

"Well, don't you sound excited for a Sunday evening."

It wasn't Mike. Her stomach and her heart sank a little. "I'm the best telephone answerer in the tricounty area," she said, trying to keep the brightness in her voice. The speaker on the other end was female and Ellis was afraid to find out who she was. "Mike is not here right now. I am taking his messages."

"Hello, Ellis," the voice on the other end said. "I am Michael's mother. I hear you're his girlfriend."

"Yes," she swallowed. *Damn.* "If he told you about us then it must be true."

"He did. What he didn't tell me is that he wasn't going to be home this Sunday. Where is my child tonight?"

"Pittsburgh. With Colin." Ellis bit down on her lower lip. He hadn't told her. That seemed right. He was upset with her about his father. Ellis wished Mrs. Edwards hadn't called. It was hard enough to speak with a boyfriend's mother. It was much harder when said boyfriend was holding a grudge. "Oh, I thought he mentioned Colin was taking him for his birthday."

"Ah," she said softly. "Colin did mention it a few weeks ago. I thought Mike would have told me. He always lets me know when he is going to be away for my calls. I think my son might be angry with me."

"Um-uh, what's makes you say that?" Ellis's voice grew unnaturally high.

"His father called and told me about their last meeting."

Shit.

"Please don't talk to me about this," Ellis said in a rush. "I don't even know you. I really can't get involved in this heavy family stuff. It gives me angina."

"Okay, honey." Margie chuckled. "I won't. Mike did say you were adorable."

"He said that?" She wrinkled her nose. "Adorable? It kind of makes me sound like a puppy. Don't you think?"

"Colin said you looked like a young Sophia Loren."

"Oh, Colin." She sighed. "Such a big stinking liar, but I'm beginning to think I should dump your son for him."

"That is one hell of a compliment, but I knew if my son was dating you then you had to be beautiful."

"I'm also a little fat and not that annoying skinny-girl-who-thinks-she's-fat, fat. But the I've-got-a-teen-in-my-size kind of fat. Did he tell you that? I'm the first chubster he's dated." She smiled. "He's so sweet about it. He gets mad at me when I call myself fat. But I'm not putting myself down. I like the way I look. I'm simply stating facts. Like the sky is blue. I have a big ass. Grass is green and Ellis likes cupcakes." She sighed. "And here I am rambling to my boyfriend's mom, like an idiot. I wish you would have stopped me."

"Don't worry about it, sweetheart." She was quiet for a moment. "He needs to be loved, Ellis. Can you do that?"

The question, phrased like that, shook her. She didn't know how to answer except to tell the truth. "I love him," she said aloud for the first time. "Very much, but please don't tell him that."

"I won't. Now tell me a little about yourself."

They ended up talking for two hours. By the end of

their conversation Ellis had a new respect for Margie Edwards.

Mike crawled into bed with Ellis after two AM. They hadn't planned to leave Pittsburgh until morning but Mike asked Colin if wouldn't mind getting back a little early. The game had been fun, the seats incredible, the hotel nice, but he couldn't let himself fully enjoy his weekend. His mind wandered to Ellis. He was in love with her and he didn't want to be.

When Mike crawled into bed with her his heart stopped its irregular beating. His breathing slowed, and for the first time in two days he felt normal. It was the scariest feeling in the world.

"My boyfriend's back," she said sleepily. "That or there's a burglar who smells really yummy." She placed her hand on his scruffy cheek. "I'll take either one at this point."

"Hello, Ellie. I missed you."

"You had better say that." She slid closer, looping her arms around him. "The next thing you should say is that you bought me a present."

He swallowed hard, the panicky feeling surging. "I did." He kissed her. She tasted like sleepy warmth, like home.

She broke away after a moment, her eyes straining to see him in the dark. "What's wrong?"

He was silent, while his mind screamed: *I don't want to love you this much. I'm not sure I can handle it.*

"I want to make love to you now." He kissed her forehead, her eyelids, the tip of her nose. "Can I?"

"Of course," she whispered.

He covered her body with his, all the while wondering how he was going to put a stop to this intense love feeling.

Chapter Twenty-three

Everybody Loves a Happily Ever After . . .

It's the reason we love romance novels. We read those lovely little epilogues and usually find the hero and heroine married with a couple of kids or a baby on the way and everybody is happy. Of course real life isn't so neat but it still got me wondering about real Happily Ever Afters. I believe that people do achieve them. But are Happily Ever Afters the same for everybody?

Ellis watched Mike enter her office and for the first time since they had met her heart didn't leap with excitement upon seeing him. It had been five days since she'd laid eyes on him. There had been some communication, phones calls on the first day, texts on the second, but silence from then on. That wasn't like him.

Ellis had known something was wrong the day he came back and nothing felt right or good or the same. They celebrated his birthday Monday by going to a nice restaurant in town. He said very little during dinner while she went on and on rambling about whatever topic came to mind. It was the first time they shared no smiles, no easy conversation. It reminded her of her last few months with Jack. She hated herself for the comparison but that's what it felt like.

When she asked him what was wrong he claimed he

was tired. When she tried to leave him alone to rest he pulled her into bed and took her body but there was no love in their lovemaking.

The day he left for Pittsburgh she'd felt so hopeful, so in love. She was learning to trust him, to let her guard down. For once she was allowing herself to see him in her future.

It was the biggest mistake of her life.

"Hey," he said softly.

"Hey," she responded.

She wouldn't look at him and Mike knew he was in trouble. He knew he had hurt her with his silence, with his absence, but he needed the time away from her to think. He needed to decide what he was going to do with the rest of his life. Now he knew. He wanted to spend it with her.

It took five days of torture. Five days of misery, of being solely in his head before he understood what love was.

Life sucks without her, asshole.

Now he had to return to her, his tail tucked between his legs, and beg her forgiveness. She was seated on the couch in her office, wearing the tight red sweater that made his heart leap into his throat every time he saw her in it. Her hand moved rapidly as she expertly stitched a delicate piece of white fabric. He watched her for a moment, waiting for her to say something, anything. It would be so much easier for him if she spoke first. He had no idea how to apologize, how to tell her he loved her, no clue how to explain why he needed time away from her to think.

Her smooth plump lips stayed tightly shut. It wasn't going to be easy for him to take the cowardly way out.

"Ellis." He got down on his knees, pulled the fabric out of her hand, and placed his face in her lap. She was warm and soft. She felt good. She felt like home. He waited for her to run her fingers through his overlong hair.

They stayed folded in her lap.

"Did you cheat on me, Mike?"

The question hit him like ice water.

"What?" His stomach flipped, then plummeted. Other women simply didn't exist when she was around. "No, baby. I didn't. I couldn't."

"It's over, Mike." Her words came out as a choked whisper. "I can't do this with you anymore."

"No." He gripped her hands. She still wouldn't look at his face. "I didn't cheat. I just needed a little space to think. I'm not good at this, you know. I freaked out. I wanted to make sure I knew what the right thing was."

"This is the second time you've done this. Things get real and you disappear. You got mad at me for not trusting you enough to share my life with you. Why is it okay for you to do it to me?"

"It's not and I'm sorry but you don't understand."

"I don't understand? Damn it, Mike! Of course I understand. You can't handle this—us. I knew this was going to blow up in my face. You asked me to trust you, to let you in, and just when I did, just when I thought that we might have something good, you screw me over. I was right about you."

"You don't know anything, Ellis." He stood, looming over her. "You're the one who was dead set on ending things. You doomed us before we even started. You were the one who kept me at arm's length. How the hell I am supposed to compete with that? I walked away for five damn days. You were never there to begin with." He pointed an accusing finger at her. "You've been looking for a way out for weeks."

"Don't you dare turn this around on me." She rose from her seat, poking him hard in the chest. "I was trying.

And even when I was unsure about us I never not saw you. I never hid myself away."

"No, you just did everything else to keep me at a distance," he shouted. "You kept expecting me to treat you like he did. I'm not your fucking ex."

"No? We were fine until you went away. What happened last weekend?"

"Nothing! I didn't cheat on you."

"Maybe not this time, but I know you. There's a reason why you never had a girlfriend. There's a reason you've gone through so many women. And no matter how much I care about you, I have to put me first. This is the first time in my life where I'm in control and I can't—I won't give you the power to make me feel like shit."

A sharp bullet of realization dawned on him. "You're never going to get over this, are you? You're never going to be able to trust me."

"I tried and look where it got us."

"It was five days, Ellis. I didn't see you for five days."

"No, Mike it was more than five days. It was ever since you went away to Pittsburgh. One moment you were with me." She touched her heart. "Here. And the next moment you were miles away."

"I told you I needed to think."

"Well, I need to think about me, too, and I'm at the point in my life where I don't have the time or energy to waste on being unhappy."

"Fine." He felt heartsick and soul sick and sick to his stomach all in the same moment. "I'm done fighting with you. I guess this is good-bye."

Ellis stood at her parents' door for a long time. She didn't have the energy to raise her hand to ring the bell. It was all spent trying to keep the tears at bay. She escaped her shop after Mike left. When Cherri gave her a curious look

Ellis claimed a stomachache and flew out the door. There was only one person who could make her feel less wretched than she already did. One person who would put things in perspective and stroke her hair and make bad things seem not so bad.

Sometimes a girl just needed her mother.

Ellis wondered if she'd made the right decision breaking up with Mike. Was it worth the horrible heartache? She loved him more than she thought was possible. But what was love without trust? She didn't trust him and it wasn't fair to him to have to live with that.

Despite her best efforts she had started to dream of a life with him. A marriage. A forever. How stupid.

"Ellis?" Her father flung the door open, his expression worried. She gave him a wobbly smile. He had pumpkins on his tie and gray sweatpants that clashed horribly with his neatly combed salt-and-pepper hair and starched white shirt. "You took six minutes to knock."

"Hi, Daddy." She stepped inside. "I came to see Mom. Is she here?"

"She went jogging at five oh five." He shook his head. "She usually runs anywhere from forty-five to sixty minutes." He lightly touched her back, leading her to the couch. "Your eyes are glossy. You are upset. Yes?" He studied her face. "What has displeased you?"

She wasn't sure what about his robotic words brought on the tears, but they started. Not elegantly, not quietly, but big loud sobs. Her father looked at her, his expression horrified.

"No. No. No. No. No. Oh, Ellis please do not cry."

She wanted to stop but she couldn't help it. She buried her face in his shirt, seeking comfort she knew he wasn't capable of giving. "I broke up with Mike."

He patted her head awkwardly as he tried to make

sense of her words. "Has he done something to displease you?"

"Yes—no." She wasn't sure anymore. "I'm sorry." She tried to compose herself. She hadn't meant to break down. When she'd made the decision to end things yesterday she didn't expect to feel so shitty. She knew going in that things weren't going to last. Why was she crying now? "I messed up your shirt."

"It can be cleaned." The look of horror was still present on his face. "Tell me what happened. Michael told me he was committed to you. Your mother likes him very much. I thought he was much better than the last boyfriend."

"He was. Oh, Daddy. It's fine. I'm okay." She wiped her still-leaking eyes. "I'm just hormonal." She lightly kissed his cheek, understanding that receiving affection was difficult for her father. "Thank you for letting me cry all over you. Is there any chocolate?"

"I always have some here for you. It's in the kitchen, in the cabinet over the sink." He patted her head again. "Would you like to stay for dinner? Your mother took tofu out." He frowned. "We could get deli. You like roast beef with pepper jack cheese and horseradish."

"Yes, Daddy, I do." She rested her head on his shoulder. "Can I sleep over tonight?"

"You can move back in. I don't like it when you have a boyfriend."

"I'm not moving back in. Can we watch *The Muppet Movie*?"

"Whatever you want."

She smiled, feeling marginally better. Sometimes a girl just needed her father, too.

Mike stared at a spot on his living room ceiling for hours. There was a smudge, a gray imperfection in the white paint. Focusing on it helped keep his mind off Ellis and the burning anger he felt whenever he thought about how quickly he'd screwed things up with her. He had been in love a little over a week and he sucked at it.

His mother had called him earlier even though Sunday was two days away. Their conversation was stilted. She tried to bring up his father but Mike shut her down. He didn't want to get into it with her. He didn't want to argue anymore that day. Not with another woman he loved. So he asked about his sisters, the floral shop, anything that didn't require many words on his part. His mother obliged, filling him in on all the happenings around his hometown. But that thread of conversation ended quickly, and his mother brought up Ellis.

He hadn't known the two of them had talked. Ellis hadn't told him, but he shouldn't be surprised by that. He wasn't around for her to tell him. Apparently his mother really liked Ellis. He heard the smile return to her voice when she spoke of their long conversation. This time he didn't stop his mother from talking about a subject that pained him. He didn't have the heart to tell Margie that Ellis had dumped him. And he certainly didn't want to share that their breakup was 99 percent his fault.

He needed to get her back. Hours of introspection and solitude told him that. He knew she had trust issues. He knew her last boyfriend had been a dick. He should have been there to reassure her. He should have talked to her, but he was no good at talking about his feelings.

A brisk knock on his door shook him from his depressed musings. He hoped it was Colin, there to distract him. He wished it was Ellis there to forgive him, but he knew that was an impossibility. She wouldn't come back. If he wanted her he was going to have to get her. But how?

He opened the door finding neither of the people he expected. "Walter?"

Before he could process that Ellis's father was at his door a fist flew in his face, knocking him off balance, physically and mentally. It was a really good hit. "What the fuck? You hit me!"

"She was crying." Walter's face was red. His lips smoothed in a tight line. "You made my daughter cry. You told me you cared for her. I thought you were going to be good to her. I thought you were going to make her happy. But you made her cry and you deserve to be punished."

Mike was at least five inches taller and thirty years younger than the angry academic before him. He could destroy this man if he wanted, but he knew that that wouldn't earn him any favors with Ellis. Still, getting punched in the face royally pissed him off.

"You tell your daughter that I didn't want this breakup. That I admitted I don't ever know what to do when it comes to her. That she makes me so fucking crazy I feel like beating my head into a goddamn wall. That being with her is not easy but it's the only place I want to be." He shook his head. "Shit! Don't tell her any of that. You and your whole family need to leave me the hell alone."

Walter blinked at him for a moment. "Phillipa makes me want to scream sometimes. There are times I want to stuff a sock in her mouth to prevent her from talking." His expression grew thoughtful. "But when she is silent I need to hear her voice. When it first happened I thought she had bewitched me. She told me that I was in love with her. You must be in love with my daughter. "

"For the love of God, I'm not having this conversation with the man who just punched me."

"You're going to have a black eye. I suggest putting ice on it." Walter nodded. "My mother made me take boxing lessons in high school. She was afraid I was going to get beat up because I am . . ." He blinked at Mike again. "Dina calls me a freaky brainiac. Would you like to accompany me to a bar? I will buy you a drink. Please do not take it as an apology, though. I am not sorry I punched you. I do not like to see my daughter cry. I will punch you again if it happens."

The whole Garret/Gregory clan was insane. Not a normal one in the bunch, and yet he was prepared to be saddled with them for the rest of his life. *Shit*. He was going to have to marry Ellis. Not want to, but have to. She was that missing piece for him, and he needed to think of a way to get her back.

"Yeah, let me get my jacket. I need to hear more about those boxing lessons."

"Don't be a putz. Men freak out all the time when they realize they are in love. Go tell him you're sorry and get him back."

Apparently Phillipa thought Ellis's choice to end things with Mike was a bad idea but Ellis stayed firm with her decision. It was for the best. She wanted more from him than he was able to give her, and it was unfair of her to wish for things he clearly said he didn't want. She deserved to be loved completely. It took her two years with the wrong man and a few weeks with the right one to realize that. Even though sadness made her heart heavy, she took her mind off it by throwing herself into her work. Before she knew it a week had passed.

Belinda's mother came to the shop every day to help her with the tailoring that Ellis could no longer handle. Belinda and Cherri were doing a fabulous job running the shop. Thanks to her happy brides' word-of-mouth advertising, business tripled. Clothes were flying off the racks and Ellis was getting offers to make more than just bridal gowns. One teenager begged her to make a gown for her Snowflake ball. The girl only had two hundred dollars and Ellis was swamped with work but she agreed to make it.

"See," she mumbled as she stitched the sapphire-colored material, "you don't have any time for men. Your career is booming. This is what you wanted."

"Talking to yourself, Smelly?" Dina walked into her office, a pout on her pretty face.

"Hey," she said, wondering why her sister was visiting her shop so early on a Saturday morning. "What's up?"

"I broke up with him."

"Oh, I'm sorry, about . . ." Ellis couldn't remember the guy's name at the moment. Pogo? Rory? Milo? She shook her head. "I'm sure you'll find the right guy for you." She had said that phrase so many times, the response had become automatic.

"I don't know, Ellie." She walked past Ellis and gracefully slumped onto the couch. "I'm going to be thirty-four next year. I think I might have already met the one and let him slip through my fingers."

Ellis held in a long-suffering sigh. She was in no mood for Dina's complaining. Ellis had been fighting back misery all week. Dina had no idea what it felt like to really be in pain, to really feel heartbreak.

"I should look up Mike."

"Would you stop talking about Mike!" Something inside Ellis snapped. She was sick of hearing about Dina's twisted fantasy of Mike, sick of her sister's constant immature bullshit. "He dumped you nearly five years ago. Things would have never worked out between you two, and if he was so crazy about you he never would have left you in the first place. Mike Edwards does not want you. It's time to grow up, Dina. It's time for you to get a real job and stop asking Mom and Dad for money. It's time you stop acting like a spoiled brat and behave like everybody else your age because at this rate you're going to be forty years old and still hanging out in bars with kids half your age. And if you can't see how pathetic that is, then God help you."

Ellis clapped her hands over her mouth as soon as she heard the final word come out. She was supposed to be getting closer to her sister, not saying mean things, no matter how true they were.

"I'm sorry, Dina. I didn't mean that."

"Yes, you did." Her eyes filled with tears. "I can't believe you're such a nasty bitch."

Her sister's words were like a slap in the face and for a moment Ellis was torn between anger and guilt. "I'm so sorry, honey." She rushed to her sister's side and gripped her hands. Guilt as usual won out. "Please, forgive me."

"I don't know if I can, Ellis." She tore her hands away and stood. "I need some time to think about it."

She stomped out of the room, reminding Ellis of the times she'd done so as a teenager. She had been too hard on Dina. Dina's father never loved her like a father should, like Walter loved Ellis. Maybe she was entitled to act a little selfishly. And maybe Ellis was once again making excuses for her big sister.

Chapter Twenty-four

Mike scratched at the new growth on his chin. He'd neglected to shave that morning, as he had for the past two days. He looked like shit. His eye was still black from Walter's punch. His head throbbed, and he hadn't felt like himself. He was missing Ellis and part of him wanted to kick down her front door and force her to realize they belonged together. But the rational side of his brain held him back. She probably needed time to cool down. Or, the thought he hated to think, she didn't love him. Not as much as he loved her. So he held off, biding his time, hoping that the shitty feeling would magically dissipate or that some other woman would come along and make him forget all about Ellis.

Fat chance. Other women didn't exist for him.

"You okay, Mike?" Lester asked as they walked down Barnum Street. They were on their way to interview a suspect in a breaking and entering. The item stolen was a twenty-gallon fish tank filled with pricey saltwater fish. The suspect was the woman's ex-husband. The case should be easy to solve.

"Yeah, I'm fine."

"You having woman problems?"

Mike shrugged, not wanting to talk about it with his partner.

"Me and my wife got into a huge fight before I proposed to her. It was about her loudmouth mother. I can't stand that old bat. I was so glad when she moved to Boca Raton two years ago I nearly got down on my knees and kissed the ground."

Mike tuned out as Lester went on in detail about his mother-in-law. Normally Mike found Lester's stories amusing, but he couldn't focus today. Instead he took in the scenery of Barnum Street. He hadn't spent a lot of time in this part of town. It wasn't as clean and shiny as the rest of Durant. It was nowhere near seedy, but the town's one and only pawnshop was located on this block as well as some of the older shops.

His eyes fixed on a fat bald guy in a tracksuit walking out of a convenience store. The man looked familiar and Mike racked his brain trying to figure out where he knew him from.

And then it hit him like a MackTruck. He was the man who'd robbed Ellis's store, the same man whose face he'd studied every morning for weeks.

"Motherfucker." He took off toward the man, who was so startled that he didn't even bother to run.

"What the fuck's your problem, man?"

Mike punched the bastard in the face. "That woman you hit and robbed is my girlfriend." He backhanded him. "How do you like being slapped around? Make you feel powerful, big man?"

"Mike!" Lester grabbed his arm before he could knock the guy out. "What the hell are you doing?"

"This is the guy who hurt Ellis. You saw her face. I'm going to kill him."

"No! Wait!" The man put his hands up in defense. "He paid me to do it."

"Who?"

"Her ex."

Mike flew out of the police station as fast as humanly possible. He barely heard Lester's warning for him to wait for him . . . or for backup. Probably both. Mike needed to get to Jack. He needed to find that weaselly smug punk ass.

The first place he thought to go was Agatha Toomey's. Normally he would look the guy up in the database but he didn't know Jack's last name. The Jack Toomeys that came up didn't fit the description and Mike didn't have time to investigate. Jack's aunt would know where he was.

He spotted a green VW Bug in the driveway and knew he was in the right place. He was going to have to play it cool with Mrs. Toomey. He couldn't let his emotions rule him or else the woman would give him nothing. Maybe he should have waited for Lester or another officer to question her but his mind wasn't functioning correctly. Jack had hurt Ellis for the last time.

He knocked on the door of the white Colonial and waited. When the door didn't immediately open he knocked again, then he banged. This time the door opened, the skinny little hag's face twisted with distaste as soon as she spotted him.

Calm down, he warned himself. *Don't let on.*

"What do you want?"

Good question. *Blood* didn't seem like the appropriate answer. He pulled out his badge. "I'm Detective Michael Edwards and I have a few questions for you."

"Who is it, Aunt Aggie?"

Mike's blood boiled. Jack stood behind his aunt in a three-piece suit. His face lost all signs of color.

"You fucking bastard." He pushed past the lady, entering her home uninvited. Jack fled toward the back. "Coward," Mike yelled. "You can't even act like a man now."

He caught up with Jack quickly in the den, grabbing him by the collar and slamming him into the wall so hard the plaster cracked. "You hurt her, you son of a bitch." Mike smashed his fist into Jack's face, hearing a satisfying *thunk* when his knuckles met Jack's jawbone. "What kind of man does that to a woman? She didn't deserve that."

"She wasn't supposed to get hurt. He was just supposed to scare her!"

"Jacky!" his aunt cried in the background.

"Scare her," Mike roared. "He split her face open. She needed stitches. Now I'm going to do to you what he did to her." He slapped Jack with the back of his hand, but this time Jack was prepared and delivered a punch of his own. Mike barely felt the impact. He was too pissed off.

"If she'd kept her mouth shut things would have been fine. I always told her that her big mouth was going to get her in trouble."

Mike's fist connected with his gut and Jack doubled over in pain.

"You leave him alone," Agatha screamed. "My Jack was too good for that slut anyway."

"Shut up, Aunt Aggie," Jack cried. "You don't get to talk about her like that. You know I love her."

Love her? The words were like gasoline on a fire. Mike loved her. Jack had no idea what love was.

He body-checked Jack, sending the smaller man flying. He advanced on him, his heart pounding, his brain buzzing. No rational thought entered or left. Jack's face twisted in fear.

Good, Mike thought, wickedly. *Now he can feel what Ellis felt. Now he can know what it's like to have his dignity robbed from him.*

Jack staggered to his feet, grabbing a lamp off the nearest end table. "You stay away from me, you animal." He threw it, and it exploded on the wall behind Mike, shards of it slapping Mike's face. Warm blood trickled down his cheek but it didn't stop him from moving toward Jack.

He picked up the antique table next. It struck Mike square in the chest but it didn't stop him.

"Are you fucking RoboCop?"

He grabbed Jack again but not before the man delivered a quick punch to his eye. It started swelling immediately, making it hard for him to see. Mike rewarded that blow with two back-to-back punches, backing Jack up into the sofa. One of them tripped and they both went down. Jack tried to get in a few more punches as they landed, but Mike expected them and countered, knocking Jack's head so hard on the floor that spit and blood flew from his mouth.

"You're going to kill him," he heard and then he felt a searing pain in his arm. The bitch did it. She stabbed him with a ballpoint pen.

"Mike's been hurt. You need to get to the hospital." It was the phone call every wife or girlfriend of a police officer dreaded.

Ellis said nothing to Lester's statement. She just dropped her phone and left her store.

Lester was waiting for her at the emergency room, his face grim. She opened her mouth to speak but her heart was lodged in her throat. "How—what—Is he okay?"

"He looks like hell, but he's a tough one. He'll be fine."

As soon as she heard those words a little bit of the pressure eased from her chest. "What happened?"

"Mike found the guy who robbed you. It turns out that your ex set up both of the robberies on St. Lucy Street as a scare tactic to get you back. When Mike found out, he found that sneaky bastard and beat the shit out of him."

"Oh no." Ellis grabbed her head. "Oh God." She wasn't really surprised that Jack had set her up. He was used to getting what he wanted no matter what he had to do to get it. But Mike . . . "He's going to get into major trouble for this."

"He's going to prison."

Ellis's eyes shot up to Lester's. "Mike's going to prison?"

"No, sweetie. Your ex is, and so is the guy he hired to do the job. Toomey confessed. They are going to get some serious time for it. Mike's just going to get his ass handed to him by our captain, but he ended up solving the case. Now folks around here won't be so afraid anymore."

Guilt pounded in her chest. "All of this happened because of me. I—I should move to Russia."

"Don't go blaming yourself. Seems to me like you're the type of girl men lose their minds over."

"Which is exactly why I should be single."

Lester shook his head. "Go see your boyfriend and do us all a favor. Take him back. He's been a mopey shithead all week."

She nodded once before she turned away.

"Mike." Tears flooded her eyes when she saw him. *Horrible* wasn't a strong enough word to describe how he looked. His face was nearly unrecognizable. Both his beautiful eyes were blackened. His cheek had long red scrapes. His perfect lower lip was swollen.

He was surprised to see her, and her heart broke. He looked so alone sitting on that hospital bed, bare-chested and bruised, his arm bandaged and in a sling. "Elle."

"What did you do?" she cried.

"Don't cry, honey. It's really not that bad. You should see what I did to him." He looked helpless for a moment. "Come here."

She hadn't realized she'd frozen in the entrance to the

tiny room. She almost didn't want to move closer, because if she did she knew she wasn't going to be able to leave with her heart.

"Please." He grabbed her with his good arm as soon as she got close enough. The tears ran faster as she viewed him up close. His face looked more damaged at this angle.

"Why did you come?" he questioned.

"Why do you think?"

"Because you love me."

"No." She shook her head. "It's not true." She wouldn't admit that to him, even if he already knew.

"No?" He wiped the tears from her cheeks. "Not even a little bit?"

"Not at all," she choked. She lightly ran her hands over his face, careful not to further hurt him. She needed to touch him, to make sure he was really with her and alive, and okay. "You shouldn't have gone after him. He's not worth it."

"I had to and I'm fine. I promise. Please stop crying." He put his arm around her waist and brought her closer. She looped her arms around him, smelling his familiar scent mixed with blood and sweat. Damn, she'd missed him. She didn't realize how heavy the ache was in her chest until she saw him again. It was as if she had been suffocating for days.

"Shh." He rubbed her back, trying to soothe her. "It's okay."

"You look like shit."

"That's my girl. Insult me again."

"You're an asshole." She smoothed kisses across his forehead. "Don't ever scare me like that again."

"Ellis, I'm sorry."

She slapped his chest, causing him to wince. "You're right. You are sorry."

He cupped her face, lightly bringing her mouth to his. "I'm so sorry," he whispered before he kissed her. "I want to come home."

"No, Mike. Don't do this to me."

"Yes." He kissed her again, held her tighter. "I miss you. I need you."

That did it. Her heart cracked open. It had been too hard without him. He was right: She loved him too much to push him away. And after what he did for her, risking his body to go after Jack, she couldn't deny him. She didn't want to let him out of her sight. What if Agatha had been crazier? What if the pen had been a knife? What if it had been his chest instead of his arm? The thought of never seeing him again made her knees buckle and her heart skip beats.

"I hate you."

"Sometimes I hate you, too. That's why we belong together."

She laughed through her tears. "You planned this, didn't you? You made it so I couldn't stay mad at you for very long."

"Yeah, and I also planned to have your father punch me in the face."

"What!"

"This black eye." He pointed to the left side of his face. "Came from your father the day you dumped me."

"He punched you?"

"Yeah and then he took me out and bought me whiskey and told me all about your family."

"Is that why he was gone for so long?" She blinked. "I thought I saw a truck pull up in front of the house."

"That was Colin." He grinned at her and then winced. "I got good and drunk with your father. He's actually really fucking funny when he's had a few."

"What? *My father?* He drinks?"

"Only whiskey. He wouldn't even let me buy a beer."

Ellis couldn't wrap her head around what Mike was telling her. "And he punched you?"

"He loves you, honey. He would do anything to stop somebody from hurting you." He locked eyes with her. "And so would I."

"Fine," she sighed. "You win. Just don't make me regret it."

"You won't." He kissed her, and at first it started off gently but then he increased the pressure and the heat, opening his mouth and letting the desire flow. It was all need, that kiss. A sign of how much they had missed each other.

"Hey! Knock that off," somebody barked, causing Ellis to jump and knock into Mike's swollen face.

He swore, she apologized and then turned around to see an older doctor who somewhat resembled a bull dog. "The way you're hurt, you shouldn't want to kiss anybody."

"My girlfriend is very beautiful, Dr. Laughlin." Mike gave the man a cheeky grin. "I couldn't help myself."

"Well, you better try. There's to be no sex tonight. Do you understand me?"

"Of course not." Ellis blushed, pretty sure her face was now scarlet.

"He's got bruised ribs, and the pen went into his arm about an inch. Normally I wouldn't have to warn anybody to keep it in their pants, especially those who refused pain medication, but you, sonny, seem to need extra warning. No sex."

Mike narrowed his eyes. "For how long?"

"Mike!" She blushed again. "Don't worry, Doctor. We'll follow your instructions."

Chapter Twenty-five

Don't ask. You really don't want to know.

A kid poked me in the behind and when I turned around to look at him he said, "You've got a big butt." Ever wanted to know the real answer to Does My Butt Look Big in This? Ask a kid. Ever want to tell someone the absolute truth? You can't or won't because you're an adult and terribly afraid of hurting someone's feelings.

A cold rain fell on Durant three days after Ellis brought Mike home from the hospital, which caused them to make a mad dash from her car to his town house.

"Shit," he cursed softly and briefly pressed his hand to his side. He did it so discreetly she almost missed it.

He was healing and never complained but Ellis still worried about him. The doctor told him it would take at least three weeks to heal. No work and no exercise. Mike usually grew a little cranky when he couldn't run, and that combined with his two-week suspension left Ellis concerned about his mood. But he seemed happy. As happy as a person with a stab wound, two black eyes, and bruised ribs could feel.

"You okay, Detective?"

"Yeah." He nodded, taking her coat to hang on the rack. "I'm fine. Help me pack my clothes. I'm thinking we can order some Chinese and light a fire tonight."

"Can we drink wine, too?"

"Only if it costs less than ten bucks a bottle."

"Ah, cheap. My favorite."

She grasped his hand and led him into his bedroom. He hadn't slept there since he left the hospital and tonight would be no different. They were there to pack the majority of his clothes. His toothbrush sat besides hers in the bathroom, and his mother called him at Ellis's house. It seemed things were getting more serious again. She missed him and was glad to be with him again but a voice in her head warned her to guard her heart.

"Sit down, Mike. I'll pack for you."

"I can do it." He opened his closet door and reached for his duffel bag on the top shelf. "Holy fucking shit." He froze, his arms in midair, his face draining of color.

"You done posturing, Mr. Macho?" She gently wrapped her arm around his waist and led him to his bed. "Sit."

He obeyed.

"I'm fine. It's just gas pains." He exhaled. "Give me a minute."

"How about I give you fifteen?" She rested her hands on his shoulders. "I'll pack for you and then we can go home and I'll run you a bath and feed you and then maybe give you a neck rub."

He lifted her shirt and pressed a kiss to her belly. "Men don't take baths."

His lips felt like heaven on her skin, and her eyes drifted shut. "What are you doing?" He kissed her again, his lips touching all over her belly. Part of her was self-conscious that his whole attention was focused on the part of her body she hated the most, but the rest of her was getting turned on. It had been too long without him. "Stop that!"

"I don't want to." He unbuttoned her jeans, slid them over her hips.

"How can you be aroused right now? You were gasping in pain a few moments ago."

"It hurts more going to bed with you every night and not being able to make love to you."

"We're not supposed to have sex. The doctor said so."

"He won't know if we don't tell him." He slipped his hand inside her panties. She was wet, had been since the moment he set his lips on her skin.

"I'm not having sex with you." She crossed her arms over her chest even though his fingers were probing between her legs, lightly stroking her inflamed nub. It took everything in her willpower not to open her legs and encourage his exploring.

"Fine." In a surprisingly graceful move for an injured man, he swept her on the bed and peered down at her. "All you have to do is lie there. I don't need much from you."

"Bastard," she muttered. They both knew she wasn't passive in bed.

He grinned, then propped himself up on his elbow and proceeded to unbutton her shirt.

"I should have worn a sweater." She relaxed, resigned to the fact that her boyfriend would not be discouraged. "Why didn't you try anything this morning? Or last night, for that matter? I was wearing much less."

"I knew you were going to say no." He kissed the hollow between her breasts, scraping his teeth against the lace on her bra.

"I'm saying no now." Her eyes drifted shut as he suckled her through the fabric. Her thoughts were becoming less coherent. Her body was starting to ache with neediness. Damn, she really had missed him.

He switched breasts, sucking her nipple hard through her bra. She moaned and it caused him to look up at her with smug satisfaction. "But you don't really mean it."

"Mentally, I do." She bit her lower lip, trying to regain some control. "My damn body isn't cooperating. It must have missed you."

"It?" He took his mouth from her skin and raised a brow. "What about you?"

"Me? Oh, I can barely stand you. I lost seven pounds while we were broken up. My sugar intake went down by thirty-five percent."

"I thought you felt different." He looked up at her, concern replacing his lust. "I don't want you losing any more weight. Okay?"

He was insane. She was twice the size of other women but she loved him for making her feel so damn good.

"Why? A few more pounds and I could be a whole size smaller."

"Ellis, I'm not joking." He frowned.

"Okay, Mike." She sighed. "I didn't lose weight on purpose, you know. If I could do that I wouldn't be in this predicament now."

"And what predicament is that?"

"Unable to get rid of my chubby-chasing boyfriend." She grinned at him, then pulled his face to hers for a long kiss. "I kind of missed you, too. Okay? You happy now?"

"I think we should live together." He slid her shirt off her shoulders, kissing each piece of bare skin that was revealed.

"What?" It took her a moment to process his statement.

"I want to share a place with you." He unhooked her bra. "You know, have my mail delivered to your house. Wake up every morning and go to bed every night with you. Have my home be where you are."

"Oh." She didn't know what to say to that. Questions crowded her head so quickly she couldn't make sense of a single one. Was it too soon? Was it the right thing to do? What did this mean for their future?

What do you want to do?

The answer was clear. "Okay, but I'm not moving in here. Your next-door neighbor gives me the creeps."

He chuckled and kissed her deeply. "Good. Now be a good girl and help me get naked."

She carefully undressed him, being extra gentle around his sore ribs, and pushed him down on the bed. "I'm not sure how to go about this without hurting you."

"Just get under the covers and I'll take care of the rest."

She obeyed him and snuggled against him, feeling his erection brush against her side. He kissed her throat as he slid one hand between her legs to rub her inflamed flesh. She sighed as his familiar touch both comforted her and aroused her. "So you really want to live in sin with me, sir?"

"Sin?" He looked confused for a moment. "It wouldn't be that way for very long." He took her hand and guided it to his heavy sac, prompting her to stroke him. "That's one of those serious conversations we need to have soon."

"Oh." She smiled, but warned herself not to get her hopes up yet.

He sucked in a breath as she slid her hand up his throbbing shaft. "I've missed you so much, baby." He settled himself between her legs. Her flesh was now slick as he pressed against her. "You feel so good against me," he whispered. He cupped her breast, kissed her ear, and rubbed his lower half against her. He was driving her crazy. But then again he always did just before he slid inside of her.

"Oh! Excuse us," they heard. Mike froze.

"I thought once he hit thirty we would stop catching him in the act," another voice said.

Mike let out a stream of curses so violent that Ellis's ears burned. He turned his head, giving Ellis a view of four women and one man crowded in the doorway. Their expressions ranged from mortified to amused.

"Don't you people knock?"

"The door was open," the older woman said.

"I don't care," he bellowed. "Get out and shut the damn door." Once they were gone he collapsed on top of Ellis, his head settling between her breasts. She could tell by his labored breathing that he was trying to control his anger.

"Mikey," she started softly. "Who were those people?"

"My family."

"I'm not going out there," Ellis said for the tenth time. "And you can't make me."

Mike couldn't help but smile at her. She sat naked on his bed, her arms crossed over her chest, her cheeks brilliantly red. "You have to." He struggled into his shirt ignoring the pain that tore through his chest, and knelt before her. "I want them to meet the girl I'm crazy about." He kissed the back of her hands. "Please."

"First my parents almost catch us in the act, then your whole family walks in on us going at it, and now you expect me to walk out there and say how do you do like nothing happened? No thank you. I'd rather die."

He fingered the locket he'd given her that hung between her breasts. "You can't stay in here all night—and trust me, if we don't make an appearance soon they're coming back to get us."

"Fine." She rose to find her clothes, her hips softly swaying as she crossed the room. "But you're taking me away for Christmas, somewhere far away where no family is allowed."

"I'll book the tickets tomorrow."

Mike tried to maintain his righteous anger about his family busting in on him but he couldn't. It had been nearly two years since he had made a trip to Buffalo and despite his feelings about his mother keeping his father's problem a secret, Mike was happy they had come. He'd missed them.

Ten minutes later he led Ellis out to the living room, where all his sisters, one of his brothers-in-law, and his mother sat expectantly.

"Hi," he said, greeting his family. Ellis buried her face in his back. "This is my very embarrassed girlfriend, Ellis. Ellis, these very rude people are my sisters Candace, Lara, and Janice. Lara's husband, Remy, and my mother, Margie."

"Hello." She waved but did not move from behind him.

"Oh, honey." Margie came forward and pulled Ellis away from Mike and into a hug. "Don't be so embarrassed. I've caught Mike with a girl more times than I can think of."

"Ma!"

"Shut it, Michael. The girl knows you weren't a saint. All that matters is that you're being a good boy now."

"He is," Ellis muttered. Her face was molten red. Mike felt so sorry for her he rescued her from his mother's embrace.

He tucked her into his side, kissed her forehead, and studied his family. "What are you all doing here?"

"Well," his oldest sister Candace started, "we heard you got the crap kicked out of you and we came to see how you are."

"Yeah," Lara, the next in line, added. "You look like crap. Can you even see out of your left eye?"

Lara's husband Remy said, "Judging by what we just walked in on, I'd say the man is feeling pretty damn good."

"Your family is as bad as mine," Ellis said in wonder. "I thought you came from semi-normal stock."

"Sorry to disappoint you." Janice grinned at her. "But the real reason we all came here was to check you out. Our brother has never been serious about a woman. We wanted to make sure you didn't brainwash him. Mom says you're nice but we needed to see that you weren't a total bitch. Oh, and we heard our father was stalking Mike and wondered why the hell we weren't getting any of that action."

"Janice!" Mike snapped.

"What?"

He wondered if his mother would swat him if he gave his sister a good pinch like he used to when they were kids. "How long can I expect the pleasure of your company," he said through gritted teeth.

"Well, little brother," Candace said. "We've got the kids waiting back at the hotel, with Bobby. Thank God we didn't bring them here." She rolled her eyes skyward. "I would have had a hell of a time trying to explain why their uncle was squashing that nice lady."

"Candace!"

"We're staying till Black Friday," she answered quickly. "We're going to go down to the city for the parade and then we were hoping to have dinner with you and Ellis."

"Oh." He looked down at Ellis. He had forgotten all about Thanksgiving. The fight with Jack, the subsequent suspension, and the reunion with Ellis had pushed the holiday right out of his mind. "Is that okay with you?"

"Oh, good God yes. Every year my mother subjects us to a tofu turkey and forces my father and I to sneak out to the diner for their Thanksgiving special. I think we would be happy for a reprieve." She looked at Margie and then back at Mike. "Lara, Janice, and Candace, would you ladies like to come see my store? I'll give you a huge discount if you want anything." She pulled away from him and kissed his cheek. "Talk to your mother," she whispered. "I'll be back in an hour."

"Remy, would you mind driving?" She gave him a dazzling smile. "I hate driving in the rain." She glanced at the clock. "Should I pick up some pizzas and have everybody meet back at our—my house for dinner?" She blushed. "Mikey?"

He smiled at her little slip of the tongue. "I'll do it. I'll have them delivered and meet you at home later."

"Okay." She gave him a shy smile and pushed his siblings out of the house.

He watched her through the window until they pulled off into the dreary afternoon.

"You're in love with her," his mother said, jolting his attention away from Ellis.

"Yeah."

"Are you going to ask her to marry you?"

He nodded.

Her eyes filled with tears. "I'm very happy to hear that." She rushed over and gave him a bone-crushing hug. "She's good for you."

He patted his mother's back and kissed her forehead before he set her away from him. "You losing weight, Ma? You're looking good."

She grinned at him and did a dramatic turn so he could admire her. "You think so? I've been feeling like an old bag of bones. Do you mind if we sit down? The long drive took it out of me."

"Of course. Do you want something to drink? I don't have much. I'm not here a lot."

"I guessed. When were you going to tell me you were living with her?"

"Eventually, I just asked her today. When were you going to tell me Dad was a drug addict?"

She swallowed. "I wondered when you were going to get around to asking me about that. Could you get me a big glass of water before you start yelling at me?"

He retrieved the water and sat on the couch beside her. "Go on."

"I always planned to tell you, but I didn't know how. Things got bad between us before he left. He was disappearing at night, not showing up for work during the day, and there were a few times I had to go searching for him in the bad part of town in the middle of the night. One night we had a huge fight after I found him passed out and I told him that it would better off if he left because I'd rather live without him than have one of our kids coming home to find him dead. Two weeks later he was gone." She looked at him helplessly. "I wanted to tell you a thousand times but there was no right way."

"Okay." He kissed his mother's soft cheek and patted her hand.

"Okay?"

"Yup." He shrugged. "I just wanted to know why."

"You're not mad?"

He was surprised to find that he wasn't. It bothered him that his mother chose to keep him in the dark for so long, but after the past couple of weeks he knew it was time for him to let some things go. "Not anymore. Ellis helped me to see that I was being a jackass."

"I'm glad. Now let's talk about when I can expect some grandchildren."

"This bride is going to be the death of me," Ellis sighed the next day as she studied the dress that Audra Landry has commissioned.

It was nowhere near done because of the intricate hand-beading that still needed to be applied. It was lovely without it. Ellis knew that the bride and her pushy mother would be very happy with the finished product. That was, if they stopped calling her to make changes. This time Audra wanted the dress cut two sizes too small because she was on a juice cleanse that promised to take twenty pounds off.

"I can't do it," she mumbled. "I've been on every diet under the sun and I know that one doesn't work. You only lose water weight, not real fat, and then you're so damn hungry you want to gnaw off the leg of the first person you see. I can't let her do this."

"What's that, Ellie?"

She looked over at Mike, who was going over her books at her computer. "Oh, I wasn't talking to you."

"I can tell, but I figured I better say something before somebody hears and tries to send you to a nuthouse."

"You wouldn't let them take me away, would you?"

"Not if I could help it." He extended his arms to her. "Come here, baby." She curled in his lap and rested her head on his shoulder. "Don't let that bride make you crazy. You're the designer. You do what you need to do."

"Can I be temperamental?"

"Of course." He smoothed his hands down her back. "Be a total bitch. Your work is good enough to warrant it. As soon as we're done here, I want you to call her back and tell her you're not going to do whatever crazy thing she wants you to do this time."

"I will. I'm glad you're here." She nuzzled his neck. "I thought you would be a big pain in the ass but you come in quite handy."

Once again he had organized her orders, putting them into a user-friendly spreadsheet. She now knew how many dresses she had to complete, how much time they would take to finish, and the cost of materials all in one place, instead of scribbled on loose pieces of paper.

"Glad to be of service." He rested his lips on her forehead. "Your business has quadrupled in the past three months. You might want to think about separating the clothing store from the dress shop. The store next door is vacant."

"You think so?" The idea of expansion had been on

her mind a lot lately. Belinda had been offering up her nest egg on a daily basis, but she had yet to accept the offer from her best friend. She didn't want to take Belinda's hard-earned money—but Belinda worked as hard as she did. Ellis couldn't run the place without her. Maybe Belinda deserved to own a piece of the shop. "It just seems like such a big step. I don't know how we would manage." She looked up at him. "I'll do it if you quit your job and help me run it."

"I would, if you could stand working with me every day and living with me, too."

She kissed his cheek. "You're sweet but I couldn't ask you to give up your job for me."

He shrugged. "Being a cop isn't that much fun anymore. And I like being in the store with you." He lifted her hands to his mouth. "If you want to make a go of the second store I want to do it with you."

Damn it. Shit. That wall around her heart finally crumbled. She reached up to kiss him.

"Hey, Smelly—oh what do we have here?"

Ellis froze at the sound of Dina's voice.

No. No. No. No. No. Shit! No. She hadn't told her sister about Mike yet. She had pushed it to the back of her mind when they had that fight.

She lifted her lips away from Mike and shut her eyes. This was all her fault. It could have been avoided if she hadn't been such a coward.

Chapter Twenty-six

Fat Hollywood

Why is it when actors and actresses gain weight for a role they are heralded? When I gain weight over the holidays nobody cheers for me, much less nominates me for a damn Oscar.

Renée Zellweger balloons up to a size fourteen and it makes the nightly news.

Charlize Theron eats a hamburger and the world applauds.

So I propose an award for everyday fatties like you and me and I call it the Chubby Flubby . . .

"What's wrong, baby?" Mike looked worried for her.

"I didn't tell her," she whispered.

"What?" Mike's face grew stormy. Ellis knew that things were about to come to a head.

Dina smiled at them, flipping her long auburn hair over her shoulder. "You didn't tell me you were seeing anybody," she said.

Ellis lifted her gaze to meet her sister's. Time to put on her big-girl panties. "I am. I've been dating him for months."

"Aren't we good at keeping secrets?" Dina moved forward and extended her hand. "Hi. I'm Dina and you're a hunk."

She didn't recognize him. *WHAT!* Dina had gone on

and on about how Mike was the one that got away, about how he was a man she could love, and now she didn't recognize him.

"Dina. This is Mike," Ellis said dumbly. "Mike Edwards."

"It's nice to meet you, Mike." She gave him a flirty smile.

"Dina. This is Mike. From four years ago."

"You don't remember me?"

Dina frowned in confusion. "Mike?" She squinted. "Ellis, how could you?"

"I'm sorry for not telling you but I didn't do it on purpose. I didn't do anything wrong. We ran into each other a while back ago and hit it off."

"You didn't do anything wrong? You let me go on and on about him. You kept trying to discourage me from hooking back up with him. And the whole time you were plotting to steal him from me."

"Wait a minute," Mike interrupted but Dina ignored him.

"You're such a bitch. How did you do it, Ellie? Did you tell him I was dead? Because if he knew I was still single, there's no way in hell he would want to be with you. I'm the one who has it. You don't. I can't believe you would stoop low enough to steal my boyfriend."

"Don't go there, Dina." Ellis stood and confronted her sister. "Don't you dare."

"Did you drug him? Is this you getting back at me for that little incident we had four years ago? Or are you still mad because you think you saw him first and I took him from you? God, you're pathetic. No real man wants you so you have to go after my sloppy seconds."

"That's it!" Mike stood and charged toward Dina, but Ellis blocked his path with her arm. "You're not going to talk to her like that."

"What?" Dina's mouth dropped open. "You're defending her?"

"Mike, let me handle this. I should have told her months ago. She has a right to be mad."

"No she doesn't." He shook his head in disbelief. "Nobody has the right to speak to you like that."

"Oh Lord." Dina threw her hands up in frustration. "She has brainwashed you."

Mike pushed past Ellis and got in Dina's face. "She hasn't brainwashed me." His voice was deadly. "Your sister makes me happy. She's beautiful and smart and everything you could never be. I was never your boyfriend. You didn't even recognize me when you walked in the damn door," he spat. "You want to know the truth about that night? I was going to fuck you and forget you. We never had a shot, but your sister and I are in it for the long haul so you better get used to seeing me around and if you can't, you can screw off. I will not have you speak to my girlfriend that way. I will not have you push her around and make her feel guilty for your shitty life. It ends today, Dina. You act like a grown-up or you go to hell."

Dina recoiled as if she had been slapped. "I see how it is." Her eyes filled with tears. "Good-bye, Ellis."

She watched Dina go, a heavy pain settling on her chest. She didn't know why she hurt. She knew her sister. She'd known how Dina would react. Nothing had changed since childhood. Ellis wasn't going to give up Mike, but she couldn't stomach losing her sister.

She took a deep breath and rested her hands on her desk. Breathing had suddenly become difficult.

"Are you okay?" Mike eased his arms around her waist and pulled her into his chest. She exhaled.

"I should go after her. I need to apologize."

He spun her around and tipped her chin up so that his

blue gaze could bore into hers. "No. You will not apologize. You didn't do anything wrong."

"She has every right to be mad. I didn't tell her about us. I'm surprised you aren't mad at me, too."

"I am mad at you."

"Oh." She looked away from him for a moment. His gaze was too intense. "I'm sorry."

"What is with you, Ellis? What's it going to take for you to trust me?"

"I—I do but—"

"No buts. This is bullshit. I don't think you—"

She put her hand over his mouth to stop his flow of words. "Please stop talking. I don't want to fight with you tonight. I want this to work. I want to be with you."

He pushed her hand from his mouth. "Then why the hell didn't you tell her about us? We went out half a dozen fucking times. Only a delusional person would think she had some sort of tie to me."

"Dina is delusional. But I didn't tell her for the reasons you think." She took a deep breath, trying to make sense of it herself. "It has nothing to do with you. Dina and I have a difficult relationship. And we were just starting to smooth things over. I didn't want anything to come between us, so I didn't tell her. I wanted to. I really did, but I was too afraid to risk it. I'm crazy about you, Mike, but you can pick up and leave or decide one day you're sick of my bullshit. Dina is my sister forever."

He shook his head sadly. "We are not temporary. When are you going to figure that out?"

"I—I . . ."

"This is about Jack, isn't it?"

"Excuse me?" she asked, shocked that Mike would bring him up.

"He treated you like shit so you assume that I will, too."

"Mike, don't." She didn't want to think about him now, or about her past with Dina, about all the times her big sister had put her down and pushed her away.

"Answer me."

"I don't know," she shouted at him. "He called me a fat pig. He told me I was disgusting, that nobody else would ever want me. That he was embarrassed to be seen with me. You know what he said the last night we were together? That having sex with me was like being with a broodmare and that he was surprised he could get it up half the time." She pushed his chest as the tears started to form in her eyes. "Are you happy now?"

"Ellis . . ." All of the anger seemed to drain from his body.

He kissed her wet eyelids, then her cheeks, and finally her trembling mouth. She hadn't realized that she was crying until he did. "I wished I could have killed Jack for you. If he wasn't in jail I would. You know what he said wasn't true." His kissed down the hollow of her neck. "You know I can't get enough of you? I'm crazy about you, Ellie, and I don't care who knows it."

"Mmm," she moaned as he comforted her. She wanted to tell him, that she loved him, but something held her back. She wanted to hear the words from him first. It might be a foolish thing to want because she already knew he loved her, but she needed to hear it. For her it would make everything real. Then she would have no problem admitting what she'd felt for so long. "Let's go home. I need for you to love me right now."

Even though Thanksgiving had come and gone in a blur, it was a good one. It was one of the few times Mike was surrounded by his family. He had been with his mother and sisters' families before, but this was the first year he'd spent the holiday with a woman by his side. Ellis opened up her home and along with his mother prepared a Thanksgiving feast. She was so cute scurrying around, trying to make things perfect, trying to make sure all their guests were happy. He watched her instead of the football game. To everybody else she seemed fine but he knew her better. Her bright eyes were a little dull. The fight she had with Dina was still bothering her.

He didn't understand how she could miss somebody who only took from her and never gave, who always went out of her way to hurt her. But Ellis wanted to be close with her sister. It was a relationship that he would never understand. He shouldn't even try because he had his own issues to work out.

Which was why he called his father. Harry was still in town, staying at the best hotel Durant had to offer. His father walked into the quiet bar wearing a suit and tie. It was surreal to see him dressed that way with his hair neatly combed. Harry had been captured in Mike's memory wearing a pair of faded blue jeans and a plaid work shirt. The man before him looked powerful. The man before him was a stranger.

"If I had known this was a special occasion I would have dressed better."

Harry looked down at himself and gave Mike a cautious smile. "Oh, the suit? I had a meeting in the city this morning. I just got back." He signaled the bartender who brought over two imported beers to the table.

Mike waited till the server left before he spoke again. "Why are you still here, Dad? You said you weren't going until we talked. We talked. You're still here."

Harry stared at his beer for a moment. "Did you think that was talking, son?"

"Maybe not, but tell me how I'm supposed to act when my father tells me he left because he was an addict."

"I guess you have a good reason to hate me."

"I don't hate you."

Harry raised his eyes to meet Mike's gaze, looking hopeful. It made Mike's stomach twist with discomfort. "You don't?"

"I talked to Mom. She explained some things. I don't hate you anymore, and I'm not really mad, either." He shook his head. "I don't know what I'm feeling."

"You're hurt. I hurt you when I left. But I had to go, Mike. I couldn't let you see what I was really like then."

Mike held up a hand to silence his father. "I understand, but I'm not sure what you want from me. We can't pick up where we left off. Twenty years is a long time. I don't know you."

"I know that, but I would like to get to know you again. I've made something of myself. I have things to offer you now."

"I don't need anything from you. I'm thirty-three, not thirteen."

"Think about that pretty girl you've been seeing. I can help you get a really nice rock to put on her finger."

"I don't need your help buying an engagement ring. It's done."

"What about her business? The buzz about her is good but she'll need a lot of capital to take it to the next level. A loan is out of the question. I had her checked out and it will be a few more years until a bank signs off on a loan of that size. I can give you what she needs."

"You had my girlfriend checked out?" He was caught between irritation and anger, feeling like his privacy had been invaded, that a piece of him was exposed. "You had no business doing that."

"I wanted to know about you. What better way than to learn more about the most important person in your life?"

The offer of money made his skin crawl, but Mike thought about Ellis for a moment. She loved making dresses. When he watched her work he saw passion glow from her that he had never seen before. It could make her dream a reality. He could make her business strong. Make it so she wouldn't have to worry about money anymore.

"Why do I feel like there's a catch? What do you want from me?"

Harry sighed and raked his fingers through his graying hair. For once he looked every bit of his sixty-six years. "I want to spend time with my son. Maybe offering you money isn't the best way to do it but I don't know any other way to get you to see that I want back in your life and nothing will stop me until I find a way in."

"Why now, Dad? Why wait twenty years? You must have been clean before now. You must have been clean for some time if you were able to make that much money."

"I was wondering when we were going to get around to that." Harry sighed heavily. "I went to Mexico to lick my wounds. I knew I had to get clean in order to get your mother back." He looked Mike in the eye. "You know she's the only woman in the world that makes my damn heart pound when I hear her voice. But Mexico can be a destructive place for a man whose problem is pills. For a long time I still used. Not to cover up the pain in my back but to make myself numb from the pain here." He tapped his chest. "I missed your mother and your sisters. I missed you to the point of pain. I started working with a private boat charter company during that time. I wasn't doing well for myself but I was doing okay. I was feeling useful. Little by little they started giving me more responsibility. And little by little I felt like a man again and realized that I didn't need pills to make me numb. Ten years had passed and the owner left the company to me. I had something then. But I didn't feel like it was big enough, like I was successful enough to show my children. So I busted my ass for another year. I got contracts with the big cruise ships that port in Mexico. A year later I was rich. I knew I had something to be proud of then, to leave my children. So I booked a flight home just in time to see you graduate from the police academy. I was going to surprise you then, but I looked at you and saw that you were a man and that you had made it on your own. So I tucked my tail between my legs and went home. It took me another nine years to realize that just because you may not need your old man anymore, he still needs you. So I'm going to do whatever I have to do to get my wife and family back. And even if you still don't want anything to do with me, you aren't going to stop me from reclaiming the rest of them."

It was hard for Ellis to ignore a summons to her parents' house for dinner. She loved her folks, tremendously so, but tonight she'd rather crawl into bed than spend three hours with them. Being a bridal gown designer was harder than she imagined. The honeymoon period was over. One bride canceled her wedding. One bride moved hers up. Ellis's sewing machine died, which halted her work for nearly two days, and now Mike was back at work. She missed him around the shop. He kept things running while she created. It made her think about taking him up on his offer. But she wouldn't ask him to quit his job. She had no idea where they would be a year from now. They had yet to say *I love you.* Ellis knew the words weren't important, but she was beginning to long for them.

"So . . ." Phillipa occupied the easy chair and studied Ellis and Mike. They had been sitting on the sofa for the past ten minutes, making small talk and waiting for dinner to arrive. "How do you kids like living together?"

"Hate it," Ellis said. She couldn't shake the feeling that her mother was up to something. "He expects me to share my closet with him."

"That's nice." Phillipa responded, clearly distracted. She glanced at the clock for the fifteenth time. "I put you two kids down as your father's guest for the university's Christmas party. You're coming, right?"

"I'm planning on landing on the moon that day. So I can't go but I'm glad because I can't stand to see you wear that poop-brown suit you wear every damn year to the party."

"Good—What?" Her focus snapped back to Ellis as Mike let out a chuckle. "What's wrong with my suit?"

"It's ugly. Now spill it, hippie. What are you up to?"

"Don't hate me." She raised her arms in defense. "But I invited your sister over. You know I hate it when you two fight." She glanced at the clock. "She should be here in about five minutes. I told her to be here half an hour ago."

Irritation passed through her. Her mother was always trying to make things better between Dina and her. Phillipa thought that placing her daughters in the same room would magically cause them to resolve all their issues. Her realist mother was a dreamer.

"Dinner should have been here seven minutes ago." Walter entered the room, his eyes moving from the clock to the door. "Dina should have been here twenty-eight minutes ago."

As if magic conjured her Dina strolled through the door, her hair loosely curled around her shoulders and her body wrapped in a houndstooth coat that looked like it cost a fortune.

"Hey, Smelly Ellie. Hi, Mom. Hello, Walter. How are you, Mike? What's for dinner?"

She dropped her coat on the chair Phillipa had vacated and headed into the kitchen.

Mike locked eyes with Ellis and raised a brow. She knew what he was thinking. *What the hell?* But it was always like that between her and Dina. Ellis knew she was forgiven when Dina breezed in and acted like nothing had happened. All her life she thought being ignored by her sister was better than arguing with her. Maybe that was changing. She wanted to breathe a sigh of relief. It was what she had done in the past. She hated not speaking to her sister. Ellis didn't want to go through life estranged from her only sibling. But this time she was finding it hard to choke down the bitterness she tasted when she watched her sister walk through the door. She was finding it hard to forget those nasty words her sister had flung at her during their last fight.

The doorbell rang before Ellis could process it all. Mike stood up and helped her to her feet. She could think later. Now it was time to eat.

Dinner that night was an awkward affair, at least for Ellis. Mike sat by her side while they dined on Italian but neither of them had much to say. Phillipa, however, had plenty to talk about and kept the conversation going by herself for nearly an hour. Dina contributed, too, telling them about the new job she'd gotten at a large upscale department store in the city.

"I used your name to help get my foot in the door, Ellis. I knew you wouldn't care. I wasn't sure about you designing clothes for a living but it helped me get a better job. Who would have thought you would be known in the fashion industry?"

Ellis didn't respond to her sister's backhanded compliment or say anything more than "Pass the pepper" to her the entire meal. So when the last plate was cleaned Ellis made a dash for the kitchen, volunteering to slice the tiramisu for dessert.

"You okay?" Mike's strong arms folded around her, and she smiled as some of the stress leaked from her body.

"I'll be much better once you take me home."

"You mean you're not enjoying the most awkward dinner ever?" He kissed the spot behind her ear that always melted her bones. "I know she's your sister but she is the most self-centered person on the planet."

"You dated her," she pointed out.

"We didn't do much talking."

"And yet you never slept with her." She turned in his arms. "Why not?"

"You interrupted us. Remember?"

"Yeah." Her cheeks burned. "I still can't get the image of you in those Calvins out of my head."

"But those Armani boxer briefs you got me for my birthday should be replacing that image nicely."

"Wear the red ones to bed tonight." She kissed his chin. "They'll put me in a festive mood."

He slid his hands down her back as he groaned. "Let's get dessert over with quickly. We need to get you to bed early tonight." He held her tightly against him for a moment, dropping his voice to a whisper. "You don't know how grateful I am to you for interrupting us that night. Sometimes I kick myself for not getting to know you better four years ago, but I know I wasn't ready then. Hell, I'm not sure I'm ready for this now." He laughed softly. "But I can't imagine not being with you and I want you to know that you're stuck with me for a very long time." He pressed a soft lingering kiss to her mouth. Ellis's eyes were about to flutter shut when she noticed they weren't alone anymore. Dina stood watching them from the doorway, her face twisted in a painful expression. Ellis gently removed herself from Mike, wondering how long they had been watched.

"Sorry," Dina mumbled as her heels clicked on the hardwood floor. "Walter was wondering what was taking you two so long. He said you should have been out eight minutes ago."

Mike could barely hide his annoyance with Dina and gave her a look that told her so. "I'll carry the plates out. Are you going to be okay with the coffee, Ellis?"

She nodded, accepting his kiss to her forehead before he quit the room. Dina remained where she was.

"He really loves you. Doesn't he?"

"I think so."

"Mom says you two live together."

Ellis nodded. She was having a hard time forming words. There was so much she needed to say to her sister and yet she could think of nothing to start with.

"She's says that you didn't tell me because you didn't want to mess up our relationship."

Ellis nodded again, now understanding that no matter when she told her sister about Mike, the fight couldn't have been avoided. Because the fight wasn't really about about Mike.

"Say something," Dina pressed.

"I'm not sorry for loving him, Dina. I won't apologize for it."

Dina's expression hardened for a moment, and Ellis could have sworn hatred flashed in her sister's eyes. Then it cleared, and Ellis thought her imagination was playing tricks on her. "I still wish you would have told me."

"But I didn't and now it's over."

"I want my sister back." Dina stepped closer and kissed Ellis's cheek. "Don't be mad at me." Ellis kept her body stiff but Dina wrapped her arms around her and hugged her tightly. "I was mean to you. I was a big fucking bitch but I was surprised, okay? And I couldn't stop myself from turning back into the girl who was always a little jealous that somebody loves you more than me. So please don't be mad at me. I love you."

Ellis relaxed a little. "I love you, too." She was never

really mad in the first place; more hurt than anything. She tried to let the bitterness drain from her body, but it was slow to leave.

"Good." Dina smiled as if her words made everything all better. And for Dina things might be better. But Ellis knew that things would not be smooth sailing for them from now on no matter how much she wanted them to be. "Because I'm going to Mom and Dad's Christmas party next week and I want my fashion designer sister to help me pick out a dress. Since you seem to have taken the last hot guy I know, I'm on the prowl again and I heard there are going to be a lot of cute, single, brainy men there." She grabbed empty mugs from the counter. "Grab the pot. We'll go shopping on Sunday."

Every year the University of Durant Science Department rented out Coco's, a local restaurant, and threw a big Christmas party for the staff and their families. It was an event Ellis went to nearly every year. Scientists were pretty damn fun when they were tipsy, and Ellis was hoping this year she would get a glimpse of her father enjoying himself.

"See if you can get my father to drink tonight," Ellis whispered to Mike as they entered.

"Most women want their fathers to stay sober at events. My girlfriend wants her father shitfaced."

"What can I say? I'm a classy lady."

"That's why I'm with you." He wrapped his arm around her waist and pulled her in for a quick kiss.

"Yuck." Dina said. "Do you think you can abstain from PDA tonight? It's gross."

"Hi, Dina," Ellis greeted her sister. "I didn't know you were here."

She rolled her eyes. "I came with Walter and Mom. You know he's such a time freak."

"I'm going to get a drink." Mike kissed her cheek. "You want a Bay Breeze, baby?"

"Thank you."

He squeezed her shoulder and walked away. He hadn't acknowledged Dina. And Ellis could tell by the look on her face that Mike's shunning bothered her. She was going to have to talk to Mike later. She only had one sister, and they had to make it work.

"You look great in that dress, sister," she said, trying to soothe Dina's bruised pride.

"Thanks," Dina replied absently as her gaze traveled around the room. "Do you see any hot guys here?" She glanced back at Ellis. "Why am I asking you? You don't seem to have a type of your own."

Ellis ignored the little barb thrown her way and searched for her parents. "Do you know where Mom and Dad are? I want to say hi."

"I think they are sitting at a table in the back room. Why don't you go find them? I'll be around."

Mike watched Ellis as another one of her father's colleagues led her to the dance floor in the main room. She was a huge hit with the nerdy set. She barely had two seconds to sit down that evening because professor after professor kept asking her to dance. Mike let her go, watching as her face lit up with each invitation. It was one of the few times he wasn't jealous of other men. He couldn't blame them for ogling his girlfriend. She wore a red lipstick to match the satin dress that hugged her body and left a large part of her creamy back bare. Vivid images of her nude body flooded his mind. He couldn't wait to peel her out of her dress. He wondered if he was going to be able to wait long enough to present her with one of her Christmas presents. He was going to take her away to Aruba as soon as she finished with her current orders. It was to be the first time they were going to be truly alone, and he couldn't wait.

"Who would have thought that my sister would be belle of the ball?" Dina slid into a chair next to him.

Mike looked around the table before he acknowledged Dina. It was empty. The party was well into its fourth hour. Many people had already left, and those who hadn't left were shaking it on the dance floor. "Your sister is gorgeous. Why wouldn't she be the belle of the ball?"

He looked into the next room, hoping to catch a glimpse of Ellis in the crowd. He failed to see her through the mass of bodies getting down to "Party Rock Anthem." After this song was over he was pulling Ellis out of there and taking her home. He had some plans for her tonight.

"Ellis wasn't a cute kid, or teenager, and don't even get me started about how she looked from eleven to thirteen," Dina said offhandedly. "I couldn't even describe her as a person, more like a blob of chub with a mess of brown hair on top."

Mike took a sip of his rum and Coke, trying to ignore Dina's comment and trying not to make one of his own. He didn't want to engage in conversation with her, but he couldn't be rude, either. Dina was going to be his sister-in-law one day, and he knew Ellis would want them to be civil. At that moment Mike was finding it very hard to be around her. There was something ugly about Dina Gregory.

"What a difference a few years make." He glanced at his watch.

"Do you love her?"

The question caught Mike off guard and this time he looked at Dina. "Yes. Very much."

Dina shifted her chair closer to him and lightly placed her hand on top of his. "I need to know how it happened. How did you end up with Ellis?"

"We ran into each other, Dina. It's just like she said."

"But there's more to it," she pressed. "I want to know exactly what happened."

Mike removed his hand from beneath hers and folded his arms across his chest. "I think that's something you should ask your sister."

"But I can't. You're the one topic we can't talk about. You have to know how awkward this is. It's not normal for us to share men."

"You aren't sharing me," he pointed out. "We were over a long time ago. We never were really together in the first place. I'm serious about your sister."

"I get it." She rolled her eyes high in her head like a teenager. "Tell me how it happened. Did you know she was my sister when you bumped into her?"

"Not at first." A smile tugged at the corners of his mouth when he thought about their first meeting. "But . . ." He was about to share the events that threw them together but he remembered who he was with and thought better of it. "Ask your sister."

"No, Mike." Dina slid her hand up his arm. "I want to talk to you now. Tell me what it is you love about her that you couldn't love about me?"

He moved back in his chair. He wasn't expecting that question and sure as hell didn't know how to answer it.

"Tell me the truth." She inched closer to him, and he could smell the alcohol on her breath. Her eyes were glassy. Her speech a tiny bit slurred. She was drunk. "I need to know what's so damn lovable about her."

Shit. Why hadn't he noticed sooner? This conversation was over.

"You can still have me. I can see why you like my sister. She's normal and steady and boring. She's who you can go home to every night. But I'm who you can sneak around with during the day."

Mike shook his head. Dina looked as if she didn't believe what she was telling him. Like she hated herself for saying it. "You're drunk. You don't know what you're saying." He looked around the room, hoping to find Walter and Phillipa so that they could get her out of here. "Where are your parents? They need to take you home."

"I'd rather go home with you."

He turned back to tell her no when her lips came crashing down on his and her arms twined themselves around him.

Chapter Twenty-seven

Men Who Got Fat . . .

Why doesn't anybody ever talk about famous men who gain weight? Kirstie Alley puts on four pounds and it's on the cover of every magazine. Double standards piss me off. Nobody snaps a picture of Jack Black every time he shoves a doughnut down his pie hole. So here's a list of actors who've gotten fatter.

Alec Baldwin.
Marlon Brando. (Well, actually people did talk about it but not as much as poor Kirstie.)
Steven Seagal.

Dr. Marlon Bradshaw sure could cut a rug at seventy-two years old. Ellis's father's oldest colleague had spun her across the floor for nearly ten minutes before Ellis cried exhaustion. He reluctantly let her go, telling her that if he was thirty years younger he wouldn't stop until she was his wife. It made her smile. She would gladly return to this Christmas party next year.

Ellis Garret. Nerd sex goddess.

"Ellis." Phillipa grabbed her hand as she made her way off the dance floor. "I think we're going to head home. Can you ask your sister to meet us at the entrance?"

"Sure. I'm exhausted. You nerdy people sure know how to have a good time. I'll get Mike and we can walk out together." She paused before she left. "And I'm burning that pantsuit later. This is your last function in that thing. You're a size four, for heaven's sake, and you can't find something a little more flattering?"

"I don't know why you keep calling my suit ugly!"

"Because it is."

"Walter!" She sniffed at Ellis and turned to find her husband, who was never more than five steps behind her.

"Yes?"

"Do you think my suit is ugly?"

Walter glanced at Phillipa and then to Ellis. His mouth smoothed into a straight tight line.

"Walter!" Phillipa gasped as Ellis walked away laughing.

She entered the back room where her family had camped for the night and saw only a few people there, including a couple making out at a table in the corner. She frowned, wondering where Mike had gone off to. He was supposed to be watching her bag. Knowing he wouldn't take it with him to the bathroom, she journeyed farther into the room. The couple making out was sitting at the table they had occupied all night. How the hell was she supposed to look for her bag with two slobbering people in the way? She shrugged. The way the women had her hands gripped on the man's face, Ellis was pretty sure they wouldn't notice her at all.

But as she got closer the man seemed familiar. Dark hair. Broad body. Chiseled jaw. He looked like her Mike. The woman wore a black dress. Her hair was auburn.

No. It can't be. This isn't happening.

Everything slowed in that moment, including her heart. A physical pain ripped through her. Starting at the pit of her feet, it shot up to her brain until she wanted to scream. She trusted him . . . but secretly she always wondered if part of him still thought about Dina. She always wondered if he was really ready to devote himself to her. How could a man who never had a serious girlfriend be ready to make such a big commitment?

Mike shoved Dina off him, and she landed inelegantly on the floor.

"What's your fucking problem?" she shouted at him. "It was just starting to get hot."

"Are you insane?" he bellowed. "I'm with your sister."

"Are you, Mike?" Ellis choked.

His head snapped up. He stepped over Dina and reached for her hands, but Ellis pulled away.

"Ellis, don't." He grabbed her. "She kissed me. You know I would never cheat on you with Dina."

"With Dina?" She yanked herself away from him. "*Ellis, I would never cheat on you period*. That's what you should have said."

"I'm sorry." He shook his head, his expression somewhat like a wounded animal. "But you should already know that."

"Ellis?" Dina stood up, smoothing her dress over her hips. She had tears in her eyes and for once Ellis didn't care. Her sister, her only sibling, the person she had always loved more than anything had betrayed her.

"I don't want to hear it." She screamed it. The words flew from her mouth, and Dina recoiled as if she had been punched. "Why do you hate me so much? I've spent my whole life trying to love you while you've spent your whole life trying to make me feel insignificant. You've ruined every important thing in my life and I have forgiven you time after time but this time it's too much. Why Mike? You knew how I felt about him. Why don't you think he's good enough for me?" She shook her head. "I don't want to know the answer. I never want to see you again."

"Ellis, no!" She rushed forward. "I'm sorry. I love you, but you don't understand. I—I—"

"Your sorrys mean shit to me," she spat. "You don't love me. If you did you wouldn't be able to do this to me."

Mike gingerly placed his arm around Ellis's shoulder. "Baby, let's go home. You don't need to be around her anymore."

"I can't do this anymore." Her heart had hardened and slammed shut. She couldn't take one more heartbreak.

"Ellis, look at me." He cupped her face in his hand and forced her to make eye contact. "I didn't kiss her. She forced herself on me. You know me. You know I would never do that to you. With anybody."

"In my head I know that, Mike." Her tears started, running down her cheeks and over his hands. "But when I saw you with her I was transported back to four years ago when you walked past me for Dina. I keep waiting for that day to happen again. I keep waiting for you to break my heart and I've decided I can't live like that anymore. It's not fair to you."

"No, this isn't fair to me." He backed away from her and slapped his chest. "Your reasons are bullshit. You can't let the past dictate the rest of your life. You can't let fear ruin a good thing. I'm committed to you. For the first time in my life. I don't know how else I can prove it to you. But I swear to God, Ellis, if you walk out on us I'm not coming after you. I won't chase you anymore. You have to trust that I'm not going to hurt you."

"I can't. I'm so sorry." She pushed herself away from him and fled the room. Her parents were waiting by the door, and as soon as they saw her they circled around her.

"What happened?" Phillipa's eyes immediately filled with tears. She shook Ellis. "Tell me what happened to you?"

"Dina." She choked on her sister's name. "I caught her kissing . . ."

She couldn't say the rest. Her father took her by the arm and led her out, Phillipa hurrying behind them.

"That's it," Walter snapped. "I'm done with her—her bullshit. You've let it go on for too long, Phillipa. We are done supporting her. I do not want to see her in my house. Do you understand me? I want no arguments out of you."

"Walter, she's my daughter! You don't understand what she's been through. I can't cut her out of my life."

"Ellis is your daughter, too, and she's hurt. I can't stand by and watch it happen anymore. I am taking her home. You make your choice. Are you going to put her first this time or not?"

Phillipa looked tortured for a moment, but she took Ellis's hand and nodded. "Of course, Walter. Of course."

Mike picked up the nearest glass and flung it at the wall. The glass shattered but didn't put a dent in his anger. She had no faith in him. How could he have fallen so hard for a woman who didn't trust him?

"Shit." Dina walked back into the empty room. "My parents left me here. How am I supposed to get home?" She looked at Mike. "Could you . . ."

"Go to hell." He clenched his fist. He would never hit a woman even though this one deserved it. "Don't you get it, Dina? Don't you get how big this is? Your sister is done with you. You went too far."

"No." She shook her head. "She's mad but she'll forgive me. She always does."

"Not this time. You betrayed her." He turned away. Walking out was his only safe option.

"I didn't," she called after him. "I—I was testing you. I wanted to make sure you really loved her."

"Bullshit! You weren't testing me. You were trying to hurt her. I used to blame Jack for her being so screwed up but it's you. You're her sister. If you can't love her how can she expect anybody else to? Do us all a favor, Dina. Drop off the face of the earth."

Ellis hadn't been able to get out of bed in two days. She physically couldn't manage, and she hated herself for it. She hated that she was so weak. When she had dumped Jack she swore no other man would ever have the power to hurt her like this. But Mike had managed to sneak in and steal her heart. It would be a long time before she got it back. If she ever did.

Phillipa crawled in bed with her as she had numerous times since Ellis had begun squatting at her parents' house. "Do you want to eat, honey? Please say yes. Your father has been outside the door pacing like a madman. He'll get you whatever you want. He said he'd even drive into the city to get you those bialys you like."

"I'm not hungry."

"I know, sweetie." She smoothed the hair off Ellis's face and kissed her forehead. "I know you feel like dying. Is it wrong that I'm secretly enjoying your misery because it gives me the chance to baby you?"

"Yes. It is. It's very, very wrong." She reached for her mother's hand. "And I do feel like dying. Why is that?" A fresh wave of tears formed. "I thought I was stronger than this."

"You're not weak. You're devastated and if you thought you could go on like everything was normal after you walked in on your sister kissing the love of your life, you're delusional."

"But I broke up with him. I'm supposed to feel empowered, not like shit."

Phillipa sighed. "I wanted to ask you about that. Why did you break up with him?"

"I should have never dated him in the first place. I knew Dina was never going to be okay with us. He's the reason we didn't speak—"

"No, Ellis. That's not a reason. Mike has nothing to do with you and Dina. She had a hard time accepting you when we brought you home. She hated Walter, and she hated the fact that he loved you so much when her own father couldn't be bothered with her, and she took it out on you. I blame myself because I tried to overcompensate to make her feel loved and in the process I was harder on you. But you had such potential and I need for you to know that I have always loved you just as much as I love her, even if it didn't feel that way sometimes."

Her voice grew raspy as her tears started to flow. "I should have stopped it when you two were little. I'm sorry that she did this to you and I'm sorry that you're in so much pain now, but you know I can't throw Dina away. I'm not expecting or asking you to forgive her but I can't cut her out of my life, even if I'm disgusted with her behavior. She's my daughter, too, and I still love her."

"I know, Mom." Ellis hugged her mother tightly, hating that she was so upset. "I'm not asking you to do that, but I'm done with her and I need for you to respect that."

"It kills me that my girls can't get along, but I will respect your wishes. Your father isn't allowing me to give her any more money and he's right. I should have made her be responsible for herself a long time ago." She pulled away from Ellis and stroked her cheek. "I'm going to try harder to put your feelings first from now on."

"I never felt unloved by you, Mom. I don't want you to think I did."

She shook her head. "Then why are you throwing Mike away?"

Ellis froze for a moment. The same thought had snuck into her head more than once.

You're a big dumb dummy. You shouldn't have let him go.

"I'm not. I just—"

"You are. If you can give me one good reason to leave him, I'll never mention it again."

"He deserves—" she started.

"Not a good enough reason. If you're ever going to be happy you're going to have to let your guard down and take the risk."

Chapter Twenty-eight

"I can't look at your ugly face anymore, Edwards," Colin said in disgust.

"Then go home," Mike retorted, not lifting his head off the couch. It was Saturday night and for the second weekend in a row Mike chose to spend it parked in front of the television with a couple of cold beers and an industrial-sized bag of potato chips. He hadn't bothered to get dressed that morning, only brushed his teeth to wash the bad taste from his mouth. Colin had taken it upon himself to spend every free moment he had with Mike, hovering over him like an anxious mother hen. It was unnecessary, Mike wasn't going to off himself. He wanted to be alone.

"No, because if I leave you'll piss away the rest of the night alone. So what, your girl dumped you like a moldy sack of potatoes. You've been walking around like a zombie for the past two weeks. It's time for you to stop wallowing in your own filth and get back out there and on top of somebody else."

"I love her," he said. He didn't want anybody else but he wasn't as depressed as his friend thought, either. He was more pissed off than anything.

"I know you love her! Call her, for fuck's sake. Tell her you want her back. Tell her you'll do whatever she wants."

"Not going to happen." He scratched his new growth. "She walked out and I'll be damned if I go after her. She should have trusted me." He had been waiting for days for her to come back, to come to her senses and realize that she was throwing away a good thing.

He'd bought a fucking engagement ring for her. He wanted to marry her. He wanted forever with her. Hell, he still did. He stopped himself from pulling it out of his drawer a hundred times. His pride wouldn't let him go crawling back to her. He didn't want his proposal to seem like it was groveling.

He knew Ellis well enough. He knew that she wouldn't believe a proposal at this point was genuine. So he kept his mouth shut. He was through chasing after a woman who couldn't trust him enough to be faithful.

"You shouldn't have kissed her sister."

"I didn't," he yelled. "You know me better than anybody else. You know I would never cheat on her."

"Yeah well, I also know how you were a couple of years ago. Haven't you been with more women than you can count? And didn't she walk in on you as you were about to shag her sister in her bed? Damn it, Mike you've got to admit that she had a valid reason to disbelieve you. Hell, she should have never given you the time of day in the first place."

"She didn't want to," he mumbled, disgruntled. Damn Collin. A few words from him and he was ready to throw his principles out of the window. He glanced at his phone as thoughts of calling her entered his mind. He shook the feeling off. She broke up with him. He would not go after her. "I'm not calling her."

Colin jumped out of his chair and winged the cordless phone at Mike, causing him to wince as it connected with his stomach. "Do it. I know how you feel. Breaking up with the woman you love feels like having your balls ripped off. I couldn't have Serena back but you can make things right with Ellis. She loves your sorry ass."

Mike looked at the phone and then back to Colin, struggling with his decision. He knew she loved him, which was why he was having such a hard time accepting the breakup.

"Call her, Mike."

The phone rang and Mike answered it before he had time to make up his mind about Ellis.

It was Lara. Her words so rapid he could barely make sense of what she was saying. But the message sank in and fear took over.

"I'll be there as soon as I can." He stood up and tossed the phone on the coffee table.

"What's wrong?" Colin stood, too.

"It's my mother. She's hurt."

Ellis stared bleary-eyed at her dress form. "If I keep this up I'm going to need glasses before I hit thirty."

She had been hand-beading for the last three days. The dress looked spectacular; every time she looked at it she was amazed that she could create such a garment. Even though the dress was glorious as it stood, she still had two days of intricate work ahead of her. Audra wanted more beading. She told Ellis that she wanted to blind her guests when she walked down the aisle. Ellis sighed at the request but agreed even though she thought it was slightly tacky. Audra's mother was good for business. The woman had gone as far as setting up a meeting with a buyer for a large bridal salon for tomorrow. There was talk of mass-producing Ellis's dresses for the world. Ellis Garret could be a household name.

It was exciting and happening faster than she could

process. It could be life changing, but Ellis wasn't as over the moon as she expected herself to be. For the past two weeks she had been numb to everything. Her business was booming, she and her mother were closer than ever, and for the first time in nearly a year she wasn't afraid of not being able to pay her bills. But instead of wanting to shout from the mountaintops she wanted to crawl into bed and fall asleep.

"Ellis." Colin walked into her office, his face drawn.

Ellis's stomach dropped to her shoes. She sat down, not wanting to hear what Colin had to say. She knew he had something important to say because her ex-boyfriend's best friend wouldn't be here unless he did.

"If he's not okay I don't want to know." She buried her face in her hands as nausea rolled through her. She couldn't bear the thought of him . . . not in her life.

"He's in Buffalo. His mother had a stroke while she was driving and was in a bad accident. They aren't sure if she's going to make it."

"Oh no." Ellis removed her hands from her face. She was torn between relief that her love was okay and tremendous worry for the most important person in his life. "How is he?"

"How do you think he is, love? She's in critical condition at Buffalo General."

He walked out then. His message was unmistakable. She had a decision to make.

The slow steady beeps of his mother's heart monitor were driving Mike insane. Smells of the quiet ICU attacked him. Antiseptic mixed with fear and death plagued his nose. Coughing, the soft murmurs of visiting families, the hushed tones of the hospital staff as they shared grave conversations flooded his ears, and for the past ten hours he had absorbed it all. Somehow it robbed him of the energy to lift his head. So he stared at the space on the floor between his feet. He couldn't look at her anymore. The woman in the hospital bed wasn't his mother. The face he could clearly picture in his mind was distorted. Her smooth white cheek was now a deep purple and swollen to twice its normal size. Her head was wrapped in a bandage, sewn up with more stitches than he could count. She hadn't woken up since he'd walked in the door countless hours ago. Coma. The doctor had told him it was the best thing for her at the moment. The injury to her head was critical, and deep unconsciousness was best for her healing.

She had to pull through this. Mike demanded it, not only to extend her life but for his own selfish reasons. She needed to see her grandchildren grow, to see him marry the girl he loved.

He was alone with her now. His sisters were gone for the night, each with a family and a life that had to keep going despite this. They had husbands and families to surround them, to keep them propped up, while Mike felt as if he were sinking into the ground.

He heard soft footsteps enter the room and didn't bother to look up. All day nurses had been in and out to check on his mother. After the fifth hour he stopped waiting for an update on her condition. There was no change. The doctor had no answers for him. She couldn't even tell him if his mother was going to live or die.

Soft fingers ran through his hair, and he inhaled. The scent of vanilla, soap, and sweet spice infiltrated his senses and blocked out the nauseating hospital scent. He was dreaming, missing Ellis so much that he could almost feel her touch on his skin.

"Mike?" Lips brushed his forehead. "It's late, baby. Come with me."

* * *

Mike couldn't stop staring at her. He was afraid she was a mirage, but she wasn't fading away. She stood before him in the hotel room she had rented, her hair damp, her body wrapped in a fluffy white towel. He didn't expect her to be here, not after what had happened with Dina.

He grasped her hand, bringing it to his mouth to kiss the backs of her fingers. "You're here." He spoke for the first time. He had been so overwhelmed before that he couldn't force the words out.

"Where else would I be?"

At her store. Phillipa still spoke to him. He knew about her meeting. He knew about the chance she had to make her dreams come true. She couldn't miss it for him.

"What about your meeting?"

She ran her fingers through his hair. "What about you?"

The back of his throat burned as he pulled her down next to him on the bed and hugged her tightly. "I don't know what I'll do if she doesn't make it."

"Mikey . . ." She kissed his cheeks. "I wish there was something I could say to make you feel better."

She didn't have to say anything. She was with him and that was enough. He pushed her down on the bed. Unshed tears stung his eyes. Her smell, the way her full soft body felt pressed into his, her sweet words made him realize how much he needed her in his life. How could he have let her walk away?

"Baby." She wrapped her arms around him as his chest heaved, kissing the tears from his face. He slipped his hand beneath her towel to touch the soft flesh of her belly. He just needed to touch her, to feel her to remind himself that he wasn't alone anymore. The tears streamed down his face a little harder. He squeezed his eyes shut, nearly choking as he tried to stop them from flowing.

"It's okay, love," she soothed as she ran her fingers through his hair. "Don't try to stop them."

It was then he broke, all the emotions that he'd felt for the past two days flowing out of him.

Chapter Twenty-nine

Letting It Go

I was cleaning out my closet and I came across the sexy little one-piece I bought last season. Immediately thoughts of the last time I wore it came crashing back to me. "Your thighs are too big to be walking around in that one-piece. You should be wearing the fat-old-lady kind with the skirt attached." I immediately told myself to shut it. I was tired of wearing bathing suits that looked like they were made for a seventy-year-old. But then that same little horrible voice said, "Is that cottage cheese you've got growing back there?" At that point, tired of feeling nutso, I shoved it back in my closet behind my old prom dress. It's winter; I've got six months before I have to think about that again.

Ellis hadn't moved from her spot for the last two hours. Their hands were linked; her fingers were a little numb, but she wouldn't let go of Mike's hand. For the past two days they had sat vigil at Margie's side waiting for any sign that she was going to awaken. Her condition hadn't improved but neither had it worsened. Mike had been silent about his feelings but Ellis could feel the worry seeping out of him.

"Are you hungry?" she asked with a touch to his face.

He blinked at her, his mind elsewhere. He had barely registered anything she had said all day.

"Mike? Do you want me to get you something to eat or drink?"

"I'm fine." He tugged her out of her chair and into his lap, wrapping both his arms around her. "Sit here for a while. You make me feel grounded."

"Anybody would feel grounded with a giant boulder sitting on top of them." She kissed his chin. "But you're sweet."

"Hello, kids." Mike's father, Harry, walked in. He looked eerily like his son. They even wore similar black sweaters. "How's my girl today?"

Harry bent over to lightly kiss Margie's bruised face.

"There's no change, Dad. The doctors haven't said anything all day."

"My poor Margie girl," he whispered. "You don't deserve this." He stood, his eyes slightly misty, and faced them. "You think she'll take me back?"

"You'll have to woo her, Mr. Edwards." After twenty years apart he still loved her. Ellis knew the damage he had caused but deep down she wanted Harry to succeed. She wanted Margie to be happy with the man she'd married nearly forty years ago.

"Harry," he corrected. "You think so? How did Mike get you?"

"Oh, him?" She glanced at his son. "He kept feeding me and now I love him like a fat kid loves cake."

Harry chuckled. "I like you, Ellis." He looked back to his former wife. "I'm going to track down a doctor. If her condition doesn't change in twenty-four hours I'm flying in a specialist from the city."

He rested his hand on Mike's shoulder and squeezed it before he walked out of the room.

Ellis turned in Mike's lap to rest her head on his shoulder. "He loves you. Have you forgiven him yet?"

"I'm on my way there. I spent so much of my childhood thinking he was perfect and so much of my adulthood thinking he was evil. But he's just a man who is as flawed as the rest of us."

"You sound so wise. When did you come to this realization?"

"Thirty seconds ago. I haven't seen him since he offered me money to spend time with him."

"What?"

He nodded. "At the time I thought it was a dickish thing to do. He can buy everything else but he can't buy me. And then I figured that only a desperate man would try to buy his son's time." He glanced at his mother. "In light of this I think I understand why he did it. If he dies tomorrow and I ask myself, Am I happy with the way we left things, would I be happy with the answer?"

"Would you?"

"No, because I still love him and I can tell by the way he looks at my mother that he still loves her."

Ellis's eyes misted at Mike's sweetness. "I hope they remarry."

"Do you?" He kissed her forehead.

"When she wakes up your mother will realize how empty her life has been without Harry and take him back. Then they will have a big wedding in Buffalo where your sisters will be bridesmaids and you will be the best man."

He smiled softly at her daydreaming. "Where will you be?"

She thought about it for a moment. Where would she be? It was the wrong time to think about their relationship. She wanted to be with him, but she wasn't sure if they could make things work. The more she thought about it

the more she realized that she'd been too quick to walk
out on him. But maybe it was for the best in the long run.
Maybe she still needed time to figure out herself, and
maybe he deserved somebody who would trust him without question. He deserved somebody who wasn't always
waiting for him to break her heart. "Making all the dresses.
Duh."

"Of course." He was silent for a moment. "You really
think she's going to wake up?"

"I know she is. This is just a bump in the road."

"Hmm." He kissed her forehead once more. "I love
you, Ellie."

She froze for a moment, not sure if she'd heard him
correctly. "What?"

"I love you." He frowned. "Why do you look so surprised? I've told you that before."

"No, Mike, you haven't."

"I had to have . . . I told everybody else I did." He
shook his head and locked eyes with her. "I'm in love
with you. You knew that, right? I fell for you when you
stuck your tongue out at me that night in the bar."

"Ugh. You did? That wasn't one of my finer moments."

He shrugged. "That's when it happened. It's like you
punched me in the heart."

"Hmm." She cuddled into him. "I fell in love with you
way before that. It was when I saw your tight ass in those
Calvins."

He gave her a half smile then sobered. "Did you really
have no idea that I was in love with you? Is that why you
broke up with me?"

She leaned in to kiss him, because she couldn't find
the right words to explain to him why she did. He had finally said he loved her. It was the best feeling in the world
but as much as she was glad he said it, it didn't change
anything. She loved him but she didn't know what it

would take for her to let the wall completely slip from her heart. He wouldn't understand that she'd ended things for his sake. So that he could be happy in the long run. "I love you so much," she whispered into his mouth, before kissing him deeply again.

"When a woman wakes up in a hospital she would like to hear some answers, not the sounds of her son and his girlfriend making out. And who makes out in their mother's hospital room? And why can't I feel my left arm?"

Chapter Thirty

She was leaving. Mike stood in the doorway of their hotel room watching Ellis pack with a sinking feeling. She hadn't heard him return from the rehab facility where his mother was going to be spending the next six weeks. She moved quietly and efficiently, stuffing her meager belongings in the small duffel bag she had brought with her. He knew she had to go back. She had missed her meeting, taken time away from her business and her customers to be with him, but he didn't want her to go.

"You're going."

She startled and turned to face him. He admired her for a moment in her white vee-neck sweater and those tight blue jeans that always made the blood rush from his brain. She was barefoot, her high-heeled brown boots resting on the floor in front of the bed. He had spent nearly every minute of the past four days with her and yet she was still a sight for sore eyes.

"How's your mother?" she asked, ignoring his statement.

"My father is spoiling her like a two-year-old so her spirits are good, but physically she is going to need months of physical therapy and a major change in her lifestyle. She's not so happy about that. My mother has lived off stress and caffeine for the past twenty years. I don't think she knows anything else."

"I'll have my mother come to visit. She can teach her all about the benefits of yoga."

Mike shut the door behind him, fully entering the room. "My father wants her to give up the flower shop and live with him, but she's torn. I know she loves him, but she's having a hard time giving up her independence."

Tears formed in Ellis's eyes.

"You're leaving," he said once more.

"I love you, Mike." She rested her head on his chest, sliding her cool hands beneath his shirt to break the tiny distance between them. "Please, don't hate me."

He did a little, but he slid his arms around her and held her. He couldn't say he didn't expect this. She hadn't answered him in the hospital. And when she greeted his questions with kisses he knew they were doomed.

They loved each other. They were good together. Why couldn't they make things work? But this time he knew it had nothing to do with him. This was all on her. There was nothing more he could say to convince her. He knew how he wanted to spend the rest of his life. It was up to her to decide how she wanted to spend hers.

"If you need anything at all, let me know." She kissed his cheek. "Okay?"

He nodded, unwilling to tell her that she was what he needed, unwilling to demand she forget her silly reasons and give them a shot.

"Thank you for coming, Ellis. I'm glad that you did."

She nodded and pressed soft kisses to his mouth, whispering that she loved him half a dozen times.

Don't let her go. Every bone in his body screamed at him not to let her walk out. But he just couldn't keep fighting for her when she was so hell-bent on walking away.

Christmas passed quietly for Mike. He'd left Buffalo a few days before, confident that his mother was being well cared for by his father. Ellis was probably going to get her wish. Mike had walked in on his parents kissing the day before he left. His father was on his knees before her, her face cupped gently in his hands. An odd feeling tore through Mike seeing his parents like that. It made him miss Ellis, but he pushed the thoughts of her out of his mind. It was easy to be angry with her for giving up on them, but he would not allow himself to be bitter. She was there for him when he needed her the most. It counted for something.

His father had bought a town house on Lake Erie, telling Mike that he was replanting his roots in his hometown with his best girl. The two of them spent a lot of time talking. His father now called him daily, as if trying to make up for years of lost conversations. Mike was okay with that. He was glad to have him back.

Moving back to Buffalo crossed his mind. He no longer had anything in Durant, save Colin and memories of college and his first love. Maybe it was time to move again. To put down roots of his own. He had come to Durant to find himself, and he'd found love. Unfortunately, he fell in love with a woman who couldn't be with him. If he moved to Buffalo he wouldn't be afraid of running into her at the coffee shop, or wondering if every blue car that passed by was hers. He could move on. He had been happy with her. Maybe he had a shot of being happy with someone else.

Fat fucking chance.

He ignored the nagging thought in his head and that deep-down feeling that told him he was never going to get over her. Disgusted with himself, he powered on his laptop and did a search for real estate in Buffalo. Thirteen minutes into his search the doorbell rang.

It's probably Colin, he thought as he shut his laptop and glanced at the clock. His friend had been around a lot lately, usually bringing food or alcohol with him.

When he opened the door he didn't see his friend. Dina faced him.

"What the fuck are you doing here?" he asked, ready to slam to door in her face.

She did this. She fucked everything up.

"I need to talk to you." She placed her hand on the frame so he couldn't shut the door. "Please. Five minutes and then you'll never see me again."

"What?"

"Can't I come in?" She looked into his place. "I'm freezing my ass off out here."

He stepped aside to let her in but refused to let her get farther than the coatrack. "If you're trying to proposition me you can forget it. I thought I made it clear—"

"God, no." She rolled her eyes. "I came to tell you that you have to get my sister back." Dina's face softened as emotion filled her eyes. "She's miserable. I can take her being mad at me but I can't take how sad she is. It's like somebody died. So you have to go back and get her, okay? Tell her you're sorry. Buy her some jewelry. Just make her stop being so sad."

"Why do you care?" he snapped then turned away, unable to look at Dina. "You spent your whole life treating her like shit. Excuse me if I have a hard time believing you."

"I was horrible to her. I wasn't happy so I wanted Ellis to be unhappy. Everybody has always liked Ellis better than me. Even our parents. I hated the way Walter looked at her like she was some sort of precious little angel. I hated how she could talk to him when I never found the right words to say. My mother, too. Every time she calls me she mentions how proud she is of Ellis. How good she turned out. It makes me feel like shit. And the only way I could make myself feel better is by ripping her apart, knowing that no matter what I did she would always love me. I tested her. All my life she has been the only person who really just loves me." She scrubbed her thin hands over her face. "But I still wanted her to fail at something.

"I knew the way I felt about my sister was wrong, but then you came along again. You, the only guy who ever dumped me, fell in love with my sister. I didn't kiss you because I wanted you. I kissed you because I knew if Ellis was alone I wouldn't feel so alone. But it backfired. She's alone and I still feel like shit. She's gray, Mike. I don't know how to explain it but it's like somebody put her light out. You've got to get her back."

Dina's explanation made sense, and as much as he wanted to blame her for the breakup he couldn't. Ellis didn't want him. "She's the one who walked away. I'm tired of chasing after her."

"But you've got to!" Tears flashed in her eyes. "Walter loves her but he's hardly ever said it and doesn't know how to show her. Then there's my mother, who told her but spent most our childhood chasing after me. Ellis practically raised herself. And then there's me who probably loves her more than anybody else but is so fucked up that I can't be around her without hurting her. She's never had anybody chase after her. Nobody who has loved her the way she needed to be loved. That's why she keeps pushing you away. She doesn't know how to be loved. She's stubborn. I know her. She thinks she's being noble by letting you go. She thinks she's too hard to love. But she's being stupid. You need to get her back. "

He walked away from Dina and sank down on his couch, his mind racing with everything she'd said. "How?"

"It's easy. Don't give her a choice."

Chapter Thirty-one

Get Happy

"No one can make you feel inferior without your consent."
—ELEANOR ROOSEVELT

Lesson of the day: Try to love yourself, even if it's a little hard sometimes.

"Ellis!" Belinda screeched her name from the storeroom, and Ellis sighed.

What now?

She put down her needle, rubbed her aching head, and met Belinda in the next room. "Yes, darling?" she answered wearily.

"Um." Belinda stared down at the large white envelope in her hand. "I think you need to open it right away. It says it's from some law office."

"No fucking way," she cursed as she took it from Belinda. What now? All of her dresses had been completed on time. Her bills were paid. Her customers were happy. Unless these people were offering her a job, she couldn't see an upside to opening it. "You open it."

She handed it back.

"No way." She shoved it back. "You open it right now, Ellison Garret. You're the boss!"

"I don't wanna be in charge," she whined. Her feminist mother would be horrified to know this, but it was times like this Ellis missed Mike.

Yeah right, dummy. You miss him every waking hour.

Oh shut up!

You shouldn't have let him go.

He was so good at the business stuff. All Ellis wanted to do was create. "Fine. I am woman. Hear me roar." She tore open the package and scanned it. As a lawyer she knew what a lawsuit looked like, and the papers usually didn't come in the mail.

"Oh." She looked up at Belinda. "We have a new landlord. It looks like they bought our store and the one next door."

"Really?" Belinda peered over Ellis's shoulder. "Who are we paying rent to now?"

"I don't know. Probably some corporation." She flipped to the second page and scanned down. Her mouth dropped when she saw a familiar name on the document. "No."

"What?" Belinda pulled the papers from her hand and looked. "Shut up!"

"Hey, guys." Cherri walked in, her arms full of hangers. "What's going on?"

Ellis took the papers from Belinda, who was still staring in disbelief. "I've got to go."

Ellis pounded on Mike's door. His car was in its space. The lights inside were on. He'd never officially given up his place even though they had lived together for those few weeks. Part of her was surprised that he was still in town. A bigger part of her was relieved he hadn't left.

"Yes." He opened the door and blinked at her as if she were a stranger, as if he hadn't pulled some major crap and interfered with her life.

"You bought my store!"

"No." He folded his arms over his massive chest. "I didn't buy your store. I bought the building it's housed in."

Unsatisfied with his answer, she picked up a wad of snow and flung it at him. "Don't screw with me, Mike Edwards. What the hell are you playing at?"

"Hey!" He ducked and then grabbed her arm and yanked her into his apartment. "I'm not playing. I thought real estate was a good investment so I bought the building."

"Bullshit! Why did you do this, Mike?"

"You broke up with me," he said, as if his move was the logical next step.

"I broke up with you, so you buy my store?" She couldn't believe him. "Are you insane? Where did you get the money from?"

"Yes, I'm insane, but only because you made me this way. And I borrowed the money from my father."

"Keep talking." She slapped his chest, forcing him backward. "I want to know why."

"You know why! I'm in love with you and I can't understand why you keep pushing me away. I'm not going to give you up, Ellis. I love you and if I have to buy your store to get your attention I will, because every time you write out a rent check you'll think of me. Or if the heat goes you'll have to talk to me. Every day you'll have to walk around knowing that I own the place where you spend most of your time. And every day you're going to have to think about me loving you."

"I already think about you loving me all the time," she said more to herself than to him.

"Then why did you leave me?"

Good question.

"I don't know." She turned from him and placed her head on the wall. He was behind her instantly.

"Yes, you do!"

"I—I . . ."

"What?"

"I'm a nut job! And I've been hurt before. I don't know if I'll ever be sane. I don't know if I can ever let all of my baggage go. So I push you away because it's easier than waiting for you to push me away first. You have no idea what it's like in here, Mike." She pointed to her head. "I keep waiting for the day when you look at me and think, *She's fucking insane. Why am I with her?*"

"I already think that, baby," he said gently as he spun her around to face him. "But then you smile at me, or kiss me, or say something that makes me laugh and my question gets answered. I'm with you because I love you."

"Why, Mike?" She looked into those fierce blue eyes. "Why do you love me?"

"I don't know why." He put her hand over his heart. "But I can't seem to function without you. I've been with so many women—"

"Not helping!"

"Listen. I've been with so many women and you're the only one who has ever made me feel anything. You're the only one I love. You're the only one I would quit my job and put myself into tremendous debt for."

"You quit?"

Holy shit! He's nuts, too. Breathe, damn it. Breathe.

He had given up everything for her. For her. He had put her first. If she couldn't let him love her now, then she didn't deserve to be loved.

"Yeah, I'd rather spend my days helping to make your dreams come true than investigating stupid crimes. And I don't think you should sell the rights to your designs. I bought the shop next door because I believe in you and I think we can expand on our own. I could help you with all the business stuff, and Belinda can do all the front-of-the-house work. All you would have to worry about is making dresses. All you have to do is say yes."

It was exactly what she wanted.

"What happens if I don't say yes?"

"Then I will spend the rest of my life hounding you. I'll be unemployed so I won't have anything better to do. This is your dream. It's so easy to grasp. What's holding you back?"

She stared at him for a moment. "I don't want to be your girlfriend anymore, Mike," she said, choking on the words.

"Why?" His face fell. "Just tell me why?"

"I want to be your wife," she shouted. "I want to be married to you, okay? I want your last name. I want you to love me like my father loves my mother. I want it all from you, Mike. It may be selfish but I want everything with—"

"Stop!" He walked out of the room, and she slumped against the wall feeling miserable. She knew that saying all that might push him away, but she wanted forever. She had known that for a long time. It was the only thing that would make her feel better about them. Partnership sounded wonderful but if she was going to risk her heart it had to be for keeps.

He stormed back in, a little black box in his clenched hand. "I've had this for over a month." He got on his knees, opened the box, and showed her a large round-cut diamond in a vintage setting. "I was planning to propose but you dumped me and ruined everything. And now when I'm busting my ass to try to get you back, you jump three steps ahead and force me to rush my proposal. Are you happy now? Are you going to call your mother and tell her that we got engaged during an argument? How romantic!"

She looked at the ring and back up at him. *Astonished* was not a big enough word to encompass how she felt.

A month? You're an idiot.

"You've got great taste, Mikey."

"Ellis," he growled.

She bit her lip to keep herself from grinning. "Ask me nicely. And make sure you tell me how pretty I am. And make sure you promise to still love me even if I get really fat and need to be weighed on a truck scale. And—"

"You've got to be a ball buster even during my proposal." He stood, palmed the back of her neck, and brought his lips down on top of hers. "I'm not going to ask." He kissed her jaw, the underside of her chin, the place behind her ear that made her quiver. "I love you. I don't tell you enough but if I have to spend every day of the rest of my life making you believe that, I will. You have to marry me. Life is no good without you." He crushed his mouth to hers, giving her one of those sweet hot kisses that made her fall for him in the first place.

"Tomorrow," she said when he came up for air.

"What?"

"I want to get married tomorrow. Let's go to city hall."

He looked at her disbelief. "The bridal-wear designer doesn't want to have a wedding?"

"No. I wasted enough time with you. I was stupid. I was wrong. I'm so sorry."

He pressed her against the wall and kissed her. "Do you know how much I love hearing that I was right?"

"Don't get used to it. You only get one of those every ten years."

He grinned at her. "I'd marry you right now but our parents wouldn't appreciate that."

"Fine," she relented. "But I don't want a cake. I want Black and White Cookies."

"Okay."

"And you're going to do the electric slide."

He hesitated for a moment. "Fine."

"Oh, and I want our first dance to be to Baby Got Back."

"Ellis," he groaned.

"I love you, Mikey." She smiled as she hugged him.

"I love you, too."

Epilogue

Ellis lay beside her husband in their new bedroom. They'd found an old Victorian in Durant and spent months remodeling it to make their home. She smiled even as exhaustion seeped into her bones. Tomorrow she would be celebrating two years of marriage to the man of her dreams and she barely believed how her life had turned out. From lawyer to designer. From not knowing how to love to being filled with it.

"Ellie?" Mike wrapped his arm around her and kissed her forehead sleepily. They were tired from the move and had just sent their families home for the night.

Mike's mother recovered from her stroke and did end up remarrying Harry, but only after making him chase her for a year. They settled in a beautiful condo on Lake Erie but spent most of the year traveling the world. Her parents were still essentially the same, except her mother had recently made the *New York Times* best-seller list with her book *Woman Up: A Feminist's Guide to Life, Love, and Happiness*. She now spent her off days lecturing around the country, doing talk shows, and dragging Walter with her.

As for Dina, apologies had been made and accepted but they were distant. Dina moved to California, where she met a nice older man and moved in with him. A year later they were still going strong.

"Hmm?" Ellis snuggled closer to Mike, sliding her hands up his bare chest. "Wanna fool around?" Two years later and she still couldn't get enough of him.

"Yes." He reached under her nightgown and gripped her behind. "But I wanted to talk to you about something first."

She opened her eyes at the seriousness of his voice. "What is it?"

"I know we decided a long time ago that we weren't going to have kids but I want to reopen that discussion."

Ellis gulped.

Shit.

She turned away and pulled the comforter over her head to cover her burning face. "No."

"No?" He yanked the blanket away from her. "You don't want to have kids or you don't want to talk about it."

"Mike, please," she begged. "We cannot talk about this right now."

"Why not? We don't have to decide tonight, but I want to discuss it."

"Ugh!" She turned over. "There is nothing to discuss because I'm already pregnant."

"What!" His eyes bulged. "When the hell did this happen?"

"When I stopped taking my birth control two months ago."

"WHAT!" He gripped her shoulders. "You're two months' pregnant."

"Yeah." She grinned. "You've got quick swimmers, buddy."

"Ellis, why didn't you tell me? What if I didn't want to have kids?"

"Well, you were going to have to suck it up. I wanted a baby with blue eyes and dark hair and I was going to get one." She grew serious for a moment. "I know you want to be a daddy. I see it in your face every time you look at a kid. And I know that I wanted to give you that gift."

"But—but . . . Is this what you want?"

"Do you think I would voluntarily subject myself to pounds and pounds of weight gain if I didn't?"

"A baby?" He stared at her in amazement and then shoved the comforter down to bare her body. He pushed up her nightgown to cup her belly with his large rough hand. "You're going to give me a baby."

"Yes . . ." Her eyes grew misty. He looked so damn happy.

"When were you going to tell me!" he yelled.

"Tomorrow on our second anniversary, jackass. You ruined the surprise."

"Oh." He grinned at her. "Sorry." He bent to pepper kisses on her stomach. Then in a move that shocked the hell out of her, he jumped up on the bed and screamed, causing her to jump.

"Ah! What the hell was that for?"

"I'm happy," he said when he returned to her. "You've given me all I ever wanted."

Don't miss Sugar Jamison's next delightful novel

Thrown for a Curve

Coming in 2014 from St. Martin's Paperbacks